IMAGINATION

PAUL LUDFORD is now retired, having spent time as an apprentice cutter in a corset factory, waited at tables on an ocean-going mail/passenger ship, operated printing presses, and worked his way up to management level in an international insurance company. Not content with taking life easy after early retirement, he spent two seasons caring for two charter cruisers operating on the Solent in the South of England. He also spent several happy years meeting people and listening to their stories as he drove a bus between Portsmouth and Brighton, probably his most enjoyable paid occupation.

When not sitting at his keyboard, Paul now spends much of his free time building and operating a large model railway in a room at the bottom of his garden. This is Paul's second self-published book, the first being a novel entitled *MISSY*

First published 2020

Copyright - Paul Ludford 2020

ISBN 978-1-913663-29-2

The right of Paul Ludford to be identified as

The author of this work has been asserted by him

In accordance with the Copyright, Designs and Patent

Act 1988

Printed in Great Britain by

Biddles Books Limited, King's Lynn, Norfolk

CONTENTS

SALLY 7
THE OLD BOOKMAN 34
DANCING PARTNERS 44
THE APPRENTICE 61
THE HANDBAG 83
THE RESCUE 94
THE CASTLE 113
CHANCE ENCOUNTER 120
OPERATION ROSY 133
ONE YEAR ON 143
THE MUCK SPREADER 151
ABANDONED 161
WEB TALK 185
MANY HAPPY RETURNS 191
THE INVENTORS 212
THE MUDLARK 218
THE RETIREMENT 234
THE GIFT 246

THE CLOWN	250
PLANE TALKING	266
TRADITION	272
THE CAPTAIN	283
PURE WHITE	301
ON THE LINES	311
DRIVING HOME	318
RESTITUTION	336
DUMPTY	353
NO GOING BACK	358
GOLDIE	365
THE SENTENCE	378
THE TAILOR	382
GLORIA	402
THE CAMP	416
BABY TALK	438
A SPECIAL DAY	446
THE SPITFIRE	463
GOLD FEVER	479
IMAGINATION	512
THE BENCHES	530
DEEP WATERS	544

SALLY

The scruffy black and white dog trotted over the cobbles, stopping now and then to sniff the foot of a gas lamppost, or the corner of a shop front. He was hungry and out searching for scraps. In the last street, he had come across a metal bin which, amongst other rubbish, revealed the stale remains of a pie. He dealt with that in a matter of seconds. It wasn't enough however, if anything, it made him more aware of his need for food. He knew where to go for the most promising offerings, The Square where there would always be a stall or two. The one he was heading for was good for meat scraps, mostly offal. He needed to be alert however. This was not his territory. He was not a member of the pack that roamed here, his torn right ear bore the evidence of that. Thinking of that encounter he felt the need to mark his progress. He made for a convenient door step and cocked his leg. Before he was able to release any urine, he was two foot in the air as his breath left his body. *'Get the hell out of here you filthy vermin, pee on my doorstep, would you? Beat it!'* The nameless stray didn't stay long enough to see who owned the hobnailed boot that had connected with his soft underside. With a 'Yelp' and tail between his legs he was gone.

Two streets later, and with a sore stomach, whether caused by hunger or the result of the kick, he didn't know, he was closer to The Square and very much on the alert for any of the pack. So far, so good. His senses were on edge, every odour, every sound filled his pointed head. That's how he heard the cry. Soft. Muffled. He stopped, ears pricked, nose sniffing. Could this signify danger? The sound was coming from an alley to his left. Hunger and pain momentarily forgotten, he lowered his body closer to the ground to present the smallest target possible, and moved cautiously toward the alley. There, the sound that had stopped him in his tracks. It was louder now. High pitched. He stopped at the entrance to the alley, sniffing. A rumbling noise blotted out the high-pitched sound. Horse's feet ringing on the cobbles. A brewer's dray rumbled passed. Two huge shire horses pulling the laden cart. A man in a leather apron with a black bowler hat perched on his head, holding the reigns. The dog drew back from the cobbles and into the alley. He knew better than to get under the feet of such beasts. The dray moved on, a leather bucket swinging from a steel hook at the back.

The cry, now becoming a wail, penetrated his ears. Looking into the gloom, the dog could see a wooden crate resting on the doorstep of one of the buildings. He instinctively knew this was the source of the sound. Silently he crept forward, hackles raised. One look was enough to tell him the bare chubby arm waving in the air at the side of the crate was a human puppy. Could this strange sight bring the possibility of food, he wondered? Throwing caution to the wind, hunger overcame him as he lifted his front paws to the edge of the crate. The baby had shifted the blanket which might previously have been covering her. She was red faced as she howled her protest of hunger. Her hands formed two tightly clenched fists.

Her eyes were closed. None of this was of interest to the dog however. He had first smelled, then seen the curved glass bottle which was dripping its content of milk. He climbed further onto the crate until he was able to reach the teat. He licked the cold milk until the drops were gone, at which point he attempted, without success, to bite through the rubber to get at the milk within the bottle. The baby girl continued to wail between sharply drawn breaths. So loudly did the child wail, that the dog failed to hear the door at the top of the step start to quietly open.

***

The elevator wheel at the top of the headframe stopped turning as the cage came to rest at the platform level. A stream of weary coal-blackened men emerged and, after handing in their name tags, walked stiffly down the wooden ramp to the locker and shower room. Turning under the luke-warm water one of the men was approached by his best pal whose muscular body was already transformed from black to pink.

'Alright, Jack?' the friend enquired of the rotating minor. 'Want me to scrub yer back for you?'

'Yea, that would be great, Charlie. You all done?'

'Sure thing, first out of the cage for a change. You comin' to the dogs tonight? I fancy me luck on the third race, 'ad a good tip off.'

'Yea, that's the general idea Charlie me old mate. Ethel's going to the workers club for Bingo so I'll be able to come out without feeling guilty about leaving her on her own for the evening.'

'That's grand. How's your Ethel getting on now? I imagine it's all taken it out on her, what wiv the baby being still-born. My Shirl reckons it can take months, even years to get over a thing like that.'

'Yea, well. It's been five months now. We wanted that baby so bad,' replied Jack as he towelled himself off. 'Four years we'd been trying. She still blames herself, carrying on at the mill for as long as she did. I told 'er that it wasn't 'er fault, but there's no convincing 'er. I asked the vicar to 'ave a chat with 'er last week, but that didn't do any good. She just moons around the 'ous, 'ardley saying anything. Bingo's the only thing that takes 'er mind off it for a while.'

'I'm real sorry, Jack. It must be 'ard for both of you. Any 'ow, praps you'll 'av a bit o' luck at the stadium tonight. Come on, get yoursen dressed and we'll walk down together.'

***

'Get out of there you mangy animal! Go on, Get!' If the shouting hadn't frightened the dog, the stiff broom certainly had the desired effect, for it shot out of the alley as though the whole pack was after it. 'What's that doing on my doorstep?' The sudden shout and yelp of the dog had caused the baby to momentarily stop wailing, perhaps instinctively thinking that food was about to be thrust between her lips. 'Oh, my god, it's a baby! You poor little

mite, what are you doing down there?' Having propped the broom against the door frame, Ethel bent down and lifted the wooden crate from the step. She quickly glanced both ways along the alley before stepping back through the doorway with the crate in her arms. 'You poor little thing, you must be so cold and hungry. Who would do a thing like that?' The rhetorical question was answered with a piercing wail from the interior of the crate as the concerned woman gently placed it on the kitchen table. 'There, there, come on, let's have a look at you … Oh, you're all wet, you poor sweet thing. Let's get you sorted.' Having lifted the baby from the crate, Ethel spotted the partly filled feeding bottle with its, still intact, teat. Placing the wailing child temporarily back in the crate she quickly filled the blackened kettle and placed it on the range. Having assured herself that the child was safe for the moment, she rushed up the narrow stairs to the small bedroom that she and Jack had prepared all those months ago. She quickly gathered all that she would need before descending back to the kitchen. '*Feed, wash, dress*', she thought throughout her rapid preparation. '*Such a pity my* milk dried up months ago, cow's milk it'll have to be, no choice.'

Just over an hour later, the sleeping child was tucked firmly in the rocking cot that Jack had made with such care and love for their own baby all that time ago. Ethel carefully placed a multi-coloured quilt over the tiny unexpected guest. As she did so, she recalled the anticipation and all the happy hours she had spent on it during her confinement. She sat on the kitchen stool and looked down at the sweet face of the baby, a girl she had discovered as she had cleaned her up. *'How old?'* she pondered? *'No more than a day or two I shouldn't wonder, and judging by those filthy rags, wasn't expected. Or the mother was on the streets.'* Reluctantly getting to her feet and stepping round the cot, Ethel left the kitchen and made her way to the coal hole outside the back door. With a small hand-spade, she filled the scuttle with the minor's perks and returned to the kitchen where she built up the fire in preparation for cooking Jack's dinner, his favourite, rabbit stew. The rabbit had hung for a few days after her husband had caught it with the aid of one of his ferrets. Ethel made a bit more of an effort over the meal by roasting the potatoes instead of making mash. She also made a plum pudding for afters. She really wanted to soften him up for the plan that was forming in her head.

***

'Oh, you're back then, Anne. Blimey, you look proper poorly. Where y' bin? Fought you'd gone fer good. Ere you ain't gone an' got rid of the baby 'ave ya?'

The young girl staggered across the room and fell onto the stained mattress where she curled up into a foetal position and allowed the tears to stream across her face. Her friend watched the heaving shoulders of the kid she had taken under her wing seven months before, after spotting her stealing an apple from a stall. Now, although she was puzzled about the whereabouts of the baby, she was savvy enough to know that she should leave Anne alone for a while. Although she had had little idea of what she was doing the previous week, she had helped to deliver the baby. In fact, she was quite pleased with her achievement, and in the few days the baby had been in the room, as inconvenient as it had been for trade, she had become quite fond of it. Little Sally had introduced a warmth and softness into her hard existence.

Life on the streets was indeed hard. There was little trust and many dangers. Mavis had never had a friend she felt she could trust, until Anne came along. She felt guilty for introducing the girl to the trade, but they had to live and pay for the rent on the hovel that served as both home and a place of business. It couldn't be helped. At first, she had tried to confine Anne to 'Gentlemen' who just wanted company, someone to just listen as they rambled on about whatever. Inevitably the girl had been drawn in to the depths of the stinking trade they depended upon.

As the afternoon light began to fade, enough to soften the ugliness of the almost bare room with its torn wallpaper and damply stained ceiling, the girl gave a loud sigh and struggled to a sitting position on the mattress with her arms tucked around her raised knees. 'Sorry

Mave, I didn't mean to scare you. Do you need the room to yourself for a while?'

'No Luv, nobody comin' today. 'Ow ya feelin' now you've 'ad a good weep?'

'Mave? I've done something awful and stupid.'

'You're scaring me Anne,' said Mavis in alarm. 'Where's Sally? What 'ave you done wiv 'er?'

'I left her.'

'What do you mean? You left her. Left her where?'

Anne didn't reply, she just sat there, arms clenched around her knees, and rocked backward and forward, backward, forward, backward … 'Anne! Listen to me. Where did you leave Sally?'

'I can't do this anymore, Mave.' Anne's voice rose to a shout. 'I can't, I just can't. How can I continue looking after that baby like this? How can I entertain those creeps when she's asleep a few feet away? How can she survive in this hell hole?'

'Where have you left her, Anne?' asked Mavis while clutching Anne's shoulder to stop the rocking. *'Look at me! Where ... is ... Sally?'*

'She'll be okay. I left her on someone's doorstep with the bottle in her mouth. I covered her up nice and warm, I really did.'

'Oh, that's all right then!' replied Mavis while releasing Anne's shoulder. 'How could you? I can't believe what I'm hearing. Take me there. We'll get her back.'

'No! It's done. She'll be better off,' replied Anne with a loud sniff and turning away from her friend.

'Right! I'm off out. You can stay here and stew for all I care.' The door slammed behind her as Mavis walked along the cobbled street, tears streaming down her cheeks.

***

The neatly dressed middle-aged lady peered into the window of every shop she passed. She also looked closely at any young woman, or girl, who passed her by, particularly if a perambulator was present. She had lost count of the cities, towns and villages she had included in her fruitless search. She had no reason to think this particular city would be any different, but she must try. For whatever else could she do? Although still smartly dressed, she was aware how much she had aged. She thought back to a time when life had been uncomplicated, although perhaps a little dull and meaningless. She had had no specific purpose other than to run her household with the aid of a housekeeper, a maid and a gardener who also drove the horse and trap when required. A modest household to be sure, but one in which she had been content, even happy at times.

Elizabeth had married her husband nineteen years previously. There had been little love at that time and even less as time passed. She was very much aware that Lionel had married her for her money and status. Her family background was one of diminishing wealth. Being the third daughter of an Earl and the last to be *"married off"*, as she had overheard her father describe it, her dowry had been modest and, as she had suspected, disappointing to her husband. Their Hampshire home was comfortable and well furnished, sitting in ten acres of the South Downs. Life for her had been rather mundane, that is, until little Anne had come along. Anne had become her life, the reason for her existence. She doted on the baby who, too quickly, had become a happy playful child. Mother and daughter were often seen together walking the lanes or browsing through the village shops. As a child Anne was best described as pretty, but as the years rolled on it was clear that young men found her attractive. It was a shame that Lionel had had little time for the girl, for it had been a son he wanted, a son to follow him into the banking world. That was not to be, for she had never again conceived, perhaps the lack of love had a lot to do with that, she often thought.

In her sixteenth year Anne needed her mother's company less and less. She was often away from the house when lessons were over. She claimed to have been *"just walking"* when Elizabeth enquired. Perhaps she had been partly responsible for the event that turned all of their lives upside down. She should have been a lot firmer with the girl, and allowed her less freedom. Lionel was seldom at home, claiming to be busy in the city, although Elizabeth suspected that he was keeping a mistress. Otherwise things may have been different. *'Water under the bridge now. What is done is done.'*

As she wondered the streets of this particular city, Elizabeth recalled the awful scene in their dining room when Anne had bucked up the courage to tell her and her father that she was with child. She replayed the scene in her mind as Lionel had thrown down his knife and fork, sprung out of his chair and pulled Anne from her own. Before she had had time to react, her husband had frog-marched her precious daughter through the door. He was shouting, swearing and banging, to the point where Elizabeth feared for Anne's life. By the time she had managed to reach the hall where she found Lionel leaning against the front door, Anne was gone.

'Where is she?' she cried.

'Where she belongs, on the street,' snarled her red-faced husband.

'Let me out, Lionel. I must go to her.'

'No! You stay here, woman. It's all your fault. You spoiled her with all that doting. Well now she's dead to us. I will not have the shame of a bastard in this house, is that clear?'

There was no way Lionel was going to allow her out of his sight that night, or through the following day. She recalled the bruises on her wrists where he had held her. She had fought him, scratched him, slapped him, all to no avail. Anne was gone. Her marriage was gone, her reason to live, was gone.

Elizabeth had spent several weeks in bed. She was in shock. Her illness was real, although the local doctor was unable to put a name to it. He had simply prescribed bed-rest and had left a bottle of medicine which tasted fowl and did nothing to lift her from the dark place into which she had sunk. Mary, her loyal maid, had tended her needs and slowly nursed her back to some semblance of health. It wasn't until the end of the second week of her illness that Mary had apologetically informed her mistress that the master had packed some bags over a week ago, and was gone.

Now, Elizabeth continued to peer through the windows of one shop after another, in one street after another. She had come to realise that this had become a hopeless cause. She even began to doubt that her daughter was still alive. Now, she was peering into a general store but not able to see into the gloom, so she stepped inside to look around. A few customers, but not the one she was seeking. She made for the door when an assistant standing behind the highly polished counter asked, 'Can I help you madam?'

Turning to look at the man she replied, 'No thank you, just looking.' With that, she turned abruptly back to the door and bumped into a young girl who had clearly been crying. 'Oh, I'm so sorry. Are you alright, dear? You look quite upset.'

'Yea, I'm okay fanks. Just 'ad some bad news, that's all.'

'Can I help?' It was clear that the girl was very poor, judging by her clothes.

'Na, I'll get over it fanks, (sniff) me friend 'as just lost 'er baby, that's all.'

'Well at least take this to dry your eyes.' Elizabeth had taken a handkerchief from her purse and was holding it out to the distraught girl.

'Fanks missus.' The girl dried her tear-filled eyes before blowing, rather loudly, several times into the fine material. She thanked the kind woman as she held out the handkerchief.

'No, no. You keep it, dear,' said Elizabeth as she attempted to hide a shudder. 'I hope your friend will be okay, you must be fond of her.'

'Yea, I am. You could say Anne's been like a little sister ever since I found 'er wanderin' the streets while carrying.'

'Did you say *Anne?*' asked Elizabeth stepping back.

A minute or two later the two of them left the shop together. This time it was the older one who had tears streaming unheeded down her cheeks. Her blurred vision, combined with her haste almost caused her to trip over the black and white stray dog sniffing around the shop doorway. Ten minutes later, she stepped into the dark room.

'Anne?' In the shadows, a movement. 'Anne, is that you?'

'Mummy?' no more than a whisper.

'Anne!! Anne, it's me, your mother.'

'Mummy!!! Suddenly, out of the shadows a figure swept into Elizabeth's arms.

***

The front door slammed closed. Ethel listened to the sound of Jack's hobnailed boots dropping to the hall floor one after the other, the usual routine. 'Something smells good, Eth. By god, I'm famished. Is that rabbit stew I can smell? Must be something special, it's not one of our birthdays, is it? Or perhaps our anniversary?' Having relieved himself of his boots, coat and cap by the front door, Jack entered the kitchen. 'Hello Luv, give us a kiss. You off to Bingo tonight then?'

Before she had time to answer, a contented gurgling noise came from the cot which was out of sight behind the, now open, hall door.

Turning to see what had made the unfamiliar sound, Jack enquired, 'What was that?' In a single stride he reached the door and swung it closed, thus revealing the cot. 'A baby? You're looking after someone's baby? Who's is it? How much they paying you? You didn't mention it. Are you sure it's wise, given your ...? well you know what I mean. It's in Rose's cot, the one I made. What's going on, Eth?' The baby continued to gurgle and kick her chubby little legs as Jack looked down on her.

'She's ours, Jack. Remember you suggested the vicar should come round for a chat. He told me I should pray for another baby. I did and, well, here she is.'

'But that's not possible,' replied Jack as he stood scratching his head. 'Where did it come from? What 'ave you done, Eth?'

'I ain't done anything, Jack. The angel's brought her and left her on our doorstep.'

'You mean, it's been abandoned? And on our doorstep?' Jack replied.

'No, not abandoned, she's a gift.'

'Well you can't keep it. It's not ours to keep. I'll 'ave to tek it to the rozzers.'

'No!' shouted Ethel, her hand covering her breast. 'I saved her life, I cleaned her, I fed her, I clothed her and I cuddled life into her. You can't take her from me.'

'Are you mad? We could end up with a twenty-year prison sentence for kidnapping. Even if the baby was left on our doorstep that doesn't give us the right to keep it, don't you understand? I have to take her in.'

'Please, Jack!' cried Ethel grabbing hold of her husband's arm. 'No one will know. We'll keep her hidden, or pretend we're looking after her for a member of our family. That's it, we can say I'm her aunty. Who will argue with that?'

Taking hold of both of her shoulders and looking directly into his distraught wife's eyes, Jack said, slowly, 'My dearest darling girl. The true mother will know, or whoever left it there will. They could come back at any time and claim her, or blackmail us. A person who could abandon a baby in such a way is more than capable of anything. Can't you understand that? If we keep trying, we could 'ave a baby of our own one day, the doctor said that, remember?'

'But Jack, she's so lovely, look at her. Don't you want to pick her up and hold her?'

'Yes Eth,' replied Jack, shaking his head. 'I can see how she has taken your heart, but it doesn't change anything. It's unfortunate that you had to deal with her, and I can see what she means to you because of that, but she isn't yours and you're not her mother, and never can be. I'm truly sorry my love. I'll tek her down after dinner.'

'So, you'll be happy for her to end up in an orphanage then?' snapped Ethel.

'Maybe she will, maybe she'll end up being adopted into a wealthy family, I don't know luv. But at least you won't end up in prison. Now, let's have some dinner while she quiet.'

Neither of them spoke as they tried their best to swallow a meal that they would normally relish. When the baby started to whimper, Ethel left her half-eaten meal and bent over the cot to pick her up. Jack did his best to avert his eyes. He had no intention of bonding with this infant who was soon to leave them. His heart was heavy as he considered the harm this episode would do to his frail wife. Would she ever be able to recover? Would she ever forgive him? He doubted it on both counts. Suddenly, there came a heavy knock on the door. Both husband and wife jumped.

'Oh my god!' cried Ethel, 'It's the police! Quick, help me to hide her.'

'Don't panic,' said Jack while getting to his feet. Let's just calm down and see who it is. Stay there and keep hold of the baby. Ethel stood trembling, as Jack left the room. She stood and listened to murmuring at the front door, although strain as she might, she was unable to hear a word. She stepped back against the sink clutching the baby tightly to her breast as several footsteps sounded down the passage. The kitchen door swung open to reveal two women entering behind her husband. One was smartly dressed, the other, no more than a girl, in what could only be described as rags.

***

It was eight months later, that Ethel returned to the little terraced house, having been out shopping. She had spoken to no one other than the shop assistants as and when necessary. Jack had been so tender with her. She knew that he was trying his best to lift her spirits. Their love-making had been gentle and sweet. He was spending more time in their small and enclosed rear garden. She had stopped going out to Bingo now, preferring to sit and listen to the wireless while Jack amused himself with the black and white dog, they had taken in. She was sure she had seen that dog before, but could not think where. It had readily made itself at home and was proving to be a comfort to them both. At last she arrived home, walking was taking it out on her these days, *"What with the bump an all"* as she was fond of saying to Jack. As she let herself into the house, she nearly stepped on a letter which had landed well away from the door. In a very neat hand, it was addressed to both Mr and Mrs, so she propped it on the mantel for Jack to open when he returned from the colliery. The dog greeted her with a wagging tail and a lick of the hand. 'Hello Scruffs, have you missed me? Look what I've got you. A nice bone from the butcher, let's put it in your dish.' Soon, she was sitting in her small armchair, dog at her feet, and knitting needles clacking away nineteen to the dozen.

Having eaten his dinner that evening, Jack helped Ethel with the washing-up before settling in his worn but much-loved armchair by the fire, pipe in one hand, letter in the other. The dog was laying on the rug with his jaw resting on Jack's slippers. For a moment he shut his eyes and contentedly listened to the clacking knitting needles, and the occasional fall of burned coal in the fire. *Bliss, what more can a man want?* he thought to himself with a smile. After a moment, he once again slipped the letter from the envelope and read it quietly to himself.

The Grange

14th November 1907

Dear Jack and Ethel

It was such a pleasure having you here to stay with us last week. I hope your journey home was not overly stressful. As you could see, Anne has now fully recovered from her ordeal and is turning out to be an amazing little mother. You saw that Sally was crawling and we have to keep our eye on where she is trying to go and on what she is reaching for. I am thrilled that you will soon be enjoying the feel of your own baby in your arms. Speaking as a proud grandmother I can say how delightful that is.

Anne is very excited at the prospect of her friend Mavis joining us soon. I am sure we will be able to help her, possibly even take her into our home as a companion for Anne. We will see. Please let us know how things go with your confinement. We look forward to seeing you all in the not too distant future.

With my kindest regards

Elizabeth xx

Jack gave a nod, slipped the letter back into the envelope and looked down at his dog who was now on his feet looking up at him. 'Okay Scruffs, I know, you don't have to tell me. It's walkies time. Come on then,'

The End

THE OLD BOOKMAN

Early morning sun glances off the partly open window. The old man sits on the rumpled bed and looks around the room. An oak wardrobe, a small cupboard on which his old black and white TV sits. Nothing on the screen but a thin layer of dust which is only seen when the sunlight reaches that corner. In fact, nothing has been seen on that screen for over a year now. Familiar pictures and photographs hang on three of the walls. He sits and puzzles over the photographs of people who have long ago moved out of his life. He has no idea who most of them are. He shakes his head and lets out a long sigh. All too much.

Pushing himself to his feet he winces as the familiar ache in his right hip diverts his clouded thoughts. He stands unsteadily until the swaying room settles down, allowing him to shuffle the few steps to the basin where he places liver-spotted hands on both sides and bends forward to examine the face in the mirror. *'Need a shave, when was the last time? Day before yesterday .... I think.'*

He turns on the hot tap, places his left hand under the flow and waits for the cold to turn to warm, then hot. With a satisfied nod he pops the plug into the hole and waits for the water to reach the overflow before turning off the tap. As he washes his face with a blue flannel, blue was always his, he hears shouting on the other side of the door. *'Terry .... Always shouting, don't know at whom or why.'* He rinses his face before drying it on a freshly laundered towel. A final look in the mirror, taking in the silver hair, now covering his large ears. *'Need a haircut, but next week will do.'*

The old man shuffles over to the wardrobe, turns the iron key and pulls the doors open. He is pleased to see that all is neat and tidy, just as he likes it, just as he left it. He takes his time dressing. Although he has various choices, he prefers to wear the same baggy grey trousers, a long-sleeve striped shirt, *'seems okay, may have worn it yesterday ... and maybe the day before.'* He has selected a maroon cardigan with football shaped buttons. Sitting on the single arm chair to put on his woollen socks he notices the twittering of sparrows in the branches of the tree which is on a level with his window. With one sock on, he rises from the chair and takes the two steps necessary to stand before the window to look for the brown feathered creatures. *'Shame I can't open it further'.* He turns and looks at the clock which is fixed to the wall above the TV. *'Time to go, must get the shop ready for opening time. Can't keep the customers waiting, that would never do. Now where did I put those shoes?'*

Taking a last look around the room he lets himself out onto the grey pavement. Looking first to the right then the left he satisfies himself that it's all clear to step out. He gently closes the door then remembers that he has left the key in his room. Once again, he is in the room looking around for a key which isn't there. *'Oh yes, I remember, I don't need one now.'* Back on the pavement with the door closed but not locked he listens to the shouting emanating from Terry's door, shrugs and turns in the direction of the book shop which is the centre and purpose of his life. He is not able to walk so fast these days. He has to favour that painful hip and remember not to put too much weight on that leg if he can help it. He has refused to use a stick, although there is one tucked away somewhere in his room. *'I wonder where that stick is, haven't seen it for a while now, just as well, I don't like it anyhow.'*

As he slowly progresses to his destination the old man thinks about his wife, Edith. A beauty in her day, and so clever with her paint brushes. *'I wonder if any of the pictures on my wall were painted by her? Flowers I seem to remember, yes that's it, flowers and butterflies. Must look when I get home. Shame she left me, oh when was it, seems a long time now. Still, it's nice when she comes to visit, always so chatty and telling me her news. I hope she manages to find time to come to the book shop today. She may bring some of my favourite toffees, the ones with nuts in them.'* Up ahead he can see a young lady pushing a trolley of some sort. A familiar site. As he gets closer, he recognises her face. *'Not from these parts. Somewhere hot I imagine.'*

'Good morning Brian, are you off to your shop?'

'Yes, I am. Lots to do. Have to get all those books back in order.'

'Work never done is it? Just like mine. Still it's nice to be busy. See you later then Brian. Mind how you go now.'

As the old man shuffles away, she shakes her head and watches him move slowly away thinking that he ought to have his stick. Further on, the old man stops to gain his breath for a few moments. As he does so, an elderly lady steps onto the grey pavement and, leaving her door wide open, slowly walks toward him. 'Good morning madam,' he says, remembering just in time that he is not wearing his old trilby which he would surely have lifted. The old woman glares at him and passes by, pressing herself against the wall as she does so.

At last the old man reaches his shop. The door is open and he is pleased to see his assistant sitting at a long table, scissors in hand, cutting what looks like coloured crepe paper. 'Good morning, Brian. Thought you would be along soon. The books are all ready for you. I'll make you a nice cup of tea when I've finished this bit. We're making paper bonnets today, in time for Easter.'

'Good morning Rose. Glad to see you're keeping busy, gives a good impression to the customers. Right then, I'll make a start, makes no difference how often I do it, it always seems to get muddled doesn't it?' Rose pauses from her work and sits back as she watches Brian remove and inspect the first book on the line of shelves. She has become rather fond of this gentle man whose whole life seems to have been wrapped around books. She knows that he used to own a large antique book shop in the busy high street until a fire had destroyed it a few years back. Such a tragedy. Now he spends his days re-living that which is lost to him forever.

Brian, with an orange duster in his hand is humming an un-recognisable tune to himself as he continues his work of love. Neither of the two speak as they enjoy the brief moment of quietness. Rose eventually rises from her seat and leaves the room, to appear five minutes later with a tray of tea and biscuits. 'Here you are Brian, not too much milk, just as you like it, and some shortbreads.' At that moment Brian frowns as the familiar scrape of Mrs

Hardacre's walking frame becomes more and more noticeable. He is not pleased.

No sooner is she in the room, having banged her walking frame into the door as she enters, she has started one of her usual rants about her family who, it would seem, studiously keep their distance. 'Worthless they all are. Don't give a damn about me. It's all a big plot, just after my money, that's what it is. Well, see if I care, they can all rot as far as I'm concerned!'

'Oh, come on Mrs Hardacre, you don't mean that,' says Rose. 'From what I've seen, they care for you a lot. One or other of them often come in here with you to help you choose a book or try your hand at some of my ideas.'

'Books! What do I want with books? I can't see them without my glasses and they can't be bothered to help me find them.'

Brian sighs and tries to ignore the commotion but is not helped when an elderly lady he has not seen before comes into his shop. Rose immediately eases herself away from the muttering Mrs Hardacre and walks over to the new lady. 'Hello, I'm Rose and that's Brian over by the book shelves. If it's a book you're looking for, he's your man, or perhaps you would prefer to ……'

'No, it's okay, it's a book I'm looking for, but I've forgotten its title.'

Hearing this, Brian enters the conversation by asking, 'What was the book about, do you remember?'

'Oh yes, it's about a horse …… I think.'

'And have you read this book about a horse?'

'What horse?'

'The horse you think is in the book you're looking for.'

'Why would I want a horse with a book?' With that, the lady hesitates, looks around the room and, having located the door, walks out.

The morning moves on, Brian stacking and re-stacking before slotting the books into alphabetic order, Rose teaching a number of ladies of varying ages and abilities how to make bonnets. It is soon after the old man has had his morning coffee, along with all present, that a middle-aged lady walks through the door. She is carrying a number of bags. Brian turns his head to see who has entered and quickly puts down the book he is dusting. 'Edith! So glad you were able to come. Thank you. As you can see, I've been busy as always. Have you been doing lots of paintings? I would love to see them. Have you brought any with you?' With that he says to the room generally, 'This is my wife, Edith, come and say hello.'

'Dad ……. Dad, I'm not Edith, I'm your daughter, Susan. Remember? Mummy died soon after the fire. The shock when she thought she had lost you.'

'Died? …. Edith dead? ….. Why was I not told? You could have told me.'

'Dad, I have told you, I told you again on Saturday when I was in with Jimmy, your grandson. Remember?'

Brian looks shocked and tears fill his eyes. 'Yes … I remember.'

'Come on, Dad, let's go down the corridor to your room. We can talk about it there. I've brought you some Brazil

Toffees, you like them, don't you? I do like this nice grey carpet. Dad, why are you wearing just one sock?'

The End

DANCING PARTNERS

It had been raining heavily as we made our way to the local community hall, my duffle bag over my shoulder. Normally I wouldn't bother to carry an umbrella but, on that occasion, I did so in order to keep the bag and its content as dry as possible. Vivian had wanted to call for a taxi, but I deemed it to be an unnecessary expense. She was not too happy with me after stepping unawares into a deep puddle in the deserted precinct. Maybe my laughing at her didn't help. However, her mood had improved by the time we had changed into our dancing shoes and taken to the floor. She was now a competent dancer, having joined our group some seven or eight months previously. On her first evening, she had insisted on partnering me. Against my better judgment I agreed but have since had cause to regret it. She had been a total beginner, while I had become quite proficient in most of the ballroom dances by the time she had joined the group. Had I known then, that my sister would refuse to be partnered by anyone else, I would have been firmer with her all those months ago. Admittedly, with her increased proficiency, dancing with Viv had become more pleasurable, but I would have preferred it if she had gained the confidence to dance with other members. This is the thought that was running through my head on that rainy evening during the coffee break, when I noticed the young lady. She had walked into the canteen accompanied by Miss Clements, our dance instructor. Holding her cup and saucer, she was introduced to Ivan who had been a member for years and who was often asked to partner new members until they had gained a little confidence.

As much as I would have liked to meet the young lady during the break, the time had passed and we were back on the floor, going through the steps of the quickstep. Not an easy dance for a beginner I would have thought. Viv and I were quite confident with this dance, which allowed me time to watch the rather attractive newcomer. I noticed that she carried herself well and her movements were graceful, although hesitant as Ivan led her through the steps. At the close of the session, by the time I had changed out of my dancing shoes, the girl was gone.

I was kept busy during the following week. An apprentice electrician at the local dockyard has little time for leisure. There were always text books to be read at home, as well as theory homework. I sometimes found time to join some of the lads for a game of football on Saturday mornings, but my passion was ballroom dancing. I would often be the butt of good-natured teasing by the lads on Saturday evenings down at the social club when the juke box played one rock-n-roll number after another. At some point during the evening, one or other of them would select a Jim Reeves track and urge me to choose a girl with whom to smooch dance, as they called it. The trouble was, I was awfully shy, and could never get myself to chat to the girls. I had never bucked up the courage to ask for a date.

I enjoyed those Saturdays, but inevitable I would find myself looking forward to Wednesday evenings and the ballroom dance classes. During that particular week, I found that I was occasionally thinking of the girl and hoping she would come again. Why that should be I had no idea, for I hadn't spoken to her and I very much doubted that she had noticed me. Lucky old Ivan, I don't suppose he even noticed how attractive she was. I recalled that she was about the same age as myself, maybe twenty-three. Her shoulder length hair was jet black and shiny enough to catch the light. I particularly liked the way it curled upward at the collar, and the bounce as she moved in time with the music. She was maybe an inch or so shorter than me. Her smile was infectious, the way it turned up the creases on the corner of her mouth. A delicate shade of pink lipstick emphasised the fullness of her lips. Her eyelashes were long with a delicate upward curl. She had worn a pale lemon knee-length dress with a white belt around the waist. I recall how, during the second session that evening my mind kept wondering, to the extent that I made a number of errors in my steps, much to the annoyance of my sister.

At last, Wednesday evening arrived, fortunately this time, without the rain. As usual, Viv held on to my arm as we walked the relatively short distance to the hall. I love my younger sister very much, but I was beginning to feel annoyed that she insisted upon being my partner at every session. Shyness seems to run in our family and I sometimes wondered how Viv and I had ever come into the world. As we neared the hall, I asked, 'Viv, why don't you have a go at partnering someone else for a change. It would be added experience for you, and I know Miss Clements would prefer you to circulate. What about that Edward? He's not a lot older than you, a good dancer, and I've seen him watching you.'

'You sound as though you're trying to get rid of me,' she replied. 'I like dancing with you, we're a good team, aren't we?'

'Yes, but dancing is meant to be a social activity, where you get to meet people, build relationships. I know you're not happy being with people you don't know, but you have to make an effort. Otherwise how will you ever get to know anyone?'

'No, please let me stay with you,' she pleaded as she stopped walking and looked up at me. 'I feel confident with you. I'm not sure that I want to carry on if it's not with you.'

'But Viv, you won't always have me to lean on. I love you, but there will come a time when we both have to think of the future. You'll want to marry and have children, and so will I. We both need to make an effort to meet other people, otherwise how will we ever find that special person with whom to share our lives?'

'I understand all that, but I'm not ready, Bruce. Can you give me a bit longer?' Not feeling able to hurt my sister, I reluctantly agreed, but with the warning that she must make an effort to combat her nervousness about taking another partner in the near future.

I was relieved to see, on our arrival at the hall, that the young lady had come back. She had been detailed to dance with one of the older ladies this time, there being a sad lack of men in the group. My determination to get to know her during the coffee break led to disappointment when she was surrounded by various women for the duration. I think Vivian noticed my interest in the new member because she attempted to dominate my attention while prattling on about something that I failed to take on board.

My frustration continued over the next four of five weeks as Sue, at least I had learned her name, made remarkable progress with her dancing, whilst I made no progress in weaning my sister off of her dependence upon me. However, I did notice that Sue had developed a habit of watching me as we carried out our routines. I even caught an occasional smile over her partner's shoulder whenever we happened to pass closely. Selfishly, I was pleased that she had yet to find a regular partner and therefore spent most of the time with older members, usually women.

What was I to do? How was I ever going to partner this lovely girl without hurting my sister? I had become infatuated by Sue, I had to admit to myself. I couldn't get her out of my mind. The longer I left it, the harder it became. She must have thought, after all those weeks, that I was not interested in her. After all, we were more or less the same age, in fact, apart from Vivian and Edward, who thankfully hadn't shown any interest in Sue, we were the only members below the age of thirty, and we still hadn't really spoken to each other. If only she knew the things that went through my mind on return home on Wednesday nights.

Suddenly, everything changed. It was Saturday and I was invited to play for a local team which was a player short. Of course, I accepted the invitation and enjoyed the game, particularly as I managed to score one of the three goals which led to victory. I couldn't wait to get home and tell my parents and sister how well I had done. I was rather disappointed when I found the house empty, and shocked when I found the note saying that they had taken Vivian to casualty following an accident on her bicycle. A suspected fractured ankle and cuts to her face and arm, the note said. I had to get down there, to see Viv for myself. When I eventually caught up with them, mum and dad were sitting quietly in a waiting room. 'Hello, Bruce.' Mum pointed to a plastic seat opposite them. 'She's been gone for about twenty minutes. The cuts are not too bad, but will need a few stitches. She's having an X-ray to check the ankle but the doctor is fairly sure that it's a sprain.'

'Thank God,' I replied. 'I had all sorts of things running through my head.'

'How did you get on, son,' asked dad.

'We won. I scored the second goal. They may even allow me onto the team on a regular basis.'

'Well done, that's great,' he said with genuine pleasure. 'Looks like you'll have to find yourself a different partner on Wednesdays for a while, I can't see Viv dancing for a few weeks,'

A few minutes later, a wheel-chair was pushed into the crowded waiting room by a porter. My sister, looking somewhat embarrassed, looked up at me from the chair and said, 'Thanks for coming, it's just a badly sprained ankle. They say I can go home but mustn't put any weight on it for a week, and to continue resting it for a few more weeks after that. No dancing I'm afraid.'

'Thank the Lord it was nothing worse,' said mum, taking Viv's hand. 'Never mind dancing, it's bed for you my love. Now let's get you out of here and into the car.'

'Have to go to pharmacy first, mum. For strong pain killers.'

It was another hour before we arrived home that afternoon. My complaining sister was helped upstairs to her bedroom by dad. Later that evening, after a hastily prepared meal, I went up to Viv's untidy teenage girl's room to keep her company for a while. 'Are you cross with me?' she asked. 'You won't have a partner for a few weeks.'

'Oh, don't worry about that, sis. I don't imagine it will be too difficult to find someone who doesn't mind dancing with me.' There was no way I was going to let on that I was seriously looking forward to Wednesday evening. In my imagination I could feel Sue in my arms, her radiant smile beaming up at me. I determined to get to the hall early to ensure that I would get Sue before any of the oldies nabbed her.

Wednesday came, and sure enough, after having explained to Miss Clements that Viv wouldn't be coming for a few weeks, it was she who suggested that I might partner Sue. 'It will be good for her to partner someone her own age for a while,' she said while looking down at her membership list. Shortly after, Sue entered the hall and was told the news about Viv and the fact that she was to partner me in her place. My heart gave a leap when I saw the broad smile crease her face as she looked at me.

Having changed into our dancing shoes, I walked this lovely girl onto the floor for the first time. She moved quite confidently as we tried to come to terms with the Viennese Waltz, not the easiest dance, particularly with a new partner. The music was stopped frequently as Miss Clements talked us all through some of the finer points regarding poise. It was so good having Sue in my arms and I could tell that she was comfortable with me from the outset. The Foxtrot was the last dance of the first session, a more familiar dance for both of us, so-much-so that we were able to chat while moving around the floor. 'I've been looking forward to this, Sue,' I said. 'I noticed you the first week you came in, and I've wanted to dance with you since. Unfortunately, my sister's a bit possessive and won't dance with anyone else at the moment. I keep telling her that she must, but she won't listen.'

As she listened, Sue beamed up at me and replied, 'I'm sorry for your sister, Bruce, but not sorry you want to dance with me.'

'You dance very well, Sue. You've come on in leaps and bounds in the short time I've been watching you.'

She gave a soft laugh and replied, 'Well, I think Miss Clements would have something to say if I started leaping around the floor.'

We continued chatting over coffee, getting to know each other a little. At one point, Edward came over to us and asked, 'No Vivian this evening?' I told him about the accident and the fact that my sister would not be coming for a few weeks. 'Do you think she would mind if I paid her a visit, Bruce?' he asked.

'No, she won't mind, I'll give you our address later.' As he walked away, I was secretly wondering how Viv would get over her shyness and handle his visit. *Oh well, it's done now,* I thought. Then it hit me. *He likes her! Is that why he hasn't shown any interest in Sue? Why hasn't he taken the plunge and asked Viv to dance with him?* It was at that moment that I knew I also needed to take the plunge. Feeling nervous I asked Sue if she would allow me to walk her home that evening. To my relief she instantly agreed. During the second session I felt as though I was floating on air, particularly as I noticed that Sue was holding me more tightly as we moved together. Later, as we walked beneath the street lighting, we found that we had plenty to talk about and we relaxed into each other's stride and company. As we crossed the main road, I plucked up the courage to take her hand. She made no comment when I failed to release it as we continued on our way. I would have walked like that for miles, but all too soon, we were in her street and outside her apartment block. We stopped at the foot of the steps and I turned to face this girl with whom I was feeling so comfortable. *What now? Do I shake hands? Can I kiss her? What is she expecting?* 'Well,' was the best I could say.

'Thank you for walking me home, Bruce,' she said, looking up into my eyes. It was then that I realised I was still holding her hand, so I gave it a squeeze and simply said, 'See you next week then.' I walked away, heart thumping. *Oh, you stupid fool, why didn't you at least kiss her on the cheek?*

It was on the following Saturday afternoon that Edward arrived at our front door. He was clutching a box of Black Magic and a bunch of flowers. *Wow!* Although Viv was resting mainly on the lounge sofa during the daytime, at that moment she was still in bed as far as I knew. I felt guilty that I hadn't mentioned Edward's intended visit to her, mainly out of fear of what she would say to me. 'Hello, Edward, nice of you to come round. I think Vivian is still in bed. Come on in, I'll let her know you're here.' As we passed the foot of the stairs I called up, 'Viv, are you decent? You've got a visitor.'

Most likely thinking it was one of her school friends she shouted down, 'Okay, I'm decent, bring her up please.'

'Okay, Edward, I'll lead the way.' I imagine I had a smirk on my face as we mounted the stairs, for I couldn't wait to see my kid sister's reaction when this boy walked into her bedroom. Cruel? Yes, I suppose it was, as this was confirmed by the sight of Viv flinging the bedclothes over her tussled head when she saw who had stepped in behind me. 'I'll leave you to it then,' I said with a grin as I walked out and down the stairs.

'Who was that? enquired my mother as she stood in the kitchen doorway with a frown on her face.

'Oh, just a boy from the dance group. Who knows, he could be your future son-in-law.'

On the following Wednesday, I asked Sue to be my regular dancing partner. 'What about your sister? Won't she want to continue with you when she's back?' she asked.

I gave her a wink and replied, 'I don't think so, somehow.'

It turned out that Sue and I were natural partners. She was soon dancing with confidence, and I'm sure my dancing skills improved considerably. I continued walking her home, holding hands all the way. We found that we shared the same interests in music, films and books. I was pleased when she even confessed that she liked watching football. It wasn't until the third week that I finally bucked up the courage to kiss her at the door to her apartment. At first it was a tentative move on my part, a gentle kiss on the cheek. However, Sue wasn't going to settle for that. She put her arms around me and kissed my lips. It was amazing. I'm sure my heart stopped for a moment as we held each other closely and she responded warmly when I allowed my lips to part.

Weeks became months. I was in love. I had had no other girl in my life. Sue was the first and the one I had been waiting for. Regardless of the fact that my mother advised me to date other girls, *"Just to be sure,"* as she put it, I had no desire to do so. I wanted Sue, and I wanted her to become my wife. There came an evening, three months into our relationship, when Sue invited me to her apartment for the evening. We had both shared how much we liked musicals, particularly *'The Sound of Music'*. The plan was to have a meal and watch the video together.

Sue's flatmate was away for the weekend, so we had the place to ourselves. That was an amazing evening. We watched the film, we drank some wine, we ate chocolates, and we couldn't resist dancing along with the performers at one point. We never did get around to eating a meal, as my proposal of marriage and Sue's acceptance sort of took over the evening.

Did I stay for the night, you may well wonder? That's for me to know. Suffice it to say that we married a short time later, and our little boy loves dancing whenever we put a musical on the telly. I wonder why it's *'The Sound of Music'* he particularly likes? Oh, and for the record, his Aunty Vivian never did marry.

The End

THE APPRENTICE

The young man, who looked considerably younger than his twenty-one years, walked along the front of The Royal Beach Hotel until he reached the corner where the car park continued around to the back. It was to the back of the hotel that he was heading, for he had remembered, just in time, that he should not use the front entrance. As he stepped along the side of the grand old building, he was aware of the ever-diminishing sound of the waves which were constantly rolling onto the shingled beach. In its place, came the sound of a petrol driven lawn mower which came into view as he reached the rear corner. Sitting on the green machine, a gardener was carefully edging around one of the many rose beds which were in full bloom. Feeling somewhat strange, dressed as he was, in brand new dungarees beneath his old tweed jacket, he gave the gardener a friendly wave before following a wooden sign indicating the direction of the tradesman's entrance.

Upon reaching the newly painted door, the young man checked his wrist-watch to be sure that he was on time. *'Ten minutes early, that's good. Now to find where to go to reach the maintenance office.'* Standing in the wide lobby he looked around to get his bearings. Ahead, there was a stone staircase which could be going anywhere. On his right, a plastic sign on a closed door indicated that this would be the direction to be taken by anyone delivering goods to the hotel. On his left, was a door, also closed, bearing the plastic legend STAFF ONLY. *'That's the one I imagine, let's have a look.'* Grasping the brass handle and on the verge of turning it, a raised voice exclaimed, 'That's staff only, you want this door for deliveries.' The owner of the voice was a young lady dressed smartly in the hotel uniform consisting of navy-blue knee-length pleated skirt, and jacket of the same colour, only with the addition of yellow piping on the collars.

'Hello,' replied the grinning young man, turning around to face the lady. 'You don't understand, I'm new here, I'm the new apprentice in the maintenance department. My name's David, I'm to report to Mr Thomas at nine-o-clock. I assumed this would be the way to go, would that be right by any chance?'

'Oh, I see. Sorry, you'd be surprised how many people don't seem to be able to read. I'm Felicity. You would normally find me in reception when not running an errand for the chief receptionist. Go on through. On second thoughts, I'll take you to your Mr Thomas so that you don't get yourself lost.'

'Thank you, um ... Felicity, that's kind of you.'

'Not at all, it's no trouble, we wouldn't want you to be late on your first morning, would we? This way.' David followed Felicity through the door which led into a long stone-floored corridor. He was struck by the all-pervading smell of oil, polish and cooking. They passed various doors, some open, others closed, but the young man had no time to look at them as he followed behind Felicity who was saying something about the recent warm weather, which David was unable to catch as her high heels click-clacked on the floor. At the far end of the corridor they turned sharp right where an open door revealed a large workshop consisting of a variety of machines, benches and offices. There were a number of dungaree clad figures moving around or standing at benches clutching tools. Following Felicity and feeling somewhat conspicuous, David found himself at the door of the middle office in which he saw Mr Thomas who he had met the previous week. 'Good morning, Cyril. I found this young man at the door, says he's to report to you,' said Felicity cheerfully. 'I'll leave him in your tender care. Bye.' With that, the helpful young lady gave David a wink and headed for the corridor.

'Good morning, David. Nice to see you again,' said Mr Thomas rising from his cluttered desk. I've put you with Matt, he's expecting you. A good man, you'll learn a lot from him. He's been in this hotel for fifteen years or so, and before that, spent some time in the Merchant Navy, tankers I believe. Not much about plumbing he doesn't know. If you're ready? I'll introduce you, and …. good luck.'

Walking across the workshop floor, David was impressed by the abundance of equipment the hotel needed in order to function. Plumbers, electricians, carpenters, and decorators, seemed to be the main disciplines but he was sure there were others. It was plumbing and electricity that he was mainly interested in at this point, and he was pleased that he would be starting with plumbing. Mr Thomas led David to the far end of the room where a man, he assumed to be Matt, was examining a pump of some sort with various bits laid out on his bench. 'Matt, I would like to introduce you to David, the new apprentice I spoke about who will be working with you today,' said Mr Thomas when they had reached the bench.

Straightening himself from the bench, Matt looked David in the eye and shook his hand warmly. 'Welcome to the mad-house young man, soft hands I notice, we'll soon get those hardened up. Okay, Cyril, leave him with me. I've a few basic jobs on today to get the lad started.'

'Right then, see you later, David. Don't forget the staff meeting this afternoon,' said Mr Thomas as he walked over to one of the other members of the maintenance team to exchange a few words.

'Okay, David, leave your jacket over there on that hook and let's get started. We need to go to floor five where there's a reported leak. Bring that bag of tools over there,' said Matt while pointing to a shelf alongside the bench. 'So, you want to make a career of plumbing then? You could do a lot worse. Plumbers are always in demand. Pipes are our bread and butter.'

'Actually,' replied David, 'I'm more interested in a career in hotels.'

'Well then, hotels are full of pipes and pumps and whatnot, so you'll have a field day if you make a go of it, like me,' Matt answered proudly as they walked along the corridor back the way David had come some ten minutes previously. Passing through the staff door they turned to the left and climbed a flight of the stairs before reaching another closed door which Matt pushed through. Leaving the echo and bareness of the stairs behind, David's world suddenly changed as he stepped onto a green carpet in a wide corridor decorated with crimson flock wallpaper, and along which he noticed many pictures suspended on the walls. There were also a number of polished tables upon which fresh flower arrangements were displayed. 'This way, lad. We take the lift from here.'

Two minutes later, the dungaree clad figures emerged onto another richly furnished corridor on the fifth floor. Turning to the right, Matt said over his shoulder, 'Okay, lad, it's number five-two-three we want. It's occupied but I'm told the guests are out at the moment. I have a skeleton key, something that should always be kept secure when you get one.' Once in the room, Matt made straight for the tastefully tiled bathroom. 'Okay, let's have a look and see what the problem is.' A cursory examination of the shower soon revealed the problem, as water dripped from a joint on one of two pipes running down from the ceiling. David, still holding the heavy bag of tools, stood in the bathroom doorway watching Matt as he rubbed his thumb on the joint. 'Okay lad, this should be a quick one. Put that bag down and pass me the large screwdriver, it should be on the top.' David quickly saw the screwdriver, which he passed to Matt who glanced at it before saying, 'No, not that one, I want the left-handed screwdriver.'

'The left-handed one? Um …. I'm not sure there is one, replied David with a puzzled look on his face.'

'Oh blast! said Matt. 'Don't tell me someone's borrowed it without a by-your-leave. You'll have to go back down to the workshop and ask if anyone has the quarter-inch left-handed screwdriver. Quick as you can, mind. We have a fair bit to do and Cyril, that's Mr Thomas to you, wants it done before the end of the day as the new owner is expected this afternoon.'

Once in the workshop, David called out to the room in general, 'Has anyone got the quarter-inch left-handed screwdriver please?' The question raised a few chuckles and a frown from Mr Thomas, before one of the men walked over and offered a large screwdriver to the young man who reached out to receive it.

'No, not that hand, mate, you have to carry it in your left hand, like this, see?'

'Oh, right, if you say so,' replied David who immediately turned and headed for the door. In his hurry to get away he failed to notice Mr Thomas standing in his doorway shaking his head.

Back in room five-two-three David handed Matt the screwdriver, having firstly checked that it was still in his left hand. 'Thanks lad, I've got this sorted now, I'll just give it a final turn.'

David watched as Matt used the screwdriver, then said, 'Hang on a moment, you're using your right hand.'

'Course I am lad, I'm right-handed ain't I?'

'But why did you want the left-handed screwdriver?'

'It's obvious ain't it? It's because the leak was from the left-hand pipe. My my, you do have a lot to learn, don't you? Okay, we're done here. Second floor, room two-twenty. No warm water-flow. You carry the bag. Trot trot, no time to waste.'

Walking to the lift at the far end of the corridor, Matt asked, 'Where were you before this, then, Dave?'

'I prefer *David*, if you don't mind. I more or less came here straight from Uni. This is my first job.'

'Oh, I see, university education and now an apprenticeship. Covering all your options then?'

'Something like that,' replied David with a grin.

'I can see you're smart, smart enough to find me a left-handed screwdriver at any rate,' chuckled Matt.

As they made their way to the next job, David marvelled at the grandeur of the building and the feeling of comfort and calmness. They passed a few guests who politely nodded to them with smiles. David was very much aware of the quality of their dress and jewellery. 'Right, this is the one, David,' said Matt. 'Hope we can get this sorted before lunch break.' It was a double room with a balcony situated at the front of the hotel and overlooking the sea. The suite was currently unoccupied. Matt walked directly to the large beautifully furnished lounge. There, he made his way over to the wall opposite the balcony doors. Placing his ear to the wall he tutted and remarked, 'Just as I thought, need to check this out. Right, David, I'll take the bag, you come over here and place both hands on the wall, like this. That's it, now put your ear against the wall, here. Over a bit ... that's it, perfect. I'm going up to the room above. What I want you to do is to keep pressing on the wall and listen.'

'What am I listening for?' asked a mystified apprentice.

'You'll know it when you hear it, lad. I'm off. Keep pressing and keep listening.'

***

'Where's David?' enquired Mr Thomas of Matt. 'Don't tell me you've got him listening to a wall?'

'Just a bit of fun, Cyril. Won't do him any harm. I expect he'll do the same to some apprentice, given time.'

'Somehow, Matt, I don't think so. If you'll take my advice, you'll go easy on him. Don't forget he's here to learn. And make sure you take him a coffee when you've had yours. We don't want him to miss his break, do we?'

'Okay, Cyril, will do. He'll be okay. Somehow I think he'll have a big future in this hotel.'

'Yes, Matt, you could be right,' replied Mr Thomas with a grin.

Meanwhile, David was sitting on the balcony admiring the view, and taking the opportunity to relax. *'Yes, I think I'm going to enjoy my time here. I know I have a lot to learn but it's certainly going to be worth it.'* As he sat back and lifted his arms to the back of his head enjoying the sun on his face, he thought about that charming and very attractive Felicity. *'I wonder if she's free tonight?'* he mused with a huge grin on his face. Hearing the entrance door open, he managed to close the balcony doors and regain his leaning position, just before Matt re-entered the lounge.

'Here you are lad, as busy as I was up there, I managed to get you a cup of coffee, I hope you take milk?'

'Yes, that's very kind, thank you Matt.'

'Good, get that down you, then it's on to the next assignment. This one's sorted now, just a sticky valve between floors, nothing a skilled plumber couldn't fix in a jiffy.' Very quickly, David swallowed the lukewarm coffee and replaced his empty cup in the saucer. 'What's the next job?' he enquired.

'You can leave the tray here. We'll pick it up on the way back. Next *assignment*, we don't call them jobs, is on this floor. A runny cistern. Elderly lady in residence. Been here for years. A nice lady, she'll take to you, no doubt. She likes 'em young.'

Soon, they were at the entrance door where Matt rang the doorbell button. This was followed by the rattle of a chain before the door moved to reveal a narrow gap where a wrinkled face beneath pure white hair appeared at the height of David's midriff.

'Yes? Who is it? Oh, it's you Matt. Just a moment while I get this silly chain off.' With that, the door slammed shut and there followed a great deal of rattling and cursing which lasted a full minute before the door swung fully open. 'Come in then, don't just stand there like a lemon,' the lady said rather loudly. 'I won't bite. Oh, who's this then?' she asked while looking at David who had stepped out from behind Matt. 'Maybe I will bite, if I could just find my teeth.'

'Now now, Betty, behave yourself, we don't want to frighten our new staff member on his first day. This is David and he's here to help me with your water problem.'

'Oh, he's a doctor then? Do you want me in the bedroom young man?'

'No, Betty, it's the runny cistern in your bathroom we came to look at,' replied Matt with a smile.

'Pity, never mind, off you go, you know where it is.'

Following Matt and gingerly stepping passed the old lady, David was suddenly shocked by a sharp pat on his bottom. As a result, he managed to get into the bathroom ahead of Matt. 'My, you're a keen one,' Matt said with a grin. 'Okay, I can see the problem here. I'll get the top off while you run down and ask anyone in the workshop for an orbital phallus.'

'A ballcock, yes I've got it, Matt. Any particular size?' responded David with a resigned smile.

'You're all the same, you youngsters. Size isn't everything you know. They're all the same here, lad. So off you go, I expect you back in ten minutes, and no making eyes at Betty as you go through.'

So, David's first morning passed very quickly and he found that he actually enjoyed the time spent with Matt. He had expected to be the butt of various jokes so no big surprises there, although, he had plans of his own where Matt was concerned. On completion of their last assignment for the morning, Matt said, 'Okay, lad. Lunch time. How did you find it this morning?'

'Very interesting, I felt particularly pleased with the wall listening. I never knew you could feel a wall tremble as much as that one did. And the grinding sound was interesting. I suppose it was ….'

'What grinding noise?' said Matt in sudden alarm. 'Did you say, *"trembling?"*

'Why, yes. Isn't that what I was supposed to feel?' replied David while trying to maintain an innocent face.

'Come on, let's go, grab the bag,' said Matt as he rushed for the door.

In very quick time Matt reached the room in question and instantly went to the wall. He was followed by David who sauntered along the corridor, carrying the bag and whistling a popular tune. Entering the apartment, David lowered the bag to the floor and retrieved his mobile phone from his pocket. Once in the lounge, he raised his phone and looked at the screen in which he could see the irate plumber with one ear and two hands pressed to the wall.

'Smile.' Click. The image was captured.

The plumber stepped back in surprise. 'Why, you young devil!' His face turned into a frown, to be quickly replaced by a smile. It wasn't long before the pair of them surrendered to uninhibited laughter, the kind of laughter that breaks down barriers, releases tension and cements friendships. 'Come on, lad, let's go and have some lunch,' said Matt as he began to recover while wiping the tears away from his streaming eyes with his dungarees sleeve. 'I'll carry the bag this time, you bring the coffee tray.'

***

On entering the staff dining room, the first person David saw was Felicity who was sitting alone by a window overlooking the car park. She had not noticed him so looked up in surprise when he said, 'Mind if I join you?'

'Sure, help yourself,' she replied with a broad smile. 'Knives and forks are over there on that small table.'

Having collected his cutlery and placed his loaded tray on the table, opposite Felicity, David said, 'I was hoping I'd see you here.'

'Oh, and why would that be?' she responded as she placed her used cutlery on her cleared plate.

'You know, friendly face in the midst of strangers, that sort of thing.'

'Well, it won't be for long. I've finished my lunch and must get back to the desk to relieve Patsy.'

'Listen, before you go. Are you doing anything this evening? I wondered if you would like a stroll along the prom, maybe have a beer in the *Ocean View*. All very harmless.'

'That's a bit forward isn't it?' replied Felicity as she arose from the table. 'We don't know each other. I don't usually go dating with men I've barely spoken to.'

'Please say "Yes", What better way to get to know each other, and I feel I need a friend here.'

'I don't know,' replied Felicity. 'Maybe if you're still here in a month's time we could think about it. You may not take to the job. Work in a hotel can be a bit pressurised you know. You have to be committed. I love this hotel and am prepared to give it my best, that's how you will have to be if you are to survive.'

'Believe me,' responded David. 'Nobody could be more committed than me. Please allow me to walk you out this evening …. Please?'

'Okay, but don't read too much into it. Meet at the pier entrance at eight. That's the earliest I can get away.'

'Great! I'll be there. Thank you.'

'Now, I must go. Don't forget there's a staff gathering in the ballroom this afternoon. We'll get to meet the new owner. Now, eat your bangers before they get too cold.'

With that comment, Felicity walked away and stacked her tray. She looked back at David as she left the room, wondering what it was about him that caused her to accept his invitation for the evening. Then she realised that she was actually attracted to him. *'Impossible.'*

***

The afternoon proved to be of extreme interest to David. The silly jokes were forgotten and the teaching stepped up as David came to realise the extent of the work being carried out behind the scenes in the hotel. Matt was a good teacher and was extremely patient as David fumbled his way with the intricacies of soldering a good joint. Fifteen minutes before four, they had finished their last assignment of the day and had cleared away and washed up. Along with the other members of maintenance, who were free to attend, they made their way to the ballroom amidst much speculation as to what kind of person had inherited their hotel.

'Let's hope it's someone who's prepared to be hands on,' Matt said to David as they took their seats on the back row. 'Last thing we want is an absent owner. The last one was amazing, bless him. Always around to help out, advise and listen. We'll miss him.'

'Popular then?' responded David.

'None better. A good man if ever there was.'

At that moment, David became aware of someone taking the seat alongside him and, turning to look, was pleased to see Felicity settling down and smiling at him. 'Hi.'

'Hi.'

The low murmur of conversation amongst the gathering of staff, who's duties had enabled them to attend, ceased as Mrs Night, the Manager who had worked in the hotel since leaving school some thirty years ago, walked through the door, accompanied by a slightly balding middle-aged man. Together they stepped up onto the low stage where normally a band would lead the dancing. 'Good afternoon ladies and gentlemen. Thank you for coming to this informal gathering. I know you are all very busy so we won't keep you long. I would like to introduce you to Mr Bishop who will say a few words.'

The low murmur of conversation that arose following the introduction of the unsmiling gentleman, ceased as he stood, placing a finger inside his shirt collar to ease it away from his neck. It was clear to the assembled staff that Mr Bishop was nervous. For a moment or two he looked along the rows of expectant faces, stopping only when his sweeping glance reached the back row. 'Ladies and Gentlemen, I know how fond you all were of the late Mr Shaw ….. and I am sorry for your loss …. He built this business up …. through his dedicated commitment …… to what it is now ….. a hotel of international acclaim. He asked me to tell you personally that he has arranged for each and every one of you to receive a bonus according to length of service ….. as an expression of thanks for your hard work ….. and your friendship. His hope was that your …. commitment and support …..will be equally enjoyed and valued by your new owner. So, without further delay, as Mr Shaw's close friend and solicitor, I have pleasure in introducing you to his nephew, the new owner who assures me that, with your help, he intends learning, with hands on, every aspect of the running of this hotel….. David Shaw.' As he said this, his eyes moved to the back of the room and he raised his hand to beckon the owner forward.

All heads turned as the bewildered staff looked to see the new apprentice, still in dungarees, on his feet and saying something to the plumber who had been sitting alongside him.

'Thank you, Matt. I enjoyed my first day enormously. See you at eight thirty tomorrow.'

Then turning to the receptionist who had her hand covering her mouth, he said, 'Forgive me, Felicity. I really wanted to invite you out for our first date before you found out. Otherwise you would probably have felt too awkward to agree. I'll be at the pier at eight. I hope you'll be there.'

The End

THE HANDBAG

Having finished the morning task of scrubbing their front door steps the three ladies dropped their scrubbing brushes into their respective buckets before congregating on the cracked flagstone pavement outside Mrs Flack's terraced house, their usual meeting place at this time of the morning, weather permitting. This was a pleasantly warm spring morning with the possibility of blue cloudless skies for the remainder of the day. A welcome break following the constant rain of the last four days.

'Give us a fag Lil, it's your turn I think,' said Doreen. 'I could do with a puff.'

'Yea, me too,' chipped in Doris, the youngest of the three. 'I won't 'ave any till me old man rolls in from the pub at tea time.'

'Anyone would fink you two were skint the way you go on,' muttered Lil as she reached into her pinny pocket for a packet of Woodbines and a box of Swan matches. After offering the open packet to her two neighbours she took a cigarette for herself, placed it between her lips and took a match from its box before striking it on the side and holding it out for the others to suck the smoke into their lungs.

'Ahh, that's better, 'elps to clear me 'ead,' sighed Doreen before taking in another puff of smoke. 'Ad a right old barny wiv our Ted afore 'e left for the yard this mornin. 'Im an' 'is pigeons, 'e'll sleep with 'em if I allowed it. He let 'is breakfast go cold 'cos 'e 'ad to check on 'is champion before the race tomorrer. *"You fink more of that bird than you do of me,"* I told 'im. Know what 'e said? 'E said *"Yea, praps I do. At least it don't nags me all day long."* Me? Nag? What's 'e on about?'

'You two going down to the Bingo later?' enquired Lil.

'Yea, I'm comin' I feel a big win comin' on,' replied Doris. 'I could do wiv a few more quid in me pocket.'

'Me too,' said Doreen. I fancy that new caller with his clickety-clicks.'

'You fancy anyone in trousers what's younger than you and what ain't got feavers,' said Doris with a chuckle. 'I remember that baker who used to come round wiv 'is 'orse n cart. You bought so much bread it was comin' out yer ears.'

'Yea? And what about that knife sharpener bloke?' replied Doreen indignantly. 'You 'ad so many knives sharpened I thought you was goin' to a one-woman war somewhere.'

'Watch out you two,' whispered Lil. 'It's that weird old biddy comin' out over the road.'

The three of them fell silent as they stared at an elderly lady who had just stepped out of her porch onto the sunlit pavement. Without looking at the three silent glaring figures she opened her large handbag and dropped her front door key into the opening before quickly fastening the clasp. Before walking away from the house, the white-haired lady gave her front door a final push to check that it really was locked. Stepping away from the door she looked up at her front bedroom window to be sure it was firmly closed, then, still without looking at her three neighbours, she limped up the cobbled street, leaning heavily on her stick.

'Stuck-up cow!' said Doreen in such a way as to be sure the elderly lady would hear. 'Who does she fink she is? Never speaks, never scrubs 'er step. And what's she got in that huge 'andbag she always carries around? That's what I'd like to know.'

***

Step by slow step the old lady limped away from the three women, her handbag clasped firmly in her left hand. More and more, as arthritis curled her fingers and weakened her knees, the bag seemed to become heavier and heavier. It couldn't be helped. She had to keep it with her at all times. The street was one of the longest in this neighbourhood. So many people lived in the small terraced houses, each with a bow window straight onto the pavement. There seemed to be more cars parked along the kerb than there had been when she moved in some three years earlier. She still knew none of the residence, although she was familiar with the sight of the ladies opposite who always gave her the evil eye whenever she left the house or opened her door to pick up her milk bottle and place the previous day's empty in its place. This was a close community and she supposed it would take many years to be accepted.

The old lady was in the habit of counting off the lamp-posts and, as expected, at the fifth one the sleek tabby cat emerged from under a parked car and rubbed itself against her legs. *Hello my furry friend, and how are you today? Have you caught any mice? Not sparrows though, I hope.* The cat purred its greeting as it sniffed at the handbag which hung just above the old lady's knees. *No, there's nothing in there to interest you, little one, but look what I have in my coat pocket. A nice bit of cheddar cheese, I know you like that, don't you?* As best as she was able, she bent down to give her friend the nob of cheese and a scratch on its cheek. With its tail in the air the cat gave a final rub on the lady's leg before slipping under the car.

It took twenty minutes to reach the end of the street where she pressed the button on the post in order to stop the main-road traffic. The green man appeared on the small screen, accompanied by the usual bleeping sound. As usual, before she had reached the safety of the opposite pavement the green man had changed to red and the waiting cars had started to inch forward in a threatening manner. *Why are people so impatient these days? I had no choice over there. If conditions weren't right you just had to sit it out.*

Approaching the sheltered bus stop, the old lady noticed a young man, possibly in his twenties, standing at the stop. He was wearing a dark suit and a trilby hat. This caused her to feel uncomfortable as she drew nearer. With each faltering step she clutched the handles of her handbag ever tighter. She hoped the number 700 would be along soon, although it was often late if it had been held up at the railway crossing further back. Reaching the stop, the lady eased herself on to one of the plastic seats, clearly not designed for comfort. All the while she kept her eye on the young man who was periodically looking at his wristwatch.

'Have you any idea when the 700 is due?' the young man suddenly barked. Alarmed by being addressed so suddenly and in such a way, the old lady stood up and clutched her handbag to her chest. She gave no reply as she inched a little further away from the man. 'Sorry, didn't mean to make you jump, it's just that I'm late for an interview.'

Interview. That's what they called it when they came for us. "We need you both to come for an interview down at Headquarters." Interview indeed. Well I hope this young man is able to walk away from his interview. My husband never did. At least my friends were able to get me away from them when they had tried to drive me to the place where I had falsely indicated they would find what they were looking for. But not before I had lost my finger nails and tongue.

'That looks like it coming now ... yes I can see it's a 700. Are you alright now madam? Would you like me to take your bag as you get on?' the man asked while reaching out his hand to assist her. Once again, the old lady shrank back and clutched her handbag, this time with both arms around it. 'Okay, please yourself. After you,' he said as he stepped aside, allowing her to step onto the platform and show her concessionary pass. Following the lady onto the platform after she had taken her seat, the young man gave the driver his destination and offered up a ten-pound note. 'She's a funny one,' he said to the driver. 'I think she was afraid I would mug her and steal her bag.'

'I wouldn't mess with her, mate. She used to be in the SAS and the French Resistance during the war. She's a regular on this bus, but I've never heard her speak.'

'Wow, you can never judge people, can you? What's in that bag that's so precious, do you know?' asked the amused and amazed man.

'Some think it's her old pistol, but that's just a bit of nonsense. Must get on, I've got some time to make up.'

***

Half an hour later, at a small village just outside the city, the regular 700 bus climbed the short hill before reaching the bus stop by the old post office which had been closed for the last eighteen months. The bus door swung open and an elderly lady carefully stepped down onto the kerb. She was holding a large handbag in one hand and a walking stick in the other. When the bus moved away the lady slowly crossed the relatively quiet road and made her way to the war memorial a short distance away. Starlings were chattering in the trees and the old lady stopped for a moment to listen, a sound which she particularly liked as it invariable made her happy to hear the friendly chatter as the fussy birds shared their news with each other. One big happy family, as she preferred to think of them. At last, she reached the memorial and immediately made her way to the other side, where the names of the fallen were honoured. She froze in horror.

Much later, tears streaming down her cheeks, the old lady limped along her street blindly passing the terraced houses. She even failed to notice the tabby cat who appeared from nowhere to follow her along the street. *How could they? How could they do such a thing? It's so cruel and mindless. All those brave men who gave everything for such people. Black swastikas painted all over the stone and the plaque. Why? Why? Why? I wish I could get my hands on them. I could kill them!*

As the old lady painfully limped passed the last few lamp-posts she became aware of the voices from across the road.

'There she is again, old Mrs Stuck-up.'

'Bet she's been boozing somewhere, what with 'er limp and stick, she can barely keep 'erself upright.'

'Spect that's why she ain't got a man. Nobody would 'ave 'er. 'Ere do you reckon that bag's full of Gin bottles so she can't bear to leave it behind when she goes out?'

'That's right, old lady, you get inside so we don't 'ave to look at the likes of you.'

Fumbling with her door key while holding on to bag and stick, the old lady managed to get the door open and stepped up into the passage. Tears still streaming down her cheeks unchecked, she stumbled into the parlour where she placed the bag on the table. Opening a door to her dresser she pulled out a stiff cardboard box about the size of an OXO tin. Not having been open for many years, the trembling lady finally managed to prise off the lid before lifting out a number of grease packed cartridges. Moving back to her bag, she unclipped the fastener and lovingly lifted out the M1917 Revolver. The same one she had used in France all those years ago. Having finished her task, she limped slowly down the passage to her front door.

The End

THE RESCUE

If there is one thing I love early on a warm sunny Saturday morning in August, it's a fried breakfast lovingly prepared by my beautiful wife, Coleen. Even after three months of marriage I still get a thrill out of referring to my childhood friend as, *Wife*. The thought of spending the rest of our lives together fills me with wonder and awe. I can't imagine life without that amazing girl by my side, not that I've ever tried. We had become inseparable friends on the first day that we met. I was the new boy in the class. No friends, no familiar faces. The teacher, Miss Hudson, introduced me to the class of thirty-three boys and girls who stared at me with varying expressions, smirks from a few of the boys, smiles from several girls, indifference from the majority.

'Now, let me see,' said Miss Hudson after the introduction, 'Janet, you collect your books and belongings from your desk and go and sit next to Phillip, I know you get on well. Is that all right with you?'

'Yes Miss, I wanted to move anyway, thank you,' said Janet as she started gathering her belongings from under her desk lid.

'Okay,' said Miss Hudson. 'Now, Ronald, you can sit at Janet's old desk next to Coleen. She will help you settle in, is that not so, Coleen?'

'Yes Miss,' replied the pretty girl whose shiny black pigtails caught the light from the window alongside her as she nodded her head enthusiastically.

At some point during the arithmetic lesson that followed, something hit the back of my head, causing me to drop my pencil and swing round in my seat. At the back of the room, three desks from my own, there were two boys watching me closely, one grinning, the other with the same smirk I had seen earlier on his face. Before I had time to react further, Coleen was out of her chair and storming up the aisle. Before I was able to get to my feet, and also before Miss Hudson had time to intervene, Coleen had pushed the smirking boy from his chair and was standing over him shouting, *'Collins, you leave him alone or I'll get you in the playground and make you eat dirt. And that goes for anyone else who wants to see how tough I am.'*

Before the boy had time to crawl away from his upturned chair and Coleen's feet, the angry teacher rushed up the aisle and took Coleen by the arm before sweeping her to the front of the class. 'Coleen Phelps, what do you think you are doing? I will not tolerate this kind of behaviour in my class. I'm surprised at you. Come and see me after the final bell this afternoon.'

That was the first day of our friendship which survived the punishment dished out to Coleen by Miss Hudson, and my anger with her for showing me up as a weakling in front of the class, when I saw her in the playground before bell the next morning.

Now, forking a piece of sausage into my mouth I looked into Coleen's open and fresh face and said, 'How about coming down to the boat with me this morning? We've nothing planned, it promises to be a fine day, and the varnish is completely dry. We could sail round to the estuary and up the river for a lunch in The Jolly Rover. I want to check the rigging is all running as it should, anyway. What do you say?'

'Well, I had thought about popping in to see your mum, possibly help out in the garden. She's not expecting me though.'

'Well there you are then. We're invited over there for Sunday lunch tomorrow anyway. So, we'll see her and dad together. We can do the dishes and be away in half an hour. Are you on?'

'Okay Honey, you know I can't resist being out on the water. Let's do it, and lunch is on you. By the way, didn't you say you were going down to the Lifeboat Station today? Something about meeting a new volunteer, as I recall.'

'That's okay. We can call in there before going on to the boat yard. He's supposed to turn up to meet the skipper at ten. It's just an induction before going down to Poole next month for basic training. Won't hold us up for long.'

Forty minutes later, we were walking down to the harbour amidst holiday makers and day trippers who were also heading in the same direction. I could imagine that the bay was going to be packed throughout the day. Sunbathers, swimmers, castle builders, kite flyers, strollers, surfers, they would all be there on this fine day. In shorts, T-shirts, and yellow wellies, and carrying my waterproof ditty bag for mobiles and watches, we passed souvenir shops, cafes, fish-n-chip restaurants and other usual sights to be seen in a popular holiday resort. I know that some of the locals resent this annual invasion, but I don't mind, although I have to admit I prefer the off-season when the town returns to some sort of normality. As usual, I was wearing my pager which was suspended on a cord around my neck. It had not sounded for over two weeks now, a straight forward assistance to a private motor launch which had picked up a line around its prop. I was hoping that today would be free of any alarms as we continued our walk to the boat yard via the Lifeboat Station, for I was really looking forward to our sail up the river and the lunch we would enjoy together.

Soon we were at the Lifeboat Station where the large doors were fully open to allow holiday makers to look at the two orange coloured boats as well as the various photographs and plaques displayed. I was pleased to see the elderly volunteers, Mr & Mrs Watkins, serving in the RNLI shop alongside where appropriate merchandise was sold. They had been doing this for as many years as I cared to remember, and had been very welcome guests at our wedding. Together, Coleen and I entered the shop and greeted the couple. 'Morning Ron, Coleen, good to see you both,' replied John as he looked up from a small sales ledger on the counter. 'The skipper's in the crew room with the new lad, if you're looking for him.'

'Okay John. Are you both well?' I enquired.

'Yes, thank you,' responded Nel. Never better. We're off to the bowls club after this.'

I loved this place. It was like family and I was pleased that Coleen had agreed to become a volunteer once she had finished her Open University course. Together, we made our way upstairs to the crew room where we were able to meet the new volunteer who, all being well, would at some time in the future, become a fully trained crew member.

'Ah, here he is. Luke, I would like you to meet my deputy, Ron Chalmers, and his charming wife, Coleen,' said Ben, the skipper, with a big smile on his rugged face. 'You'll soon get to know everyone, Luke.' Turning to me, Ben continued, 'I've warned Luke that it will take a while to work up to Crew status but that, if he sticks to it, it's just a question of time.'

'Hello, Luke,' I said, 'Welcome to the team. I look forward to getting to know you. Listen to this man, there isn't a thing he doesn't know about boat handling. Salt in the blood, ex-Royal Navy. A great skipper.' Turning to Ben I said with a wink, 'That'll cost you a beer or two later, skipper. Right, me and this wench here are off sailing. If you get a shout, you're on your own.'

'Ha! As if you'd do any good, you don't know a reef-knot from a bow. Don't go bumping into any innocent fishermen while you're out there in your little sail boat. And don't teach this beautiful young lady any of your bad ways.'

'Don't you worry about that, skipper. I didn't know what bad ways where till we were wed. She knows them all.'

With a laugh, Ben replied, 'Off with you, have a good time and think of us poor souls working our hearts out here while you swan around, and don't call us if you capsize.'

Leaving the Lifeboat Station, we soon left the happy throng of visitors behind as we entered a narrow cobbled lane between rows of cottages which had seen the Royal Navy press gangs as well as smugglers in their time, each cottage individual in style and condition. The inevitable seagulls, with their constant hungry cries, passed overhead or perched on roofs or crooked chimneys. This was home to me and I could not imagine ever living anywhere else. I was so thankful that Coleen had also fallen in love with the town during the many holidays she and her parents had spent with us after my parents had decided to move here when my school days were over. There had never been any question of where we would live after our wedding, and thankfully my work at the local brewery paid our rent.

At the end of the lane the cottages gave way to a small nature reserve before reaching the mouth of the estuary. The sailing club, to which we were heading, owned a wooden jetty which was built some eighty years ago and which stood alongside a public slipway. My Firefly dinghy gleamed in the sunshine, having had three coats of varnish recently applied. She was squatting on the launching trolley where I had left her the previous weekend, her name, *Little Gem* newly painted on the transom. The original cotton sails were hidden within their protective covering which I quickly removed. We were ready to go. A glance at the water's edge confirmed what I already knew, that the tide was some three hours before the ebb, which would enable us to have an easy reach up the river to our destination, The Jolly Rover.

'Okay, sweetheart, you take the stern I'll take the bows. Shouldn't be too difficult between the two of us. Ready to go?'

'Yes. Let's do it,' Coleen replied.

In less than four minutes Coleen was standing thigh deep in the sea, holding on to *Little Gem* while I hauled the launching trolley back onto level ground. Quickly rejoining her and casting my wellies into the bows alongside Coleen's, I paddled into the water and held the gunwale while my nimble wife swung herself aboard. Still holding onto the dinghy, I watched as Coleen unfastened the foresail and hauled it up the mast before securing it to one of the cleats. She then dropped the centre board, before taking the tiller and giving me a nod. We were away and I was climbing in over the transom. With Coleen steering into the light wind toward the open sea I cleared the mainsail and hauled it to the top of the mast. Immediately, *Little Gem* heeled to starboard while I took up my position on the portside gunwale to balance her.

'Okay sweetheart, you keep the helm, bring her round slowly and watch out for an unexpected jibe. With the wind as it is, we shouldn't need to do a controlled jibe till we reach the bend near the village. You happy with that?'

'Yes, I've got her,' replied my wife who was now skipper with me crewing. I had no concerns, as she had become a competent helmsman during the previous season when we were both looking forward to our new life together. Sailing, rock climbing, hill walking and classical music were passions we both enjoyed, and we were in complete harmony with each other's feelings and moods. The sun shone down on us as we were gently caressed by the following breeze. The bows lifted slowly with each passing wave. The chuckling of water under the stem was music in our ears. The peace and quiet of the moment, was a balm to our busy lives. All was right with the world.

My pager broke the silence!

'Damnation' I exclaimed. 'Missed that one, I'll call them on the mobile and see what's afoot.' With Coleen steering us upriver on an easy reach I had time to recover my phone from the ditty bag and dial the Station. Hearing Tina's voice after the fourth ring I said, 'It's me, Ron. I won't be able to respond, what's happening?'

'Hello, Ron. We've had a call from a private cabin-cruiser, twenty-three miles south. Fire in the galley, one casualty, burns, quite severe. They're preparing the

Tamar, full crew expected, four already here. A helicopter is already on its way. ETA thirty-five minutes.'

'Okay Tina. Thank you. Sorry I won't be involved this time.'

'You can't do them all, Ron. Enjoy your lunch. Must go. Bye.'

The line went dead. Suddenly the day had changed. I could never relax when the crew were out without me, but I was determined to make Coleen my priority for once. Placing my mobile back into the bag I grinned at my wife and said, 'All in hand. A helivac, severe burns, a private craft had a galley fire. We'll let them get on with it while we enjoy ourselves. Right, move over, I'll take the helm for a bit, help me to take my mind off of it.' That was never going to happen however, for twenty minutes later the helicopter flew directly over us on its way to the sea. Our sail up the river continued. We were both silent, each in our own private thoughts. Every instinct within my being was screaming, *Turn back.*

The banks of the river in which we were sailing were becoming closer on both sides. Open fields, in which black and white cattle grazed, had given way to dense woods with trees growing right down to the water's edge. We had passed no other craft since leaving the estuary. My attention was momentarily aroused by the sight of a cormorant perched on a dead tree branch, which was partly immersed in the water on the right-hand bank. The large black bird was drying its wings which were spread wide apart. I was about to point the bird out to Coleen when my mobile rang from within the bag. Coleen quickly pulled it out and answered it. I watched as her smile changed to a look of deep concern. Having listened for no more than a few seconds she said, 'Hold on, Tina, I'll pass you over.' With that, she slipped onto the stern seat, handed me the instrument and took the tiller from my hand.

'Hello Tina. What's up?'

I listened to what the Station controller had to say, then abruptly said, 'Were on our way, keep us informed please.' I quickly switched off the phone and handed it back to Coleen. 'I'll take the tiller, love. We have to go back. They need us. Ready about!'

As only a competent crew can do, we turned the Firefly on a sixpence and in less than half a minute we were flying close hauled on the port tack. Without a word having been spoken Coleen was leaning her body weight well out on the starboard side. This was my favourite point of sailing. Speeding through the water with the ever-present possibility of a capsize. Very soon we were fast approaching the river bank and we expertly went through the drill of putting the dinghy on to the starboard tack while maintaining maximum speed. So far, Coleen hadn't questioned my actions. Knowing me as she did, she would realise that what we were doing was important and that I would explain as soon as possible, and this was the moment.

'The Tamar is still out and won't be free for a long time. The Station's had a second call, this time a young person caught in a rip and drifting out to sea on a surf board. Fortunately, they had surplus volunteers who attended the first alert but too late to join the crew. They have taken the B Class, three on board. They're searching now. A few minutes ago, they received a third call. A lad out on one of the offshore rocks, paddled out in a canoe, he's fallen from the top. He was able to dial 999 on his mobile. He's sure that he's broken his leg. The Fowey Trent Class is on its way but that will take over forty minutes. We've been asked if we can make our way to the rocks to see if we can spot him.'

Following this rather lengthy explanation, I was relieved to see the determined look on Coleen's face and the brief nod of her head. There was no need for further words between us. We both knew what to do and what was expected. I could never, after the event, put a time on it, but much sooner than I would have imagined, we had left the calm river and emerged from the estuary to meet the incoming waves. We were both soaked as spray broke over the bows of our little dinghy. Soon, Coleen was using the baler to prevent too much water slopping around our feet. As we approached the cluster of offshore rocks Coleen suddenly pointed. Following the direction indicated by her arm I quickly spotted something red on a ledge near the foot of the largest rock. *'That's it!'* I shouted. 'There's a small pebble stretch a short distance away from him. I'll beach her there. Be ready to let go the mainsail when I say. Lift the centre board now. As soon as we touch, don't hang about, take the painter and jump over the bows. We may not get a second chance. Are you okay with this, love?'

'Yes Ron. Let's do it.'

Beaching the dinghy was easier than I had imagined. No sooner had Coleen jumped onto the pebbles than I had joined her, and together we hauled *Little Gem* partly out of the breaking waves and had tied the painter to one of the rocks scattered among the pebbles. I noticed the canoe was safely nestled among the rocks. Climbing the slippery rocks to the ledge on which the casualty was sitting, proved to be more difficult and I was thankful for the experience we had gained the previous year while on an outward-bound course in Wales. As it turned out, the casualty, a fifteen-year old boy, had been able to break his slide down the steep slope in several places where small bushes and outcrops had come within reach. He was fully conscious and able to tell us that he was unable to move his left leg without extreme pain. We could immediately confirm that it was badly broken. He also had a gash on his forehead and the skin on both hands was badly torn. While Coleen stayed with the lad, I returned to the dinghy and took the mobile from the bag to call the Station, relaying our position and giving details of the injuries. Having been told that the Fowey boat would be with us in about ten minutes, and that the helicopter would return to our location after they had delivered the burns casualty to hospital, I unrigged the cotton mainsail which would serve to keep the lad relatively warm. After that, there was very little we could do, apart from to keep the lad talking and to stand and wave when the Trent Class came into sight.

It was late in the afternoon when, having secured *Little Gem* in the boat yard, we arrived at the Lifeboat Station where the Tamar was being hosed clean by the maintenance team. In the crew room there was a buzz of conversation as various accounts of the rescues were being re-told. The lad on the surf board was no worse for his experience, although a valuable lesson had been learned. The lady suffering from burns would carry scars for the rest of her life, otherwise she would apparently make a good recovery in two or three weeks. The private cabin-cruiser, owned by the lady's friends, was secure in harbour, having been towed in by the Tamar. Coleen and I were regarded as heroes, much to our embarrassment and *Little Gem* was toasted by these sea-hardened friendly men and women, with orange juice. Clapping me on the back, Ben said to the room in general, 'Looks like we now have a third boat in our fleet, the Firefly Class. We can soon strip off all that shiny varnish and get a tin of orange paint from B&Q …….'

'Touch that varnish and you're history, skipper,' I responded with a laugh. At that moment I noticed Luke, the new recruit looking on with a bemused look on his face. Addressing him I said, 'Welcome to the team, Luke. You can see what you're letting yourself in for. Salt of the earth, each and every one of them. Always ready to put their own lives at risk, but if they go anywhere near my *Little Gem*……' With that, I was well and truly scragged.

'Come on, Ron. Don't think you're getting out of it this easy. You owe me a meal,' said Coleen as the group started to break up. 'Let's go home and shower, then you can take your *BIG GEM* to The Jolly Rover for an evening meal. This time by car, and don't bring your pager …… or mobile, or else.'

The End

THE CASTLE

'Sire!

'What is it, Sir Drysand? Can't you see that I'm busy taming this falcon? I left word that I was not to be disturbed unless there should be a dire emergency. So, unless you ……'

'But, if you please Sire, this is an emergency, such as you would, no doubt, wish to be informed.'

'I do not *please,* as you suggest, neither am I interested in your so-called emergency. Last time it was sand in the thunder box and the time before ….'

'Sire, I assure you that you will, nay must, be interested in this emergency.'

'Oh, very well, but it had better be good, otherwise I will have you hanging by your thumbs over the lookout parapet again, you know what that feels like, umm?'

'Yes Sire, my thumbs are now longer than my hands and keep flapping about when I pour wine into your silver goblet.'

'Enough of this drivel Sir Drysand. What?

'What?'

'Yes, what? Good god man! What is it that you think will please me?'

'No, it won't please you, if you please, Sire.'

'And you wonder why it's Sir Sandiman that I send out to watch over my sand, I mean land. At least he knows where his brain is. Now then, while I place this hood over the pretty head of my beauty here, you can gather your Knightly wit and try to remember what brought you here to risk my wrath. Ha, ha, that's funny, I like that, "Risk my wrath", say it quickly, Risk my wath, Wisk my wask. Go on, you try it.'

'Risk your wrath?' Easy, Sire. I'm always doing that.'

'No not *your* wrath, fool … *Mine dammit!* Why are you here anyway?'

'Sorry, Sire. I nearly forgot. The enemy is drawing nearer by the minute.'

'Why didn't you say so, instead of all this drivel. How near?'

'How near what?'

'How near … *please?*……. I can't believe I just said that … How near to this castle?'

'Well, if you look through a telescope, but you can't because they haven't been invented yet, but if you could ……'

'Get out! Get out! You gormless, brainless sham of a knight. Go and find where you left your horse, get on it (if you can) and ride out to the enemy to find out when we will be surrounded. And if they drown you, I'll send you to the kitchens to wash greasy pans, without soap, for the rest of your miserable life. Now, get out!'

***

'What did he say, Sir Drysand?'

'He said that I did right to inform him, Sir Sandiman. He bids that you ride out forthwith to assess the situation and report back to me. To me, you understand?'

'Then I will take my leave, my lance, and my shield, and tilt this monstrous and impertinent salt incrusted devil, see if I won't.'

'I wouldn't, should I be you, but I'm not, so you must do what chivalry demands. Good luck Sir Sandiman. Oh, by the way, where do you hide your purse? Should you need to send for it, you understand?'

'Nay, Sir Drysand, This I cannot tell you, for my Lady Sandra would not like you to fumble through her drawers.'

'Of course not, off you go then.'

***

'Sire!'

'Oh, what is it now, Sir Drysand?' I was just about to take a bath. I try to do so at least once a year you know.'

'Yes Sire, this has often been drawn to my attention when standing down wind.'

'Yes, well you should try it, although looking at the rust on your armour I doubt you would ever get it off. Out with it then. Is it the rats, or maybe Jehovah Witnesses at the drawbridge? Just drop it on them if it is, they want to go to heaven after all. Or perhaps we are out of brandy, or dolly mixtures, or …….'

'It's the enemy, Sire. They're filling the moat and will soon be beating against the castle walls. Arrows have no effect, neither does boiling oil. Sir McSandringham has tried to scare them away with a lusty tune on his bagpipes, but to no avail. Although it did make our archers run for cover with their hands over their ears. Both of them.

'Both ears?'

'No Sire, both archers, we only have two now, since you trained your favourite eagle to pick them up and drop them in the Keep.'

'Yes, well that was a mistake, I meant it to pick up the spent arrows, not the archers. Anyway, never mind that. I will forgo my planned bath, and come up to the battlements and see what is to be done. When the enemy spots me they will surely turn tide and retreat. Lead the way, Sir Drysand, while I choose which helmet to wear. Impressions count you know.'

***

'Ah, there you are Sire, I surmise that choosing a helmet must be hard, since the sun has moved beyond the hill during the time you must have been in dire need of a serving wench's opinion on the matter. I must inform you that, regardless of your swift action, all appears to be lost. The south wall has collapsed, and with it, the round tower bearing the straw pole with the lolly-wrapper flag. The next wave of the enemy troops will surely take the three remaining walls, and reduce us to wet sand. What is your advice, Sire?'

'The only thing we can do. Let us crawl back into our shells and wait for the next lot of children to start us all over again, Sir Drysand, or should I say, Wetsand?'

***

'Come on, children, time to go. The sandcastle is gone, just a load of old shells left now. The tide is still coming up and the sun is gone. It's a funny thing, I thought I heard the distant sound of bagpipes just before your castle collapsed.'

The End

CHANCE ENCOUNTER

Last night had been particularly bad, it was as though Hitler intended to wipe out dear old Portsmouth, five nights in a row with hardly a let up. As if that were not bad enough, our engine played up something rotten. Probably all the dust we had to keep driving through to get to our next call. Mavis was brilliant, never batted an eyelid, just got on with the pick-ups, all matter of fact, while I cringed with each bang and sound of falling masonry. At least we didn't have a situation like the previous night when we had a rescued woman in the back who was hysterical and unable to speak. She had kept trying to get up from the stretcher, hitting me in the process. She had a compound fracture to her right leg and had clearly lost a lot of blood. She could have done herself some serious harm if I hadn't restrained her.

I don't think I'll ever get used to it like the others seem to have done. My Reg never wanted me to do this job, said if I want to do my bit why don't I stick to knitting woollen gloves and scarves for the troops like his mum does. Worthwhile, I'll give it that, but I need to be more involved in saving the country, know what I mean? Thought about joining the air-force but didn't fancy being posted away from home, what with my dear old mum's arthritis. Then I met Mavis in a café down Commercial Road, had to share a table, with it being so busy at lunch time. We got into conversation over a spam sandwich like you do, and before I know it, off she went with these accounts of saving lives in bombed buildings. I'd done a bit of first-aid in the Guides so I reckoned that was something I could do that's worthwhile, and it even meant I could keep my part-time job at Woolies, and still manage a night shift with the brigade. Well, the long and short of it is, that after an interview and an embarrassing medical, least said about that the better, I got the job and even got teamed up with Mavis who does the driving and sticks her head under the hood to do all the mechanical stuff which is all a bit beyond me.

So here I am, at the end of another really bad shift, still in my dusty uniform, sitting upstairs on the number 5, heading for home, assuming it's still standing that is, having a Woodbine and thinking of my Reg who reckons he can get some leave for our wedding next month. I do hope so, don't fancy coming out of the church only to wave him good-bye. All being well, we can have a two-day honeymoon in Bognor. Soon as I get home, I'm going to join me mum for breakfast, assuming she's waited, then have a one-inch-deep bath and a nap before walking round to see Dot for a fitting. Hope our houses weren't too badly shaken. Dot's my best friend from school and has kindly offered to run up a satin wedding dress for me, out of a party frock she had for her 21st last year. Cor, won't I look grand, even got some nylons I've been saving since before the war, so won't have to draw a black line down my calves.

I see the driver's having difficulty weaving his way through the traffic and rubble. Haven't moved for ten minutes. I'm going to be ever-so late getting mum sorted, and she'll be worrying her socks off. Wonder what the problem is?

'Sorry everyone, you'll all have to get off. Driver says we can't get any further cos there's an unexploded bomb ahead in Fratton Road and we can't back up.' It's the bus conductress having appeared at the top of the stairs to make her unwelcome announcement. Wearily I lift myself from the seat and shamble down the aisle along with the other passengers. There are no complains or comments, we're all used to this kind of disruption in our lives now, and what's the use anyhow? 'Had a busy night luv?' the clippie asks me as I descend to the platform at the rear of the bus.

'You could say that,' I reply. 'Went out ten minutes after the sirens sounded, and hardly saw the depot again till knocking-off time.'

'Well, I admire you lot, and the lads from the fire brigade, out in the worst of it while the rest of us hunker down in the shelters. Sorry we can't get you home. Far to go?'

'Down New Road to Copnor, won't take long provided the way through is clear, although it could be a problem, as Copnor was badly hit during the night. Spent most of the night clearing casualties from there, and the night before. St Albans got it, not much of it still standing from what I could see.'

'Oh my gawd!' exclaims the clippie. 'I was only in there last Sunday, took my aunt to the morning service. You run along luvvy, get yer 'ead down, and best of luck to you and your mates.'

I pull up my greatcoat collar, adjust my gas mask strap to a more comfortable position, and hunch my shoulders as I start my trudge along the bomb-littered diversion away from the danger of the unexploded bomb. A dog trots up to me, wagging its tail. He sniffs my outstretched hand before trotting off, tail no longer wagging, toward several bombed-out houses, one of them with the remains of a bathroom sink suspended over empty space, curtains billowing out from half of a window frame. Is the dog looking for an owner? A home? Probably. There are so many stray dogs and cats scavenging in the streets these days.

As I approach the end of New Road, which surprisingly shows little sign of bomb damage, I become more and more aware of the smell of burning, wood, paint, rubber and something that begins to turn my stomach. Smoke lazily drifts into the early morning sky from several locations. As I follow the course of one of the rolling black plumes, a lone Spitfire flies passed, almost low enough for me to see the pilot. What can he see as he gazes down at the burning city? So many gaps where once stood proud buildings, no doubt. Even the magnificent Guildhall is now reduced to a shell. How does that now look from the air I wonder? Oh, I do hate that madman with his silly moustache. How could such a proud nation as Germany have allowed him so much power? My thoughts are interrupted by the clanging of a bell as a fire engine sweeps toward Copnor Bridge and heads for the tightly packed housing district into which I am about to enter, helmeted firemen hanging from the sides, smoke blackened faces grimly peering ahead.

I walk over the humpy railway bridge just as a steam train slowly passes under. I am unable to see it over the parapet, but can tell it's a goods train by the clanking of the trucks. Probably taking stores and equipment to the dockyard where it will be loaded into the grey warships moored alongside the jetty. At least the trains are still running even though Fratton and the goods yard took a bit of a hit last night, and the night before. My mind suddenly conjures up a picture of my Reg, looking all smart and proud in his sailor's uniform the first time. How we all laughed when he described the difficulty he had, getting it on, what with the vest, the tight shirt and the separate collar with all them cords and ribbons attached. But, by 'eck, he did look the dog's dinner, bless him.

Nearly home now, can't wait to get my aching feet up, with a nice cuppa and a bit of toast with dripping. Now I'm thinking about it, I'm starving, didn't get to eat during the night, too busy. Hello, what's 'appening over by Baffins Pond? Looks like a little kid trying to get away from someone. Why, that's Betty from the post office, holding his arm, what's going on then?

'Mornin' Betty, who's this then, was he dipping in your shop?'

'Oh, hello dear, no nothing like that. Looks like 'e's lost, found him asleep among the bins in the yard. I caught 'im as 'e tried to leg it. I can't get any sense from the little lamb, every time I try an' find out where 'e lives 'e just starts crying.' All the while, the little lad is trying to escape from Betty's firm grip. It's then that I notice the dried blood on his left thigh and one of his forearms. Also, a large graze on his forehead. I stoop down to take a closer look. Beneath a layer of dirt and grit I can see that the boy is in need of first aid, which I should be able to deal with. The boy warily watches my movements as I finish my cursory examination and stand up. 'Well, I suppose we'll 'ave to get 'im to the cop shop.' says Betty as she hopefully looks around as though looking for an irate parent.

'Okay Betty, you have to open up, if I can get him home, I'll see what I can do about his cuts, and I'm guessing he's hungry. Then I'll take him to the police station.'

'Are you sure? You look about done in, but I suppose that would be best. Here, take his arm, or 'e might run again.'

Once again, I stoop down and ask the child, 'Would you like to come with me, I expect you would like a biscuit and a glass of milk? Then we can see about finding your mummy.' For a moment the child looks me in the eye and my heart melts as I see the pear-shaped tears run from his eyes, leaving trails in the dirt on his cheeks. Slowly I take one of his hands in my own and am relieved and touched when I feel the soft pressure of his clasp. It's just a matter of a few minutes before I am able to turn the corner and anxiously check that our house is unscathed, as indeed, are the others in the street. The boy is content to follow, and although I ease my hold on his little hand I am warmed by the tightening of his hold on my own hand. As I unclip the latch on the garden gate, the front door just beyond, swings inward.

'There you are, Amy, I was so worried when you didn't … Who's this? Oh, the poor little tyke, he's hurt, where did you find him?'

'Hello, mum. It's a long story, I'm all right, it's this little fellow we need to sort out. Get the kettle on, there's a luv.' Turning to the boy I say 'Nothing to be afraid of, let's go and find you a biscuit, shall we?'

Twenty minutes later, with the boy sat on the kitchen table munching some toast which had followed three biscuits, I survey my work on leg, arm and forehead. My mother, who had assisted me by constantly replenishing the warm water, is telling me about the previous night's air raid, and how she had spent the duration in next door's Anderson shelter. 'It was a bad'n alright, as you could see, our street was okay but Coleridge Road got a right bashing. Old Walter knocked on the door first thing to tell me The Fitzroy got clobbered, not a brick standing. In tears he was. He'll have to drink in The Plough now, if they'll have him, that is. Still no word out of this little tyke yet. He'll be eating us out of house and home if you don't sort him out soon. I'll just nip out and get some coke from the coal hole, see if he'll talk to you on your own for a bit.'

With that, my mother eases herself through the back door, coal-scuttle in hand, allowing the door to slam behind her. Suddenly the boy gives out a loud shriek, and scampers down from the table to disappear beneath. 'It's okay, sweetheart, just the door closing, you can come out now.' I wait, but there is no sign of the boy moving. I stoop down, and lifting the hem of the table cloth, peer under to see the boy sitting with his back to the wall clutching his arms around his drawn-up knees with his chin lowered to his chest. 'Oh, you poor, poor thing, you've been bombed out, haven't you? Have you seen your mummy since that bad thing happened?'

'Want my mummy, I want my mummy,' came the sudden wail as the boy crawls forward and clutches my legs. 'I want my mummy; they took her away. I runned after her but couldn't catch up.' Now the tears are streaming down his face as he sobs 'Mama, mama, mama.'

As he hiccups the events of what had happened, I manage to grasp a vague picture of what he has been through. It seems that he and his mother had had to take shelter under the stairs. There had been no light, just pitch blackness in the turmoil of explosions, falling masonry, and clanging bells, until the blackness was shattered by orange and red flashes accompanied by a loud crashing noise. The boy had clung to his mother who was groaning and not able to move. Realising that she was badly hurt, he knew that he had to go next door to get the lady to help. Easing himself from the rubble, virtually all that was left of his house, he stumbled over bricks and fallen beams in the darkness, with only the flash of explosions and the red glow of various fires to show him the way. But there was nothing he could see that he recognised. Where the lady's house was supposed to be, there was a smoking pile of debris. In the confusion, he was very frightened and lost. After a long time of searching for anything familiar, he came upon a charred post box which he knew was only two doors down the road from his house. It was then that a sudden flash had enabled him to see the ambulance and the stretcher being carefully slid into the back. At that moment, he had seen his mother's face as she frantically struggled against the person holding her down on the stretcher.

'That's about the last of it till we can get more,' grumbles mum as she pushes through the door with a quarter-filled scuttle. 'What's up, you look as though you've seen a ghost.' Glancing down at the boy, she asks,

'Why's he hanging on to you like that? Has he been able to tell you anything?'

'Yes, mum, I need a cup of tea, then I'm going to take him to The Royal Hospital where I took his deaf and dumb mother the night before last.'

The End

OPERATION ROSY

Cautiously, the two figures emerged from the shadowed alley. Wild eyes scanned the street, both ways. No movement, no sound, apart from the distant murmur of traffic. No danger. Or was there? What was that rustling in the nearby hedge? A black cat silently steps onto the pavement, tail raised and shaking at the tip. Disdainfully, it looked at the two furtive figures who were both unconsciously holding their breath. Another quick look around, paying particular attention to the shadowed areas. The cat had vanished into the darkness by the time the leader was satisfied that they had not been seen, and before focusing his attention on his younger companion.

'You okay?'

'Yea, that cat got my heart beating, could feel it thumping in my chest.'

'Yea, me too. Wonder what happened to Coochie? Last I saw of him he was way behind us trying to get over that last wall. He'll have to take his chances, we can't wait.

We know Sandy was nabbed. He's probably having to answer some awkward questions right now. Shame, he was doing okay back there. Okay, let's move, keep your eyes peeled and no talking till I say so, clear?'

'Don't worry about me, Roy, I want this as much as you do, lead the way.'

Rifle straps fitted snugly over shoulders, arms lightly swinging, they cautiously walked along the pavement, keeping as close as possible to the shadows. The road they were following was a downhill stretch, with a number of streets intersecting it. They hurried across the first junction, hoping that there would be no vehicles approaching, Pete, the younger of the two, following closely behind the dark slightly stooping figure of his older brother. He had not been sure if Roy would allow him to come on this raid and was pleased, if a little nervous, if he was being honest, when he had relented. He suspected this was only because Sid had dropped out, and he had been convenient to make up the numbers.

Suddenly, Pete's thoughts evaporated as an approaching low murmur quickly became a roar as the headlights of what turned out to be a motor cycle appeared from the intersection they were about to cross. Together, the brothers pushed themselves into the bushes of the corner plot, hearts beating. Almost without a pause the rider eased his machine around the corner and accelerated down the hill with a loud roar and rapid change of gears. The smell of the exhaust, mingling with the heady aroma of Honeysuckle, permeated the air.

'Phew, that was a close one,' breathed Roy. 'Thought the game was up then. Right, almost there now, let's get out of these bushes and watch out for any movement.'

It was only the day before that the raid had been planned. There were supposed to have been four members of Roy's gang taking part, it was mere chance that Pete had been allowed to participate. It was as they drew closer to their goal that he was beginning to regret that chance. *No, he must not think like that. Committed now. Can't let Roy down.*

'Okay, this is the one,' whispered Roy. 'Remember what I told you. You stay here and keep watch, but try to stay out of sight. If there's any sign of danger, do the owl signal. This won't take long, in two minutes time that beauty will be done for.' Pete gave a nervous nod of the head as he unhooked his rifle and held it firmly in his hands. He glanced both ways along the road before turning back to Roy, but to his surprise he found that he was alone. He heard a feint scraping noise on the other side of the head-high wall, then a low curse.

Silence

Tempted as he was to peer over the wall, Pete continued scanning the street, first up hill, then down, then up again. *All quiet on the Western Front.* With that thought Pete had to supress a giggle. Nerves he supposed. *Keep calm and concentrate. Where is he? Come on Roy, you've had time to commit a murder, let alone scrump an apple.* At that moment a searchlight lit up the scene, well actually a door shaped light spread across the highly manicured lawn on the other side of the wall, just as Roy plucked the rosy fruit from the little apple tree.

OYE!!!

For a split-second Roy froze in the shocking light spilling from the open kitchen door. But, oh dear! It was not the blinding light that gave rise to the boy nearly messing himself, oh no, it was the shocking sight of the silhouette of the huge Police Constable Gillham, filling the open door frame, that loosened the boy's bowels.

'Bloody 'ell …. RUN!!' Dropping his wooden rifle, Roy shot across the lawn and leapt for the wall, dropping the purloined apple in the flower bed as he did so. Feet scrabbling for purchase, arms momentarily resting on the top, he managed to cock one leg, then the other over the top. For a brief eye watering moment, he glanced back and, to his horror saw the still booted PC Gillham, braces hanging down to his hips; shirt sleeves half rolled up; pounding down the concrete path and heading for the closed gate.

'I'll get you, you little turd. Steal my apple, would you? Come 'ere!'

As Roy dropped to his feet, he became aware that Pete had already taken off down the hill. The chase had started. The two boys had stopped pretending to be brave invincible commandos and had taken on the mantle of children in a panic. Very quickly, Pete arrived at the first corner and shot around it with Roy now close behind. Legs pumping; arms bent and moving like engine pistons; heads down; they ran as they had never run before. But it was proving to be not quite fast enough, for they were constantly aware of the steady beat of PC Gillham's studded boots pounding the pavement behind them, *and getting closer*. Without thinking, for any question of thought had evaporated, they ran to the only place where they would be safe …. Home. Not a good plan as it was to turn out.

'Nearly there,' panted Roy. They were running down the last street before skidding round the corner into their own road, and near safety. They ran passed their front door, instinctively knowing that the beast would be on them before the door could be opened by dad, or mum. Instead they ran two houses further, to where an ally looped round and took them to their back door which was never locked until bedtime. The door slammed shut behind them and both leaned against it, gasping for breath and thanking their lucky stars. That is, until the loud rat-a-tat-tat on the front door knocker, accompanied by the sight of the unmistakeable silhouette of the police constable, appearing through the frosted glass, announced imminent doom to the brave commandoes, well, not so much brave commandoes, as terrified children.

Sinking down onto the kitchen floor, the boys listened to the murmured conversation taking place at the open front door, but were unable to hear what was being said, for their mother had closed the hall door, leaving them alone in the kitchen.

'Did you know that house was PC Gillham's?' asked Pete.

'No, I'm beginning to wonder why Coochie had so much trouble climbing that wall earlier, he's a good climber and it was him who told me about the apple. Gillham's house is on his paper round, he must have known. Wait till I see him tomorrow, that's if I'm still alive.' At that moment the kitchen door was opened by their mother.

'Into the hall you two.'

The two boys slowly got to their feet and followed their mother into the hall, where PC Gillham was standing alongside their father. For a moment nobody spoke. The policeman was the first to break the silence as he turned his stony gaze away from the boys and addressed their father.

'Will you do it, or shall I?' was all he said.

Glaring at the quaking boys, their father folded his arms and responded, in a gruff voice 'I'll do it.'

***

The following morning, Saturday, there's a knock, on PC Gillham's front door. With a sigh he throws down his morning paper and removes his pipe from between his lips before carefully placing it on an ash tray which is in the shape of a frog. 'What now? Can't an honest copper have any peace on his day off?' To his surprise, as he pulls the door open, he's confronted with the site of the two boys from last night's fiasco. One of them, the shorter of the two, is rubbing his bottom. 'Well you two have got a nerve. What are you doing here?'

Roy replies 'Please sir, I mean constable, we've come to say we're sorry. Our dad told us to come.'

'Oh, you have, have you? Is it sorry because you got caught, or sorry because you've been told to be? Which is it?'

'Not neither of them, sir,' pipes in Pete. 'We really are sorry. We didn't know it was your garden and that it was the only apple you had. We just wanted to play commandoes and do what it says, you know, "He who dares, wins." It was just a bit of fun.'

'A bit of fun that spoils things for other people,' replies the policeman sternly. 'Most of my job involves catching people who spoil things for innocent folk. Do you want to grow up to be one of those nasty individuals?'

'No sir, we don't. We'll do anything to make it better for you, honest we will.'

'Well, maybe I believe you, and maybe you've learned a lesson. Let me see ….Tell you what, you come through into my garden, and on the way, we'll collect some string and a pair of scissors.'

Out in the garden, PC Gillham leads the boys over to the fruitless apple tree and says, 'Can you remember where you jumped over my wall last night?'

'Yes, over there,' replies the mystified Roy, pointing to the exact spot.

'That's right son. Now then, you go over there now, and you'll see something red lying on the ground in the middle of the flowers you trod down. Go and fetch it.'

The policeman and Pete look on, as Roy bends down and picks up the object. He stands there for a moment looking at the object in his hand, then turns and shouts, *'That ain't real, It's plastic!'*

'That's right son, all is never what it seems, is it? Now you can tie it back on the tree for me, then we can go in and find some lemonade and biscuits and have a nice little chat.'

The End

ONE YEAR ON

'You may ask, why have I come here, to this particular spot, on the beach, on this particular day. Don't you remember, my love? Surely you do. This day exactly two years ago? The day they told you. The day you wept and asked me to take you away from the fear and the pain. The day our world fell apart, when the real became the unreal, and nothing any longer felt solid and safe. I held you here, on this spot. I so much wanted to protect you, as I always said I would, as you came to expect and understand. Nothing could, or would, harm you while I had strength in my body. Little did I know.

When you heard those dreadful words, you looked at me with such faith that I would sort it out, as you always expected and as I always seemed to manage. But not this time, my love. Forgive me, for this time it was all beyond my reach and, as it turned out, beyond the ability of the doctors. Oh yes, they tried their best, but we knew, didn't we? You even warned me that we could only expect two years. We could not have known then that it was to be just one year. What I would give to have another year with you, another month, or week, or even a day. Still, we were blessed with forty-four years together weren't we? From teenagers, to mid-life. Forty-four good years, although we did have our ups and downs, didn't we? Do you remember the time you threw my packed drawer of papers and documents, drawer and all, down the stairs, because you were fed up with the amount of time I had to spend on them? How we ended up shouting at each other, then sitting on the hall floor crying, then laughing till our sides ached?

Did you ever realise that you were a great inspiration to me? Did I ever tell you? Perhaps not. You had only to walk into a room and everyone took notice. When you spoke, all would listen. You had your thoughtful and serious side, but most of all, I remember your sense of fun, your infectious laughter. Your one-year battle didn't diminish any of that. You were still the source of great strength for those who needed it ……. for me

I miss you so much my funny girl, oh how I miss you. It's in the quietness of the night that I am most lonely, and in need of your touch. It's been a year now. How quickly that time has gone, and how much it has dragged. I know, that sounds contradictory, but the whole of my life seems to be that way now. Fun quickly turns to sadness, laughter to tears, hope to despair. Since you have been gone, I have imagined seeing you on two occasions. One when I spotted you walking away from me in a shopping precinct. She was your build, your height, and her hair, pure white. I knew it couldn't possibly be you but I had to catch up to be certain. On another occasion, I was working in the garden pulling weeds, at least I hoped they were weeds, for a brief moment I stood to stretch my aching back and, as I did so, I glanced at one of the conservatory windows, and there you were staring through the glass, presumably checking on what I was pulling out of your tenderly loved flower bed. In that moment my heart felt as though it had leapt out of my chest. Slowly I laid down my trowel and walked up the path to the open door. As I came nearer, your head became a cushion on top of which there was a white towel I had left there earlier. Needless to say, tears of bitterness unashamedly flowed.

If you were physically here now, you would surely be standing with the waves lapping up your thighs. Your skirt would be wet from when it had come loose after being tucked into your knickers. You would be attempting to jump over each wave, inevitably making yourself even more wet. How you loved being in water; sea, lake, river, pond, puddle, it made no difference. Apart from the love of a good bonfire, this was your element. Such a child, so easy to please. I remember the time, while on holiday, we were on a sandy beach which had many rocks and pools. You were delighting in the various rock shapes and colours. You wanted to pick up some of the larger ones in order to take them home, to be placed in the garden. I refused to allow this, as I was concerned about the weight our old car was having to cope with, which included pulling our caravan. With your crazy logic you stated that the rocks could be placed in the caravan so that the car would be okay. You accepted my refusal, even made a joke of it, and I have regretted denying your request ever since.

We were so young when we married, weren't we? You twenty-one and myself only twenty. You presented me with a beautiful baby daughter, two months before my twenty-first birthday and not so long after, a fine son. We were so proud. Everything we possessed, was second hand, all except the lovely pram we splashed out on. Better than a Rolls, although thinking about it now, a Rolls would have been better than our sit-up-and-beg Ford Popular. That old Ford was a god-send to us when we were courting wasn't it my love? Do you remember the evening when we were parked on top of the hill looking at the lights below, amongst other distractions, when there was a knock on my driver's side window? On winding it down we were confronted by a gypsy boy from a nearby camp, who boldly told us he would go away if we gave him five shillings. How we laughed!

Thinking about it now, laughter was never far away from us, was it, my love? Even at your funeral service, laughter was a predominant factor as various stories about you were presented to the packed congregation. They particularly liked the one about you phoning me at work to tell me you had broken the bathroom window. I had said not to worry and that I would replace the glass when I got home. What you didn't tell me was that you had somehow wrenched the whole window frame from the wall while sitting on the sill, legs inside, body outside, trying to clean the window. What about the time I arrived home from work only to find that you and our un-born daughter were stuck under the roll-top bath which you had crawled under two hours previously to dust the wall behind it. Yes, my love, life with you was unpredictable but fun.

Now, here I am, standing by the sea, waves lapping at my feet, my head filled with memories, but my heart is empty. How can I go on? How can I face the years without you? They said it would get better after the first year. I have to believe them for it cannot be any worse than it is now … can it? My darling girl, can you hear me? Have I been rambling to myself these passed two hours? Where are you? I'm so pleased that you had a strong faith. You told me that you knew where you were going, but that you were still afraid. Of course, you were my love, but it was okay and natural to be afraid. I remember the look you had in your eyes when you stared at our house from the car as I drove you to the hospice, the day before you died. You knew at that moment that you would never see our home again. How I ever found the strength to say to you the next day, when you were taking your last feeble breaths *"It's okay to go, my darling, you don't need to struggle anymore,"* I shall never know.

My own faith took a serious dip after the funeral, when reality kicked in. I wanted to shout at God for taking you away from me. I wanted to rant and to punish Him. How could He do this to us? My one enduring thought is that if we are ever to be together again, I have to hold on to my faith, so that I can eventually take the same journey you have taken.

I'm going now, my love. Tonight, I will, no doubt laugh and cry, as I look through the photographs of you. Something I will, no doubt, continue to do with each passing anniversary over the years. Oh, by the way, your garden is looking great. Are you still talking to the plants, as you always used to?'

The End (Or is it the Beginning?)

THE MUCK SPREADER

'Perhaps sir, you would like to explain why you were caught in the act of muck spreading all the way up The Mall, from the Palace to Marble Arch.'

'That's easy sergeant, one of your lot saw me.'

'What I mean is, why did you decide to drive your tractor into London in order to cause so much havoc?'

'Didn't.'

'Do you mean to tell me that it wasn't you, caught driving that tractor?'

'No.'

'No, what?'

'No, Sergeant.'

'You're telling me that it wasn't you?'

'No, Sergeant. Yes, it was.'

'Then why did you say "No"?'

'You asked me if I decided to drive my tractor into London to spread the muck, I said that I didn't decide to do that, but I never told you that it wasn't me, because it was.'

'Oh, I see ..... I think ...... Why did you do it?'

'Do what?'

'Spread that sh … muck all over the place.'

'It was the 'orses.'

'Oh, come now, we all know it wasn't horses, you were seen carrying out your vile act with your spreader.'

'No, it weren't the 'orses what did the spreadin', it was them that gave me the idea.'

'The horses gave you the idea. How did they manage to do that?'

'Well now, you see, I was watchin' The Troopin' of the Colours on our telly with my Flo, and I 'appened to notice the 'orses weren't too proud to drop their doings on the road, Queen or no Queen. Then I see one of those there contraptions sweepin' the muck from the road soon after the Queen and all them soldiers 'ad gone by. I said to our Flo, "Oh, oh, look at that, in our day we used to 'ave to take our shovel and bucket into the street after the 'orse and carts 'ad gone by, but the Queen 'as a contraption to do it for her." That got me thinking, *Of course, she 'as such a large garden, she needs tons of the stuff, she could never do it with a shovel and bucket, it would take her all night.'* Well it so 'appened that I 'ad a full load in my spreader, that I 'ad no need of, so, being a loyal subject, why don't I give it to Her Nibs. Flo thought it were a good idea too, mainly 'cos she were fed up with the full spreader being parked by the kitchen window for the last two months.'

'You mean to tell me that you intended delivering your pile of muck into the Palace?'

'Oh no, sergeant, that would be daft, I was aiming to take it round to the back garden, knock on the back door and ask Her Nibs where she wanted it. I expect she would have wanted to pick some of it up to 'ave a sniff to be sure it was well-rotted enough. You would be surprised what a difference a week or two makes to the ....'

'Okay, I get the idea. So, you drove your tractor into London. From where, If I may be so bold as to ask?'

'From 'ome'

'And where might that be?'

'Oh, there's no "Might" about it, it's there alright.'

'My giddy aunt. Where is "There"?'

'Where is there, what?'

'HOME! Your home. Where is it?'

'It's in Itchybottom.'

'Are you trying to take the p … p … patience out of me?'

'No, not me, sergeant. Itchybottom is right alongside the M4, well to be exact, it's on both sides of it, but when they come along with all that road-building stuff, they split my Itchybottom in two. What a cheek! Anyhow, it didn't take many minutes to get my load onto the M4 and …….'

'What? Do you mean to tell me you drove your tractor and muck spreader along the M4?'

'No sergeant.'

'I thought you said you drove it onto the M4.'

'Oh no, that weren't me, that were our Flo. I was sat on the spreader holdin' the valve shut. Y' see, the valve's a bit loose an' it needs a bit of holdin' with a spanner. I told Flo to stay in the right-hand lane 'cos she's a bit cross-eyed and don't see so well on her left. It was a bit of a laugh watchin' the faces of some of them drivers as they slammed on their brakes. We had three lanes of queues behind us after a bit, seemed to go back for miles. It were a good job we were in front of it, else we might 'ave got held up.

'I don't believe this is happening to me! ……. Constable Blaker?'

'Yes Sarge?'

'Is this the first of April?'

'No Sarge, it's the third of June. Why?'

'Oh, never mind, get on with whatever you're doing. Now then, sir, let's get to the bit where you flung the muck all over The Mall, shall we? I can't wait to hear your explanation for that.'

'Well, it was a bit tricky getting through London, not having one of them Tom-Nav things. Our Flo got 'erself a bit flustered when she drove into an Underground entrance and 'ad to reverse out into the traffic. She'd never done that before, and got 'erself stuck between a bus and a posh car without a top. It was then that, for a moment, I lost my grip on the spanner. I lost some of me muck on the back seat of the car, well to be 'onest, quite a lot. The lady wasn't too 'appy, especially when she waved her fist at me and knocked her wig off 'er 'ead. Bald as a chicken's bum. I shouted to rub some of the muck on 'er 'ead, to make 'er 'air grow, but by then our Flo got 'er gears sorted and we were off. It were interesting when we 'ad to cross that lifting bridge over the river. We got 'alf way across, when the tractor engine suddenly stopped. It was nice of them to have lights flashing at both ends and putting the barriers down to protect us from the traffic. It took me twenty minutes to get the old girl started again, and when I looked over the rail at the river I was amazed when I noticed a big ship had bumped into the river-bank and 'ad swung round, blocking the river. "Someone ought to learn 'ow to drive that thing," I said to our Flo. "Could 'ave caused a nasty accident." It's a shame, I lost a load of muck when I had to let go of the spanner. Still, there was plenty left for the Queen. I knew she would still be grateful when we dumped it in the Palace garden.'

'You managed to create the longest tailback ever known on the M4, then you caused panic on the whole London Underground System when they thought it was under attack, not to mention upsetting a lady who will, no doubt, be on a councillor's bench for months, if not years. Not satisfied with that, you prevented Tower Bridge from lifting to enable our newest Destroyer to enter London on a Royal Navy exhibition, designed to demonstrate how nothing is able to stop, or damage her. You managed both, in a mere twenty minutes. They obviously didn't take muck spreaders into account, did they? I should lock you up right now and throw the key into the Thames, but at this moment, nobody is allowed anywhere near the river, as there's a big security clamp-down. Now, tell me what happened next.'

'Well, it's all a bit disappointing really. We get to the Palace and park up at the front. Our Flo gets off the tractor and approaches a soldier to ask 'im where the back gate is so we can dump our load. He must have been deaf or something 'cos he just stands there holding his gun with one hand and his nose with the other. Then one of your lot comes up and tells us to 'op it. Well, I can tell you, are Flo was in a right state. She jumped back onto the saddle, (that's seat to you), slams the engine into gear and takes off, round the fountain and up The Mall. I 'ad no warning, I slips off the back of the spreader and gets my welly caught in the valve, which then springs open. Flo has no idea we're flinging the muck, and that I'm sitting on my arse being dragged along behind, with me welly stuck in the doings.'

'So, it was Flo, I mean your wife, and not you who was driving when the policeman stopped you at Marble Arch?'

'Was it?'

'You said it was you, at the beginning of this statement ……I think.'

'Okay sergeant, she asked me not to say anything, but it was the Queen. After she saw us from her bedroom window, she couldn't resist the dung, so she jumped on her bike and caught us up, demanding that we "stoorp". Well our Flo wasn't 'avin any of that, and said we was takin' it back to Itchybottom where it would be appreciated. Then the Queen jumped up and dragged our Flo from …'

'GET OUT!!! OUT, OUT, OUT!'

'Excuse me sarge.'

'What is it constable Jenkins?'

'We've just brought a man in, who was found digging a hole on the centre court of Wimbledon Stadium. He says he's prospecting for gold, as he's heard how the players make a fortune there. He's already twelve-foot down …..Sarge? …..Sarge? ….. That's funny. He was here when I came in …. Sarge?'

The End

ABANDONED

The shabby terraced house in the centre of Portsmouth bore all the marks of a near miss which had happened some three years ago in the height of the blitz. Where there had been six homes between number 73 and The Dragon's Head public house there was now only a bomb site, which had become a makeshift night-time shelter for a few people who had lost their homes for various reasons. It had also become a playground for the local children where dens could be erected and imaginary enemies, usually Germans, could be fought with wooden rifles. No 73 had been shored up following that devastating night when the bombers had concentrated their efforts on trying to obliterate the dockyard which serviced and supplied the warships. Colin, at the age of ten, was the older of two brothers. At this moment he was sitting on a wooden cross-member which formed a part of the structure holding up the wall which used to be the partition between No's 73 and 75. He was swinging his bare legs as he watched his brother attempting to climb the structure, some seven feet below his scuffed shoes.

'Come on, Dan, you can do it,' called Colin encouragingly. 'Just put your left leg on that bolt sticking out by your hip and your right hand on the nail by your head.'

'It's alright for you, you're bigger than me,' moaned eight-year old Dan in frustration, 'I can't reach the bolt, I'm gonna go and call for Jack and see if he can come out to play. Do you wanna come with me?'

'Naa, I got some thinkin' to do. Now the summer 'olidays 'ave come I wanna think about what we can do for the six weeks. You go, I'll see you later, and don't go talkin' to any old men, you know what 'appened before.'

As Dan stepped down from the rubble onto the pavement, Colin gazed across the road to No. 62 where Pam lived. They had become close over the last few years, sitting together in school and often sharing their individual lunches, hers packed in a red OXO tin, usually spam sandwiches, his, fish-paste sandwiches wrapped in newspaper. He thought about the kiss they had exchanged last night in the alley behind her house. She had just had her tea and was allowed out for an hour. It was the first time they had done it and he remembered the taste of jam on her lips. He would be careful not to let his mates know because they thought kissing was sissy as was evident by the groans and catcalls if ever such a thing occurred during a cowboy film in Saturday morning pictures. Pam's house was intact, as was the line of terraced houses, from one end to the other, on her side of the street. This being Sunday afternoon, he knew that Pam, having had her dinner, would soon be allowed out. They had planned to go down to the shore together, to have a paddle. The tide would be high and the water relatively warm. He particularly enjoyed paddling with Pam as it often created the excuse to hold her hand when she stepped over an obstruction beneath the still water. Colin experienced a momentary feeling of guilt that he had not told Dan that he was going down to the shore, for his brother would have loved to come with him. Normally he would have welcomed Dan's company, however, today he wanted to be alone with Pam without the responsibility of watching out for his young brother.

Half an hour later, with sea water over his knees and threatening to reach the legs of his short trousers, Colin held out his hand to help Pam step around a dumped pram which was half submerged. With little conscious thought, he looked through the clear water at the wheels, thinking they might be useful for making a go-cart, but he could see they would be useless for that purpose.

'My dad's coming home on Wednesday,' stated Pam as she released Colin's hand. 'He wrote to let us know. He's got his demob and will be finished with the Air Force for good. My mum cried happy tears. We're going down to the town station to meet him. You can come if you like, I asked mum and she said it's okay. Please say you will.'

For a moment Colin hesitated, before replying, 'Alright, as long as yer dad won't mind.'

'Course he won't, he's fond of you and Dan. Remember, on his last leave, how he took you down to his shed and carved you an aeroplane, saying it was like the Wellington Bomber he had to navigate?'

'Yea, it's brilliant, it's hangin' up in our bedroom between our beds.'

'You'll come then?'

'What about Dan?'

'He can come too; mum knows how you always like to stay together.' The two of them fell silent for a while as they paddled parallel with the shore until Pam quietly asked, 'What about your dad, has your mum heard when he's coming home, yet?'

Colin continued pushing his brown legs through the water for a while before wiping both cheeks with the back of his right hand. 'No, me mum 'asn't said anyfing'

There was an awkward pause before Pam said, 'Well I expect you'll hear soon, perhaps his ship hasn't come home yet. We ought to go back now and dry our feet. Mum said not to be home late 'cos my aunt Hilda's coming over for tea.'

After watching Pam wave and close her front door, Colin reached his hand into the letterbox of his own front door to grasp the string which held the suspended key. Pulling the key through the letter box, he caught a whiff of the familiar smell which permanently lingered in the house. A musty, damp smell combined with over-used cooking fat and general neglect. Quietly closing the door behind him, Colin crept down the dimly lit passage. He paused at the bottom of the stairs to listen for any sounds coming from above. Nothing. It was likely that this new *uncle* whom he had never seen before, had left. Not wanting to take any chances, he slipped through the dingy and airless back room which led to the tiny kitchen. There, he saw the remains of breakfast. Half a stale loaf and a bowl of dripping still on the table, Also, an open woman's magazine with an ashtray resting on top, clearly intended to hold the page open revealing the horoscope section. The ashtray was full of cigarette butts, each with lipstick stains on the end. As quietly as possible, Colin cut himself a slice of the bread before looking in the cupboard over his head to see what was there. As he expected, there were two jars of paste and an un-open tin of spam. Paste it would have to be. He rinsed out a cup under the cold-water tap, making sure there were no lipstick traces, and filled it with water, to drink with his bread. He hoped that Dan will have been invited into Jack's home to eat, as was often the case. Colin took his meal into the middle room where he could sit in the only armchair, and read an old comic while he ate. No sooner had he sat down, the front door slammed shut and he heard his mother's footsteps coming along the passage, high heels making the familiar hollow sound on the lino.

'Oh, you're home then, where's Dan, is he with you?'

In middle years, the mother of the two boys habitually attempted to take years off her appearance, by the application of heavy make-up. She wore a red beret which failed to hide her greying hair. Her pale blue blouse was undone at the top thus revealing an ample cleavage of which she was proud. Her grey skirt was short enough to reveal legs which once may have been described as shapely.

'No, he's round Jack's, 'spect he'll be 'ome soon.'

'Well, I can't wait, your uncle's outside in his car, he's taking me up north, for some business I have to deal with, you'll be alright, your dad'll be home soon. He can look after you, till I get back. I've left five bob on the dresser so you can get some food from the corner shop. Don't spend it on sweets.'

'How long you goin' for, mum?'

'Just a few days, I'll be back before you know it. Right, I'm off then. Look after Danny boy, bye, luv.'

With those words, Colin's mother paused in the doorway and looked at her son for a moment before turning to clip clop down the passage, leaving the overpowering smell of cheap perfume lingering in the air.

'MUM!' shouted the boy, but his cry was masked by the hollow thud of the front door as it slammed shut. Jumping to his feet, sandwich and comic forgotten and slipping to the floor, Colin ran into the empty passage, reaching the front door as the sound of a car, rasping through its gears, gave way to silence. Colin turned around and, with his back to the door, sank to the floor and sobbed into his folded arms. A few minutes passed before the letterbox above his head suddenly opened, as a small hand reached through to grasp the string. Colin came to his feet and carefully opened the door for his brother.

'You've been cryin', what's up, someone beat you up 'ave they?' asked Dan with a wide grin on his face.

'SHUT UP! SHUT UP! SHUT UP!' shouted Colin. I thought you were going to Jack's. Why are you back 'ere?'

'He wasn't in. Where's mum?'

'She's gone.'

'Gone where?'

'How should I know? She just said she 'ad to go north, but I fink she's left us. She said dad would be 'ome soon, but 'e won't 'cos he's dead. I saw the telegram that came before Easter, it said "Missing, presumed dead." He ain't ever comin' 'ome.'

'But who's goin' t look after us?' asked Dan, now showing alarm in his voice.

'No one. We'll 'ave to take care of ourselves. But you mustn't tell anyone, do you hear? If anyone finds out we're on our own they'll separate us and put us in a home for orphans. So, don't tell, not even yer best friends. We'll be alright. You see. I can earn a few bob, doin' errands for people, and I know 'ow to make scrambled egg and baked beans on toast, and stuff like that. Don't start sniffling, come on, let's go down the corner shop and get some grub, mum left us five bob. 'Spect we can buy some bacon and some eggs; I can do us a fry-up.'

***

Irene Coleman awoke with a start as the bell suspended above the shop door bounced on its spring with a resounding clanging noise. There had been no customers for the previous twenty minutes, sufficient time for Irene to settle on her stool and close her eyes, *just for five minutes,* she had told herself.

'Well bless my soul, look who's come in, would it be sweets you'll be wanting? Not much choice I'm afraid, what with this rationing.'

'No, it's not sweets, Mrs Coleman. We want somethin' for our dinner, somethin' easy to cook. We thought bacon would be a good idea.'

'Sorry, Colin, I'm out of bacon, sold the last an hour since. How about some tripe? No? Tell you what, run along and ask your mum to come round, so I can sort you all out.'

'NO! ... I mean no, I can't do that, she's got a bad 'ead and wants to stay in bed. What else you got?'

'I see. A bad head is it? Let me see now ......' Looking under the counter, Irene reluctantly reached for the pork sausages she had been keeping for her and her husband Fred's supper. 'Do you know how to cook sausages? A bit of lard in a frying pan, prick each one with a fork and keep turning them over till there nice and brown. Don't turn the gas up too much.'

'Yea, I've seen me mum doin' it. 'Ow much?'

'You can have four for thrupence. Have you got that much?' Taking the wrapped sausages, Colin fished half a crown out of his trouser pocket and handed over the money.'

Pocketing his change and turning to the door, Colin said, 'Ta, Mrs Coleman, spect you'll be seein' a bit more of me now. I'm tryin' to be 'elpful for me mum. May be back tomorrer. Bye.'

The bell clanged as the two boys exited through the door. *'Poor little mites. What chance have they got with that floozy for a mother? So, it's a headache she says, more like a serious hangover if you ask me. Looked as though they had both been crying.'* With those thoughts running through her mind, the kindly middle-aged shop owner walked round the counter to the door, flipped the OPEN sign to CLOSED and slid the two bolts across, before locking the Yale. Satisfied that all was secure in the shop, Irene stepped through the dividing curtain which led through to her cosy living room where her husband was seated, with the black and white spaniel at his feet on the rag mat in front of the empty fireplace.

'All locked up then, luv?' said Fred as he looked up from the sports page of his Sunday paper. 'Wish you didn't have to open the shop of a Sunday afternoon. Sit yourself down, I'll make us a nice cup of tea.'

'Thank you, dear, that sounds good. You know how much the locals like to pop in for the odd bits they need, sometimes just for a chat. Too many widows around these parts these days, they need the company. I've just had the Golding boys in, wanting something for their supper. Something not right there, you mark my words.'

'Well, whatever it is, it's none of our business. Want a biscuit with that tea?'

***

Throughout the following week, Colin was often seen knocking on doors along the street and within the neighbourhood, asking if there were any odd jobs he might do for a few pence. It was not unusual to see Dan with bucket and spade, following the various tradesmen with their horse-drawn carts. Manure was always useful for the back yards. The observant neighbours might have noticed that the two scruffy boys were becoming more so, as the days went by. This was particularly noticed by Irene on the, almost daily, visits by Colin as he pondered over the food counter and shelves. On the following Sunday, when Colin entered the shop, Irene could no longer hold back as she asked, 'How's your mother, Colin, I haven't seen her all week? Seems you're doing all the shopping now.'

'Hello, Mrs Coleman, she ain't too bad, but still not up to goin' out. How do you cook liver? I've never done that before.'

'Can't your mother tell you? She has often bought liver for your dinner.'

'I don't like to bother 'er, she ain't up to it yet.'

'Colin, if you don't mind me asking, when did you last have a good wash, and change your clothes?' asked Irene who was unable to ignore the smell permeating the shop.

'None of your business, gotta go now.'

'But you haven't bought ….' Too late, the door had opened and closed to the insistent ringing of the bell which was now bouncing silently on its spring. *'Well I never. Something's wrong here. I'm going round there tomorrow no matter what Fred says about it.'* Irene and Fred had never had children. After two miscarriages and a still-born little girl they had stopped trying. Irene was now finding that her dormant maternal feelings were becoming evident. She had always been fond of the regular children who came into her shop, but she had stronger feelings for those poor boys whose father had been killed so recently, and whose mother seemed to be going off the rails, even more now than before. The father had been such a nice gentle man. *'That woman never deserved him.'*

The following morning, having had a breakfast of Marmite on toast, Colin made an attempt to wash his and Dan's underpants, vests and socks. He had boiled up sufficient water to three quarters fill a galvanised bucket. Having found a half empty box of washing powder behind the shabby curtain under the kitchen sink he threw the clothes into the water. Kneeling over the bucket he swirled the hot water around with the wooden tongs he had seen his mother using. He was in the process of rubbing each garment on the skiffle board when a loud knocking on the front door echoed down the hall. Quickly rising to his feet and drying his red raw hands Colin crept through to the passage and up the stairs as the knocker sounded again, even more insistent this time. Silently he entered his mother's bedroom and from behind the edge of the musty net curtain he peered down to the pavement. There he saw a man in raincoat and trilby hat, peering into the front downstairs window. *'Cripes, it's the rent man. Please don't let Dan come home till he's gone.'* Colin quickly retreated from the window as the man took a step back to peer up at the bedroom window. Sitting on the unmade bed, he waited silently and listened. There was another loud knock followed by the rattle of the letterbox, then a loud voice. 'I know you're in there Mrs Golding. You're seven weeks behind with your rent. If you don't come into the office and settle up this week, we'll have no choice other to send the bailiffs in. Don't make us do it.'

At that moment, having temporarily closed the shop, with a sign telling the world that she would be back in ten minutes, Irene heard the rent man's threat as she approached the gap alongside No 73. Quickly she stepped off the pavement into the weeds and long grass which had so quickly taken over the site. Clearly the man hadn't noticed her as he straightened up and, with his back to her, walked further down the street to other addresses on his books. Irene waited for a few minutes, to be sure that the rent man was gone, before stepping back out onto the pavement and along to the front door of No 73. Taking a final look along the road, to be sure the coast was clear, she reached for the knocker, paused for a moment then rapped it hard. At the same time, she stooped down to peer through the letterbox just in time to see Colin's head draw back into the stairs recess. 'It's alright, Colin,' she called through the opening. 'He's gone now, please come and open the door. It's Mrs Coleman, I know something's wrong and I want to help you.'

Silence.

Again, Irene peered through the letterbox but this time there was no sign of the boy, or the mother for that matter. With a sigh Irene used the knocker and waited.

'Hello, Mrs Coleman, what are you doing here?'

With a guilty start, Irene spun round to be confronted by the younger brother, Dan. He was clutching a rather smelly empty galvanised bucket and an equally smelly spade in his other hand. 'Oh, you made me jump, Dan. I just wanted to have a word with your mother to see if there's anything I can do to help.'

'Well, she isn't here, she … Oh I shouldn't have told you that!'

'Where is she? I thought she was poorly in bed.' At that moment the boy burst into tears, dropped the bucket and spade and buried his face into Irene's coat. Instinctively she put her arms around the thin body and gently rocked him till his sobbing eased away. 'It's okay, Dan, you can tell me. What's happened?'

Looking up into Irene's eyes and wiping the snot from his nose with his shirt sleeve Dan burst out, 'Mum's left us.'

'What?' When was this? Easing herself onto one knee to be at eye level with the boy, Irene gently asked, 'Has it been over a week since she left? I remember you both coming into the shop for food last Sunday.'

'Y..yes, we've b..been on our own s..since then,' replied Dan between sniffs. 'Colin's been l..looking after me.'

'Here you are luv, use this hanky,' offered Irene as she rose to her feet.

'Is there a problem?' To her relief Irene looked up to see Mr Webb calling across from the house opposite.

'Oh, hello Mr Webb, I heard you were home from the RAF, your Pam told me on Tuesday. She was so excited about going to meet you, and the boys went with her and Mrs Webb I understand? Speaking of Colin and little Dan here, yes, a big problem it would seem. Their mother left them on their own over a week ago.' It was at that moment that the front door to the house slowly opened to reveal

Colin peering at them. 'What can we do?' asked Irene. 'We can't let them stay here like this. We have to tell the authorities.'

'No, please don't tell anyone,' cried Colin in alarm. 'They'll put us in an 'ome and we won't see each other anymore! We're doing alright. We can manage.'

'No, son. You can't stay here on your own. Apart from anything else, there's a law against it,' replied Mr Webb who had crossed the road to join them.

'And there's also the question of the rent,' chipped in Irene. 'If it's not paid, you'll be evicted. You heard what the rent collector said. They'll send in the bailiffs if it's not paid next week. No, we have to notify the authorities.'

'Tell you what,' said Mr Webb decisively. 'You can come over to our house until we can get things sorted. We've got a spare room. You'll have to sleep together but I don't imagine that will bother you. What do you say?'

***

On the following Wednesday, Irene glanced out of her shop window and was delighted to see Mr and Mrs Webb with their daughter and the two boys, leaving their house and carrying all that they would need for spending a day on Southsea beach. Mrs Webb had called in to the shop earlier to buy extra food and treats for making a picnic. She was pleased to inform Irene that the boys were settling in well and how much they appreciated their new clothes and sandals. She also commented on how close Pam and Colin had become, almost like brother and sister. She had gone on to say that efforts were being made to foster the boys out to a local family who were able to take both boys so that they would be able to stay together and also be able to stay in their own school. When asked, Mrs Webb had replied that the police had had no success in tracing the mother. *'Well at least they are safe and well fed now.'* Thought Irene as she worked on the new window display.

Later that day, just after closing-time and as Irene started peeling potatoes for a fish pie for their meal, there was a knock on the side window. 'Can you get that, Fred.

I expect it's someone wanting to buy some fags or something. Tell them we're closed.'

'Alright, dear, I'll see who it is.' A short while later, Irene pricked up her ears as she heard Fred's raised voice, through the curtain. This was followed by the sound of booted feet clumping across the shop floor and into the living room. 'Rene, you'll never guess who's here,' said Fred as he poked his head round the kitchen door.

'Well, it's too early for Father Christmas, luv, tell me.'

'No, you put that knife down in case you drop it, and come and have a look,' replied Fred with a huge grin on his face.

'Oh my God! It can't be,' uttered Irene when she at last came into the living room to see the uniformed father of the two boys standing in the middle of the room. 'Mr Golding, how is this possible? It was rumoured that you were dead. I just don't believe it.'

'Well believe it, Mrs Coleman, because I'm not a ghost, I'm flesh and blood and very much alive. Although for a while back there that could have been so much different.

My ship was torpedoed, and sank just off the north coast of Africa. This is what I was told anyhow, I have no recollection of what happened. I was concussed and somehow washed up on the shore, most likely days after the sinking. Somehow or other I had apparently lost my identity tag, perhaps in the explosion. I eventually ended up in a hospital where it was discovered that I had lost my memory. I didn't know who I was and how I ended up there, and neither did anyone else. It was apparently four months before glimpses of my past began to emerge. This eventually led to my identity being established, along with the details of the sinking of the ship. But enough about me. Do you know where my family is? I tried the house but no answer, the key used to hang behind the door, but that's gone. Have you any idea?'

'Fred, go and make us all a nice cup of tea while I have a little chat with Mr Golding, there's a luv.'

An hour later, Norman Golding stood outside No 62 watching two adults slowly walking up the road, accompanied by a girl and two boys. They were carrying several bags between them, they were laughing and chattering, they were getting closer. Suddenly they halted and peered ahead. They had noticed the tall sailor standing by their front door with a huge grin on his face. The quietness of the street was broken in the most wonderful way possible ……… 'DAD! It's our Dad!' The two adults, with their daughter, stood together as they watched two boys rush into the outstretched arms of a loving father.

The End

Were we to go further, we would discover that Norman had sufficient back-pay to settle the rent, that Colin and Pam eventually married and had two boys of their own, that Dan went into the Royal Navy and became a Chief Petty Officer, that Fred & Irene were able to adopt two sibling teenage girls, and that nothing was ever again heard of the mother who abandoned her two children.

WEB TALK

With great care, Drogom slowly carried out his daily ritual of rubbing each leg over an adjoining one in order to clean away any particles of his last meal. He remembered just how tasty that midge had been; small but rather juicy. He assumed that it had recently been sucking the blood of a Human Being, a young one judging by the taste.

'Oh, how good life on the web can be at times. Was it only yesterday when I completed this particular web, nicely suspended between the handles of the gardener's petrol lawn mower?'

He had contemplated building the web on the wing mirror of the car which squatted on the drive, but the last time he had done that, he had had to endure a bone jarring journey, leaving his beautiful home somewhat dishevelled. No, that was a lesson to be remembered in future. No cars.

'Seven legs completed, just one more to do, then time to retreat to the lawn-mower handle, and wait for dinner, which will surely come to me. Yes, perhaps a nice tasty bluebottle.'

Twanggggg.

'Wassat? Let's have a look …… Oh drat. Just a wasp. They are so much trouble, and not particularly good eating. Now if it were to be a big fat honey bee, that would be different. Wasps are so stupid. Why do they always look like airborne rugby players? Anyway, this one didn't even have the sense to get himself properly stuck. Just a wing-tip I see; can't be bothered to nab it.'

'Go on, you daft excuse for a helicopter, shove off out of there before I change my mind.'

Bzzz Bzzz Bzzz Bzz Bzzzzzzzzz … Thwonk

'At last, took him long enough. Now for a nice nap before dinner.'

Two hours later, having had a nice dream in which he had built a beautiful web with ten attachment points much to the admiration of that large hairy female spider he so much wanted to get to know, he awoke to an insistent buzzing close by, momentarily fading then returning, then fading again. A quick run to the far side of his web brought the fly into view.

'Could be dinner. Now let me see if I can entice that fly into my web.'

'Excuse me, little fly. Would you like to take a rest on my nice cosy web?'

'No, I would not like (bzzz) to rest on your web, sir.'

'But surely you have had a tiring day zooming around doing whatever it is you are doing?'

'No sir, I can (bzzzzz) for hours and hours. It's such fun bashing my head into windows and pretending I didn't know it was glass.'

'Well I can't see the attraction myself, but whatever turns you on. Apart from that, you seem to be a sensible fellow, why don't you come and land on my fine silky web so that you can tell me all about window bashing.'

'No, I don't think I will, (bzzz) thank you for the invitation.'

'But look how fine it is, and how you can see the rainbow effect when the sun shines on its surface. How can you possibly resist a closer look?'

'Sir, you may think your web is rather grand but, (bzzz) if you will excuse me saying so, it appears to be full of holes.'

'No, you sil .. um ..silver winged friend, they are not holes you see, they are the carefully structured and symmetrical spaces which separate the individual strands which make up the structure. Should you care to settle on one of the strands you will undoubtedly be able to appreciate the skill which went into my trap ….. um … trapeze-like creation. It's all about angles, struts and strakes. So, little fly, will you join me, perhaps for dinner?'

'No, thank you, sir. I would prefer not to be around when you have your meal, for it may not be to my liking.'

'Little fly, I do so admire the skill you display with you're flying. Are you able to loop the loop?'

'Oh yes, that's so easy, it comes in very useful when avoiding the occasional rolled-up newspaper during the odd times when I enjoy buzzzzzing around the heads of humans. Strangely, they appear not to appreciate the display.'

'Well then, little fly, you are speaking to one who likes nothing more than to eat …. Um, I mean, *greet* a skilled acrobat. I would love to see how close to my web you can get when flying upside-down, have you the nerve to do that?'

Bzzzz bzzzz

'You missed it, sir. I did it so fast you were unable to follow with your …. Um, how many eyes have you got anyway?'

'Six.'

'I don't believe that. I also don't believe you can make that silky stuff from inside your body.'

'Can.'

'All right, show me. If you can prove it, I'll (bzzz) sit with you on your web and you can enjoy my company over dinner. You must go to the middle of your web (bzzz) and then lower yourself down as you let the silk come out of your body.'

'That's easy, on the end of my line I'm a spider glider, watch me.'

Sure enough, the spider was able to suspend himself between the lawnmower handles, until he had almost reached the grass box. Having done so, he couldn't resist showing off to the cheeky little fly who was soon to be dinner. So, he swung in an ever-increasing ark until the crow, who had been watching the whole encounter from start to finish, swooped.

'Ho hum.' said the little fly with a smile. 'That's life.'

The End

MANY HAPPY RETURNS

The object resting in the mud close to a rubbish skip outside a house which is in the process of being renovated, has been there for the last three days. Although rather dull and dirty now, it was once bright and attractive. The object is made of two different metals, one being a gold coloured nickel-brass and the other a silver coloured nickel-plated alloy. This particular object was manufactured by the Royal Mint in the year 2018 and was sent, along with many others, to a High Street bank from where it was circulated to the general public. The value of this object is one-pound sterling and, not altogether unreasonably it's therefor called a *'Pound Coin'*. Having said that, the true value of our pound coin is very much dependent upon the person who currently owns it. To a wealthy person, the individual value is relatively little, whereas to an eight-year old boy, to own such a coin is to be regarded as most fortunate when one considers how many gob-stoppers can be purchased in the local sweet shop with such a desirable object.

And so it is, that an eight-year old boy, who, shall we say, answers to the name of Alfie .... or Kid .... or Pest ... or Oi ... well you get my meaning, whilst investigating the contents of the afore mentioned skip, hoping to find anything saleable, happens to tread on the particular area of mud that is, until this moment, partly obscuring the dirty coin. At first, Alfie has failed to notice the sudden revelation as his head is inside a cracked toilet bowl which is resting on top of the pile within the skip. With posterior sticking up and legs waving in the air our boy has decided that this is not a dignified posture, even for an eight-year old whose bottom can be clearly seen through several holes in his somewhat grubby shorts. With hands resting on the rim of the bowl, he heaves himself out of the pan and lands rather clumsily in the mud on all fours. Yes, you've guessed it, that's when the variably valued coin becomes something highly desirable as it is picked up from the mud, spat on, and rubbed down the leg of Alfie's shorts.

'Cor, what a find, and on me birfday an' all', our boy says out loud whilst his train of thought runs to a number of possibilities such as sweets, comics, cakes and rides in the funfair. In his young mind he has spent his pound coin several times over. In fact, he would need to find at least another ten of these coins in order to pay for those treats which have filled his head. That's why his instinct is to crawl around on hands and knees, in the mud, in the vain hope of finding more. Having accepted that his coin is the only one likely to be discovered, Alfie walks away from the site and, with the coin clutched in his muddy hand, for both of his shorts pockets have holes in them, he makes his way to the corner shop at the end of his road.

The shop owner is an elderly gentleman of Asian origination who is well respected within the community for his kindness and patience. Alfie enters and makes straight for the sweet shelf where he spends forty minutes choosing the selection which will cost one penny short of a pound. It would be fair to say that the patience of the gentleman might be wearing a bit thin when, at last, with a loud sigh, and muttering under his breath, he drops our one-pound coin into his till before slamming it shut. The coin will rest there among several other one-pound coins for no more than ten minutes before the till suddenly shoots open, spilling daylight, well shop light, onto the various loose coins within, before crooked fingers sift through the numerous one-pound coins and extracts several, including the one which was once lost and muddy but which now has a shine as a result of having been spat upon and rubbed on the rather dirty leg of a pair of shorts. 'Thank you, Mrs Lamb, here is your change, you take care now and give my regards to Mr Lamb'.

Karen, the lady in question, is dressed in a loosely fitted yellow and white dress and a white straw hat with a yellow ribbon trailing down the back. With a smile and a nod, she slips the coins into her purse and swings the shop door open to the tinkling of the small bell above the opening. She is aware that she mustn't be late for the bus as she can't afford to miss her appointment with the doctor. It's rather dark and stuffy, as well as fluffy within the zipped purse resting in a zipped handbag. It's also somewhat jerky as Karen has just spotted, and runs for, the No.9 bus, well actually there are three No.9s coming along together in a line, not at all unusual, for reasons irate passengers who have been waiting at the bus stop for half an hour for a ten minute service, are unable to comprehend, but which makes perfect sense to the bus companies. We digress. The jerking stops, our one-pound coin, along with a few others, is extracted from the purse and the chatter, chatter, chattering starts, following the rather abrupt entry into a coin machine which is mounted close to the bus driver's left hand as it holds and spins the steering wheel.

Chatter, chatter, chatter, chatter, chatter, chatter. A sudden jerk, the chatter, chattering stops.

A swishing sound.

'Two to The Park, please.'

'Four pound-thirty.'

'Um, I've only got a twenty-pound note, is that alright?'

'You're the third one this morning. Do you think this is a bank, or something?'

'Sorry.'

'It'll have to be in one-pound coins.'

With a great deal of muttering and lever-pressing the pile of one-pound coins sinks down and, without warning, our coin shoots back into daylight and slides into a metal tear-shaped bowl along with fifteen others and an odd assortment of other denominations. The young man gathers the coins, with an embarrassed smile at the driver, before pocketing his change and scanning the interior of the bus till he spots his girlfriend who is already seated by a window one row from the back.

'He's a bit of a misery, isn't he?' says the young lady whose name is Lynda.

'Yea, got a smile out of one of them last month. Thought that was nice, till I realised my fly was unzipped.'

'Oh, Rob, you didn't go to work showing the world what you've got, did you?' replied Lynda as she discreetly glances at Ron's lap for reassurance.

'Never you mind miss nosey parker, let's just say I cheered up the girls in the typing pool.'

'I bet, there isn't one of them below the age of fifty, I expect a few of them felt a bit feint. You weren't wearing those ones with *"Too Hot to Handle"* printed on the front, I hope,' says Lynda with a chuckle.

After a fifteen-minute journey, the couple alight from the bus and make their way to the park entrance. Arm-in-arm they walk to the pond at the centre of the lawned area and find a bench which is surrounded by ducks which are busily nibbling at the ground. Lynda turns to Rob and assures him, 'I'm going to take a walk then return here to sit while you're in your head office this morning. I can see the windows from here and I can try to guess which one belongs to your boss and how your meeting is going. I'll be okay till you come out, then we can have our picnic while you tell me what happened.'

'You're sure you'll be alright? It seems a long time for you to wait.'

'I'll be fine, I'll have a coffee and a bun in an hour or so then it'll almost be time. Oh, that's a point, I need some money, can you lend me a few pounds?'

'Of course, here take this.' With that, Rob reaches into his trouser pocket and produces all the loose change he had been given by the unhappy bus driver.

'I do hope it goes well, Rob. Just think, we could be married this time next year if it does.'

'Well, let's wait and see. Wish me luck.' For a moment, Rob holds his childhood sweetheart in his arms while he kisses her soft lips, then hurries away to the park exit. Our coin is now safety nestled in Lynda's purse, that is, until she has taken a walk around the park and steered herself to the park café.

Shortly after seating herself on the terrace, Lynda selects a pastry from the menu and awaits the service of a staff member. 'Good morning, madam, may I take your order?' It is a plump middle-aged lady dressed in a black and white uniform who had glanced over to Lynda's table while clearing another a short distance away. Half an hour later, with the bill paid and before getting to her feet, Lynda reaches into her purse and extracts a one-pound coin which she leaves on the table. Yes, this is our coin as you might expect. It rests there between an empty cup and saucer and a plate for a while, during which time a thin shabbily dressed elderly man shuffles past the table and approaches the entrance to the café. At that moment our waitress, whose name is Gwen, emerges from the interior with a smile on her chubby face. 'Good morning George, would you like to go round to the back, I'll give you a nice cup of tea and one of yesterday's rolls as soon as I've cleared the tables.'

Before doing as instructed the man holds out his gloved hand and we can now see our one-pound coin sitting in the woollen palm. In a raspy voice he breathes, 'Morning kind lady, this was sitting on that table over there, can't leave money lying around, you never know who might come along and nick it, do you?'

'Why thank you George, tell you what, finders-keepers I say, but only at this café and only this morning. Since you are able to pay, you go and sit at an empty table in the sunshine while I go and get you a nice cooked breakfast and a big mug of tea, how does that sound?'

'That sounds tempting,' the elderly homeless man wheezes 'But one pound wouldn't pay for that and it's all I have.'

'Tosh and tish! Go and do as I say, back in five minutes.' True to her word, not much more than five minutes later, the waitress finds George sitting at the furthest table away from the few other customers. She sets before the amazed ex-soldier a plate which holds a full-English breakfast and also the promised mug of tea. 'Here you are George, tuck in, it looks like you need it.'

'Thank you, love. You've always been kind to me when I come this way. Here's the money.' He holds out a grubby hand which is no longer hidden by an equally grubby glove.

'I don't need that, George, replies Gwen with a wink, 'You payed at the door, don't you remember? My old dad used to be in the Regiment you know. Enjoy.' George does indeed enjoy this unexpected breakfast, the first he has had for longer than he cares to remember. As he lifts his mug of strong tea, he watches a young lady sitting on a bench by the pond. She has been gazing at the office block opposite the park since he sat down at the table. *Interesting, I wonder what's going on in her life right now, I hope her day turns out to be as good as mine,* he muses to himself.

With the one-pound coin nestled in the otherwise empty jacket pocket of the ex-soldier, he gives Gwen a wave and, with a full stomach, contentedly shambles toward the park exit, as he does so, he glances back at the pond and notices that the young lady is still seated there. Away from the park and along the busy precinct George enters a *One Pound* shop and comes away with a bar of chocolate which he will later share with a friend he often finds seated on the pavement by the fountain. The one-pound coin is once again sitting in a shop till, but not for long.

In fact, it was a mere three minutes before the coin was scooped out and placed into the hand of a middle aged smartly dressed man, along with three other one-pound coins. 'Thank you,' said the man to the assistant, carelessly dropping the money into his trouser pocket which also holds a freshly laundered handkerchief. William, for that's his name, steps out of the shop, holding a briefcase, and briskly walks through the crowded precinct. He steps past hand-holding couples, a lady wheeling a push chair, a bunch of teenage girls, all of whom are gazing at their mobile phone screens as they saunter along. A man on an electric buggy, with a spaniel dog standing between his feet steers passed. A young lady stands holding out a *"Big Issue"* and looks at him hopefully. He has no time to stop, although he often buys these magazines without ever reading them. An old man in ragged clothes is shambling along in front of him, he notices how thin the man is and feels a brief sense of pity as he enters a bank to emerge five minutes later carefully checking that his briefcase is firmly clasped. At the end of the precinct he arrives at a taxi rank and immediately opens the rear door of the front car.

'Where to, Guv?' asks Trever, the driver.

'Fairmile Road.'

The taxi eases out into the traffic, its indicator flashing the intent.

'Nice weather this week, let's hope it lasts,' says Trever with a quick glance at his passenger in his mirror.

'Yes.'

Clearly the passenger doesn't want conversation, so Trever mentally shrugs his shoulders and concentrates on the traffic. The ride is brief and soon the passenger is handing over the five pounds requested along with a one-pound coin for a tip. 'Thank you, Guv, have a good day.'

'Yes, thank you,'

Trever pockets the coin and makes his way to the nearest taxi rank where, with luck, he can read a few pages of his newspaper before his next job. It's now a few minutes passed eleven and, as he turns the pages, his thoughts go to Karen, his wife, who should be finished at the doctor's by now. He has little time to ponder this however, before his rear door is suddenly opened. Once again, he is working his way through the slow-moving traffic until he is able to turn into the requested street which is close to the park. Having received the fare, and before pulling away, Trever spots a florist on the corner just ahead. Although he hasn't previously thought about it, it occurs to him that a bunch of flowers would be appropriate whatever the outcome of Karen's visit to the doctor. Soon our coin is resting in the scent filled interior of the shop which has a far different aroma to that which was experienced in the hand of an eight-year-old boy who has been grubbing about in a skip, not to mention, mud.

Several customers come into the florist shop over the following half hour. Non however, have such a wide-open smile as the one who is looking so pleased with himself and the world in general. 'I would like a dozen red roses please.'

'Certainly sir,' says the shop owner. 'A celebration perhaps? Or an offering for forgiveness? Just my little joke, I can tell it's celebration time by the look on your face.' As she wraps the flowers she continues, 'Don't mind me. She'll love these, lucky girl whoever she is. Have a nice evening,' she says with a wink. 'Two pounds-fifty change, take care now.' Yes, our coin was one of the two. Clutching the wrapped flowers, Rob makes his way through the precinct to the park entrance with a skip in his step. Soon the ornate gate comes into sight and with a glance in both directions he crosses the road and passes through to the contrasting quietness of trees, shrubs and lawns, a relief after the hustle of head office and busy streets. She is seated on the familiar bench, not looking in his direction as she is gazing at the building overlooking the park. With a wide grin on his face he approaches the bench from behind and reaches around his girl with the roses clutched in his hand. Before Lynda has time to react, Rob swings around the bench and immediately drops to one knee.

'Lynda, will you marry me?'

'Rob, you *got* it! Oh well done, I'm so happy for you, for both of us.'

'You haven't answered my question my love, will you marry me?'

'Of course I will, you silly sausage, and thank you for the roses, they're lovely. Lynda buries her head into the wrapping and inhales deeply. 'How lovely, but can we afford them?'

Easing himself from his knee Rob leans over and kisses his new fiancé before sitting by her side. 'Yes, we can afford these, and a lot more, my love. I've been promoted to Department Manager with a big salary increase, starting next month, and, guess what? A company car. We can set a date now, how about next spring?'

'Oh Rob, that's wonderful. Spring seems so far away, I don't want to wait that long, what's wrong with September?'

'Wow! Even better, let's do it!'

Rising to her feet, Lynda takes Rob's hand and says, 'Come on, let's give these boring sandwiches to the ducks, and have a nice meal in the pub over the road. I feel like celebrating and you can tell me all about the new job, it sounds very important. Have you got time?'

'Oh yes, my love, the boss has given me the afternoon off. He's not as bad as I thought. I'll be seeing a lot more of him from now on.' So that's how our one-pound coin arrives in the *Red Dragon* public house.

Two hours later, the love birds, having enjoyed a three-course lunch and paid the bill, head for the pub door, arm in arm. The one-pound coin is left in yet another till. As they reach the door, they step aside as William, who is still carrying his briefcase, enters the bar. He is accompanied by a younger man sporting a waxed moustache and dressed in slacks and sweater, they spot an unoccupied alcove table and make their way over. 'What will you have?' asks the younger man.

'A pint of bitter please.' The young man goes to the bar and orders the two beers which he carefully brings back to the table. William takes a sip and wiping the froth from his lips with the back of his hand says, 'Thank you. I needed that.'

'Least I can do, glad you like her. She's a fine lady. Twenty-three years old and will never let you down as long as you treat her right. She's quick as well, as you discovered. I have loved her since the day I first stripped her down. No hidden blemishes, no nasty surprises. She has an even temper and, to me she is also very sexy. A lovely shade of green and throaty sound when you put your foot down. Thirty-five miles to the gallon on a run, only two previous owners. We agreed sixteen thou. You were grinning from ear to ear when you were on the test drive so I'm assuming we have a deal?'

'We do, yes it's a deal.'

'Cash only I'm afraid, hope that's what's in the briefcase.' The young man nods in the direction of the briefcase, which is resting on the bench beside William.

At that moment, the pub landlord walks over to their table, 'You forgot to wait for your change, sir, Twelve pound-fifty.'

'Oh thanks, here take five and have a drink on me.'

'I'll do that, thank you, sir.'

Once the landlord has moved back to the bar, the briefcase is opened and the contents is discreetly transferred to a hold-all. The young man hands the car keys and papers over to William, writes a receipt for the money and finishes his beer in one swallow. 'Pleasure to do business with you, drive carefully, good day to you.' He leaves the bar, carrying sixteen thousand pounds in his hold-all and our one-pound coin in his pocket. With a jaunty walk he makes his way to his bank in the high street where he will deposit the cash. He remembers all the problems he had with that retched car and is congratulating himself on getting rid of it. Tonight, he will take his partner out for a slap-up meal, but first he'll call in to the betting shop for a flutter on the three-thirty. Yes, that's right, the one-pound coin is destined to visit the bookmaker's shop and there it is to remain for an hour before a lucky taxi driver is able to park outside and collect his winnings.

With a smile on his face, Trever removes the bunch of flowers from the boot of the taxi and places them on the passenger seat for the twenty-minute journey home. An early finish today will allow time to celebrate or commiserate with his wife. Having parked his taxi in the first available space, a fair distance down the road from his terraced house, he switches off the engine, gathers up the bunch of flowers, and locks the doors. He has to pass the corner shop so he decides to nip in for a bottle of wine which may become handy later.

'Thanks Mr Singh, be seeing you,' he calls out as he leaves and as the shop owner places several coins in the till. Three minutes later, Trever puts his key in the keyhole, turns it and opens the door into a long passage. No sooner is the door shut than Karen, having heard his entrance, runs down the passage straight into his arms. 'Hello luv, how did it go at the doctors?'

'It's what we suspected, it's twins, Oh Trev, isn't that wonderful, imagine it, twice the joy, I'm so happy.'

'Oh, my darling girl, Karen, you are so clever, let me give you a big kiss and a hug, oh and some flowers. Wow! I should have bought champagne rather than cheap wine, well I never, twins. Who would have thought it?'

Meanwhile, another customer has come into the corner shop. She is looking through the birthday cards, specifically for her eight-year old son. Having made the selection of a card with a footballer scoring a goal on the front, she hands over her last five-pound note and waits for her four pounds change which, of course, includes a coin which, if you look closely, still bears a trace of mud on the queen's nose. A few minutes later, she is seated at her kitchen table, writing:-

"To Alfie. Couldn't afford a present so here's a quid for you to spend how you like. Love Mum. Many Happy Returns."

The End

THE INVENTORS

'Well, if it isn't my old mate, Rocky.'

'Hello Chalky, fancy bumping in to you. How are things?'

'Oh fine, fine. You know how it can be, coughs and sneezes, that kind of thing.'

'And how's your woman these days, Chalky?'

'Can't complain, Rocky. She looks after the fire and keeps it going. Produces some decent meals. Keeps the kids off when I take a nap. Keeps the old cave tidy, that sort of thing. Actually, Rocky, I've got a bone to pick with you.'

'Oh? What have I done to deserve that, Chalky?'

'Well, you've been a good mate to me, Rocky, and we've always enjoyed our games of bowls whenever we can catch enough hedgehogs to roll into prickly balls. It's only a small bone, but it has to be shared. Here, it's all that's left of the last duck I caught. A wing each.'

'Thank you, Chalky, you're so generous. Next time we have a mammoth roast, I'll send one of the nippers round to let you know.'

'That'll be most welcome, Rocky. I'm having a problem with my club these days.'

'Don't tell me they've gone and kicked you out.'

'No, not the Buffalos, I'm still the treasurer there. Someone has to keep an eye on the chippings. No, it's my club.'

'Your club? Oh, I get it. You mean your *'club.'*

'That's right, Rocky. The thing with the piece of flint tied on the end. It's bent.'

'Bent?'

'Yes, bent.'

'How did it get bent, Chalky?'

'Well, it was that big hairy mammoth that did it. You know, the one with that stupid sloth that follows it everywhere. I fancied my chances, crept up on it while it was busy grazing. I was just about to bash it over the nut when that cretin of a sloth shouts "DUCK!" So, I did. Then the mammoth turns round and says, "I think he meant me." Then he pulls my club out of my hand with his trunk and smashes it against a rock. It's bent now.'

'Against a rock, Chalky. Phew. It could have been your head.'

'Well he aimed for where my head should have been, but I was still ducked. Believe me, I got out of there quick, you can imagine. Anyway, I'm giving up on the club, unless I'm looking for a woman to clobber and drag back to my cave by her hair. They like that for some reason.'

'Wow! How will you get any dinner without a club?'

'I've invented a bow and arrow.'

'A bow and arrow. What's that, Chalky?'

'A bow is a stick with a bit of gut tied to it at both ends. You get another stick with a pointy end, place it on the first stick, put the gut at the end of the blunt end of the second stick, pull and let go.'

'I seeee … I think. Chalky, are you sure you want to give up on the club?'

'You don't think it'll work, do you?'

'No, Chalky.'

'No, neither do I, Rocky, but you have to invent things, otherwise where will we be after four thousand summers?'

'How about inventing a stick that you can point at a mammoth and it goes "BANG", and the mammoth is dead. Ha-ha-ha-ha. That would make hunting easier, and less risky.'

'I know what you mean, Rocky. Just think, we could invent something you hold in your hand and talk to cavemen on the other side of the world. Ha-ha-ha-ha.'

'That would be clever, Chalky. What about a box in the corner of the cave that shows pictures of sports like hedgehog bowls and snail racing? Ha-ha-ha-ha.'

'Yea, that would be good. You could watch pictures of cooking different meat over the fire. Or maybe not a fire, how about a box that you put your slab of meat in and it comes out an hour later all cooked. Ha-ha-ha-ha.'

'I know! What about a box that can answer all your questions, and give you all sorts of information like how to find your way to Lungdung or Liverpond? You could give it a name. How about "Dougal" That silly old duffer, Dougal, is always trying to invent things. Yesterday I saw him chipping away at a rock, trying to make it round with a hole in the middle. "What good's that" I asked him. He said he could push a stick through the hole and make it go round and round. I can't imagine what you could do with that. Ha-ha-ha-ha.'

'Ha-ha-ha, the next thing you know, he'll be trying to invent something that flies through the air. Can you imagine a lump of wood flying among the clouds?' Ha-ha-ha.'

'Ha-ha-ha, yea, you could even reach the moon and bring it down with you when you land. That would make a brilliant thing to kick around. It could become a new game. Well, it's been good bumping into you Chalky. You have to have a laugh sometimes, don't you?'

'That's right, Rocky. Must go. What's the time anyway?'

'How would I know? The watch hasn't been invented yet.'

'What's a watch? Ha-ha-ha-ha.'

'I don't know, it just came into my head when I watched for how far the sun has got.'

'Ha-ha-ha-ha.' I like the leopard skin tights by the way. Be seeing you.'

The End

THE MUDLARK

It was a warm August day in the year 1950. Although the Second World War was five years in the past, the city of Portsmouth was still showing the deep wounds and scars of the heavy bombing it had suffered. Most of the inner city was flattened and bomb sites had become the favoured playground of the local children. Little thought was given by those children as to what has caused the deep holes in the ground, for them, it was claimed territory which needed to be defended from kids from outside their own stomping grounds.

On this bright morning however, one particular twelve-your old boy had no thoughts of play, or defending his territory from outsiders. For him, it was time to work. With his hands in the pockets of his short trousers he quickly stepped along the cracked pavement of Queen Street toward The Hard which fronted the narrow entrance into Portsmouth Harbour. Hitching his canvas bag further onto his shoulder, Charlie paused at the window of a Royal Navy outfitters called *Gieves*. Longingly, he gazed at the smart uniforms displayed there. He was mesmerised by the bright buttons, each with an anchor on its face, and the gold stripes depicting the rank of an officer who would one day wear such a smart garment. Charlie's father had been a career sailor in the Royal Navy. He had proudly worn the uniform of a Chief Petty Officer and the boy still had the feint recollection of proudly sitting on the shoulders of his tall daddy, with his mother walking alongside, wheeling a second-hand pram, in which his one-year old sister rested. They were accompanying his father as he returned from leave, to a Destroyer which was birthed alongside the quay in the dockyard.

His father had never returned.

Charlie was now the man of the house in the residential area of Stamshaw which is opposite the Royal Navy Gunnery School, HMS Excellent. He loved hearing the bugle, playing *'Sunset'*, across the short stretch of water each day when the flag was ceremoniously lowered at dusk. It always filled him with a sense of pride and made the hairs on the back of his neck prickle. He knew that there would come a time when he would be wearing a Royal Navy uniform, of that, he had no doubts.

Today, however, he had other business to attend to. His mother was able to bring in a wage from the laundry in which she worked, it was sufficient to feed her two children and herself in a modest but adequate way, it also paid the rent and the electricity bills, but left little for clothing and other necessities. Charlie was required to supplement his mother's income in any way possible. As the man of the house, he had no problem with that, it was his duty. His casual job of cleaning cars in a local garage, along with his regular paper-round brought in a reasonable additional income, but when supplemented with the work he was to be engaged in this afternoon, until the tide once again flooded The Hard basin, it made the difference of allowing a few luxuries, such as soap, toilet rolls and cake or biscuits, which they would otherwise do without.

Time didn't allow Charlie to gaze into the shop window for more than a few minutes. *Time and tide wait for no man,* the boy repeated to himself as he moved on. Just before reaching the end of Queen Street the dockyard gate came into sight on his right. He could never look at those gates without thinking of the father he still missed, and then, on the positive side, how he would one day swagger through such gates in a port somewhere, and possibly salute a guard or an emerging officer. Oh, how he had practised those salutes in front of the cracked mirror in the bedroom he shared with his seven-year old sister. In fact, June was on his mind at that moment. She was a frail child, always prone to sickness and any infection going around. In spite of this, she never complained and was as cheerful as any illness would allow. She was also very cute with her blonde curly hair and she knew how to gain appreciative smiles from passing strangers. Something he would need to watch out for as Charlie loved her dearly and would never allow harm to come to her if he could avoid it. His thought turned to the new bonnet he was hoping to buy her if this afternoon's work went well, as it was likely to, on a sunny Saturday afternoon, particularly if Pompey won their match at Fratton Park.

Charlie rounded the corner opposite the dockyard gate and emerged onto The Hard. He crossed the road where a number of red Portsmouth Corporation buses were parked ready to start their next journeys through the city. He noticed that one of them was his favourite, a trolley bus with its twin poles sticking up above its roof, attached to the live electric cables suspended over the road. Those buses were fast and silent until they passed under directional points on the cables at road junctions, at which time they made a noise like a bark of thunder and sometimes a spark of carbon would drop to the road. On reaching the cobbled slipway, Charlie was pleased to see that two of his friends were at the bottom, and just about to step onto the black oozing mud. Instantly his nostrils were filled with the familiar smell of the mud which made most folk turn away in disgust but which he had come to like as, for him and his friends, it heralded the means to make some money.

Before stepping down the slipway, Charlie removed his scuffed sandals and grey socks which he placed on the seat of a rowing boat resting partly on its side clear of the high tide mark. From his canvas bag he extracted a mud stained tin can which had a length of string passing through two drilled holes at the rim. With the can at his left hip he passed the string around his waist and neatly tied it with a reef-knot.

'Come on, Charlie,' called one of his friends, a girl of his age who had tucked the hem of her dress into her navy-blue knickers and who was already standing up to her knees in the mud. 'Looks like the usual gang,' she called, 'And they're already busy.' Charlie could see that Valarie's brother, Peter, had waded ahead and was already peering up to the walkway some four metres above his head. On the walkway which led to the Gosport Ferry pontoon, there were many people passing by, most going to and from the ferry. Many were wearing the blue and white striped scarves of Pompey's football team colours, in spite of the warmth of the afternoon. Amongst these passing folk there were a large number of holiday makers and day trippers who had come out of the railway station which shared the walkway. It was those people who were most likely to be attracted to the children beneath, standing up to their bare thighs in the stinking ooze and calling up to them.

'Throw us a penny missis'

'Come on, mister, send us a thruppeny bit.'

'If you ain't got a penny, an 'alfpenny'll do.'

'Go on missis, shame the old man, show 'im 'ow good you can throw.'

'I'll duck me 'ead under fer a tanner, mister.'

'A real gent' would plop a bob in the mud, come on, 'oos a gent then?'

All the children were looking up and calling to the astonished and amused crowd above. At the same time, their young hands and arms were groping in the churned-up slime for the coins which had not been caught. Charlie and his friends worked industrially. As they became more mud-caked their individual tins became heavier. This was a good day, pretty much as Charlie had expected. He might even be able to afford to buy June a toy as well as a pretty bonnet and, maybe, his hard-working mother a new hair brush, or something. It would never occur to Charlie to spend any of the money on himself.

Three hours after their strange work had started, Charlie noticed that the tide had turned and that it would soon be time to stop their activity. However, he hoped not before the football supporters returned to the Gosport ferry, even better if Pompey had won the match to put them all into a good mood. As he searched the crowd above, Charlie noticed a uniformed man peering down at him. 'Come on, sir, throw a penny, let's see 'ow generous the navy can be.' Charlie was gratified to see the man reach into his trouser pocket and extract a coin before tossing it in his direction. The sun caught the coin which glittered as it spun toward him. *A tanner, brilliant!* Charlie managed to catch the small coin before it disappeared into the mud. After rubbing it on his blackened trouser leg he spat on it and dropped it into his, almost-filled tin can. Instinctively Charlie came to attention, as best he could, being knee deep in mud, and threw his smartest salute. Taken by surprise, and with a huge grin on his face, the sailor quickly shot his arm up to return the salute and, in so doing, knocked his peaked cap off of his head only to see it sailing down toward the black oozing mud. Charlie, of course, saw what had happened, and taking three sticky steps through the mud, managed to catch the cap before it plunged into the quagmire. Holding the white-topped cap in his muddy hand, Charlie looked up to the now bare-headed sailor and pointed to the slipway. The man gave a nod before heading along the walkway toward the main road, then onto the slipway where he was to meet a very muddy and smelly boy with a huge grin on his face and a rather muddy cap in his hand.

'Thank you, son.' The sailor said while reaching out for the cap and inspecting it. 'Glad you managed to catch it, although it looks as though I'm going to have a problem.'

'Yea, it's not looking so good is it?' replied Charlie doubtfully.

'I'm grateful, but the problem is, I've just arrived for a ship re-union this evening. The Captain, and even the Port Admiral are guests of honour. I'm down to meet and greet the Admiral and his wife on behalf of the crew after he's been met by the Captain. I can't turn up with a cap looking like this.'

'Well, I might be able to help you. You see, my ma works in our local laundry. I expect she'll be able to sort it, if you've got the time that is.'

'Really? That would be great. My name is Chief Petty Officer Small, but you can call me Lofty if you like. May I ask your name?'

'I'm Charlie and you can call me Charlie if you like.'

'Okay Charlie. We have a deal. Now, where will we find this star of a mother?'

'It's about a twenty-minute walk, well maybe twenty-five, or a bit more. It's opposite Whale Island.'

'Ah, I suspect that's in Stamshaw, am I right?'

'Yea, that's right, you know it then?'

'I did four years in *HMS Excellent*; I should know it. Tell you what, how about we take a taxi. It'll save a lot of time and I don't want to bump into any matelots looking like this, that would never do. Come on, there will be cabs waiting at the station.'

'Wow, I've never been in a taxi,' exclaimed Charlie with a grin. 'Can I just collect my things and say cheerio to my friends?'

'Sure, you go ahead, and see if you can rid yourself of some of that mud, at the bottom of the slipway. I see the tide has reached there now.'

Fifteen minutes later, a very proud twelve-year old boy stepped out of the taxi accompanied by no less than a Chief Petty Officer from the Royal Navy. He was pleased to see that his new friend had a long strip of medals on his tunic. As he stepped onto the pavement outside his home, he was hoping that more than one set of curtains would be twitching. As Lofty leaned into the cab to pay the driver, who was staring at the boy and wrinkling his nose, Charlie reached through the letterbox and deftly extracted the key on the end of some cord. 'Come in Lofty, mum will be in the kitchen cooking dinner I expect'. Together they walked down the narrow passage with Charlie leading the way and Lofty following while awkwardly holding his mud stained cap in his hand.

'Hello, is that you Charlie?' came the voice of his mother from the small kitchen as they reached the middle room. 'Have you had a good day down there?'

'Who else would it be, Ma?' Course it is, and yes, I've had a brilliant day.' As he was speaking, Charlie's mother stepped through from the kitchen and gasped as she took in the smartly dressed sailor standing in the centre of the middle room.

'Oh my god!' she exclaimed as she fell against the door frame with her hand covering her forehead.

'Oh, I'm sorry Mrs… erm, I didn't mean to startle you.' said Lofty with concern. 'Forgive me, I should have waited outside.'

'Are you alright, ma? You look as though you're going to feint.' said Charlie, reaching to support his mother who was barely any taller than her son. 'Perhaps you need to sit down while I get you a glass of water.'

'No, it's okay, Charlie. For a moment I thought it was your ……. Oh, never mind. Who is this, that you've brought in? You're not in any trouble I hope?'

'No ma, this is Chief Petty Officer Small. I'm afraid I got his cap all muddy and he needs to be smart for an Admiral tonight. I said you could probably help him with it.'

'Oh, I see … well I don't really. Mr Small, you are welcome in my house, would you like a cup of tea? Then I'll take a look at that cap while one of you explains.'

Ten minutes later, while Charlie was out in the garden washing his coins in a galvanised bucket, his mother handed the sailor a strong cup of tea and properly introduced herself. 'I'm Barbara Coldwell, you've met my son Charlie. My daughter, June, will be returning home from a friend's birthday party at any minute. Their father was in the Navy during the war, but he was killed when his ship was attacked by an enemy plane.'

'Just a minute,' replied Lofty. 'Did you say your name is Barbara Coldwell?'

'Yes, that's right. You sound surprised.'

'I don't believe this, was your husband's name Frank, by any chance?'

'Yes, he was a CPO just like you.' replied the mystified lady.

'Would you believe? I served with your husband on his last ship. I was just a rating then. He was such a brilliant leader. Kind but firm, no nonsense, but a great sense of humour when we were stood down. He and I got on quite well, in spite of the difference in rank. I had been conscripted and, I suppose because we were of a similar age, he took me in hand. We all missed him. He was the salt of the earth, well in our case, the salt of the sea.' Lofty paused for a moment, and looked at Barbara with concern. 'I can see you're upset Mrs Coldwell, perhaps I should stop talking about Frank like this.'

'Call me Barbara. It's fine. It just brought it all back, that's all. I'm so pleased you knew my Frank and how much he meant to you. Now, let me have a go at that cap and you can tell me a bit more about yourself.'

'Not much to tell really. It's all navy, ships, and oversea adventures. I prefer to be away now, since my wife, Cath passed on three years ago. I'm a bit of a recluse when on leave. I'm not very good on my own you see. I have a house in Plymouth, but I just rattle around in it, so I prefer not to spend too much time there.'

'I'm sorry about your wife, Mr Small. It must have been hard for you.'

'Lofty. My friends call me *Lofty* for obvious reasons.'

There followed an awkward silence which was broken by Charlie coming excitedly back into the room. 'Made two pound, three shillings and thrupence farthing. The best ever.'

'That's good, Charlie. I'm pleased I was able to make my small contribution.' The words were barely out of Lofty's mouth, when there came a loud knocking at the front door.

'That'll be our June, I'll go ma, said Charlie. I expect she's eaten too much jelly again.'

During this time, Barbara had been applying some sort of chemical to the cap, which was beginning to look more presentable. Lofty was amused by the sound of a child's voice describing how she had managed to eat four sandwiches and two helpings of apple pie with custard. He turned to face the door as the little girl walked into the room. She stopped when she saw Lofty sitting in the only armchair. She stood gazing at the smartly dressed sailor before quietly saying, 'I knew my daddy would return from heaven one day, I can tell it's him by his uniform, like in his photographs.'

I will leave it to the reader to decide the outcome of this story. Suffice it to say that they all lived happily ever after.

The End

THE RETIREMENT

Slowly, the loaded pallet rose from the deck of the passenger/cargo ship *Capetown Castle.* This was the last of the deck cargo, which had been loaded onto the homeward bound ship when she had called into the busy port of Las Palmas four days out from Southampton. The cavernous holds were still to be cleared of cargo, which had last seen the light of day in Capetown, South Africa. Several days' work which Bert would normally be involved in. But this was not a normal day for the lifetime stevedore. This was the day he had been dreading for the past few years.

'Well Bert, how you feeling? Last pallet today, and the last for you. Must feel grand, you lucky bugger. I said to the misses this morning, "Last day for Bert, I'm gonna miss him." Saying this, George removed his thick gloves before lifting his grubby flat cap from his bald and perspiring head. Taking Bert's hand in a firm grip he shook it vigorously. 'You've got an hour before the nobs arrive, time for a quick rinse and a mug of Dora's tea down the canteen, come on old chap, you look like you need it.'

The two close friends were joined by the three other members of their gang as they reached the top of the sloping gangway. Bert, who was leading the way, paused and looked down at the bustling quay, then along the deck of the lilac painted liner. *All those years working on these ships and we've yet to go to sea on any of them, Mave.* The other men stopped behind Bert and respectfully waited until their Ganger was ready to slowly descend to the concrete below. A great deal of care needed to be taken as the two friends emerged from the shadow of the ship on which they had been working. Although their work was finished for the day, other ships were still being unloaded or prepared for sea. Lorries and railway wagons were constantly on the move as the tall cranes continued their never-ending task of hauling pallets and a multitude of bundles up and down. Ropes and railway lines were a constant trip hazard for the unwary, although these were so familiar to Bert, he rarely gave them a thought. He had entered the docks as a fourteen-year-old labourer back at the turn of the century. A time when many of the ships he had worked on were sleek clippers or chubby two-masted schooners. Now, at the age of sixty-five, he was to receive the golden hand-shake from the Port Superintendent. In Bert's view that was a polite way of saying that he was being thrown on the scrap heap. *They don't want me anymore, Mave. Too old they say. By god, I can still lift loads these modern-day kids won't touch, unless there are three of them to do it.*

At that moment, a smartly suited gentleman approached the two men and, after removing a handkerchief from his top pocket to blow a nose which didn't need blowing, he said rather too sharply, 'Ah, there you are Mr Belling, you have just over half an hour. Kindly ensure that you are in the main company office five minutes before the ceremony, we can't have Mr Cousins waiting, now, can we?'

'He'll be there Mr Nose, I mean Nobes. Bert's just going to wash up and have a cuppa, don't you worry, I'll get him there on time.'

With that, Mr Nobes gave a loud sniff and marched away. 'Thanks, George, but I can speak for myself you know. I'm not quite in my dotage yet, in spite of what they think,' retorted Bert, perhaps a little more loudly than he meant to. *Crickey, Mave, even George thinks I'm passed it. Well I'll show them, see if I don't.*

***

At precisely six-thirty the outer office door swung open to reveal a smartly dressed young lady who was carrying a leather brief case. She stepped into the crowded room and stood holding the door as the Port Superintendent followed her in. Within the room, already waiting, was Mr Nobes who was Acting Deputy Superintendent; Mr Slade, the foreman of Quay 'D'; Mr Crimley, the office manager, with his secretary, Mrs Flint hovering behind him; and of course, Bert and the four other members of his gang. There followed a great deal of shuffling, each of those present trying to make a little clear space around themselves as Mr Cousins peered around the room.

'Good afternoon Mr Cousins, it's good of you to spare the time to come, we all know how busy you are,' said Mr Crimley. 'May I introduce Albert Belling who you may possibly have met before.' Turning to Bert he took his arm and pulled him forward so that he was forced to stand immediately before the revered gentleman.

'Ah yes, Mr Pelly, so this is your last day with us, after how many years?'

'It's Belling, and I've been here, man and boy, for fifty-one years, Mr Cousins. And yes, we have met, I once clipped you round the ear just after you joined us from college, you had kicked a ship's cat when it came off a gangway in front of you.'

'Ahem, no I can't say I recall. If I did that, I expect I deserved a sore ear. Now then,' looking around the room, 'We are here to congratulate Mr, um, Belling on reaching retirement age after many, many years of loyal service. Also, to thank him for the work he has done throughout, um …. his time.' Facing Bert directly he continued, 'To honour this occasion, I am proud to present Mr Pell ..Belling with this token of our esteem.' During the short speech the young lady had unclipped the briefcase and had removed a velvet covered box which she now handed to the Superintendent. Mr Cousins then took Bert's right hand to shake as he handed him the box.

'Speech …speech.' came the voice of two of the gang.

'Um, … said Bert, who's face had taken on a bright hue of red. 'Um … thank you for the gift and kind words, Mr Cousins.' There followed an expectant pause and an embarrassed shuffling before the Superintendent said, 'Happy retirement,' to the room in general before swinging round and making for the door. Before it swung closed the young lady was just in time to slip through behind him.

'Is that it?' demanded an indignant George. 'All those years of service and he only gets two minutes of the man's precious time? I don't believe it.'

'That's enough my man,' retorted Mr Nobes, I suggest you leave before you say something that will get you into trouble. Just be grateful that Mr Cousins could spare the time.'

'Spare the time, my arse!' yelled George.

'Come on, George, let's go,' said Bert, grabbing George's arm. It's not worth it.'

As Bert led George, and the other three members of the gang, to the door, the foreman said quietly, 'I'm sorry, Bert. It cuts me up to see how you were treated today, after all that you have done here.'

'Thanks, Tony, not your fault, still, I've got the watch now, and a bit of a lump-sum with my pension. Might even decide to take our Mave on a cruise, who knows? World's my oyster now. It's you lot I feel sorry for. Fancy a jug down *The Anchor*, lads?'

Half an hour later, the door to the Public Bar of *The Anchor*, which was situated at the east end of the docks, swung open to admit the five men. Crowded at the bar with pint glasses in their hands, conversation took on a lighter note as the friends of long standing amused themselves with the re-telling of favourite dockside stories and then speculation on next Saturday's football match between old rivals Southampton and Portsmouth. After a second pint each, Bert and George were left alone at the bar as the other three left for home.

'Are you serious about taking a cruise, Bert?' enquired George while eyeing his closest chum speculatively. 'If so, it would do you good. Get away. Meet a few people. You never know who you'll meet on one of them boats. You deserve a break.'

'Maybe, I'll have to see what our Mave thinks about it.'

'Yea, you do that, mate,' said George removing his glance away from his friend. 'Come on, let's down another. Your round, I think.'

As the two men lost count of the rounds they had consumed, the bar filled, firstly with men on their way home from work, then a bit later, with couples. The noise level increased so that all conversations were necessarily shouted. Cigarette and pipe smoke filled the dimly-lit room so that throats and eyes became sore. Bert had a great time showing off his gold watch and chain which received much interest and admiration. 'You should put that away, mate, you never know who might be getting over interested,' cautioned George while glancing around the crowded bar. 'Come on, let's go. I think it's time I got you home. Sup up, my friend.'

Slamming his empty glass onto the wet bar-top George grasped Bert's arm and guided the unsteady man to the door. There was no way he was going to let Bert walk home alone this night. During the time they had been in the pub, a sea mist had rolled in, creating a halo of light around each street lamp as they passed. With hob-nails ringing on cobbles the two men reached the front door of Bert's terraced house, where he clumsily extracted the Yale key from his trouser pocket. 'Okay, Bert, home safe and sound. Get yourself straight to bed and get a good night's sleep. I'll pop round in the morning before my shift, just to see you're all right. Good night, mate, sleep well.'

'Yea, good night, George, and thanks for everything. See you tomorrow then.'

The door quietly closed and George stood there listening to the chain-lock being set in place, then, with a shrug, he lit a cigarette before stepping out on the pavement in the direction of his own house a few streets further up the hill. *Poor old bugger, he won't know what to do with himself when reality sets in.*

With the front door securely locked, Bert crept quietly up the passage and into the parlour where he switched on the ceiling light. *Thought so, Mave's already gone to bed. Don't want to disturb her. I'll sleep in the armchair. So tired now.* With the overhead light still glowing through the dusty shade, it wasn't long before the old man was sound asleep. Ten minutes later, the velvet covered box slipped from the unmoving hand and landed with a soft thump on the threadbare carpet alongside the chair.

***

On the following Monday morning, after a sunny weekend of light gardening in his small back yard, Bert made his way on foot toward the town centre. He had deliberately gone the long way so that he would have to pass the dock gates. Here, he paused for a while to watch the familiar activity taking place beyond the gates. Lorries passing in and out; fork-lift trucks darting about between the sheds; crane jibs moving sedately up and down like a choreographed dance; tugboats nudging steamers into their births; crewmen on suspended planks painting their ship hulls; men walking up and down gangways, some in overalls, others in smart uniforms. On the water, the deep roar of ships hooters warning of impending movement into the channel, and tugs fussing and answering with their own higher pitched hooters. Each sound having a special meaning to those who were responsible for the safety of the vessels. Bert noticed that cargo was still being taken out of the holds of the *Capetown Castle* and, for a moment he stood there in thought. He knew that she was not due to sail until Thursday of that week and that her first port of call would be Madeira, four days out.

Wouldn't that be a treat for Mave? he thought to himself. *The Canary Isles. She'll love it.*

So it came about, that Bert found himself talking to a uniformed clerk at the counter of The Union Castle Line. 'Just checking, sir. You want a return to Madeira leaving on the *Capetown Castle* this week.' Knowing full well what the answer would be, the clerk asked politely, 'Would that be first or second class, sir?'

'Second please. I know Mave would love to go first class, but we really can't afford it.'

'Let me see, I have a double internal cabin on deck C, if that would suit?'

Bert thought about it for a moment, Mave would have loved to have had a cabin with a porthole, but no longer possible. 'No, you don't understand, I want a single birth, with or without a porthole. You see, my wife was killed five years ago in a car accident. It's just me now … and my memories.

The End

THE GIFT

The old man sat at his kitchen table with his coffee mug held forgotten in his gloved hand. The brown liquid was now lukewarm. A drip remained on his large red nose before gravity took over and caused it to drop onto the table's edge. The house was silent, apart from the ticking of the hall clock which his brain had shut out long ago. The room was bitterly cold. Frost had still not melted away from the north facing kitchen window. A bowl of cornflakes, now soggy, sat untouched to one side of the table. The near silence was disturbed by the sound of a large vehicle slowly passing. It had to be slow, as the snow was now deep enough to change his neglected garden into a place of magical beauty. He hadn't noticed it, or even bothered to look. His attention was fixed on the decoratively wrapped parcel squatting on his table. It was red, under a pattern of gold bells, and tied with coloured string. It was soft and a bit floppy, the size of his sofa cushions. Attached to the string was a card with a picture of a robin perched on a spade handle. The message inside was clearly written by the hand of a child. Although the card was now half closed, he could still see the name of the writer at the bottom of the partly obscured message.

The hall clock chimed the quarter hour, before returning to its regular ticking. He didn't notice. His troubled mind was recalling the last time he had received a present. Jean had given it to him two Christmases ago, just three days before she died. It was the gardening book he had been hinting at whenever they had gone to the shops together. That book had remained untouched since she had been rushed to the hospital on the following day. Boxing Day. A heart attack. Forty-nine years together, then gone. He was bitter and had become reclusive. He had ranted against the world for weeks and months after they had put his childhood sweetheart into the frost hardened ground. He was always going to go before her. He had provided for it.

They said he would get over it in time. What did they know? The neighbours tried to be kind, but slowly they gave up. Apart, that is, from one. A child. A little girl from three doors down. She had become a pain. Didn't know when to mind her own business. Always asking her mother if she can stop to talk to him whenever she caught him in the street. By ignoring her, he had hoped she would get the message and just leave him alone, like all the others.

The old man gave a loud sniff, and once again, reached out his gloved hand to fully open the card which was still attached to the parcel.

Dear Mr Fellows.

I no you don't like me much but I reely like you. I have bean saving up my 5 pees when ever I get them so I can by you a presnt for chrismas. I hope it fits, mummy thinks it will.

I now you are unhapy cos you are lonely but you don't hav to be cos I want to be *yoor frend. My teecher says chrismas is a time to giv so That's what I have done, not cos teecher says so but cos I want too.*

Lots of luv from your friend KIMBERLY

xx

Slowly the old man arose from the table and made his way to his bedroom where he opened the dressing table drawer. With trembling fingers, he removed a small green box. After carefully opening it, with tears in his eyes, he gently touched the sparkling bracelet, his last gift to his dearly loved wife. A tear rolled un-noticed down his cheek. It took a few minutes to find where the old Christmas wrapping paper was stored, even longer to find the Sellotape. Ten minutes later, the old man, now wearing his overcoat and a flat cap walked through the falling snow, head held high, to a house three doors away.

The End

THE CLOWN

*T*his is the best day of my life. The birthday cards are all lined up on the sideboard, some with large glittering number eights on the front. The one my mummy and daddy gave me is the best because, when I opened it at breakfast this morning, it said inside, that we were going to the circus. I've never been to a circus. I've seen pictures of animals and clowns, of course, but to actually go to one is like a dream come true. I can't wait, I'm so excited, and, I think that secretly so are my parents. I hope they have horses with those feathery things on their heads. I've seen them in pictures, trotting round the ring with ladies in costumes standing on their backs. I like horses very much, that's why two of my cards have horses on the front. After the circus, mummy said we can go to McDonalds for a burger, and, tomorrow two of my friends are coming to my party. We're going to do lots of different craft things.

'Okay, Janet, it's time we left. Go to the toilet, then get your shoes on. Daddy's getting the car out of the garage.'

'Yes mummy, I did a wee just now, I just need to get my shoes, then I'll be down.'

That was my mum. Well I suppose you guessed that. She said I can wear my best shoes, the ones with silver beads on the top. I've only worn them once before. That was at Bunty's party. She was sick after tea, all over her dad's feet. I expect it was the pink blancmange cos it all looked pink when I saw the slippers, and other colours, but mostly pink. I didn't eat any cos I don't like it.

'Ah there you are sweetheart. My, don't you look pretty in that dress?'

Yuk!! I don't do 'Pretty'. Attractive ... yes, but pretty is for children. Mum is a poppet, but she forgets I'm growing up. I won't say anything because today is a good day and she's in my good books.

'Now, where did I leave my keys? Handbag? …. No. On the hall table? … No, on the draining board? … No, now where *did* I leave them?'

Toot, toot.

That's dad in the car, wanting us to hurry up.

'Mummy, did you think of looking on the key hook?'

'Oh, *there* they are. Who's a clever girl then?'

Cripes! Don't push it mother.

'Come on you two or we'll be late!'

That's dad. He's just finished shutting the garage doors and is standing by his open car door calling us. We won't be late, of course, dad always likes to get to places early. Last time I had an appointment at the dentist he insisted we should leave at nine-o-clock for my appointment at ten-thirty. The dentist is only fifteen minutes down the road. We had to sit in the waiting room for ever, and did they have any comics? No, they didn't. Just boring magazines about gardening and motor cars. Dad kept telling me off for swinging my legs all the time. I did it even more, of course. All that, just to be told everything was okay. I could have told the dentist that, on the phone. He's got long hairs growing out of his nose. I couldn't stop looking at them when my mouth was wide open. He kept asking me questions about how I was doing at school.

How do you answer when your mouth looks like a cave full of pokey things?

Now we are all settled in the car, mum and dad in the front seats, of course, me in the back with Conk. Oh, did I tell you about Conk? He's a soft panda my parents gave me for Christmas last year. They wanted me to give him a sweet name like Silvester, but I didn't want that, so Conk was the ugliest word I could think of at the time and Conk he became. There's no way I would have brought the stupid thing but mum insisted. I hope she's not expecting me to let it out of the car when we get to the circus.

'Are we nearly there yet?'

Of course, I know where we are and where the circus is, so not far to go, but I can't resist winding dad up, even on my birthday and even when he's doing something nice for me.

'Not long, Honey, about forty-five minutes. You remember when I took you to the football match. It'll be around the time it took to get to half-time.'

Cripes! Does he think I don't know how long forty-five minutes is? And that football match took for ever and ever ... amen. We motor on, dad sticking to the speed limits as usual, and every so often saying something like, 'What does he think he's doing, hasn't he got an indicator? Bet it's a woman driver.' That's when he winds me up, and mum. I bet he can't cook a dinner, or sew on a button, or skip up to a hundred. I close my eyes, not because I want to go to sleep. It's a game I play, I like to guess where we are by how the car turns on corners and bends then, every so often, I open my eyes to see if I'm right. I imagine I've been kidnapped for a ransom of two million pounds. I have a blindfold covering my eyes and I'm remembering the way, so the police can catch the baddy and get our money back. I know, it's a silly game but it passes the time. I hope the circus has a lion that lets the man put his head in its mouth. That would make things easier for the dentist if he could do that. I amuse myself with my little private joke, imagining the dentist saying to me, 'Wider please, I can't get my head out.'

'Hello?'

Dad's voice brings me back just as I'm about to bite the dentist's head off.

'What's going on up ahead?'

I open my eyes and look between the front seats. There's a man standing by a van parked half on the verge. He's stepping out onto the road waving at us.

'Looks like he's broken down, or run out of petrol, or something,' dad says.

'Are you going to stop?'

Mum asked the question which isn't really a question. Mum has a way of doing that, she says things like, 'Are you going to wash your hands before you sit up at table, Janet?' It's a way of telling me to jolly well do it, or else.

'Am I heck, it's his own fault if he can't maintain his vehicle.'

Dad slows down a bit to pull around the man with the van. The man looks pleased because he probably thinks we are stopping. But not for long, as we pass him. I see his smile change to a frown. I quickly kneel up on my seat and look out the back window. Our car hasn't got rear *seat belts fitted yet. It's an old Ford something or other. The man just stands there watching us. I would be shaking my fist or something, but he just stands there shaking his head.*

'Daddy, you have to stop! He needs our help!'

'No Honey, we mustn't be late. I have to find a safe place to park when we get there, and we need to buy the tickets. We don't want to miss the beginning, do we?'

'Daddy, we've got lots of time. That man may be taking his wife to the hospital with the baby coming, it may be half way out. Or … or… he may be a plain-clothed detective on his way to catch a gang of murderers. You can't leave him there!'

'Okay Honey, but if we're late to the circus, don't blame me.'

With a loud dad-type sigh which means he thinks he's right but he's just humouring me, he slows down to find a place where he can turn around. I can't wait to see the man's face when he realises, we're coming back. As I expected, he is looking really pleased when we pull over near his van. Dad does all those twiddly things with levers and keys in the car before telling us to stay in our seats. Of course, I immediately jump out, not wanting to miss anything exciting, like pulling the baby out and slapping its bottom to make it cry and breath.

'Good day, sir. Thank you for stopping, I'm afraid this old van won't be taking me any further today. I'll have to send someone out to retrieve it. Is there any possibility you could give me a lift into town if you're going that way?'

As the man is talking to dad, I'm peering into the van to see if the baby has come. I'm disappointed to see that there's nobody in there.

'Yes, I suppose that will be alright. We're going to the circus so we'll have to drop you off there.'

I notice dad is looking at his wrist-watch as he answers the man, just to let him know that he's putting us out a bit. He can be such a grump sometimes, but he usually means well. *Dad tells me to get back into the car and allows the man to follow me in.*

'Hello, little girl. What is your name then?'

'Hello, Mister. My name is Janet and this is Conk. It's my eighth birthday today, so I'm not little anymore. What's your name?'

'Sweetheart, you mustn't be rude to the gentleman. He'll tell you his name if he wants to, but you mustn't ask.'

That's mum turning in her seat to look first at me, then at the man. She has one eyebrow raised. Anyone can see she's really asking the man for his name. Why do grown-ups have to be so complicated?

'Good day to you, madam. My name's Mr Mills. It was very kind of you and your husband to stop for me. I must admit, that had you not done so, I would have been in trouble. As it happens, I too, am going to the circus, so all's well that ends well.'

'Well, actually it was Janet who insisted we should stop, so it's her you should be thanking.'

That was dad. At that moment I loved him to bits for showing the man how kind I am.

'Why thank you, Janet. And may I wish you a very happy birthday, and I must say, that I do like the name of your little friend. Conk the Panda, it has a ring to it. Talking about a ring, do you happen to have tickets for this afternoon's performance?'

'No, we'll be buying them when we arrive.' *Mum says.* 'I hope we can get good seats.'

'Well now, dear lady. It just happens that I have a little influence at the circus. I think I might be able to ensure that you have really good seats. Why don't you come in with me after you have parked your car, and don't worry about that, by the way, I know of a good spot where it will be perfectly safe.'

Having listened to what Mr Mills had said, mum looks at dad who speaks over his shoulder while not taking his eyes off the road ahead.

'Do you, by any chance, work for the circus, Mr Mills?'

'In a manner of speaking, I suppose I do.'

'Wow! That's brilliant!' *I couldn't contain my excitement.* 'What do you do there, mister?'

'Oh, this and that, mostly between the big acts. I expect you'll see me if you watch carefully, my friend.'

'Does the circus have horses? I love horses.'

'Why yes, as a matter of fact it does. And there's even a carriage for the circus queen to sit in during the finale.'

Clapping my hands together, I can't help shouting 'Hooray!' at the top of my voice. For the rest of the journey Mr Mills plays with Conk and makes him talk, and even say some jokes. It's as though Conk has come alive in his hand. I know Conk isn't really talking, like I know that Santa Clause is really daddy, but us kids have to go along with it 'cos it pleases the grown-ups. I can't see the man's mouth moving when Conk speaks but I know the voice is coming from him. He must be a ventricle-thingy. I'm laughing so much that we are nearly there. I even see that dad has his laughing eyes when he has a quick look in the mirror. Soon we are bumping into a field that's used for football during the winter. Mr Mills points to the place where he wants us to park. It's right behind the big colourful circus lorries, some of which have their engines running. Mr Mills leads us into a back entrance, not the one where people are queuing, but a different one. We stand and wait, as he talks to someone who is wearing a soldier's uniform with a top hat on his head. Then he takes us to a special box, right next to the ringside. It has scarlet and gold material around it. Mum and dad are looking surprised and embarrassed at the same time. I am so, so, excited. The ring is covered in fresh sawdust and I can see swings and ropes hanging from the roof. Not far from where we are sitting, there's a brass band playing tunes. I know some of them but not all of them. People are coming in and finding their seats. A lady comes along with a tray of ice-cream. We choose what we want but she winks at mum and says it's free for us. I have a ninety-nine 'cos I like to see if the flake lasts longer than the ice cream. It never does.

Just as I finish eating my cornet wafer, the band plays something called a fanfare. The lights go dim and a searchlight comes onto the soldier man in the top hat. Dad says that he's the ringmaster. That sounds awfully posh. He welcomes the audience and then, to my surprise, he welcomes the guests of honour and points at us. The people are all clapping, but I don't know what for. I don't think the people know, either. I watch dad say something to mum, but I don't hear what he says, as the band starts playing another fanfare as the first act is introduced by the ringmaster. It's two men on motorbikes who jump over lots of ramps which get higher and higher, before riding through an arch which is set on fire. Following that, three ladies in pretty costumes, that show a lot of their legs, come on and do a clever juggling act with large wooden things that you see in the skittles ally in the pub garden when you're having lemonade and crisps.

After they have finished, a clown comes into the ring. He has huge white eyes and a very large red nose. He has a funny hat on his head which looks like a Christmas pudding, but this one is yellow. He has a white jacket with big blue buttons down the front and his red trousers are all baggy. The best thing is his shoes. They are orange and as long and wide as my tennis racket that I keep at *school. He's carrying a huge bucket and a step-ladder which he places in the middle of the ring. Then he pretends to be cleaning imaginary windows. As we all expect, he keeps falling off the ladder and sticking his foot through the steps when he tries to climb back up. He is very funny. The imaginary building gets closer to our seats until the clown is right above us. He is wobbling on the top of the ladder, with the bucket of water in his hand, all the children around us are laughing and screaming at the same time until ..... the ladder tips over and the clown lets the water fall all over me and my parents. Mum lets out a loud scream, even louder than mine, but then the water turns into little bits of silver paper that scatters all over us. Suddenly the clown, who had disappeared below the scarlet material in front of us, pops up his head and speaks to me.*

'Hello Janet, are you and Conk enjoying the show?'

It's my Mr Mills!

'Janet, you did me a huge favour today. Now, I wonder if you will do me another. You see, my fairy-princess isn't here today and I need someone very beautiful to ride in the carriage behind the team of horses at the end of the show. Will you do it?'

Well of course, I did. Just before the end of the show I was taken into the dressing room where a kind lady changed me into a princess with a glittering costume. I ended up riding around the ring with everyone clapping and cheering as I waved to them. It was so, so amazing. Truly the best day of my life, especially as Mr Mills later told daddy that he was the owner of the circus as well as being a clown.

***

'Janet, it's time for you to wake up now. You've had a nice little snooze and now it's time to get ready for your surprise birthday treat,' says her mother.

'Mummy, I had the most amazing dream. I was in the carriage …..'

'Later, sweetheart. We must get ready now or daddy will be waiting. Pop up to the bathroom, then put your nice new birthday shoes on.'

Half an hour later, as the little Ford Popular makes its way through the country lane, heading for town, they approach a van which is pulled over to the verge. There is a man standing beside it waving for them to stop.

'Stop, daddy!' yells the birthday girl.

The End

PLANE TALKING

The two aeroplanes were squatting comfortably on their sturdy wheels, each facing in the opposite direction from the other. Facing north, the larger of the two stood tall and proud, while the smaller bi-plane, for the moment, faced South. Each was braced, ready to receive their passengers as the dawn light increased. Bright markings caught the early morning sun which glinted on the wings of both craft. The larger plane, a Jumbo Jet, was painted silver, which contrasted with the bright red of the other. They had been parked in their respective positions since late yesterday evening. Soon they would, once again, be on the move.

'Won't be long now, Humphrey,' said Lucy. 'I think things are moving over there.'

'Yes, I think you could be right. I'm ready to go, after all this waiting around,' replied Humphrey. I've been sitting here imagining breaking through the clouds into the azure blue sky and climbing higher and higher until the clouds look like a white fluffy carpet below the wings.'

'Well, I don't need to go that high to enjoy flying,' said Lucy. 'Dodging in and out of the cloud gaps is much more fun if you want my opinion.'

'Well, I suppose that has a certain appeal, but just imagine when the clouds are behind you and you can see for miles and miles, why you can even see the curvature of the earth. Now, you have to agree, that's a sight like no other.'

Lucy thought about that for a moment before replying, 'Yes, that must be a thrilling thing to see, but can you imagine heading for a huge cloud that's the size of a mountain, and, just at the last minute, banking over to avoid hitting it?'

'Sounds exciting,' replied Humphrey, 'But I think it's a thrill when a Jumbo sinks lower and lower at the end of the journey and skims along the top of the clouds until it's time to be swallowed up by the swirling mass.'

'Well, I suppose both have their advantages, Humphrey. I know something we smaller aeroplanes can do that you Jumbo jets can't. I bet you can't loop the loop.'

'Of course not. Why would a Jumbo do such a crazy thing? Why, all the passengers would hit the ceiling and their food and drinks would be all over the show. Oh no, that would never do.'

'Well bi-planes can,' replied Lucy with a smirk. 'A bi-plane can climb clear of the ground, then put its nose down to go faster, faster, faster, with the wind whipping through the wires, until the nose comes up, up, up, then it flips over the top. Ooh I can just see it, it sends shivers into my wing.'

'I think I'd be sick if I ever did that,' retorted Humphrey. 'I know something a Jumbo can do that a bi-plane can't do. A jumbo can draw white lines across the sky. Sometimes when there are two or three, close to each other, they can make a criss-cross pattern that stays there for ages'

'*Do* you two mind?' croaked the fire engine. 'Yap, yap, yap, can't you keep quiet and let a chap snooze while he has a moments peace? Looping the loop, making lines in the sky, who cares? I'm in the serious business of saving lives, buildings, and cats in trees, do you hear me yapping about it? No, you don't.'

'Alright dear chap,' said Humphrey, 'Don't get your knickers stuck in your ladder. Can't two aviator types chew the cud when grounded?'

'Chew the cud?' Listen to me, you big fat excuse for a bird brain,' piped in the tractor which was sitting behind Lucy. 'If it's chewing the cud, you're into, you should see what we tractors have to put up with. Cud chewing beasts splattering their muck all over the place, getting into wheel treads and under the mudguards. If a tractor ever looped the loop that sh… muck would be all over the show.'

'What would you know about that, Terry? You've never been anywhere near a farm. You're always here with us flying types,' retorted Humphrey. 'And as for that fire engine, can't he ever stop clanging that retched bell?'

'The children like it,' said Fred. 'And what about that silly excuse for a bus over there, always honking her hooter. That's far worse than my bell.'

'I honk my hooter to let those aeroplanes know that there are passengers coming, only I never seem to catch up with them,' complained Bess the Bus.

'You lot are all wind, wellies, wipers, and water if you ask me. Us motorbikes can zoom through the traffic jams and make a lovely ripping sound as we do a hundred up the motorway. You can't beat that sense of freedom when we leave everything standing.'

'Wondered when Zoomy would chip in,' said Bess. 'Show offs the lot of them.'

'Now, now, friends. Let's not get personal. After all, we have to go around together.' said Humphrey while adopting his wise voice. 'I think it's time we were all on the move. Here come some kiddies with their mums and dads, and I see the dodgems are already on the move. I just can't understand how they get so much fun out of bashing into each other all day long. Well it was nice talking about flying, Lucy, for a moment back there, I felt we were really up there. Life is a bit of a roundabout isn't it, my friend.

The End

TRADITION

My name is Mary. I am twenty-three years old and a receptionist working for a large group of solicitors in the centre of Leicester. I enjoy my work which I find both stimulating and interesting. I particularly like meeting the customers as they pass through. I shouldn't refer to them as customers really for they are described as *valued clients* by the Partners. But I can't help it, for that's how I think of them. Some are quite regular and can be very friendly, while others can be more distant, even nervous, as they wait in reception for their appointments.

That's how I first met my David. He came in one day, just before lunch. He had no appointment and didn't know which of the Partners he needed to see. I could tell he was a bit anxious about coming in because I had noticed him hesitating outside the glass entrance door. Trying to put him at ease I offered him a cup of coffee from the dispenser, which he accepted. I couldn't help noticing how much his hands were shaking when I handed him the plastic cup. My heart went out to him then and there. It turned out that he had accidently run over a cat which had shot across the road as he was passing on his way to work. The daft thing is that he was riding a pedal cycle. First, he was really upset about the dead cat, but also, he was worried that he might be sued by the owner. Actually, there had been no one around at the time, so it was doubtful that anyone saw him move the cat to the side of the road where he left it for the owner to find. Anyway, I managed to get Mr Chalmers to give him ten minutes and assure him that there was no danger of prosecution or litigation.

Did I say that David came in just before lunch? I did, didn't I. Well, while he was in with Mr Chalmers, I went for my lunch break in The Black Cat Café down St Margaret's Street. It's conveniently close to our office, and the sandwiches aren't bad. I had just finished my cheese and pickle sandwich, and was half way through my coffee when the door opened, and guess what, in walked David. I must say, he was looking a lot more relaxed, that is until he saw me sitting there. Our eyes met, he smiled,

I smiled, he gave a little wave, I gave him a little wave. In the best romantic stories, I would of course say that he joined me and we talked, then fell in love. How ridiculous! But that's exactly what happened. Yes, it is!

I told you that my name is Mary. I am the only daughter of my loving and lovely parents whose names are Joseph and Ruth. Yes, we are a Jewish family and I was still living with my parents. I can't say that we are practicing Jews. We don't attend the synagogue or anything like that. But my father likes the Jewish traditions and particularly the idea of a Sabbath meal on Friday evenings. Oh, we don't do the candle thing, nor do we eat traditional Jewish meals, it's usually takeaway fish-n-chips for us on a Friday. However, ever since I can remember, my father has always started that meal by saying a prayer in Hebrew before we can tuck in. I was always impressed by this, although to my knowledge, he never spoke in Hebrew at any other time. If I ever wanted a lesson on how a married couple could have a close loving relationship, I only needed to watch my parents who loved each other to bits. There was nothing my mother wouldn't do for my father if it was humanly possible. My father always tried to please my mother. That's not to say they never had a cross word. Mother often scolded father when he did or said something wrong in her eyes, but it was all done in love.

Why am I telling you all of this? Well I suppose it's to put everything into context, as you read on.

***

David and I started dating. He was my first boyfriend and I was both pleased and relieved to discover that he was a Jew, the same as us. I don't think my parents would have minded me going out with a non-Jew, but at least, there would be no necessity of putting it to the test. We met as often as we could and very soon, in fact by the third week, we were discussing the very real possibility of marriage. David had a great sense of humour and was always keen to please me. I could see the similarities with my father, and my love for him continued to grow. I had told my parents that I was seeing a good Jewish boy fairly regularly and that he could speak Hebrew. Of course, the time came when father suggested I should bring David home to meet them and join us for a meal. On seeing David that evening, I told him what father had said. I was so pleased when he responded by saying that he would love to come to our next Sabbath meal, if that were possible, even though I had already told him about the fish-n-chips. Later, on return home from an evening at the cinema, I asked my parents if David could come on the Friday of that week. Looking up in alarm, father responded, 'No, that will not be possible. You must bring him on another day.'

'But, father, what's wrong with Friday? David said he would love to join us for that meal,' I replied.

'No! Monday, Tuesday, Wednesday, Thursday, but not Friday. It's not possible.'

'I don't understand, father. It's not as though we do anything particularly special on Fridays is it?' I could have kicked myself as I said this. Of course, the prayer was special, but I couldn't see that as a problem.

My mother spoke for the first time in this discussion, 'Mary, every meal we share together as a family is special, you should apologise to your father.'

'I'm truly sorry, Father, I didn't mean ….'

Before I had time to continue, my mother raised her hand to stop me. 'Joseph. You are a good husband and father. Let the boy come on Friday. He should see us as we are, don't you think?'

'Any day he could come, but he wants it to be Friday, iy, yi, yi, yi, If that is to be, let it be, what is a man to do when he lives in a house full of women, I ask the good Lord.'

'Oh, thank you both, I'm so happy. I know you will like him.'

'If he makes you happy, we love him already,' said mother as she placed her hand on father's shoulder and kissed his cheek.

***

That week seemed to drag as I looked forward to Friday. I was so distracted; I barely noticed the valued clients passing my desk on their way to their various appointments. It was made worse by the fact that David was unable to see me in the evenings as he was working overtime. I had to admit to myself, I was a little nervous as well as excited. Would the three most important people in my life get on with each other?

The day came, and dragged, until it was time for David to meet me at the office. I could see that he had made a special effort to look smart, to the point of having combed his usually unruly hair. He was holding a bunch of flowers which he said, with some embarrassment, were for my mother. I had promised my parents that I would buy the fish-n-chips on the way home with David, and mother had said the table would be ready, and that for once, we would have candles. With the warm paper-wrapped parcel in my bag, we walked along our lamp-lit street, hand in hand.

'Are you nervous?' I asked

'Yes, a bit. What about you?'

'It'll be okay, they'll love you. You'll see.' I replied while squeezing David's hand.

I knew it was all going to be alright as soon as we walked into our kitchen with the food. Father was getting under mother's feet, doing his best to help and being told to go and open the wine. 'Come in, come in, come in,' he said while gripping David's hand firmly. 'You are welcome in our humble home.'

'Hello David,' said my mother. 'It's good to meet you at last, and flowers! Thank you, aren't they lovely? My husband should think about buying me flowers, but does he? Go through to the dining room, all of you, I'll warm the food in the microwave and dish up.'

A few minutes later, with the fish-n-chips on our plates before us, father poured the wine and picked up his knife and fork. Mother raised her eyebrows and said, 'The prayer, Joseph, you haven't said the prayer.'

'Oh, I think we can dispense with the prayer this time, we don't want the fish-n-chips to get cold, do we?'

'Oh, it won't go cold tonight any more than any other Friday, Joseph. Say the prayer please,' said mother.

Father glowered at mother who sweetly smiled back at him. 'All right, all right, all right. We'll thank the good Lord as usual.' With an anxious look at David, he prayed the words that I could never understand, but loved to hear. The moment he said 'Amen', father picked up his knife and fork and grunted, 'Now, let's eat.' I looked across to David and was reassured to see a smile on his face as he salted his chips.

The meal went well as conversation flowed. David amused my parents with stories about his two older brothers and younger sister, and his work. All too quickly the meal was finished and mother suggested that David might like to help her in the kitchen while father and I could relax in the lounge.

It wasn't until the following day, that David told me what mother had said in the kitchen;

"Thank you, David, for not saying anything after the prayer. You see, Joseph doesn't speak Hebrew, as you

probably guessed. But those words he uses are a prayer of love, to me, to Mary and to his God. I treasure that moment, always. You are a good boy, I can tell, for your silence after the prayer told me so much about you. Please don't tell Joseph that I know about the prayer, it means so much to him"

Meanwhile, after having had our coffee in the lounge, Father arose from his armchair and said to David, 'Young man, I would appreciate a few words with you in my study, will you come through?' I assumed David was about to get the third degree, as he had probably done with mother earlier. However, that turned out not to be the case as I was to learn the next day when David recalled what father had said to him; *"Thank you, David, for not saying anything after my prayer. You see, I don't speak any Hebrew as you might assume. The prayer has become a tradition, but they don't know that I just make the words up. It has become an important part of our family life. I know it might sound silly, but it's been going on for so many years, I'm not able to stop it now. I know that my*

Ruth loves that moment and holds it in her heart. Please don't tell her the truth."

As David told me about those two conversations, he was smiling down at me and holding both of my hands. 'I love your parents, Mary. They are such loving people. I can see where you have inherited your loving nature. Please don't tell either of them what I have just told you.'

David and I were married just over a year later. We have a little girl now. Every Friday evening our little family crosses the town by bus to join my parents for the Sabbath meal. Each time, we all look forward to the moment, after we have sat at the table, when Grandpop winks at David, and Mama gives a secret smile, as her husband says his prayer of thanksgiving.

The End

THE CAPTAIN

It had been a particularly cold day. Although the snow cover had turned to grey slush there were still pockets of untrodden snow in gardens and many cottages which were still slumbering under their seasonable bonnets of white, hiding the dark brown thatch beneath. Exposed cobbles, where the slush had been swept aside by the constant movement of barrels, were icy under foot, ready to catch out the unwary. Nancy glanced up at the leaden sky, fearful of more heavy snow falling before she was able to complete her trading and start the long trudge home.

As she looked up, she gazed at the masts and rigging of the few ships which were moored to the crowded jetty. Regardless of the cold, there were crew members working up there amongst the confusing network of ropes. They were occasionally calling to each other. Nancy was unable to hear what they were calling, but their good-natured laughter was unmistakable. When was the last time she had laughed, she asked herself? She couldn't remember.

Where would those ships be sailing to, she wondered? Somewhere warm she suspected with envy, maybe Africa, or India, maybe South America. With those thoughts floating around in the mind of the thirty-seven-year-old woman, she hitched her shawl further over her head and blew warm breath into her frozen clenched hands, before carefully stepping over the cobbles with her basket tucked into her elbow. It would never do should any of the eggs fall to the ground and break. She needed every one of them to trade for the food her and her mother needed, particularly if the snow made it impossible to leave the cottage over the next few days.

Further along the jetty, Nancy watched two uniformed men walk through the open door of the tavern. Ships officers, she assumed. The sound of laughter underlined by the murmur of conversation reached her ears. There was no question of her following the men through that door to momentarily gain some warmth. She couldn't afford a warming glass of Port and, in any event, there would only be one reason for an unescorted lady to enter such a place. She momentarily stood there, listening to the tink-tonking sound of a badly played piano escaping from the closing door. Suddenly, there was a movement of traders, customers, and dock labourers along the jetty as the regular passenger stage rattled over the icy cobbles behind its four horses. Nancy stepped back to avoid the wet slush being splashed up by the prancing horses. As she did so, she accidently trod on the foot of someone who had just left the tavern.

'What the ….?'

'Oh, I'm so sorry, sir. That was clumsy of me, please forgive …'

'Say no more madam, my fault I'm sure,' replied the man while lifting his navy-blue cap. Immediately Nancy realised that he was a ship's officer as she took in the brass buttons and gold stripes on his cuffs. 'You look cold my dear, would it be too inappropriate, if not impertinent, for me to offer you a warming potato and a drink? I was just about to walk to the corn exchange where there is a cosy little shop which serves both.'

'Oh no, sir! I couldn't accept such a kind offer. I need to trade for food and return to my sick mother. She'll be hungry and in need of my attention, I'm sure.'

'I see,' replied the man who looked disappointed to be turned down. 'That was presumptuous of me. Please forgive me. You see, I've just landed and know nobody in this port. I'm the captain of that ship over there. I'm hoping to be able to buy her from the owners when I've earned enough to do so. I've had no conversation with any other than seamen for the last four months and I tend to be a bit abrupt, do you see? That's why more genteel conversation would have been most welcome. I suspect that we will be stuck in this port for at least the next three to four weeks while the agent finds us a cargo. I assure you; I had no intention of alarming you. Spending months at sea tends to dull the ability to maintain the polite conventions expected on shore. If you're sure you are unable to take up my offer? Then I'll bid you good day, madam.' Thus saying, the captain once again lifted his cap, turned, and stepped carefully along the cobbled jetty without a backward glance.

Nancy stood and watched the man till he was out of sight behind a pile of wooden crates. *"He was so good looking, in a rugged sort of way,"* she mused as she slowly stepped in the opposite direction toward the fish stall. *"And he seemed so kind. He must be desperately lonely if he can do no better than me for company, poor man."* Arriving at the fish stall, Nancy uncovered the eggs to show the fishwife who nodded before lifting out half a dozen of the eggs, in exchange for three medium sized cod. Next, the warehouse office where further trading resulted in a fair-sized scoop of flour.

"I liked the way his eyes crinkled around the edges when he smiled, and the manly smell of tobacco and tar that seemed to float in the air around him."

'I said, "How many onions do you want, luv?" enquired the warmly wrapped man on the grocery stall. 'You seemed to be miles away. I've got other customers to serve. Tell you what, give us a dozen and you can 'ave two onions, a pound of carrots and a nice cabbage, 'ow does that suit you?'

'Oh sorry. I *was* miles away. Put a couple of large spuds in with it and it's a deal.'

Walking away from the stall, the last one along the jetty, Nancy took the heavy basket in both hands and hugged it to her chest. At that moment, a large snow flake settled on her sleeve, then another, quickly followed by another. A sudden and unexpected gust of wind blew the shawl from her copper coloured hair. It was at that moment, anyone observing would have noticed how attractive the poorly dressed woman was. Lowering the basket to the wet ground, Nancy pulled the shawl more tightly around her head and shoulders. The snow-flakes were now thickening and settling. The woman lowered her head against the snow and continued walking up the main street, passing various bow windows and doorways. She was thinking of her mother and wondering if she had been able to place more logs on the fire to keep herself warm in her daughter's absence. If so, it would have been a struggle for her. Walking passed the corn exchange; Nancy noticed a sailor emerging from one of the doorways. Her heartbeat quickened, she held her breath as the man turned in her direction. He came closer, then crossed the street ducking behind a horse-drawn cart, the horse's breath creating a cloud of steam for a brief moment. The man reappeared. It was not her sailor. *"What am I thinking! The kind captain isn't my sailor, and never will be. Why am I looking at anyone who seems to be a sailor, stupid woman that I am?"*

Following an increasingly difficult walk up the lane, Nancy eventually peered through the white fluttering screen and made out the small cottage. She was relieved to see smoke rising from the tall chimney. Kicking snow from her soggy shoes she pushed the heavy wooden door open and stepped directly into the relative warmth of the parlour. 'Hello mother, it's me,' she said as she lowered the snow-covered basket to the flagstones and stepped quickly over to the bed in which the old lady was laying under a variety of covers. 'I see you managed to build up the fire. Well done, how are you?'

'Oh, you mustn't worry about me, my dear.' replied the old lady. 'Look at you, all covered in snow, and your hands and feet will be freezing. Take that wet coat off and go and sit near the fire.'

'I will, as soon as I've checked on the chickens and the goat, and warmed up the broth. Mother, you're so pale, I'm really worried about you. Perhaps I can get old Mrs Harris to come over and look at you. She may have some of her medicine made up that can help.'

'You are such a good girl, and I do appreciate all that you do for me, my darling girl, but you know all the medicines in the world won't make any difference to me. Now, if you must, go to your chickens and do what you have to do. Then come and get yourself warm.'

The door closed behind the daughter who had sacrificed so much for her. But not for much longer. She knew it was time to tell Nancy the truth. Soon it would be too late. Putting those logs on the fire had taken all her strength. She had not seen or heard from her two sons for, what was it now? Fifteen years or more? They had decided to leave the two of them, to seek their fortune. Never a word. The old lady gave a sigh and wiped away a tear with a crooked finger. Even that exhausted her. Yes, it was time.

The door was flung open again. Nancy quickly entered and closed it before shrugging off her coat. Glancing at her mother she pulled open a cupboard and lifted out two small glasses and a half-filled bottle of rum. 'This won't do us any harm, mother.' She poured a tot into each glass then gently helped the old lady sit a little higher up the bed, ensuring that she was well propped up on the pillows and well covered. She then handed one of the glasses to her mother who slowly winked at her before taking a sip.

Nancy swallowed her tot, relishing the warmth that slid down her throat and into her empty tummy. 'Right, I'll just hang the pot over the fire, then slip to my room and put on some dry stockings and slippers. You rest for a bit, mother. Here, let me take that empty glass.'

While Nancy was gone, the old lady looked around the room. Apart from the bed which took up much of the space, there was a square wooden table, an over-stuffed and badly worn armchair, a stool, a sea chest, a small dresser and a cupboard. The floor was bare. On the shelf above the fireplace was a crude painting which was intended to be the likeness of her late husband when in his twenties, now faded with age but still one of her treasures. It had been painted by one of his crew members. *"Not much here for the girl. The cottage belongs to the 'Big House' and the tenancy finishes when I'm gone, a kindness for the service my man gave them for ten years before the consumption took him. Perhaps they'll help Nancy in some way."*

The meal over, dishes and pot cleared away, Nancy made her mother more comfortable and built up the fire. Ensuring that the old lady was asleep, Nancy eased her aching body into the armchair and allowed her thoughts to return to the encounter on the jetty. She had never before, been so distracted by a man. Oh, there were the occasional farm hands and traders who had given her the eye, but she had never been interested. If the truth be told, it was the thought of her uncaring older brothers who influenced her feelings about men in general. So then, why could she not get the image of the sailor out of her mind? She slept at last. She dreamed of a sandy beach with palm trees swaying in the gentle breeze. The waves were gently kissing the sand with a sigh. A man was slowly walking toward her, he lifted his arm in greeting, he was smiling with crinkly eyes. He was still walking in her direction but was not getting any closer. He was reaching out to her but the distance between them grew, until he simply faded away. Nancy jumped as one of the logs shifted amongst a scattering of sparks in the fire. Her heart was racing. She glanced toward the bed. The old lady was still. Quickly, she left the comfort of the chair and stepped across to the bed.

'Mother?'

'Ah, so you're awake at last. You were talking in your sleep. You kept saying *"Come back"*. What were you dreaming? Can you remember, child?'

'No, mother, I can't,' replied Nancy sadly.

'Never mind. I want you to do something for me. Use that stool and see if you can reach into the loft. You should be able to feel a wooden box. Fetch it down to me.'

Without a word, Nancy did as she was asked, as she had done for as long as she could remember, never questioning anything she was asked to do by her mother.

Standing on the stool, she gave the trap door a push, but it resisted her effort. She pushed again with no success. She stepped down and moved the stool to one side before pulling the sea chest beneath the trap.

'Oh, please be careful dear,' said the old lady who was anxiously watching her daughter balancing the stool on top of the chest. Cautiously Nancy stepped onto the chest before climbing back onto the stool. She found that she was able to get her shoulders under the trap door. She pushed with all her strength until, with a thud the door swung up and over, causing Nancy to lose her balance. However, she was just able to grip the edge of the opening to save herself from a bad fall.

'Well done!' said her mother. 'Now reach around inside, can you feel anything?'

Nancy did as she was asked. She hated the feel of cobwebs on her arms and hands but continued to grope around in the darkness. With her head through the opening she could imagine the big black spiders, that had made those webs, crawling onto her face.

'Found it!' she cried.

'Good girl. See if you can pull it through the opening. Mind you don't lose your balance.' Five minutes later, a small wooden box was sitting on the bed, having been dusted by Nancy.

'Open it my dear. It's yours.'

Nancy, carefully unclipped the lid which surprisingly opened easily. Inside, she saw a leather bag tied at the neck with a leather cord. She looked at her mother who nodded. Untying the cord, Nancy was aware of lumps of something moving under her fingers. She gasped as the bag opened and revealed the contents which sparkled as they caught the muted light coming from the partially snow-covered window.

'Diamonds!' Nancy sat on the edge of the bed, entranced by the sight of the precious stones nestling in the bag. 'I don't understand. Where have they come from? How long have they been up there?'

'My dear,' replied the old lady. 'The answer to your second question is, twenty years or more. As to the first question, I don't know. It's time for me to reveal the truth to you. You see, my darling girl, you are not my daughter. Your real parents died when lightning struck their home, setting the thatch on fire. Your real father saved you when he struggled through the flames to reach you before going back in to rescue your mother. Before they got out, the roof collapsed. They were our friends. Your father pushed you into my arms before he went back into the house, and told me to look after you. Later, while searching through the ruin, your father, that's my late husband, Charlie, found those diamonds scattered amongst the ashes. You were the only survivor and therefore, wherever they came from, they are yours. We took you in. Charlie hid the diamonds from the world, saying that one day you would have them. You have been a good daughter to me, for that's what you are. My sons were happy to leave me, but you have remained loyal. And now, my child, I am very tired. I haven't got much time left to me. You must leave this place and make a life for yourself.'

'But …'

'No, don't interrupt me. I haven't got the strength. Take the diamonds, find yourself someone you feel you can trust, then sell them, but not all in the same place. One last favour, please see that I'm buried alongside my Charlie. I never stopped loving him, and I will love you, Nancy, to the grave. Now I must sleep.'

***

Nancy stood alongside the open grave, looking down at the coffin. She had run out of tears. The few mourners from the neighbouring homes had quietly left. The snow had thawed. She had noticed the suggestion of daffodils poking through a patch of remaining snow by the lych-gate when they had followed the coffin into the church yard. The hope of life at the beginning of her own new life. She had been given a month to sell the livestock and belongings before leaving the cottage. She still had no idea where she would go. As she walked away from the grave where two men were busy with their shovels, the sun appeared from behind a dark cloud. She could feel the suggestion of warmth on the back of her neck, or was that her imagination?

Without conscious thought, Nancy wandered down the familiar lane, for she couldn't bear to go back to the cottage, where only five days ago, she had fingered the glittering stones as she had listened to the mother she loved so dearly, for the last time. The dear old lady, had never awoken from that sleep. Soon, Nancy was treading the cobbles. It all looked so different now that the snow was gone and the sun was shining. The various stall holders were still going about their business, carts were still being pushed or pulled along the jetty. Men were still loading or unloading the ships. She noticed that one of those ships was gone. Was it the one her sailor had pointed out to her? She quickened her pace to see. To her relief, the ship in question was still there. *"Why should I be so pleased to see her there? After all it's only a ship."*

'Good afternoon, madam. Why if it's not my lady of the basket. I trust you are feeling warmer now?' Nancy swung round to see her sailor grinning at her and raising his cap.

'You seem to be very interested in my little ship. Would you like to come on board and look around inside by any chance?'

'Oh no, I couldn't.' Nancy replied while holding her free arm in front of her breast.'

'Don't tell me, I know, you have to get back to your sick mother, I understand, another time maybe. I have a cargo and we will be sailing to Spain once it's loaded, so best make it soon if you change your mind.'

'I have just buried my mother and …'

'Oh, my dear, I'm so sorry, I had no idea.'

'And why would you? Tell me Captain …?'

'Captain Styles, but Samuel to you and my friends.'

'Well then, Cap … Samuel. Tell me, do you take passengers in your ship?'

'Yes, we have a small cabin for that, and we provide victuals. Why do you ask?'

'Spain, you say?'

'That's right. Spain.'

'I think, Samuel, that I would like to come on board and look around after all.'

The End

The writer is happy for readers to draw their own conclusions as to how this story might end. However, should they care to read 'Deep Waters' *which follows later in this book, they will learn of the writer's conclusion, in the sequel to this story.*

PURE WHITE

It feels good to be leaving the picnicking visitors behind as I set out on a circular walk through the woods. This has been a busy time for me, with rarely a moment to find the peace and quietness my hurting brain so much needs. My fourth novel is almost complete and is currently in the hands of my Editor who will, no doubt, be suggesting various changes which will improve it considerably. I will, of course, listen carefully to her criticism and advice, for that is what she is paid for. Listening is something most of us fail to do well. We think we hear what we are being told, but so often the brain has a tendency to block out those things which seem not to be relevant to our lives or situations, or that of the person who is speaking at the time. As a fairly successful novelist I have been training my brain to look and hear beyond the obvious. I look for anything that may potentially open a crack to reveal hidden gems of facts, information or lost stories.

I am aware of the receding sound of happy children who are enjoying their time with parents, relatives and friends, as they play on the grassy area of Royal Victoria Park which overlooks the channel known as Southampton Water. A slight rustle of leaves in the shrubs nearby attracts my attention. I see a grey squirrel dart to the nearest tree and scamper effortlessly up into the canopy. These invasive American creatures often bring a smile to my lips, although I much prefer to see the native reds which are thankfully still protected in various areas of the UK. Birds are flitting amongst the trees and a large drone bee makes its erratic way passed me as I continue my stroll. I no longer hear the children at play. I am aware of the rustling leaves over my head. This is bliss. I give my thoughts free rein. It's not too long before my mother occupies the space. I know that I have recently neglected that dear person who means so much to me. She has always been there for me, through illness, self-doubt, through broken relationships. We have also shared many good times together over the years. Mum has been on her own for some twenty years now. She never got over the death of both my father and older brother during the war, dad in an air raid as a fireman, Steve as a navigator in Bomber Command. She never ceased to give thanks that I wasn't old enough to go. We seldom miss the opportunity to watch the Festival of Remembrance together on television in November. She watches it with pride, and a tear.

Without realising, my walk has taken me to a hilly clearing amongst the tall surrounding trees. To my surprise, I see that it's a grave yard. Its wooded location, and the loving care that is clearly spent on it, takes my breath away. There are hundreds of white stones scattered on the hill. I realise that most are in tidy rows. Closer inspection makes me see that most are War Graves, mainly British, although there are many Commonwealth stones and also several German and Italian ones. This is such a peaceful place. The grass is neatly mown, the stones are spotlessly clean. I walk among those stones reading various inscriptions. So young, most of them. For no particular reason, my eye is caught by a stone which is standing alongside that of a German airman. The stone is actually the same as those around, but it's the name of the

British serviceman that holds my attention. It's the same as my own. A common name; Jenkins. I bend forward and read the beautifully carved inscription:

Junior Seaman Brian Jenkins R.N.

Aged 19

Killed during The Battle of the Denmark Strait

1941

Slowly, I sink to the ground. My eyes take in the swaying trees which surround this peaceful place. A blackbird sings its melodious song not far from where I am kneeling. White fluffy clouds slowly make their way across the deep blue sky which contrasts so well with the greens of the trees. My eyes return to the grave stone, which is pure white as the sun casts its afternoon light onto it. Pure brilliant white ………

"Pure white", thinks the boy. In the midst of the grey sea, smoke from the forward guns is indeed pure white for just a few seconds, before it is quickly disbursed. *The Mighty Hood*, as Britain's largest battlecruisers was nicknamed, had been diverted to assist in the battle with the German battleship, *Bismarck*. This was Brian's first ship. He had joined the Royal Navy shortly after his eighteenth birthday. Following his shore-based training in Portsmouth he had been posted to this huge ship which was manned by a crew of over one thousand, four hundred men. His mother had been distraught when he had thrown his kit bag over his shoulder after kissing her goodbye. She had dreaded that day since the first time he had put on the navy-blue uniform. He had marched down the narrow street, head held high, ignoring the street urchins who, for a while, marched alongside him. Later, on seeing the ship, which was to be his first, and last, he had been over awed by the sheer size of her as he filed up the gangway behind other new members of the crew.

'Cor blimey,' he said to his new friend, Tom. 'She's so blooming big. I'll never find me way around her.'

'Yea, I know what you mean, Bri. 'Spect we'll get used to her once we're at sea.'

'I'm surprised anyfing this big can even float. At least we should be safe with all that armour plating and them big guns. Glad we're not on one of them frigates. Death traps if yer ask me.'

'All right you two. Cut out the gossip. Get yourselves below and stow your kit. Follow the Subby over there. He'll sort you out alongside all the other new bods.' This was a middle-aged Chief Petty Officer who had been brought back from retirement for the duration.

It was indeed several weeks before Brian could make his way around the ship with confidence. His battle station was on the ship's bridge. He was in the "Signals" section and was the relief signaller, expected to be able to use the signal lamp in Morse, as well as to be familiar with flag signalling when required. He had thought that he would love life in the Royal Navy but found that he was dreadfully home sick and missing his mother. He had always been a bit of a home boy, preferring to help out around the house, or to assist his father, a dockyard worker, in his shed with one of his wood working projects. Word had gone around that *HMS Hood* was heading for The Denmark Straits where it was expected that *Bismarck* would be on the loose. She would be joining the aircraft carrier *Ark Royal* with several other ships of the fleet. Brian had not, up to that point, been involved in any sea battles. He wondered how well he would perform his duties under fire. Would he be afraid? His greatest fear was the distinct possibility of showing fear. As the great ship had elbowed her way through the waves which occasionally swept over the bows, Brian had found time to go into his allotted crew room to write a letter home to his mother. Having finished it he re-read the scrawl, which was the best he could manage with the constant rising and plunging of the deck beneath him:

Dear Mum,

I hope you are both well and that you are not having to spend nights in the shelter. I am well and am doing okay with my job on the ship. The CPO who is my divisional chief says that I should be a good signaller before too long. We may be going in to battle soon, but you mustn't worry about me. This ship is very big and safe from anything the Germans can throw at her. I don't know when I will get any leave but you can be sure that when I do, I'll be coming straight home to see you. I miss you so much, particularly your lovely scones. I'm looking forward to riding the bike dad built for me out of old bits, and exploring the country lanes. Look after yourself, mum, and give my love to dad. I love you both so much. Your son, Brian xxx

No sooner had Brian finished re-reading his letter, the claxon sounded and seamen were jumping from their bunks to attend their battle stations. Brian arrived at the bridge and stood behind the leading signaller, as he had been trained. Looking forward through the rising sea, he was unable to see any other ships. He could tell, from the activity of the officers on the bridge that something momentous was happening. The Captain was standing at the screen with his binoculars almost constantly to his eyes. Every so often he gave clipped orders down the speaking tubes to the helmsman or the engine room. The Navigating Officer was moving in and out of his screened cubby following every course change.

Almost before Brian realised what was happening the order was given to the main guns to fire. The noise was ear shattering. Smoke surrounded the forward guns, to be instantly blown away in the wind. Brian was too curious to know what was going on than to be afraid. He watched as the guns continued to fill the air with noise and smoke. He noticed that the smoke, just for a few seconds, was pure white, yes *"Pure White ..."*

Pure white. So clean and pure. Contrasting with the green grass surrounding the stone. Who was Junior Seaman Brian Jenkins I wonder? I remember that the Battle Cruiser *HMS Hood* blew up during the Battle of the Denmark Strait. One moment, there, the next, gone. Just like that. Only three survivors apparently. Could he have been one of the crew of that magnificent ship?

The blackbird continues his beautiful song as the sun drops lower. The grave stone of Brian Jenkins, aged 19, is now in shadow. No longer pure white. This is such a peaceful place. Far from the horror of war. I look away from the stone. The writer in me had created the story of Brian Jenkins. I will never know if it comes close to the reality of how this boy, who missed his mother so much, had died in that battle.

I think it's about time I paid mum a visit.

The End

ON THE LINES

Dust and an assortment of litter swirl, from the grey platform surface, into the air as the express train sweeps through the station. The sound of steel on steel is momentarily drowned by the shrieking of the green loco's whistle, causing a child who is being securely held by his mother, to hide his head in her pleated skirt. Momentarily, conversation amongst the waiting passengers ceases, only to be continued as the last carriage sweeps passed and rapidly diminishes in size in the eyes of the three boys at the end of the platform.

'Brilliant! I haven't got that one,' says the tallest boy as he peers through his spectacles at the pages of his *Train Spotters book*.

'No, nor have I,' says the ginger haired lad. 'Lend us your red pen when you've underlined yours.'

'I already had that one,' pipes in the third boy.

'Yea, you've been doing this longer than us,' replies spectacle boy.

'The train standing on Platform Two is the twelve-twenty service to Portsmouth Harbour, calling at Porchester, Cosham, Hilsea Halt, Fratton and Portsmouth & Southsea.'

A man and woman are seen running over the footbridge, intending to catch the Portsmouth train which will stand at platform two for one more minute. The carriage door slams shut with a resounding *curlunk* as they disappear inside. The locomotive breathes a loud *hissssss* as its large steel wheels slowly turn. Another *hissssssss,* then another. Steam rises from the funnel.

'Goodbye,' calls a sailor who has his head and shoulder out of the window, looking back and waving to his wife and little girl.

'Goodbye, darling.'

'Goodbye, daddy.'

The train noises are replaced by the sound of traffic passing the station. A double decked bus, a grocery van, an ambulance with its insistent ringing bell. A black Ford Popular travelling in the opposite direction, closely followed by a Guy lorry with its load of timber. A taxi pulls into the station car park and stops at the entrance. The three boys are sitting on a bench, tucking into their lunch. Cheese sandwiches, crisps, a Wagon Wheel to follow. They are comparing the pages of their well-thumbed books. They all look up as a shunting engine continues its task of re-arranging trucks and wagons in the goods yard. A diesel, not interesting enough to go and look. They swallow their lemonade, accompanied by exaggerated burps and giggles.

'The train arriving on Platform One is the thirteen-fifteen service to Cardiff, calling at Southampton....' The announcement is swallowed up by the clanking of the green locomotive as it barges its way into the station amidst a jet of escaping steam as excess pressure is released by the driver.

'It's a Streak,' shout the three boys in unison.

'*Winston Churchill*. Wow, I've been waiting for that one for ages,' exclaims Ginger in glee. Names are being enthusiastically underlined in red ink in two of the three books, the third having already been underlined some months previously. A porter is busily pushing suitcase laden trollies as the platform momentarily resounds with the bustle of emerging passengers. Others enter the train. Doors slam with the usual *kerlunk*. Two pedal cycles are lifted into the goods compartment at the end of the train. The porter walks back along the platform, slamming closed those doors that have been left open. He raises his whistle to his lips and importantly waves his green flag.

WHOOOOF ……………………..WHOOOOF ………….. WHOOOOF …. WHOOOOF …. Click-click click-click ……………… Click-click click-click ……………….. Click-click click-click. The train gathers pace, faster, faster, faster. The last carriage clears the platform where the three boys look into their duffle bags to see if they have anything further to eat. The porter walks along the platform, picking up an empty crisp packet which has blown along from the direction of the three boys. He enters the Porter's Office for a quick brew before the thirteen-thirty-five is due to arrive. Once again, the traffic noise, along with the clanking of moving trucks in the yard, can be heard. The big hand of the station clock can be seen turning, should anyone bother to stare at it long enough.

Movement in the station has ceased for the moment, apart, that is, from a tabby cat which has appeared, seemingly from nowhere. Silently it trots along the platform, pausing occasionally to investigate something that has, for no apparent reason, attracted its attention. With raised tail, it enters the Porter's Office. The boys had not seen it, otherwise at least one of them might have tried to stroke it. A gentleman carrying a briefcase emerges from the booking office onto the platform, a lady carrying a shopping bag follows. Soon a number of people are standing waiting for their train, the thirteen-thirty-five no doubt. The three boys stand expectantly, books at the ready. A train appears from the bend. It is approaching very quickly ……. too fast? … It isn't going to stop! …The shunting diesel has just pulled its load of trucks onto the main line beyond the station. A disaster cannot be avoided! The loco, with its four carriages swaying behind it, plunges through the station and ploughs into the slowly moving trucks. Locos, trucks and carriages are scattered across the tracks. It has all happened so quickly … Silence … but only for a few seconds.

Suddenly, a giant hand, appears from the sky. The hand momentarily hovers over the rearmost carriage which is tipped half over and blocking both lines between the platforms. The carriage is carefully uncoupled from the one before it, then is lifted into the sky. The hands reappear, this time to lift a second carriage which also goes up into the sky.

'Hello Tommy. What's this? A crash? Oh dear, here let me help you.'

'Hello Dad. I didn't hear you come in. Had a good day at the station?'

'Not bad, son. Even got a fiver tip from a lady with far too much luggage. This looks a mess, what happened?'

'Oh, I got carried away with my imagination. I was a train spotter with Gary and Andy in a place called Fareham in Hampshire. I found it in your road map. Then

Tabby came in and tried to jump onto the layout. The crash happened as I pushed him off, stupid cat.'

'Well, let's get this all back on the lines, then we'll push the layout under the bed. It's nearly time for dinner.'

'Okay, Dad. Can you help me build the signal box after dinner?'

'Of course, I said I would, didn't I?'

With the rolling stock back on the lines, the layout, on its castors, is carefully pushed under the bed.

The three boys know what's coming. Suddenly there is a jerk and a quiet rumble as the day becomes darker. The blue sky on the distant ceiling is replaced by giant bed springs.

'That was a brilliant crash,' exclaims Ginger. Hope he does it again tomorrow. I wonder where we'll be? Scotland, I hope.'

The End

DRIVING HOME

Snow has been threatening for the last two hours. As Barry had driven into Farnham earlier, he had noticed that the rain was turning into sleet. Each drop seemed to momentarily flatten out on the windscreen before being swept away by the constantly moving blade of his windscreen wiper. His tyres have, so far, maintained a firm grip on the tarmac although, at this point, he is taking nothing for granted, for he can now see snow-flakes in the beam of his headlights. At the bottom of the High Street he swings the steering wheel to ease his vehicle around the bend and, it's with a feeling of relief, that he sees the bus station ahead.

His ticket machine tells Barry that it is six-forty-one. *'Good,'* he thinks, *'I can have nine minutes to relax before the return journey.'* He eases his double decker into Bay five. As he expected, there are no other buses here at this time of the evening. The last Winchester service is due to arrive in a couple of minutes, if he's on time. Barry's last passenger had alighted at the top of the High Street. He had watched him in his mirror as the man had pulled up the collar of his coat and had thrust his hands into his pockets before leaving the bus shelter to walk back in the opposite direction.

The bus station is deserted. Barry switches off the engine and resets the ticket machine and destination screen. "38 PETERSFIELD ONLY" comes up in white letters on the screen. Sleet has now given way to snow, the flakes are large. *'That's annoying,'* he thinks. *'Could have done without this, hope it doesn't start laying.'* Barry now has time to peer through the windscreen which is partly obscured by numerous snow-flakes sliding down to the bottom of the screen. He finds that he is looking for his regular passenger who is usually standing in the shelter before he arrives. *'Perhaps he wasn't working this evening,'* he thinks to himself. The small foreign man has been catching this bus since Barry started on this cross-country route back in May. He always steps onto the bus with a huge grin on his face. On one occasion he told Barry how disappointed he always felt whenever it wasn't him driving, because, as he said, he missed the smile and greeting and the fact that Barry always listened to him when sharing his concerns, in a way nobody else ever did.

Barry looks away from the partly covered windscreen to check the time on his ticket machine. *'Two minutes to go.'* He reaches into his shoulder bag to retrieve a packet of Polo Mints. With the engine turned off he is beginning to feel the cold. He continues to peer through the screen, and also double checks that there is nobody standing at the closed door. The final minute. Barry switches on the engine and presses the button which operates the door. A cold draft immediately hits him as heavy snow-flakes swirl into the bus, only to instantly melt on the platform floor. He wonders why the Winchester bus has not yet arrived, suspecting that the snow has something to do with that. Six-fifty … Time to leave. With the door now closed, Barry switches on his windscreen wipers, checks both mirrors and activates his hazard lights which indicates that the bus is reversing onto the gleaming concourse. He is very much aware of the different feel of the steering wheel as he turns it, less resistance on the tarmac. With a final check that all around his bus is clear he selects forward drive and turns his vehicle in the direction of the Exit. Suddenly, out of nowhere, his regular foreign passenger is running across the concourse through the snow, with raised hands. Instinctively, Barry presses the brake pedal, hoping not to lock the wheels on the now slippery surface. As he feared, the passenger slips on the snow and is down. *'Oh my god! Not beneath the front wheel, please!!'* The bus is stationary. Barry quickly knocks the bus out of drive and applies the parking brake. He opens the door, but before he is able to leave his seat, a grinning head appears at floor level in the doorway.

'Good evening, sir. I thought I had missed you,' says the grinning man. 'Thank you for stopping, it would have been a long walk in this snow.'

'Are you okay?' askes the shaken driver. 'I thought I might have hit you for a moment there.'

'I'm okay, sir,' says the man as he regains his feet with difficulty, one foot sliding from under him. 'I am very happy. My lady friend has just agreed to marry me. That's why I was late getting here. You're the first to be told, I'm glad about that. It's going to be such a happy Christmas Day tomorrow. We're to spend the afternoon together after my night shift and a sleep.'

'I'm happy for you,' says Barry. 'Congratulations. Promise me you won't be throwing yourself under any more buses, specially not mine. We had better get under way, I'm already two minutes late.'

With his passenger safety seated, Barry eases his bus into the High Street. Snow is settling on the road. There are wheel tracks climbing the hill between the brightly decorated shops and under the suspended Christmas lights. Just like a Christmas Card, muses Barry. Peering ahead, he spots two people standing at the bus stop at the top of the hill. They are signalling that they want him to stop. Gently he applies his brakes as he pulls into the curb. With the door now open, an elderly gentleman enquires, 'Is the Winchester bus coming, driver?'

'Well, it's not in the bus station yet. Probably slowed down by the weather. You might consider a taxi, or the train, if you don't see it in the next ten minutes. As things are looking right now, I'm becoming doubtful about getting down to Petersfield, then on to the depot in Portsmouth to park up. Sorry I can't help you.'

'Okay, thank you. I think we'll go down to the train station. Good night, and Merry Christmas. Come on Hilda, take my arm.' They are gone by the time Barry manages to ease the bus forward without losing traction on the snow. Away from the High Street and into darker roads through the outskirts of the town Barry is not able to see more than a hundred metres ahead through the blinding snow. His headlight beam is a swirl of flickering light. He is particularly careful to check each bus stop as he passes, in case of waiting passengers. None appear, although that's normal for this last journey of the day for the No.38 out of Aldershot. He doesn't expect any passengers until reaching the outskirts of Farnham where Garlic Lady will, no doubt, be waiting. Sure enough, she is there ten minutes later as he carefully pulls into the bus stop lay-bye.

'You're twelve and a half minutes late, driver. Don't you realise how cold it is waiting in this shelter? I suppose you've been wasting time drinking tea at the other end.

Well, it's not good enough. I've a mind to complain to your company.' As she continues her tirade, she is breathing garlic fumes into Barry's face, as usual.

'I'm sorry, madam. I'm afraid this snow is holding everything up. I have to drive more slowly for obvious reasons. Be assured that I will mention your complaint at the depot when I'm finished.' As Barry tries to placate the lady, he is examining the weekly pass she is waving under his abused nose, hoping that it has expired so that he can have the pleasure of telling her so, and charging her for another. Waiting for Garlic Lady to huffily move into the bus and take a seat, Barry looks into his interior mirror and sees his foreign friend grinning at him. *It takes all sorts,*' he thinks to himself.

At last, he pulls into central Farnham. The town is as festive as Aldershot had been. A large brightly lit Christmas tree is standing in the square. There is a cluster of carol singers standing beneath, some with lanterns on poles. Unlike Aldershot, there are many people standing or walking along the pavements. The shops are now closed, so Barry assumes that these people are mostly on their way to restaurants and pub, maybe even to a church for an early midnight service.

'Thank you, sir,' says the happy foreign passenger as he comes to the open door. 'I hope your Christmas is full of joy and warmth, as I'm sure mine will be. And a very happy New Year to you and your wife.'

'And to you, my friend,' replies Barry with a slight falter in his voice. 'I still don't know your name, may I ask?'

'My friends call me Todd, for they are unable to pronounce my name. You can call me Todd as well. I would like that.'

'Well, have a good Christmas, Todd. See you next year. Good night.'

'Two singles to Bordon, please.'

'Whitehill, please. Hope we make it.'

'Bucks Horn Oak, please, driver.'

'Most likely, shop assistants, finished for the day,' assumes Barry. *'I expect they're looking forward to being*

welcomed home to a warm house. Well, let's make sure they get home safely.' The bell rings a few minutes later. *'I know, I know, I've been dropping Garlic Lady off here long enough. Hold your breath, Barry.'* Good night, madam. Merry Christmas.'

'Hmff.'

'Okaaay. Hope her stockings are full of garlic bulbs in the morning, or strong peppermints.'

With Farnham behind them, the bus makes its wary way across country. There are no lights apart from a brightly decorated pub at Bucks Horn Oak where the first passenger alights into the blizzard, and quickly disappears into the darkness. Dipped headlights of oncoming vehicles momentarily make the bus windscreen glisten. The windscreen wipers are beginning to struggle. Impacted snow now forms deep ruts where traffic has passed through. Barry is now focussed on keeping the bus on a straight course. His headlights are almost useless as the falling snow-flakes simply reflect the light back to his cab. He is now becoming concerned about the advisability of continuing the journey. But what choice does he have? Bordon is not too far ahead now. However, before reaching it there is a fairly steep rise to negotiate. There is a junction controlled by traffic lights at the foot of the rise. Through the near white-out Barry sees that they are on green. He is relieved that he will be able to take the rise at a steady speed, rather than from a standstill. The lights change to amber, then red, but not seeing any other vehicle-lights he keeps the revs up and shoots the red light to tackle the rise. He is losing traction and the rear wheels are spinning. Barry fixes his concentration on the top of the rise, closer, closer, nearly there, speed dropping to walking pace, they have made it. This was the first time he had ever deliberately shot a red light when it was possible to stop in time. *'It's beginning to look as though this will be a first for many things,'* he thinks.

'Well done for getting up that hill, driver, thought for a moment you wouldn't make it. Next stop for us, please, at the crossroads. I'm a soldier, drive tanks. This lot would be no trouble for one of those. Best of luck for the rest of your journey, mate.' It's a man who has come forward to speak to him. Presumably it's his wife who is still seated, waiting for their stop.

'Merry Christmas to you both,' calls Barry as they step off the platform into thick snow. He shuts the door, checks in the mirror, and inches forward, thankful for the street lights at last. Whitehill comes soon after and, with his last passenger gone, Barry is now on his own. There is no other traffic moving, the last, having been a lorry passing in the opposite direction at Bordon. Leaving the street lights of Whitehill behind, Barry becomes concerned when he sees blue lights flashing ahead through the blizzard. It takes no time to realise that it is on a junction where he should turn off the main road to drive through a village. He sees that the blue lights come from a police Land Rover with an officer standing in the road waving a torch. Gently, Barry applies his brakes and comes to a standstill close to the parked vehicle. He opens the door as the booted police officer moves forward.

'Problem, Officer?' enquires Barry.

'I'm surprised you're still on the road,' says the snow-covered officer. 'A bus is the last thing I expected to see.

If your intention was to turn here, I'm afraid you can't. There's been an accident in the village. They're waiting for a helicopter, although how they think that's going to happen in this, I don't know. You'll have to go straight on. My advice is to forget Liss and Petersfield, even if you get that far.'

'Okay, do you mind if I stop here for a moment to phone my Controller?'

'That's okay, just move forward, clear of the junction.'

Doing as told, Barry retrieves his mobile phone from his bag and speed dials the depot number. His call is answered immediately. 'Hi Carol, Barry on the 38.'

'Thank goodness, you're the last one to account for. We've been trying to contact you, where are you?'

'Just left Whitehill. There's no signal before that, if you remember. I'm in a near total white-out. The police have advised me not to attempt Liss and Petersfield.'

'Have you any passengers aboard?'

'No. the last one got out at Whitehill.'

'Okay, that's good. You should blank out and go straight onto the A3 and return directly to the depot. We are informed that one of the southbound lanes is still open … just. Watch out for Butser Hill, it could be bad there. Phone in again if you get stuck.'

'Okay, thanks Carol, will do. See you in half an hour, or an hour … or two.'

'Just take it steady, Barry. You've only been back a week. We don't want to lose you again.' The line goes dead.

Barry selects drive and releases the brake. He is thankful that the road leading to the A3 is straight, apart from a turn at a roundabout. The large vehicle in his hands seems to have a mind of its own now. It slips and slides causing Barry to constantly turn the steering wheel to maintain a straight course. On several occasions he has to negotiate around abandoned vehicles. He is stunned by how quickly the snow has transformed his world. When he had driven up this road as little as two hours ago, everything was normal, just wet. Now, it is transformed into white shapes that bear no similarity to the reality beneath. Abandoned cars appear to be igloos, trees are the white irregular walls of a tunnel through which a blanket is constantly moving through the air in the beam of his headlights. He can well imagine how people have become lost in these conditions, death is a real reality and threat. These days, death is indeed a reality. Previously it was something that affected others. It was a distant thing, not to be dwelt upon, why should it? But now? Death has intruded into his previously contented life. So unexpected, So unfair, So unbearable. So unforgiving. So final.

The roundabout appears in the white world ahead. Barry allows the bus to slow down without touching the footbrake. He gently eases the steering wheel anti-clockwise. The headlights seem to be searching for something solid on which to focus. The rear of the bus is sliding a little to the right. *'Gently correct the slide. Come on, baby, you can do this, you know the way home. You want to be parked in the midst and shelter of the fleet in the depot. Do this for Barry.'* The bus straightens up. The A3 is ahead. The tricky thing is to take the loop which will enable the bus to settle on whichever lane is still open.

Slowly, ever so slowly, Barry eases the vehicle into the loop. He must avoid a front-end slide at all costs, for that would be a disaster with the inevitable result of leaving the road and slipping down the embankment. Together, bus and driver work as a team. They understand each other. 'This is what I call real driving,' shouts Barry in relief as man and machine come out of the loop and settle on the partially swept, but still open south bound lane of the A3. Barry knows they will get to the end of this journey where so many had not, judging by the parked vehicles on the snow covered inside lane. He is coming home. An empty home now, but still home.

It is not possible to retrieve his car which is part buried by drifting snow in the depot car park, even if it is possible to drive home, which is highly doubtful. Barry has no other choice other than to struggle through the snow by foot. By no means an easy task. Sticking to the main road and having climbed the hill that overlooks Portsmouth, Barry is relieved to notice that the snow fall is reducing. His house is in sight by the time the snow has ceased all together. There is no welcoming light in the window. How could there be? He is knee deep in snow as he reaches into his coat pocket for his keys. Every step has been a trial. He can no longer feel his wet feet, or his hands, as he fumbles with the key. The house is in darkness as he kicks the snow away and opens the front door. Now on the WELCOME mat he switches on the hall light before removing his shoes and wet socks. The house is cold. No welcoming music, No aroma of cooked food. No loving greeting. Just emptiness. Everything exactly the way he left it this morning. Checking his wrist watch, Barry sheds his wet uniform and underwear and heads for the shower.

An hour later, he steps carefully up the short path to the lantern lit porch. There is a Christmas wreath on the front door. White and blue icicle lights are suspended from the eaves. A Christmas tree can be seen flashing in the front room window. He rings the bell and the door is thrown open within seconds. 'Hello Dad. Merry Christmas. Come on in out of that cold. Here, let me help you with your coat and those boots. Your slippers are on the radiator. We've got your favourite soup simmering on the stove.' Barry's daughter is so relieved to see her father safety in her home. 'Your room is ready for you. Have you had to walk here?'

'Hello my love. Merry Christmas. Are the children asleep?'

'They should have been by now. We've not long been back from the midnight service. They're too excited and they won't rest until they've seen their Grandpops. Go up to them now, they'll be so happy to see you.'

'Thank you, love. I'll do that. Sorry I didn't manage to get to the service.'

'Well, you're here now, that's the important thing. I'll ask Phil to pour you a whisky while you're up there.'

Barry creeps into the girl's bedroom. A softly lit nightlight shines on the dresser. There is a duvet covered mound in each of the small beds, each of which has an empty stocking on the footboard. All is quiet. Or is it? Was that a soft giggle he heard? And another.

'Alright you two, you can come out now. I know you're awake.' Simultaneously both duvets are swept back to reveal the excited giggling five-year old twin sisters. He sits on one of the small beds and instantly he has a curly fair-haired head resting on each shoulder.

If you were to peer through the curtain, you would see that there is no sign of the snow beginning to melt outside. Inside however, Barry's heart has completely melted. *'This is what I battled through that blizzard for,'* he thinks. *'She loved these two so much, she will live on through them.'* A tear runs down his cheek. 'Merry Christmas you two.'

The End

RESTITUTION

Silently, the man stands in shadow, well away from the nearest street light. He watches and waits. A glance into the sky reassures him that there's little chance of the moon reappearing from behind the thick clouds. He needs a smoke, but that's out of the question. Too big a risk. Another car rounds the corner, some two hundred metres away. The hooded man shrinks back into the bushes as the headlights sweep round. All clear again. He can see the flickering blue light of a television behind the curtains in the house across the street. *'Probably watching the news,'* he surmises. He knows that that house has an alarm box attached to the front of the building. He has been walking through this street for several days now. He knows the houses he is interested in. An affluent area judging by the house prices he has seen in the village estate agent's window display. What a give-away. All is still again, apart from a fox which is silently trotting across the street a few houses down. He is aware of his lack of experience at this game. He must be careful not to make mistakes.

A front door opens a few houses from where he is standing. A child's voice, young. 'Come on, Mummy, we mustn't be late, it starts at half past seven, tell daddy to hurry.'

'We're fine, sweetheart. Plenty of time, daddy's just locking the back door. In you get, don't forget the seat belt.'

The sound of a front door slamming. This is followed by the slamming of three car doors, then the cough of a car engine starting up. Once again, the man, with all senses on alert, sinks back into the bushes. A car reverses from a drive just two houses away. *'Couldn't be better, must be going to some sort of show. They'll be gone for at least two hours I should think. Wait a couple of minutes in case they've forgotten anything.'* Five minutes later, a furtive figure walks toward the house. *'No lights on in the front, apart from a Christmas tree.'* A careful look up and down the street. *'No movement, no sound. Right, it's now or never.'* He really didn't want to be doing this, but what else could he do? Wife, home, job, all lost. Life destroyed in the space of one week. How could he have allowed this to happen? Where did it all start? He had passed many homeless people sitting on the pavement in the shopping precinct, sometimes throwing a coin into the inevitable cap, never thinking to speak to the person or look him or her in the eye. If he ever gave thought to their predicament, he invariably blamed alcohol or drugs as being the underlying cause. Must be their own fault. How far is he from joining those unfortunates? he wonders. *'I have to do this.'* He silently scans the street before walking up the drive.

He had heard the heated discussion between his friend and wife Lizzie, behind the closed door of their bedroom last night. "Either he goes, or I do. He's been taking advantage of your friendship for three weeks now. Never a penny for his keep. It can't go on."

"I know, love. But what can I do? His parents are both dead, if I turn him out, he'll be homeless. Kelly won't have him back. You know it was her dad who set them up in that house. Now that his job's gone, he's not able to pay his share of the rent. He just needs a place to stay until he can get himself sorted. You need an address to get a job, or any kind of assistance, you know that."

"Yes, but it doesn't have to be our address, I'm telling you, Mike, if he doesn't cough up some money to at least pay for his food this week, he's out, or I'm gone till he's gone."

"Have a heart, Lizzie. You know as well as I do that none of this was his fault. That cow, Irene told Kelly a string of lies about him, how he was supposed to have gone round to her flat half-cut trying to . . . well you know what I mean. She has had it in for him ever since he told her to leave him alone when she came on to him. Gerry would never have had anything to do with her, I know that for a fact. He loves Kelly to bits and he would never cheat on her. I'm sure she'll come round sooner or later when she realises her mistake in believing that bitch. We came through a lot together when we did our three years National Service. He stood up for me several times, I can't let him down now, Lizzie"

"I don't think he cheated on Kelly any more than you do, but he's got to get it sorted. He can't just stay here and moon about feeling sorry for himself. As I said, we can't afford it."

"But she won't let him come home, how can he get it sorted?"

The row had gone on, but Gerry had tried to blot it out. He had to get some cash, somehow. That had been two nights ago. He had spent the next two days walking the streets looking for job vacancies in the only trade he knew. Building sites had been laying staff off during the severe winter weather that had hit the country, particularly here in the West Country.

Standing at the back of the house, Gerry checks out the door and windows. All locked, that is, apart from one upstairs skylight window, obviously the bathroom. *'Is that the way in? Could be, if only I can get up there. Is there a ladder? The garage, the side door with a bit of luck.'* To his surprise, Gerry discovers that the garage door is unlocked, although, in the subdued glow of the nearby street light he can see that there is no hidden ladder within the empty space. *'Where would I put a ladder?'* Careful not to trip over any pots or garden furniture on the small patio Gerry makes for the far corner of the house where it would appear that a narrow path between the border fence and the house leads to the front garden. *'Bingo! Now the difficult part.'* Slowly he lifts the extending ladder and carefully manoeuvres it onto the patio without catching it on any of the border shrubs. *'So far, so good,'* he breathes. Now directly under the bathroom window, Gerry slowly extends the ladder until, with a slight clatter, it rests on the window sill. He pauses for a moment to check there is no disturbance before starting the cautious climb. After what feels like minutes but is in fact just a few seconds, he is able to place one foot on the sill as he hauls himself to full height with one hand on the skylight window frame.

A dustbin lid shatters the silence. An unseen cat disappears into the neighbour's undergrowth having attempted to shift their dustbin lid to get to the tempting smell of fish inside the bin. The lid rocks on concrete. The sudden shock is sufficient to make Gerry jump and, in-so-doing, accidently kick the ladder away from the sill, to come to rest against a drain pipe. A dog is barking in the neighbour's house. The backdoor swings open, light from the kitchen spills onto the neatly mown lawn. Gerry is a frozen statue, clinging on the sill with one arm inside the skylight. He watches the dog run around the neighbour's garden frantically sniffing at everything he encounters. The dustbin lid clatters back onto the bin. "BENNY, COME HERE, GOOD BOY. IT'S GONE NOW." The door closes, a bolt is slid into place, darkness returns. Gerry can hear the beat of his heart. He looks at the angled ladder which is just out of his reach. *'Bloody 'ell. What now? Only one way, fingers crossed.'* He pushes his arm further into the gap, lower, lower. Pressing his shoulder hard against the opening his finger tip touches the handle he is reaching for. Too far. He is unable to grasp the handle. He reluctantly withdraws his arm before carefully shuffling into a new position on the sill. This time he places his other arm through the opening and again presses his shoulder hard against the frame. *'Got it. Press harder, press . . .'* He has two fingers round the handle. Painfully he pushes the handle with all the strength he can put into those two fingers. A slight movement. Pause to get the blood back into the fingers. *'Now, or never.'* The handle moves a fraction, then more. It gives way. The window is free. He removes his arm from the skylight opening and shuffles far enough along the sill to create sufficient space for the larger window to fully open. Carefully, Gerry moves a glass ornament of some sort, possibly a dolphin, along the shelf, creating the clear space he needs to swing his legs into the room. He is in.

As he stands in the bathroom of this warm detached house which is someone's home and sanctuary, the enormity of what he is doing hits him. He feels sick, sick in the stomach and sick in his heart. He has never knowingly broken the law during his relatively short life. Maybe over the speed limit a few times, scrumping as a boy, but this? Never in his wildest dreams. He has become a burglar, a thief, a wanted man, an intruder in the lives of innocent folk who have done him no harm.

'What now?' He hasn't thought beyond getting in to a house, any house. *'Bedroom. That's the obvious place. No torch, didn't even think of it. Too big a giveaway in any*

event. *Anyone outside seeing a torch beam moving around would soon get on the phone.'* Fortunately, the main bedroom is at the front of the house and, once again, the street lamp helps him. It takes no time to find the jewellery drawer. He has no idea of the value of anything he slips into his pockets. He assumes this is a well-off family, so the jewellery value most likely reflects that. He spots some twenty-pound notes on a bedside table. *'Sixty pounds? Eighty? Time to leave, don't take any chances. Only one way out, down the stairs and out the front door.'*

With heart still thumping and pockets bulging, Gerry eases his way down the thickly carpeted stairs into the hall. The front room door is open. He enters the dimly lit room. What light there is comes from the Christmas Tree. All is neat and tidy. There are wrapped gifts under the tree, various shapes, sizes and colours. He steps across the room and picks up a shoe box shaped parcel which has clearly been wrapped by a child. There is an un-sealed card slipped into the ribbon. As Gerry starts to return the parcel to the pile beneath the tree the card slips out of the envelope to the floor. He stoops to retrieve it and, in the light of the tree, he cannot resist reading the childish handwriting;

To my lovely mummy and daddy. Thank you for looking after me so well while I am having my chemo. I know I will get better because you are always praying for me, so you mustn't worry any more. I think this will be the best Christmas ever. I hope you like the cakes I have made you.

Lots of love, big hugs and wet kisses.

Your Princess Poppy xxxxxxxxxxx

Tears are streaming down Gerry's cheeks as he replaces the card. *'What have I done! How can I ever forgive myself? I can't do this!'* Reaching into his pockets, he draws out every item of jewellery and the twenty-pound notes. He looks round the room and chooses the round coffee table on which to place every item. A quick glance down the drive assures him that he is safe to leave this warm, loving home. He makes his way back to Mike's place, hands in empty pockets and hood hiding his tear blotched face.

***

'Hello, Mate. Any luck with the job search?' enquires Mike as Gerry enters their living room an hour later.

'Fraid not. Can't even get a labourer's job let alone bricklaying. I have tried, believe me. I did something really desperate and stupid this evening,' replies Gerry.

'Oh, mate, you didn't try to . . .?'

'No nothing like that my friend, not that desperate. I'll tell you about it someday, but not now if you don't mind. You on your own? No Lizzie?'

'Yea, she went out after our dinner, yours is on the stove, by the way, beef stew. She didn't say where she was going, just out with three of her girl friends. She said she doesn't know what time she'll be back but asked that we both wait up for her. Can't tell you any more than that, it all sounds rather curious don't you think?'

'Are you worried? Doesn't sound like your Lizzie' says Gerry.

'Naa, not worried, just curious. My Lizzie knows how to take care of herself, and as for those friends of hers, I wouldn't want to get on their wrong side.'

'Look, Mike. I think it's time for me to move on. You and Lizzie have been great and I really appreciate it. However, as Sergeant Bonner would say, it's time to shoulder my rucksack and wear the tread off my boots,' says Gerry with a smile that failed to meet his eyes. 'I'll leave in the morning.'

'But, where will you go?'

'Oh, don't you worry about me, Mike. I've got a few favours to call in. I'll be okay. Right, I'll go and enjoy that stew. Perhaps a game of cards after? While we wait to see what your lovely wife has been up to.'

It isn't until nine-thirty that the two friends hear the front door being opened. They also hear voices. 'Sounds like she's brought at least one of her friends' home. I'll go and put the kettle on,' said Mike rising from the table.

Gerry starts stacking the playing cards as the living room door opens. 'Kelly! What are you doing here?' says Gerry to his tearful wife in amazement while getting to his feet.

'Oh Gerry. Can you ever forgive me?' says Kelly as she steps into his outstretched arms. 'How could I have ever doubted you? I'm such a fool and I'm so sorry, and . . .'

'Hey, hey, hey. It's okay, darling girl. Stop beating yourself up. The important thing is that you're here. I love you so much.' Hugging her tightly, Gerry kisses Kelly on her forehead then releases his tight hold so that he can kiss her willing lips. 'I think you should explain why, and how, you come to be here. I suspect Lizzie had something to do with that.'

At that moment, Lizzie and Mike enter the room, Mike carrying a tray of tea. 'Too right she had something to do with it. Tell him Lizzie.'

'Simple really,' Lizzie says with a smile. I went round to Irene's house with Dora, Belle and Betty and we pointed out the benefits of accompanying us to call in on Kelly to tell her the truth.'

'What are the benefits?' Mike and Gerry asked simultaneously.

'She gets to keep her arms and legs.'

Later that evening, after Gerry and Kelly had made love in their own bed, they sit against the pillows, each promising to always trust the other in future, no matter what. Before settling down to sleep, Gerry tells Kelly that he has to visit a family in the morning. With it being the Saturday before Christmas Eve, he is hoping they will be at home if he goes early enough. Of course, he then has to tell Kelly what he had done in his desperation.

'Do you mind if I come with you, love,' Kelly asks. 'It may make them feel more comfortable having me there to confirm what you are going to say.'

'That would be good, yes please. It will give me a bit of courage having you there beside me.'

***

'I know I did wrong in thinking that stealing would solve my short-term problem, but I was beyond all reasoning. My world had crashed. I never felt comfortable with what I was doing but it was when I saw the card that slipped out of your daughter's present to you that I came to my senses. I am so very sorry, I know you will want to inform the police, but also I would like to make amends to you in any way I can.'

'Well, young man, that was quite a speech,' says the gentleman who has allowed the couple into his house. I can see that nothing is missing, so I believe what you are saying about that. However, you have violated our home. Have you any idea at all what that feels like? I suspect you have no idea. My wife is extremely upset although we have kept all of this from our daughter who has suffered enough. Having said that, I admire your bravery in coming here this morning, you didn't have to. Also, I admire your honesty. Well, I forgive you, although there should be some form of restitution. You say you are an indentured brick layer?'

'Yes sir, I am, but there's no work at the moment, as I said.'

'Okay. Here's what we will do. Firstly, no police, I'm not pressing charges. I am the leader of a free church, that means non-denominational. We meet in our own premises which used to be a warehouse. We need to create smaller rooms within the building and we want the walls to be brick built. For how long would you say you were on these premises last night?'

'An hour, no more,' replies a mystified Gerry.

'Okay, I will expect you to work for an hour, no more, no less, free of charge. After that hour, if you agree, and if your work is up to our required standard, we will pay you the going rate for an independent brick layer. You will create all the internal walls and after that, assuming the weather allows, there is a boundary wall to be built. How does that sound?'

'You would do that for me?' gasps a shocked Gerry.

'For us. And I would never be surprised if there are members of our large congregation who would benefit from the work of an honest young man. Do you agree?'

'What can I say?'

'What do you think, young lady? Should he agree?' the gentleman enquires of Kelly with a wink of his eye.

'Oh yes, sir, he will agree, otherwise he'll have me, Dora, Belle and Betty dragging him round to your church. Thank you so much.'

'Splendid. Now I would like to introduce you to my wife, Jane, and our daughter, Princess Poppy who has an uncanny knack of bringing peace into every situation.'

The End

DUMPTY

'Come here my son, I want to talk to you.'

'I'm here Mama, and I am listening.'

'You are still very young, my child, and there is much for you to learn. You see, life can be difficult at times. There are many pitfalls, many who would pull you down given the opportunity. If you are to survive, it is right that you should understand why you are made the way you are. Our kind have evolved over many thousands of years. It is no accident that we are the way we are. Do you understand what I am saying?'

'I am really trying, Mama, but why are we so different?'

'Well all of us are different for many reasons. So much depends upon where we spend our lives, and the sort of problems we may need to overcome. Always remember, my son, that you are very special, perfectly adapted to withstand all that the weather and your natural surrounding can confront you with. As I look at you, my heart fills with pride, for you are so beautiful and so much like your father.'

'Where is my father, Mama?'

'Oh, he was needed in another part of the country where there was a shortage. I'm sure that he is having a great time, you mustn't worry about him.'

'Well, I really miss him, will he ever come back to us?'

'Perhaps, we will have to wait and see what transpires. Now, my son, you are older now, and will soon be fully grown, you may ask me whatever you like about who you are.'

'I suppose the obvious thing is the hump on my back. Why do I have that?'

'The simple answer is that your hump is fatty tissue which enables you to cross the desert without having to worry about water. When you are fully grown, you will be able to go for ten days or more without drinking. Essential when on long journeys across the desert, as it could be a matter of life or death in the hostile environment where it can be many days before you reach the next well. Did I ever tell you the story about my great,

great grandfather Dumpty?

'No, I don't think so. Will you tell me now, please?'

'Well now. Dumpty had been travelling for many days, so much so, that they were desperate for water by the time they reached a well. Everyone was fighting to get to the water because they were so dry. Poor Dumpty got pushed, and fell over the low wall into the well. As much as they tried, they couldn't lift him out, so they sent for some horses that belonged to the king of the region. That didn't help, so they gave up and went home. After they had all given up and left him, Dumpty thought to himself *"That was a nice cool bath, I think it's time to get out now,"* So he got up onto his long legs and stepped over the wall. The failed attempt to rescue the so called, drowning animal, became a legend called *Humpy Dumpty* which goes something like this;

Humpy Dumpty leaned on the wall

Humpy Dumpty had a great fall

All the king's horses and the king with his crown

Gave up on Dumpy and left him to drown

The following day they went back to look

They took a long pole with a strong metal hook

Dumpy stood there, alive and quite cool

The king was annoyed, being made such a fool.

'The legend changed over the years and Dumpty became an egg, don't ask why.'

'Wow! So that's where my name came from.'

'That's right, Dumpty my son.'

'Mamma, why do I have three eyelids?'

'A good question, my son. That is to protect your beautiful eyes when the great sand storms sweep across the desert.'

'I have often wondered why my legs are so long. Can you tell me?'

'The desert sands can become very; very hot in the middle of the day. Your long legs keep your body well above the rising heat.'

'Why do I have such long hair?'

'Ah, that is called insulation, my son. Surprisingly, your thick hair protects you from the intense heat of the sun when we walk among the vast sand dunes.'

'My feet are very big, why is that, Mama?'

'When others sink into the soft sand of the desert, your large flat feet act like platforms which spread your weight, enabling you to walk without sinking up to your knees.'

'Wow! all of these things mean that I am perfectly made to travel across the vast and dangerous desert. I can go many days without the need to drink water, I don't get blinded by the sand in a storm, I don't get too hot when the heat comes up from the sand, I stay cool when the hot sun shines down on me, and I can walk across the dunes without sinking.'

'That's right my son, wonderful isn't it?'

'Mama, why do we live in a zoo?'

The End

NO GOING BACK

A blue van is parked on the cliff top. It is old. Rust can be seen beneath the doors. The glass of one of the small rear windows is missing. A sheet of polythene fills the otherwise empty gap. The tread of the two front tyres are clearly below the legal limit. There is a large impact dent along the nearside. It is facing the sea which is glinting in the path of the setting sun, a red and silvery pathway to the horizon. Behind the parked van there are numerous small bushes, each leaning away from the prevailing wind. Only, at this moment there is no wind. All is calm. The only movement is the soaring of a few seabirds which have ceased their endless hunt for any kind of food, before they settle for the coming night. The shimmering sun sinks lower, the bottom half now lost in the inevitable descent into the sea. Regardless of the two-hundred-foot drop from the cliff edge the muffled sound of waves striking the slippery rocks beneath reaches the ears of the two young people who have been silently watching the ever-changing colour of the sky as the day gives way to the secrets of night.

They sit in the two front seats, she on the passenger side, he behind the wheel. He is gripping the wheel tightly at this moment. She is fidgeting with a hand embroidered handkerchief on her lap. Her hands are constantly folding and re-folding the soft material. She is shaking, although the coming evening has the promise of warmth, a warmth which is retained from the beautiful sunny day which saw their van approach this spot, away from their troubled lives. A small piece of paper is sitting on the front window ledge. A piece of paper which cannot be ignored, try as they might. He releases his grip on the wheel and reaches forward to inspect the words and numbers for the hundredth time. They are the same, unchanged. His mind returns to the threatening letter he had received just a week ago. His one-man business is finished.

She is thinking of her parents. Of how they have sacrificed everything to ensure her safety and happiness. Never complaining, always ready to help whenever possible. She thinks of the little terraced house in which she had grown up. A poor area, although a community which looked after its own. Half of them gone now, houses boarded up. Her parents destined to move to a high-rise block three miles away from all that is familiar to them. They have no idea that their daughter and son-in-law are to be evicted. Or that she has been made redundant from the shop assistant job she has held for less than a year. No warning, no appeal.

Life can be so cruel and also unpredictable, she thinks.

Replacing the piece of paper on the shelf he fumbles in his pocket for his cigarettes and matches. 'Want one?' he asks while watching the sun take its final dip, the deep red colour seeming to momentarily creep along the horizon in both direction before the final bow. End of show.

'No thank you, but you go ahead. I don't mind,' she replies with a deep sigh.

He places the tip between his lips and scrapes a match along the side of its box. The sudden light of the sparkling flame briefly fills the cab. He draws on the cigarette and tosses the spent match from his open window. The interior of the van seems much darker now. 'What are you thinking?' he asks through his exhaled smoke as he turns away from the windscreen to peer at his wife.

'I just can't help thinking what mum and dad will say, or do, when they hear. I just hope the shock doesn't send mum into one of her turns.'

'She'll be alright, don't worry.'

Silence descends. Both are lost in their respective thoughts for a few minutes. Ahead, the sky has become purple. The horizon can still be seen, although the cliff edge in front of the van is now difficult to make out.

The cigarette end glows in the darkness as he inhales the comforting nicotine deep into his lungs. *'Never did manage to give these cancer sticks up,'* he thinks with a brief smile on his lips. He is aware of the weight of his mobile phone in his trouser pocket, has been aware of it since he drove the van in to this beauty spot. He remembers that he had come close to bumping the barrier as he applied his foot to the dodgy brake. *'Won't take much for that barrier to go,'* he muses. *'They need to think about replacing it with something stronger.'* He flicks the still burning stub out of the window, his eyes following the glow till it expires. *'Can't risk setting fire to the grass,'* he thinks to himself.

'I suppose this old crate will end up on some scrap metal heap somewhere. It's a shame, it's had its problems but always got me and the tools to the jobs ... eventually. Still, can't be helped.' She allows a smile to reach her troubled face. 'Do you remember that time when the gear stick came off in your hand, how you had to drive all the way through the town in first gear, and the queue behind you all hooting their hooters?'

'I was thinking of the time your dad had to push me down your street just before we got engaged. It cost me free beers for a month,' he replies with a smile.

Silence.

'How will our friends feel?' she wonders. 'I think there will be a few tears. These things always end in upsets of some sort or another.'

'Are you sure you want to go through with this, love?' he enquires while looking toward the cliff edge and taking her hand in his. She is still shaking.

'We've talked it over and over,' she replies quietly. 'We have no choice, do we?'

'It would appear not. No money, no business, no home, no future. If you still feel the same, then so do I,' he says while giving her cold hand a squeeze.

'Well then?'

'Okay, love. You do know that you are everything to me. I love you so much. In spite of everything that has happened, you have always been there for me.'

'Yes, I know, and I love you, right from that moment when you accidently tipped your glass of beer into my lap as you tried to get off with my best mate in that pub. She stood no chance.' Do it now . . . please?'

He hesitates, again feeling the weight of his mobile phone which seems to be increasing minute by minute. 'You do realise that once I make that call there's no going back. We are committed.'

'I know, my sweet husband. Do it, now . . . before I change my mind. Please, just do it.'

'Okay.' He reaches into his trouser pocket and fumbles to release the phone from the folds of the material. He switches the instrument on. She watches as he keys in the numbers which are fixed in his mind. She is mesmerised by the green light of the small screen as he lifts the phone to his ear. She can hear the muffled ring tone. Three rings and a click.

'Hello? Hello, is that the European Lottery Office? . . . . Good, I need to tell you that I have the winning ticket for the roll-over.'

The End

GOLDIE

A slight breeze stirred the leaves of the Silver Birch above their heads. Beyond the hedge sparrows could be heard and yet, not heard, so familiar the sound. The melodic song of a blackbird welcoming the coming evening was more noticeable as it penetrated the sombre thoughts of the boy's father who gazed down at the mound of freshly turned earth at his feet. With one hand resting on his spade, the other on the boy's trembling shoulder, he gave a sigh as his thoughts trailed back over the years. *"The runt of the litter . . . Small . . . All the others, brown . . .. This one, corn coloured . . . No choice . . . This was the one . . . Had to wait a few weeks to collect him . . . It was worth it. Best dog I ever owned . . . Faithfull old friend . . . Never let me down . . . Loved the boy . . . Protected him . . . Taught him . . . God, I'm surely gonna miss that old hound."*

The blackbird continued its song, long drawn out notes. Like it was putting the final touches to the burial. The boy, with bowed head, sobbed as, with the sleeve of his lumber jacket, he wiped away the tears from his eyes and the snot from his nose.

'Okay Tom, that's enough now. We've got work to do.'

'I hate you, hate you, hate you!' the boy screamed. 'Why did you have to shoot him?'

'Son … he was in pain, and it was gettin' to be worse come each day. You could see that. Cruel to let it go on. It was for the best.'

'You could have taken him to the Doc's, he would have given him something, sure he would.'

'That would have been even more cruel, son. All them miles on that ol' buckboard would have finished that old fella in the most painful way possible. And there was no knowin' that the Doc would be in town and what he could have done if he wus, nothin' I would guess. That old dog is free of all that pain now, his time was up, and he knew it, and you just have to accept it boy.'

'It ain't fair, Pa, why did he have to die?'

'Time comes to us all, Tom. We gets born, we play, then we work, then we die. That's how it's always been. Eatin', drinking and sleeping is the best we get, apart from the love of a good woman and the devotion of a trusting dog. Yer Ma was a good woman and a good Ma to you. She fed you, washed you, changed you, stitched the clothes you stood in. It was the same fer her. She had the time allotted to her, twenty-four years. You won't remember, too young. But it took me a whiles to get over it, but get over it I did. All in good time. That's how it'll be fer you, boy. You'll get over it. You say you hate me. Well, that's all part of grievin'. I know you don't mean it. Why I remember just after my Jenny died, I rode into town and busted up the saloon a bit. Had to get it out of my system. Cost me a bit after, and I got meself banned fer a month, but it did me a power of good. Work up some anger if you must, kick that fool mouser, she's useless anyways, or better still, work yer breeches off with the hay bale.'

'Pa, I know what you're saying, and I'm sorry for what I said (sniff). It's just so hard. He was my best friend. He saved my life that time I broke my leg when I came off that ledge. I thought he had deserted me, but he came home to find and fetch you. And he taught me how to swim with the doggy paddle down at the pool. I reckon I would have drowned that time I fell in the river if I wasn't able to swim. Them bullies in the town school would never touch me when old Goldie was around. How am I goin' to sleep without him on my bed?'

'Well, you've had to manage these last few days, so I guess you'll just have to get used to it. I never did like that dog sleepin' on a bed. Makes 'em soft if yer want my 'pinyon. Now, how about we put this spade away in the barn and ride over to Jem's place? That bitch of his'n often has a litter. We might get ourselves the pick. Jem owes me a dollar or three.'

Hearing his father's words, Tom looked up, tears welling in his young eyes. Shaking his father's large calloused hand from his shoulder he angrily said, 'Pa, I don't want another dog. Nothing will ever replace old Goldie It wouldn't be right. How could you even say it? We've only just put him into the ground. Don't you care?'

'Oh yes, I care, boy. Don't you start thinking you're the only one hurtin.' That was my dog! I was his only master for all those years afore you came along. We shared his love and affection, you and me, we were joint members of his pack and he watched over us both. Oh yea, I care all right. I just show it diff'rent from you, that's all. Garn, it was me that had to look into those big brown eyes and pull the trigger, and you may need to do the same someday. So, don't go sayin' I don't care, cos one day you'll be the one havin' to stay strong. Now you listen to me, boy, the greatest compliment you can pay Goldie is to love another dog just like you love him, and I say "love" and not "loved" because you will always love dear old Goldie, just like I will. In that way, Goldie gets to live on in your heart, just like yer Ma does in mine. You may not fully understand yet, but you will, son.'

'Pa?'

'Yes, son?'

'Can we go over to Jem's place now?'

'Not now, Tom. It'll be dark in an hour. First thing tomorrow after milking and the eggs are in. Why don't you go and wash up, while I finish off here?'

'Okay Pa, and Pa?'

'Yes, son?'

'I really am sorry for what I said. I love you Pa. We can get through this together, you'll see.'

The man stood alone, looking down at the earth mound. Tears streaming unashamedly down his cheeks, 'Good bye old friend. We were a team, weren't we? Say hello to my Jenny when you see her. Tell her we're doin' okay down here, and that the boy will be a fine young man soon.'

***

'Howdy John. It's been a while. And young Tommy has growed a bit since the last time, when was that now? Must have been at the Warren's barn raising. My, that wus a mighty good day with all that food and fiddling. Get yourselves off them mounts and come in for coffee, Sam here will take care of 'em. My Clem's gonna be right pleased to see ya both, especially young Tommy. Ya knows how she likes to fuss the youngsters since . . . well never mind that.'

Jem and Clementine had lived in the valley for as many years as any could remember. They had made a success of rearing horses and had gained a high reputation for hundreds of miles around. Their business was running down now, as Jem was no longer agile enough to handle the hard work involved. Clementine had born two sons, the first had never reached his first birthday, whilst the second had matured into a hard-working boy who was set to take over the business, that is, until an overturned buggy had ended his life a few years back. As the three of them approached the large two storied clapperboard house the fly screen burst open to reveal a pleasantly rounded lady bearing a huge grin on her rosy cheeked face. 'Lordie, lordie, see what the wind has blown in to visit.

John and young Tommy. You must have smelled my apple pie. Come on up, John, and let me have a big hug.'

Grinning and removing his hat, John mounted the four steps onto the stoop to do as Clem said. He took in the combined aroma of jasmine soap and cooked pastry as he took this dear lady into his arms. 'Good to see you Clem, how ya keepin' these days?'

'Oh, you know. Nothing a tot of brandy now and then won't sort. My, look at you, Tom, you's nearly as tall as me now. I won't embarrass you with a hug … yes I will, come to your Aunty Clem.' Tom didn't hesitate, he was more than ready to be held in the warm comforting arms of this lady who had always referred to herself as *"Aunty"*. For as long as he could remember she had been the mother to him that he had never known. He just wished they lived closer. 'Well, don't just stand there, come on in and give me your verdict on my apple pie, I must have known my house was going to be graced with two handsome men this morning.'

Pie and coffee well appreciated, gossip exchanged, John got around to telling Jem why they had come over. He had noticed that Pips hadn't put in an appearance the whole time they had been there, so was hopeful that she was caring for a brood of pups. 'You're in luck, John. She had six not long since. Two didn't make it, so she was feedin' four. Reckon this will be her last lot now, it's time for her to retire, just like me. We'll enjoy walking the hills together, as long as this leg of mine holds up. You've got the pick of the litter my friend, and for you, no charge. Call it a birthday present for young Tom here, fer whenever his birthday is, danged if I can remember.'

'You can't even remember when my birthday is, old man, let alone anyone else,' said Clem with a smile as she heaved herself from her sewing chair. 'Come through, she's in the kitchen, least that's where I left her.' Together, all three of them followed Clem as she rolled through the lounge door. The dog's blanket-covered sewn mattress was positioned in a quiet corner of the large kitchen. As they approached, the bitch looked up at them, tail thumping on the mattress. The four puppies were play-fighting around her, with little growls and whimpers.

'Pure bred,' said Clem proudly. Father came over from Yellow Springs, cost us a few dollars but well worth it. You can take your pick if'n you're interested young man, she said to Tom.

The boy fell to his knees and held his hand to the mother for her to sniff, before attempting to touch any of her brood. *"Good boy, you're a natural,"* thought John proudly. *"You'll be okay"* 'Take your time, son. The right one will come to you.' As Tom ruffled the mother's ears, he watched the pups at play. For some reason that avoided Tom his eyes settled on one of the brood which always seemed to get the worst of the friendly nipping of its peers. He slowly lowered his hand to the mattress and waited for any kind of reaction. Something told him that it would be the one he had been watching that would make the first contact with his hand. And so it was. The little bundle of fur tentatively sniffed at the boy's outstretched fingers before a dry tongue flicked out to explore further. A lifetime partnership was forged at that moment.

'This one. I like this one,' said the boy quietly as he looked up at Aunt Clementine. 'Please, may I have this one?'

'Well now Tommy, do you suppose you ought to ask Pips, after all, she brought him into the world, don't you think she should have a say?'

Looking back at the mother, Tom said, 'What do you think Pips, will he be happy with me? I promise to look after him, honest to goodness I will.' Pips looked up at the boy's pleading eyes before licking his hand. She then turned her attention to the puppy in question, licking around its face. 'I think she's saying it's okay.' Tom said hopefully.

'And so do I young man. He's yours,' replied a grinning aunt who wasn't an aunt at all.

'Really?' yelled the boy, so loudly that the three other pups stopped their game and scrambled as close as possible to Pips. 'Sorry,' said Tom as he fussed Pips' ears. 'Thank you for trusting me with your baby son, I promise to bring him to see you sometimes so you can see him growing up.' Turning to the three adults, he asked, 'When can he come to us?'

'That little fellow is ready right now, Tommy, replied Clem. 'If it's okay with your Pa you can take him home today.' Saying that, she glanced at John to see the brief nod. 'Tell you what, young man, you get that pony of yours hitched to the buggy and you and this little fellow can ride home with Sam in style, with your daddy as escort. You can even take what's left of the apple pie. How does that suit you?'

***

'Pa? How is it possible for someone to be really sad and happy at the same time?' enquired the boy while standing at the graveside beside his father, with the puppy in his arms.

'I don't rightly know son, it's a mystery to me, but I know what you mean.' John placed his hand on his son's shoulder and together they stood silently in their own thoughts. The leaves on the tree above them rustled in the dying breeze. 'Have you given this one a name yet?' enquired John breaking the peaceful quietness.

'If it's okay with you, Pa, I want to call him Goldie.'

'That's alright with me, boy. I like the sound of that, and I reckon he would like it too.' Together, father and son continued looking down at the pile of earth, upon which a stone had been placed during the afternoon. The name *"Goldie"* had been chiselled into the flat surface of the sandstone, clear to see. As they stood there in the light of the setting sun, a blackbird whistled his throaty song, and a puppy dog licked the salty tears on the cheeks of the boy who was to become his sole purpose for living.

The End

THE SENTENCE

'You have made your choice, now you must pay the price. You will be taken to a place where your dignity will no longer be of any consequence. You will be lined up with others whose life choices have taken them to the same place as yourself. You will be closely supervised. Any objection or disruption on your part will be severely dealt with. There will be no relief. You will be forced to carry your belongings. This will seem like endless torture but the ordeal ahead is manifold and designed to break your spirit and reduce you to a quivering jelly. Your suffering will be great and without mercy.'

'Gulp.'

'After seemingly endless agony you will stand before the inquisitor who will make the appropriate checks to ensure that your route of torture is appropriate for your particular punishment. From there, you will face the corporal punishment zone where you will be divested of all that you treasure, including your shoes, before being thoroughly manhandled by security.'

'Gasp.'

'You will then be squeezed into a tube where you will be placed in your cell which you will share with two others. In this space you will be strapped down and may not be released should the tube be subject to violent shaking for the duration. You will have no space in which to exercise, so that every nerve and muscle will scream for release. Do not be surprised if your limited space is further reduced when the wall ahead of you is suddenly thrown onto your trapped knees. You will be forced to breath in all the germs that circulate in the enclosed airtight space. There will be no relief other than a tray of cardboard which you will be expected to consume within a matter of minutes.'

'Oh, my lord.'

'Your lord cannot help you. Your time will have to be faced. Once in the tube of horror you will have no possible means of escape. You should have thought about this before you committed yourself to the path of iniquity.'

'I'm so sorry, I didn't mean to …'

'Enough! Do not presume to think you can escape the un-enviable journey you have ahead of you. There will be a time of respite when you will be released from the tube, that is assuming you still have sufficient circulation in your miserable legs to allow you to leave your cell. WHAT IS THAT NOISE YOU ARE INFLICTING ON MY EARS? SPEAK UP!'

'S ..s..sorry, it's my teeth chattering.'

'Yes, you may well have cause to be afraid. Others have gone before you and having survived, vowed never to go down this road again. Be afraid. Assuming you are able to leave the tube on your own feet you will be subjected to further humiliation when your face will be minutely scrutinised. Should you be inclined to panic and allow your frayed nerves to cause you to smile, or even worse, giggle, you will be detained for further scrutiny.'

'Gulp.'

'You will then be searched, including your possessions, to ensure you are not carrying anything illegal or dangerous to the final destination where you will serve out your term. There, you will see the depressing ruins of civilisation as you know it. You will find that little remains standing. The pride of those who have gone before you, are no more. Dust, broken stones and dreams are all that remain.'

'Is there any other way?'

'There is no other way. You have made your choice.'

'I have?'

'Do you understand what is to happen to you?'

'Can't I go to Dartmoor instead?'

'I'm afraid the Dartmouth & Dartmoor coach tour is now fully booked. It will have to be the cultural tour of the Greek ruins as planned. Enjoy your holiday Mr Ludford, and have a safe flight. Goodbye.'

The End

THE TAILOR

At five thirty-five precisely the door of the tailor's shop was closed for the final time that day. The brown shutters had been lowered on both the window and the door exactly five minutes earlier. It could not be said that the door had closed behind the last customer, for there had been no customers that day, a Friday in June, nor the previous day, although on the day before that, a gentleman had walked in to purchase some boxed handkerchiefs. Business for this family tailor's shop had considerably declined with the introduction of off-the-peg clothing in the larger clothing stores within the High Street. There had been a time when a customer requiring a new suit to be fitted would expect to be seated at a small table within the confines of the shop, and offered a pot of tea along with an apology for the wait while other customers were being taken care of. This particular tailor's shop had been in the ownership of the Taylor family for eight generations. It used to be a particular favourite of serving naval officers who could be assured of being correctly dressed, having visited the shop bearing the legend "E.L.W. TAYLOR – Gentlemen's Outfitters – *Est. 1865",* all in gold lettering against a royal blue background. No, it wasn't a departing customer who closed the door, it was a slightly balding man, short of stature, who closed the door before carefully locking it. Edward Taylor gave the door a push, just to ensure that it really was locked. Satisfied, he peered over his half-moon spectacles, up and then down the road before crossing to the opposite side.

Naturally he was concerned about the business, for he was reluctant for the shutters to come down for the last time while on his watch. One hundred and fifty years that shop had stood there to serve and clothe the gentry. It all started with a barrow, of course. He often amused himself by imagining what it would have been like, standing on the cobbles and attracting the attention of sea officers who spent their lives harnessing the wind and sailing from port to port to obtain the best prices. Romantic to be sure. Edward had never been to sea, except, that is, to cross over to Gosport on the ferry. *'One day,'* he mused as he walked toward the city centre, *'I'll buy that yacht I keep promising Lesley.'* This evening he was on a mission. He knew the flower stall would be open until six-o-clock, plenty of time to buy the red roses to go with the birthday present he had bought Lesley, a gold bracelet that she had admired in a London Jewellers last week.

A ten-minute walk brought him to the shop he had been aiming for. Sure enough, they had sufficient red roses for him to be able to purchase a dozen. 'There we are luv, a dozen of the best,' said the assistant as she handed Edward the paper-wrapped bunch of flowers. 'Special occasion is it? Or 'ave you been a naughty boy?' she enquired with a wink.

'Yes … a special occasion, I mean. My wife's birthday.'

'How romantic, you'll be wantin' a card then.'

'Oh, yes, thank you, I suppose I will.'

It wasn't long before Edward was on the No. 21 bus, settled in a seat next to a rather rotund lady. He thought about the car which was securely locked in his garage.

There was no way he would consider driving it to work and parking it in Queen's Street. No that would never do. This was not the comfortable journey Edward might have wished for. The lady with whom he was seated seemed to be taking up more space than her own seat allowed. Consequently, he had to sit with one leg in the aisle to maintain his balance, particularly when the bus turned the numerous corners along the route. He lost count of the number of times his foot had been kicked or trodden on. He felt obliged to say "Sorry" each time, as also he felt obliged to retain his uncomfortable seat as the bus emptied and alternative seats became available, for he knew that such a move might cause offence to the lady and would most certainly make him feel embarrassed as other passengers would know why he had moved. It was not in Edward's nature to want to be noticed, at least, in these circumstances.

At last, he was home. Edward loved the detached Edwardian house they had managed to purchase after their wedding seven years ago. He was particularly fond of the bay windows on both floors which allowed splendid views of the well-maintained garden. The garden was Lesley's province, one which kept her busy and extremely happy. As he opened the gate, Edward noticed that his wife was where he might have expected her to be, on her knees with a trowel in her hand, in one of the side beds. Hearing the gate close, Lesley rose to her feet and walked over to the gravel path to welcome her husband home. 'Hello darling, have you had a good day?' she asked as she approached to give him a kiss.

'Hello, love. It's been quiet. We'll have to see what the future holds for the shop. It's not looking too promising at the moment. It won't support staff and I'm feeling that my time is being wasted each day, as much as I like to be there. As you know, I've had an offer from the hairdressers next door, goodness knows what they think they can do with it.'

'What are you hiding behind your back, as if I didn't know? Let me guess now … um, would it be flowers by any chance?'

'Happy birthday my love,' said Edward as he held out the roses.

'Oh, how lovely,' responded Lesley as she held the roses to her nose. 'You are so good to me, thank you.'

'Nothing's too good for you, my love. I've booked for seven-thirty at the restaurant, that gives us both time to get ready.'

***

'Okay, this is the place sweetheart,' said Phillip, 'and there's a convenient place to park, just behind that Aston Martin. Wow, that's a beauty, must have cost a penny or two.'

'Well, you can look and wish, Phil, but it will be a while before we can afford anything like that, especially as things are going, or not going I should say, at the moment,' replied Susan. 'In fact, I'm not even convinced we can afford this elaborate weekend you've planned for our anniversary, what with dinner tonight and the concert at the Guildhall tomorrow.'

'Don't you worry about that, honey. Leave the finances to me. The promised partnership will come up one day, we'll be fine. Just enjoy yourself,' replied Phillip as he held the restaurant door open for his young wife.

'Good evening sir,' said a neatly dressed waitress who was standing behind a plinth just inside the door. 'Have you a reservation?'

'Yes, Mr and Mrs Dutton,' replied Phillip.

'Ah yes,' replied the waitress with a smile. 'If you would like to follow me?'

Moving through the occupied tables behind the waitress Phillip glanced around on the off-chance that he would recognise any of the seated diners, *'One of the partners from the accountancy firm perhaps? In this kind of place, you could even bump into a minor celebrity, maybe the owner of that fab car outside,'* he mused as they arrived at their table. As they took their seats Phillip did spot someone he knew. Not a senior partner from his office, or a celebrity, but one of his old school chums. *'Ed, of all people. Taylor the tailor's son. Must be all of fourteen years. Still looks the same, smart clothes, specs, always a bit of a loner with his passion for classical music. Oh dear, I think he's spotted me. Pretend I haven't noticed.'*

With the drinks ordered, the waitress left them to study the menu. 'This is posh, Phil, are you sure we can afford it?'

'Don't you worry about that, honey. Yes, we can. Not every week perhaps, but for our anniversary, why not splash out a bit?'

'I do love you Phil, thank you. Have you seen anyone you recognise?'

'No, not even a famous actor, singer or politician, never mind, my love, I'll just have to settle for you, won't I?' replied Phillip with a wink.

***

'You're looking a bit distracted, love. Why are you staring at that couple who have just sat down? Do you know them?' Lesley enquired as she started on her main course.

'Yes, I think I know the man. If I'm right, he was in my class at school. Certainly looks like him. He used to tease me about liking classical musical, also about my name being Taylor, because my father happened to own a tailor's shop. He used to call me *'Titchy Stitchy'*. Very much into pop music as I recall.'

'So, he wasn't a friend then?'

'Oh, we got along alright I suppose. We all took every opportunity to tease or play jokes on each other. I'm sure it's him. Phil, that's it, Phil Dutton. Well, well, well, after all these years.'

***

Looking up at the waitress, Susan said, 'Soup please, and the salmon sounds nice, I'll go for that.'

Pad and pen poised; the waitress turned to Phillip. 'Sir?'

'I'll have breaded whitebait and the pie please.' Taking the menus, the waitress walked away as Phillip took a sip of his wine. 'That's definitely Titch over there, I noticed they were both looking as we placed our order. I'll have to go over and say "High" otherwise they'll think we're being rude. I won't be a moment, honey,' saying that, Phillip pushed back his chair and within a matter of seconds had approached the other table. 'High, it is Edward isn't it?' He enquired with a grin, while feeling a little embarrassed at the intrusion.

'That's right, good to see you, Phil. You haven't changed. This is my wife, Lesley.'

'Please, don't get up. Would you be happy to meet up in the coffee lounge after we've all eaten?'

'Certainly,' replied Edward. 'It would be nice to catch up.'

'Good, we'll see you a bit later then.'

***

'It's great seeing you again,' said Phillip as he and Susan approached the coffee table at which Edward and Lesley were seated. The latter had retired to the coffee lounge half an hour earlier. 'Allow me to introduce my wife, Susan'

Edward and Lesley stood and introduced themselves while shaking hands. Shortly after, with fresh coffee having been brought to their table, conversation was freely flowing and telephone numbers had been exchanged. The two ladies had immediately hit it off together and were chatting quietly while Edward and Phillip shared stories about school days and mutual acquaintances. 'So, Ed, you're still running the old tailor's shop. How's business these days, with all the competition in the city centre?'

'Not so good, Phil. People don't go for our style of service any more. It's all about haste, *'Sales'* and loud pop music blaring out, these days. I think our days are numbered now.'

'Well, it can't be paying you much, how are you coping financially?'

Taken by surprise by such an invasive question, Edward simply responded with, 'Oh, we get by, don't you worry about that, my friend.'

'Well this place isn't cheap, Ed. This must be a special occasion, are you celebrating something?'

'It's Lesley's birthday. Well, you have to push the boat out, sometimes don't you? What line of business are you in, Phil?'

'I'm an accountant, waiting for a promised partnership which never seems to happen. One day, hopefully things will improve on the financial front. As a matter of fact, we're celebrating as well, our eighth wedding anniversary this weekend, and my boat is well and truly pushed out. This meal today and a show tomorrow at the Guildhall. A great singer called "Yellow Rat" I don't suppose you've even heard of him. One of the top billings at Glastonbury this year. Great albums. Not a lot known about him. Avoids the media. Tickets are like gold dust.'

'Really? Do you have the tickets with you by any chance?'

'I surely do,' replied Phil as he reached into his inside pocket. 'I think I'll be framing them along with the programme. Here, take a look.'

Edward took the tickets and examined them for a moment. 'Well, if this *Yellow Rat* is as good as you say he is I'm sure you'll have a great time, Phil. Now, if you don't mind, I think it's time Lesley and I were off. I've got a busy day tomorrow. It was nice bumping in to you again.'

'Ed, don't be offended, but we could always help you out a bit if things get really tough, you know, financially.'

'That's really kind. Don't worry, we're doing okay, but I'll always remember that offer, Phil. Thank you.'

As Edward and Lesley briefly waved at the exit door Susan sipped her third cup of coffee before saying, 'A nice couple, Phil. Lesley was telling me how much the business is struggling at the moment. I felt sorry for them. At least they managed to have a good night out for her birthday.'

Half an hour later as they approached their car, Phillip commented, 'I see the Aston Martin has gone. I wonder if there was a celeb in the restaurant after all. I was so absorbed in looking at Ed I forgot to have a good peer around.'

***

The concert at the Guildhall was every bit as good, and as loud, as Phil had expected. At the interval, with ringing ears, he and Susan managed to reach the crowded bar, enjoy a drink and get back to their seats just before the second half. However, they had just settled in their seats when an attendant leaned over Phil and asked, 'Do you mind showing me your tickets, sir?'

'Okay, I have them here, why, is there a problem?'

'No problem, sir. It isn't generally known, but Yellow Rat likes to invite someone, with a guest, to his dressing room for drinks after the concert. Seat numbers are selected at random during the interval. I'm pleased to inform you that you have been selected. Will you be able to accept the invitation, sir?' Stunned by this turn of events, Phil was momentarily speechless.

'Sir?'

'Oh, yes. Yes please, we would be honoured to accept. Thank you.'

'Don't thank me, sir. Thank Yellow Rat. If you would like to remain seated at the end of the performance someone will come and escort you back stage.'

'Can you believe it, Honey? We're going to meet the great man himself. I can't wait to tell everyone in the office. Wow!'

As much as Phillip enjoyed the second half of the show, he could hardly wait for the end which was even more loud, and thrilling to the over excited fans. All were on their feet during the last few songs, with much waving of arms. The loud screaming of many of the female fans failed to blot out the rhythm of drums and guitars, although the words of the songs were totally lost. It took a long time for fans to start leaving when it had become clear that there was not to be a further encore. Phillip and Susan remained in their seats as instructed, until a young lady approached and asked for their seat numbers before escorting them through a discrete door near the stage. They were soon in a corridor which led to a flight of steps which ascended to a higher floor. Following the young lady, Phillip's heart was beating rapidly and his throat was becoming dry. He took Susan's hand as they arrived at a closed door where their escort paused. Turning to them with a smile she said, 'This is it; I'll leave you now. Just knock and walk in. You'll find that he is charming. Good luck.' She left. Phillip held his breath, knocked three time and opened the door.

***

There before them, was a brightly lit dressing table upon which there was a variety of jars and bottles. On one end of the dressing table was a black long-haired wig resting on a false head, also the sunglasses Yellow Rat always wears. Standing alongside the dressing table was a wardrobe with partly opened doors. Inside, Phillip glimpsed the yellow cloak he had seen less than half an hour ago sweeping off the instrument cluttered stage. Stepping inside the dressing room and closing the door behind them, they looked further into the room and noticed a large screen at one end of the apparently empty room.

'Come in, both of you. No need to be shy. Over here behind the screen, excuse me for not getting up. I'm a bit bushed after that performance. Come and take a seat, plenty of room for us all.'

'Edward? What are you doing here? Where's ....'

'Yellow Rat? You're looking at him, my friend'

'I don't understand. Do you mean to tell us that you're ...'?

'Yellow Rat. That's right, none other.'

'But ... but ... how ...?'

'Let's just say, I was discovered during a karaoke evening and it moved on from there. When I have the cape and wig on, I become a different person. A bit like Superman I suppose, only I don't have to wear my pants on the outside, thankfully.'

'But, you're a tailor. What about the shop?' asked a very confused Phillip.

'The shop is important to me; it keeps me grounded. It's a safe haven where I can be … well, *Me*. A hobby I suppose.'

'This is so …, I don't know what to say. Where does the name "*Yellow Rat*" come from?'

'Oh, I've just worked it out,' piped in Susan who had seated herself opposite Edward. Your shop is named E.L.W. Taylor isn't it?'

'Well done, clever girl. Yellow Rat is an anagram of the shop name. Fans expect that sort of name for a punk group, according to my agent. Now, what can I offer you to drink? You can see a small selection over there on the table. Lesley will be along in a moment. She likes to drive me to and from the venues in the Aston Martin.'

With a whisky in his hand Phillip enquired, 'I assume you knew who would be coming through that door, Ed? Or should I call you *Yellow Rat?*'

'Ed will do. Of course I knew. I memorised your ticket numbers when you showed them to me last night.'

'I just can't believe that my friend Titchy Stitchy, has turned out to be Yellow Rat.'

'I can't quite believe it myself sometimes, until I look at my bank statements. Apart from anything else, that's another thing I wanted to talk to you about.'

'What, your bank statements?'

'Your glass is empty, Phil, let me pour you another. Yesterday, you offered to help me out financially should the need arise. Even though things are not going so well for you. I … we were touched. Phil, I need a good accountant on my team, someone I can trust, someone I like. I would be pleased and grateful if you would consider taking it on. Full or part-time, whatever suits your situation. Should you feel you could take it on, you will like the salary I have in mind. What do you say, Phil?'

'He says he would love to accept,' piped in Susan while jumping out of her seat and plonking down next to Edward and throwing her arms around him. Edward was speechless, he just sat there with a huge grin on his face.

'Should I be concerned?' said Lesley who had slipped through the door un-noticed. With a smile she said, 'I assume he has made his offer, welcome on board, both of you. It will be good to get to know you more. Are you free to come to dinner next weekend? I know Ed would like to show his Aston Martin off, Phil. He might even let you have a drive in it, while Susan and I have a good old natter talking about you two.'

The End

GLORIA

It was a warm summer's day when I first met Gloria. She was seated on a park bench eating a pork pie. Sparrows were flitting from branch to branch in the tree above her. Their twittering a backdrop to the song she was humming to herself. Or was it a hymn? Now that I know her more, I can almost definitely say it was a hymn. She didn't seem to notice my approach, although, as I was about to pass her, without looking up she stopped chewing and said, 'Hello Olive, lovely day, isn't it?'

I stopped in my tracks and said, 'Excuse me?'

'Lovely day, I said *"Lovely day,"* she replied looking up at me.

'You called me *'Olive'*, why would you do that? It's a girl's name.'

'Really? Hang on a moment.' With that, she rummaged about in her oversized handbag and pulled out a piece of paper. Holding it up for my inspection she said triumphantly, *'Olive,* it's there in black and white. Are you telling me you're not a girl?'

'I would hope it's obvious that I'm not a girl since I'm sporting a beard, let me see that piece of paper. There, you see? *"Clive",* C.L.I.V.E. not Olive.'

Taking the paper back, Gloria held it close to her nose and said, 'Oops, sorry, I should have checked with my glasses on.'

'Well, I suggest you do put your glasses on, tell me who you are, then tell me why you have this piece of paper with my name on it.'

'Yes, glasses where did I put my glasses?' Diving back into her handbag. 'Tissues, hair brush, tooth-brush, map of London, mobile phone, spare knickers, Polo mints, ruler, tea-bag, duck food, slippers, ah, here they are, right at the bottom.' She hooked her spectacles onto her nose and ears. 'That's better, why didn't I think of that before?' She peered up at me through thick lenses and said, 'Golly gosh, you're a handsome boy, Olive'

'Clive! We've already done this; my name is *Clive.*'

'Oh yes, Clive.'

'May I ask you again, what is your name, and why am I even talking to you?'

'My name is Gloria and I'm your Guardian Angel.'

'My what?'

'Your new Guardian Angel. Your old one has moved on to someone more interes … um … challenging. She liked to stay invisible. I much prefer to be seen you know. But it's only you who can see me when I choose to be visible. Actually, I'm new at this. Being a Guardian Angel I mean. I was a B.B.S. before I got you.'

'What's a B.B.S.?'

'A Belly Button Shaper, you know, that thing on your tummy. I wonder if that was one of mine, may I see?'

'No, you may not see,' I replied while stepping back from this strange woman.

'Never mind, I'll check it out when you have a shower.'

'In your dreams. I've a good mind to phone for the police,' I replied while reaching in my back pocket for my mobile.

'Oh, don't do that, you will embarrass yourself, for I'll be invisible to them. That's why most of us G.A.s' choose to remain invisible; I was warned that things can get complicated if we decide to be visible to our bods.'

'Bods, what's that?

'You're my *'Bod'* you know, as in *'Somebody.'*

I decided then, to play along with this lady who must have escaped from her party. One of the Carers must appear at any moment, surely. 'Why did you stop being a, what is it? B.B.S.?'

Holding her forefinger up for my inspection she replied, 'My finger became sore after a while, with all that pushing into babies' tummies. Then I was put in charge of making sure the sun came up at the right time every day, but I kept getting confused when the hour changed, I kept changing the sun as well as my alarm clock. So now, I'm a Guardian Angel, your Guardian Angel. Isn't that nice?'

'No, that is definitely not nice, and don't even think of being around when I take a shower.' I was desperately looking around the park as I spoke. 'Where are your friends, Gloria? Did you wonder off? We can go and find them if you like?'

'No need, Oli … Clive. My friends are all around us. See that boy down by the pond floating his little boat? That's Wendy standing over him making sure he doesn't fall in.'

'All I can see is a boy, on his own by the pond, and that must be his mother watching from the bench on the other side of the path.'

'Oh of course, Wendy's invisible to you isn't she, and I don't suppose you can see Brian sitting alongside the mother either. You see? I'm surrounded by friends.'

Becoming somewhat concerned about this strange lady and her fantasies I began to wonder if I should escort her to the nearest police station, after all, they were bound to be informed that one of the patients from some nearby institution had been mislaid. Then again, I might be able to take her to her home myself, if it was close by. 'Where do you live, Gloria, do you know?'

'Oh, I'll be living with you now, I can't wait to see our home.'

'No, I'm sorry, Gloria, that won't be possible, I live in digs and have no spare bed in the place.'

'Oh, you mustn't worry about that, Oli …Clive. We don't sleep. We watch over our Bods when they sleep. I'll be watching over you tonight, and filling your head with lovely dreams. How about you riding over a lovely rainbow on a silver unicorn? I like that one. Or what about finding buried treasure on a beautiful island with lots of trees swaying in the …'

'Stop! You will not be watching over me tonight, or any other night. You will be safely tucked up in your own bed in whatever home you come from. Now, you finish your pork pie while I continue my walk around the park. It was nice meeting you, if I see your group, I'll tell them where you are.' I left her there, still sitting on the bench with a warm smile on her face. However, I thought it best to keep an eye on her until she was found, so I made my way over to a distant bench which would afford me a clear view of the poor lady while I ate my lunch. On my way, I looked over my shoulder to see if she was still there and was reassured when she gave me a distant wave. Turning back, I approached my bench, only to see someone I hadn't previously noticed sitting there. Oh well, not a problem, big enough for two. As I approached, I started to shrug off my backpack to get to my sandwiches.

'Hello Clive.'

'What the?'

'Wow, I got you name right first time, aren't you pleased?'

'How …?' I swung round to see if Gloria was still seated on her bench near the lake. It was unoccupied.

'Would you like to join me on this bench, It's ever so comfy.'

'Gloria! How did you do that? It's like *"Beam me up Scotty."* That's cool.'

'Yes, it is isn't it? One of the perks of the job.'

'Now look here, Gloria. I don't mean to offend you, but even if you are a Guardian Angel, I don't need one.'

'You do.'

'I don't, and I don't want ...'

'DUCK!' Instinctively I ducked, just as a football narrowly brushed passed the top of my head. 'You were saying?'

'How did you see that? It was coming from behind us,' I exclaimed.

'It's what we do,' Gloria replied with a smirk. Now what are we doing this afternoon?'

'I'M going into college to sit a test paper. You're going to go and guard someone else.'

'Can't'

'What do you mean, *"Can't?"* Just transport yourself to someone who will appreciate you.'

'I'm allocated to you, Clive. I don't think I can just go off and leave you. Hang on a moment, I'll check. Eat your lunch, oh and by the way, when you open the bag, you'll find that the chutney has oozed out of your cheese sandwich and has gone all over your doughnut.'

Once again Gloria was delving into her handbag. 'Toilet roll, rubber bands, sandpaper, here it is.' She was triumphantly holding up her mobile phone.

'Hey, wait a minute, who are you phoning?' I asked.

'Head Office, you know, up there.'

'You have to use a mobile?'

'Why not? It was more difficult in the old days, having to use a dove. It took ages to get an answer. The answer is *"No"* by the way. I have to stay with you.'

'But you haven't spoken to anyone yet.'

'Yes, I did. You see, we live outside of 'Time', I've just had a long chat with the Boss while you were looking at your doughnut. He likes you and thinks I'm good for you. So, I'm afraid your stuck with me.'

'My giddy aunt,' I groaned.

'Oh, are we going to visit her?'

'Visit who?' I asked in exasperation?'

'Your aunty. You should take care of her if she's having giddy spells.'

'No, that was just an expression of frustration.'

'I know,' replied Gloria. 'Just having my little joke. You'll get used to me.'

At that moment a sudden thought entered my head.

'No, that's for children's Fairy Stories,' Gloria said with a smile.

'But I haven't asked you anything yet.'

'You were about to ask if I can grant you three wishes. I do not have a magic wand, and wishes are definitely out. Ask me another … No, I do not have wings, that's for the imagination of artists, and I do not play a harp, much as I'd like to.'

'How can you know what I'm thinking and am about to ask?'

'I don't know. As I said, I'm new at this G.A. stuff. I rather like it.'

'Well, I think it's all a bit weird. I preferred it when you were just lost and separated from your group. I could handle that.'

For the next twenty minutes we sat in silence, with me eating cheese sandwiches and a new type of doughnut, and Gloria still eating her pork pie, which didn't seem to get any smaller. With the remains of my lunch, mainly a half-eaten doughnut, I rose to my feet and said, 'Nice knowing you, Gloria. I'm off to college. Bye.' Before she had time to answer I had hoisted my backpack onto my shoulder and had walked quickly away. By the time I had entered the college and seated myself at a desk I had convinced myself that I must have had a very quick and unexpected cat-nap in the park and dreamed the whole thing. *'Guardian Angel, Belly Button Shaper, where did that come from? Perhaps it was the cheese.'* The test was going reasonably well until I had a question about the density of the atmosphere at forty thousand feet, two possible answers, both seemed likely. I thought about which box to tick and made up my mind when a familiar voice entered my head, '*Are you sure you want to tick that one?*'

'*Oh no, it can't be!*'

'*I'm not allowed to give you the answer, Clive, just asking if you're sure, that's all, tee hee*'

I ticked the other box without replying, after all, you're not supposed to talk during these tests.

With the test behind me, I left the building and sat on a wall near the college entrance. I was alone. Or was I? 'Gloria, are you here?' Then louder, 'Gloria, where are you?' Then I raised my voice, 'Stop being a pain in the butt and let me see you.'

'I beg your pardon?' It was a girl who happened to be passing by with an armful of books.

'No not you, I was talking to my … girlfriend?'

'Your girlfriend,' repeated the girl while looking around. 'Well she has my sympathy,' she retorted before stomping off with her nose in the air.

'Your girlfriend,' The unmistakable voice came from the wall right beside me.

'No, you are not, I repeat, *Not,* my girlfriend, you're my Guardian Angel.'

'Ha ha! so you've finally caught on and admitted it. That's progress.' Suddenly there she was, sitting on the wall beside me. No pork pie.

'What exactly is your purpose, Gloria? I mean, what do you do, apart from annoying me?'

'That's easy. I look out for you, try to keep you from harm, try to guide you, although you can always make your own choices in the end. Like that question about the atmosphere.'

'But you told me the …'

'No, I didn't, I just asked you to be sure, and that's all I will ever do. The rest is up to you. I can put ideas into your head but it's up to you to decide how to use them, that's all. Before I took over from your previous G.A. I asked her how this all works. She said that she once had a Bod who fancied himself as a writer. When her Bod, Paul, wrote a really good story, it was because he had heard her voice in his head and followed her prompting. But when the story was not so good, it was when he just went ahead without listening. Do you see? That's how it is through life. Now then, why don't we go and do something interesting, I've always fancied surfing. Have we got a surf board by any chance? We have? Brilliant.'

'But I didn't … Oh, never mind, let's go surfing.'

So that was my first day with Gloria in my life. Yes, I did follow her prompting and her warnings. She eventually decided to remain invisible to me, but I always sensed she was there watching over me, and my children who would one day come into the world. I often wondered why their belly buttons were so beautifully shaped.

The End

THE CAMP

Swish-swash swish-swash baa swish-swash baa swish-swash baa swish-swash baa baa baa baa swish-swash swish baa swash baa baa.

'Will we ever get to the end of these blessed sheep? We've been sitting here in this rain-soaked lane for ten minutes,' said the man behind the wheel. 'Where's the farmer? Why isn't he here to get these retched animals moving? This is ridiculous!'

'What did you expect, dear?' replied his wife who was sitting quietly beside him. 'This is the countryside after all, it's where the animals live.'

'Not on the road,' retorted Adam with a raised voice. 'They belong in a field, or something. Not on the road. I think they must have escaped; they are clearly not being driven by a dog or a man with a whistle, like I've seen on the telly. These are just milling around and rubbing themselves on my nice clean car.'

'I'm sure the car is beyond clean after that deep muddy puddle we drove through back there, dear,' said May. 'Why don't you get out and shoo them away, or something?'

'While you two just sit here in the dry laughing at me I suppose. Kelly should do it, after all she's the one who's supposed to be spending a weekend at camp learning fieldcraft, isn't she?'

'No, we can't have her out there messing up her nice uniform, Adam. If you won't do it, I will.'

'Hang on,' replied a relieved Adam, 'I think the cavalry have arrived. A tractor's coming up behind us, and a dog running along beside it. At last.'

Adam and May, with Kelly their twelve-year old daughter, watched from the safety of the car as the farmer jumped down from the tractor and stomped up to the car. He motioned for Adam to wind down his window. 'Ahh do? Been waiting here long?'

'Only the best part of an hour,' exaggerated Adam. 'Are these animals yours?'

'Reckon they are,' replied the farmer while scratching his head beneath his stained flat cap. 'Where thee be off to in this rain then?'

'We're taking our daughter here to a Girl Guide camp. According to our instructions it should be a half mile from *"The Bull"* public house which we passed a while back.'

'That's right, it's in my top field, you're nearly there. We'll soon 'ave this lot back where they belong, then you can be on yer way. Someone must 'ave left the gate open, ruddy hikers I expect.' With that, the farmer started whistling to the black and white collie who scampered around the confused woolly wanderers, even climbing on top of them to get to his various positions. Working as a well-oiled machine, man and dog very quickly drove the sheep to the field from which they had escaped. Having done so, the farmer turned to the car and waved them through.

'Dad, I don't want to be here,' came a plaintive voice from the back seat. 'It's wet and cold, and I would rather be at home in my bedroom. Please don't make me stay here.'

'I didn't drive all this way in this weather just to turn around and go back because you suddenly don't fancy it,' retorted Kelly's frustrated father. 'You begged to be allowed to go camping. It couldn't come soon enough. Now, with a bit of rain, you decide to curl up and go home.'

'Adam,' cautioned May, 'Calm down. Of course, she's having doubts. It's her first time away from us, and conditions aren't exactly ideal, are they?' Turning in her seat to look at Kelly she continued in soothing tones, 'I can understand why you're feeling this way love, but it won't be like this all the time. I felt the same as you at my first Girl Guide camp, then I found that once I was there, I loved it. The rain will soon be gone and things will look entirely different in the sunshine, you'll see.'

The car bounced slowly along the rutted lane between the high banks lining both sides. Adam gave an occasional glance in his mirror to observe his tear streaked daughter. He was feeling guilty about the way he had spoken to her a few minutes ago. If he was being honest with himself, he would not have wanted to be dumped out here in this rain either. Returning his gaze through the rain smeared windscreen he spotted a gate ahead. A flagpole of sorts was tied to the gate post with a blue and yellow flag hanging limply at the top of the pole. 'This is it,' he said, while trying to make his voice sound cheerful. 'Hope they've got the kettle on.'

Meanwhile, on the other side of the hedge, Deborah, the Guide Captain, along with Bunty, her Lieutenant, was tapping in the last peg on the last tent. Her long suffering but supportive husband was still unpacking various items from his VW Camper. He was trying to be helpful but the pain in his back, along with the necessity for the ladies and girls to be as independent as possible, prevented him from doing as much as he would have liked. 'Sounds like a car coming up,' he called.

'That may be the Blakes with Kelly. They said they would come early in case we needed a hand. Looks like they'll be a god-send as things are going,' replied Deborah as she straightened up. She looked around at the six tents, all now securely pegged and fastened. Her team of volunteers were still busily working on the covered field kitchen or placing the hay boxes, and other various equipment in each tent, whilst trying to keep it all dry. 'Come on Bunty, let's make them a drink before we break the bad news to Mr Blake.'

With the somewhat muddy car parked near the VW, as directed by the Captain, the occupants quickly ran through the rain, and into the field kitchen. 'Good morning Mrs Stephens,' said Adam apologetically. 'We were held up by a flock of wandering sheep in the lane back there.'

'*Captain* in front of the girls, or *Eagle*, my designated name, if you don't mind, Mr Blake. Sorry about the sheep, and this rain, would you like tea or coffee?'

'Coffee for both of us, um… Eagle, please, milk no sugar. Kelly will have whatever you normally give the girls.'

'Hello, Kelly, are you all right, love? It looks as though you've been crying,' exclaimed an ever-observant Captain.

'She's getting cold feet about staying,' said May. I'm sure she'll be fine once she's settled in.'

'She will,' replied the Captain. 'We often get this with first timers. The secret is to keep them busy right from the start.' Turning to her lieutenant, she said, 'Lefty, would you show Kelly where we want all the food stored.' Turning back to Adam and May, she said, 'Usually we would leave the setting up of camp for the girls to do, but with this weather we thought it advisable to get it done before they arrive. It's a shame, but it can't be helped. Mr Blake, I have to ask you an enormous favour. You see, Tim, that's my husband, has hurt his back this morning. He twisted awkwardly while carrying some of the poles from the van. Normally he would dig the hole for the lavatory, he tried, but wasn't able to do much. Some of us ladies have had a go, but there's a lot of flint under the ground and, so far, it's defeated us. I was wondering if you would give it a go? The rest of the girls are not due to arrive till after six, otherwise I would ask other fathers to form a team.'

'I see. You want me to go out in this pouring rain to dig a loo hole in flinty soil. How can I say *No* to such a tempting prospect?'

'You will? replied the Captain with relief. 'Thank you so much, finish your coffee first, then I'll show you what we have managed to do so far.'

Five minutes later, the Captain and Adam surveyed the one-foot deep hole in the soggy ground. A scattering of flint stones broke the surface of the water that covered the bottom of the hole. 'How deep do you want it?' asked Adam as he stood on the lip of the hole with a pick axe in one hand and a garden spade in the other.

'It should be four-foot-deep,' replied the Captain.

'FOUR FEET?' gasped Adam.

'Minimum, I'm sorry. Would you like to borrow Tim's gloves?'

An hour later, mother and daughter were working together in the, now complete, field kitchen. Realising that she and Adam were not going to leave before lunch, as planned, May had offered to make soup and dampers (dumplings) for the team who were clustered together discussing the plans for the weekend. May took time to peer through the falling rain to see Adam up to his knees in the hole. At that moment he was swinging the pick axe. He looked all-in and her heart went out to him. She knew her husband was a stubborn man and that he would never give up until satisfied that he had completed the task. She was very much aware of the slowly filling Porta Loo in the camper van. Tim had offered to take a turn with the spade, but Adam wouldn't hear of it after seeing the obvious pain he was in. 'How are you getting on with the bread and butter, Kelly?' she enquired of her daughter.

'Nearly done, mum. I'm feeling quite hungry now.'

'Well, we can eat as soon as Eagle has finished with the ladies. By the way, she told me that you are to receive your cookery badge after your help this morning, isn't that nice?'

'Wow, I'll also earn my camping badge this weekend, I shall feel like a real Guide.'

'You already are a real Guide, my love. Your uniform says so. Oh, they've finished their meeting. Lefty has gone across to see how your dad has got on.'

'Mum, I'm sorry about, you know, earlier. I was really cross with dad, but seeing him in that hole, working so hard for us, I just want to hug him.'

'Well, here's your chance, my love. Looks like Lefty has told him to come in for lunch, but bags I get first hug.'

There was no let-up in the weather that day. The team enjoyed the warming soup and dampers, and expressed their appreciation before going off to prepare for the arrival of the assortment of vehicles which would be bringing the girls to the long-awaited camp. During the afternoon, the farmer very thoughtfully brought several bales of straw which he laid down in the gateway and around the entrances to the lavatory, the field-shower, and the kitchen. Whilst there, he inspected the hole and congratulated Adam for a job well done.

Before her parents left, Kelly was keen to show them the tent in which she would be sharing with three other girls over the weekend, one of them being the 'Sixer' of her particular Patrol which was named *Starlings*. 'This is my bed and I can keep my things in this hay box,' she said proudly. 'We've even got a field-shower we can use when it's our turn, but I think it will be cold water.'

'It all looks very exciting, darling. And I've seen some of the plans they have for you all. I'm sure you will have a great time, and I like your tent, it looks very comfy in here out of the rain. We have to go. Are you sure you're all right now?'

'I think so, but I wish this rain would stop. It's spoiling everything,' replied the girl who was suddenly looking a lot younger than her twelve years.

'The forecast is looking good after today, you'll be alright, you'll see. We'll see you on Sunday. Have a good time.' Both parents gave their daughter a hug and quickly walked to the car before tears could be shed by any one of the three of them. As they drove down the lane, May asked, 'How are you, after all that digging? It looked so hard.'

'Not too bad, blisters and a sore back, nothing to worry about. I'm looking forward to getting home to change out of these soggy clothes though. How do you feel about going out for a meal this evening? I'm sure you've had enough of cooking for one day.'

'Good idea. I'll phone *'The Seven Stars'* now. I've got their number in my mobile.'

It was just after going to bed that night, when a call came on Adam's mobile. 'Hello? Adam Blake speaking.'

'Mr Blake, I'm sorry to be calling so late.' Adam immediately recognised the Guide Captain's voice. *'It's Kelly, she's in tears, I'm afraid she has broken her spectacles. She had to get up to go to the toilet and unfortunately stepped on them as she got out of bed in the dark. Also, one of the other young girls in her tent was sick during the evening so everything had to be sorted out. I'm afraid it's all upset Kelly too much and she's saying she wants to go home. There's no question of you arriving here this late, are you able to come over in the morning? She says that there's a spare pair of specs in her bedside cabinet.'*

'Okay Deborah, thank you for calling us, under the circumstances I can imagine she's feeling low. We'll be over in the morning and we'll bring the spare glasses. We'll probably be there between nine and ten, is that alright?'

'Yes, that's fine. Breakfasts will be over by then. Oh, by the way, Tim is working on a temporary repair with sticky tape. We'll see you in the morning then, good night.'

Turning to May, Adam asked, 'Did you get all that?'

'Yes. It's such a shame, she's been looking forward to the camping weekend for so long.'

***

Shortly after ten, Adam turned the car into the lane opposite *The Bull*. He remembered the lane being narrower and supposed it was the bright morning sunlight that made the difference. 'Soon be there, May,' he said with a feeling of relief. The drive had taken it out of him, much more than he expected. The back pain had increased over the miles. 'I expect our Kelly will be looking out for us, and anxious to get home. Last bit then … that's funny,

I don't remember all these houses being here. Where's old Dan's farm? We must have driven passed it without noticing.' Peering through the windscreen, with the sun in his eyes, Adam could see the turning ahead, where he expected it to be. 'That's it, May.' Slowing down, ready for the turn into the field, he was surprised when an ambulance emerged from the turning and passed him on the other side of the lane. 'That's a bit worrying, I hope it wasn't one of the girls,' he said with concern. He turned the car into the field and found, to his amazement, that he was still on tarmac and that the field was now lawns and flower beds. 'Where are the tents, and where have all those houses over there come from? I don't understand. I know this is the right place.' Pulling up into the kerb, Adam slowly looked around. A kiddie play area with swings and a slide, shrubs with paths meandering through them, a pond further down, more houses further over, and shops.

Adam switched off the engine and opened his door to get out. He stood there in shock. 'This cannot be! It's just over there, where that flower bed is, that I dug the hole.'

He slowly walked to the spot where he had endured so much pain. 'Roses, how the hell did they get there?' He spotted a bench nearby, upon which sat a lady with a sleeping baby in a pushchair. Slowly he walked over and said, 'Do you mind if we join you?'

The lady edged along the seat and replied with a frown, 'Yes, that's okay.'

'I dug a four-foot-deep hole just over there yesterday, in the rain, with a pick axe.' The Eagle was very pleased, you know.'

'Was it?' replied the lady as she prepared to get up from the seat.

'Oh yes, after losing my temper over those retched sheep, it calmed me down a bit, though the flint stones were a bit of a pain.' He frowned and said quietly, 'I can't see the hole now, can you see it, May?' The lady was on her feet and walking away with the pushchair, mobile phone to her ear. Adam continued gazing around. 'That's where the camp fire will be later, May, we'll have a nice singalong.'

A few minutes later, an elderly gentleman came along the path and sat down on the bench next to Adam. 'Good morning, nice day,' he observed as he rested his stick on the side of the bench. Haven't seen you here before, are you visiting?'

'No, we've come to collect our daughter. She broke her glasses last night and got upset. We're going to take her home when we find her.'

'Oh, does she live here?' the old man enquired.

'No, she's only here for the weekend.'

'I've lived here nigh on thirty years now', said the man. 'Used to be a farm, you know.'

At that moment a car pulled over behind Adam's and an elderly lady got out of the passenger's side and walked in the direction of the bench. 'Adam, thank God, I thought you might be back here. You can't keep doing this. You'll get yourself lost. I'm going to hide the car keys in future. If this keeps happening, you'll have to go into care, and you don't want that, do you?' Addressing the elderly gentleman, May said, 'I hope he's not been bothering you.'

'Oh no, not at all,' he replied. 'He said he was here to collect his daughter.'

'She died, a long time ago. A horse accident in that lane over there, a car backfired and the horse panicked. She never regained consciousness.'

A moment later, a police car pulled up behind May's neighbour's car. The officer walked over to the bench and smiled at May. 'Thought it would be your husband again. He really shouldn't be driving. I suggest you hide the keys in future. He seriously frightened a lady a while back, talking about eagles and pick axes. Take him home, ma'am, but next time …'

'I know, I'm sorry. It won't happen again. Come on, Adam, let's go home and have a nice cup of tea and a teacake, you'll like that won't you?'

'But what about Kelly,' replied a concerned Adam getting to his feet and looking around the park.

'Oh, she's alright now. She decided to stay here. Let's go, dear.' May nodded her thanks to the police officer and led her husband back to their car.

***

Shortly after nine-thirty the following morning, with the spare spectacles securely lodged in May's handbag, Adam eased the car, once again, up the narrow lane.

'How different it all looks with the sun shining,' he commented. 'Nearly there, I see the gate into the sheep pasture is closed this time. Hello? What's going on?'

Up ahead, the lane was blocked by a gaggle of uniformed girls walking up the lane toward the familiar field. As they got nearer, May said, 'It's Eagle with some of the girls, they must have been on a ramble.' It was at that moment that several of the girls turned around and immediately one of them started waving, before running back toward the car.

'Mum, dad, it's been brilliant.' She yelled as she arrived at the open passenger window. She was beaming so much she was unable to contain herself.

'Well, you look happy, Kelly, what's changed, apart from the weather, that is?'

'We've been chasing sheep all over the place, it's taken us ages. And after we've had some juice and biscuits, we're going down to the river to do some canoeing. Did you bring my glasses? We had some sausages and beans cooked over an open fire earlier, it was lovely. And this afternoon we're going on a trail hunt. After dinner tonight we're going to organise and practise some entertainment we're going to perform for all the adults around the camp fire on Sunday evening. Me and my Buddy are going to practice a song we want to sing. And tomorrow we're …'

'Hold on a moment, sweetheart, did you say you've been chasing sheep, surely not?'

'Yes. The farmer came around very early and said that his sheep had escaped again, only this time he didn't have 'Patch', that's his dog, 'cos he's got a poorly foot and can't run. So, he asked Eagle if we could help. So, we did. They were all over the place, some in the lane and some in other fields. It was such fun. Anyway, we managed to round them up with lots of shouting and a bit of shoving. Honestly, they are so stupid and …'

'Okay, luv, it sounds as if you've had a great time,' Adam butted in, but are we to assume, from what you are saying, that you've decided to stay, because we have come to take you home.'

'Oh, please don't do that, dad. I'm having a marvellous time. The farmer was ever so, ever so, pleased with us, he said if any of us ever wanted to visit, with our parents, he would let us ride his pony, I really, really, want to do that … can I?'

'We'll see, I expect so,' replied May, 'But we'll pop in and check with the farmer before we leave today.' Reaching into her handbag she continued, 'Now, let me have those broken glasses and you can have these. I see the other girls have gone into your field, jump in and we'll drive up and see Eagle.'

The remainder of the weekend passed in warm sunshine and there was much activity around the camp. The girls spent much of their time learning new skills and generally having fun. The farmer called in on Saturday afternoon to thank the girls, and to say that the problem had been caused by a faulty catch on the meadow gate, which he had been able to fix. Also, to let them know that Patch was enjoying his rest. The problem had turned out to be a thorn embedded in one of his pads. He also brought with him a large hamper of scones his wife had baked for them, along with some jam and thick cream.

On a balmy Sunday evening, along with all the parents, the girl's weekend was rounded off with the traditional camp fire entertainment and songs such as Ging Gang Gooli and the Jellyfish Song.

Four years later, Kelly started her training to become a Leader within a Rainbows Unit. She also became a competent rider, having started learning on the pony in the farm, where she spent many weekends, helping the farmer and his wife. She once told her mother that she really liked the farm and had hoped to be offered a job looking after the horses, but that was before Dan had decided to sell up to the developers after receiving an amazing offer.

The End

BABY TALK

The branches of the tree above the park bench swayed in the gentle breeze. Dappled sunlight flickered on the occupants of the bench as they enjoyed half an hour of gossip, two young ladies, each with their babies in tow, one in a highly sprung pram, the other in a three-wheeled forward-facing buggy.

'Hello,' came a voice from the pram. 'How's things?'

'Hi, not bad, nice day isn't it?' replied a voice from the buggy. 'I've just been admiring your wheels.'

'Yes, the latest in prams, very springy. Yours is cool though. I expect it's quite fast, with that tri-chassis arrangement. I noticed the calliper brakes, very sensible when you reach top speed I imagine, especially on the downward stretches. Does your mum jog a lot? My name is Oliver by the way.'

'Yes, she's in training for the marathon as it happens. Pleased to meet you, Oliver, I'm Ethan. I like your bonnet, it's sort of fluffy.'

'Yes, have to keep up with the fashion don't you,' replied Oliver.

'I suppose you do,' said Ethan. 'My hat is okay but I sometimes think I should be wearing a crash helmet, the way we fly around the park.'

'Are you on solids yet, Ethan?'

'No, I'm still on the breast.'

'Yuk,' retorted Oliver. 'I couldn't be doing with sucking body parts. My mum tried it but I wasn't having any of that nonsense, give me a good old rubber teat any day, you can have a good chew on those.'

'Oh, I can chew mine when I feel like it, but I don't think mum likes it. When I chew, she thinks I'm finished and puts me over her shoulder for a good burp.'

'Oh, you get that treatment as well, do you? Sometimes it makes me throw up all over, ... that's better, sorry, what was I saying?'

'About throwing up,' replied Ethan. 'Was that a number one or a number two you've just done?'

'A number one. I like to leave my number two's until just after my fresh nappy goes on,' replied Oliver with a grin.

'That's wicked. Was that a smile I saw, just then?'

'No, just wind. It's a strange thing,' mused Oliver, when she puts me over the shoulder she starts bobbing, I find that quite soothing, it reminds me of being in this nice springy pram. I can be bobbed till the cows come home. She soon knows it if she dares to lay me down in my cot in mid bob before I'm ready for a nap.'

'I get the bobbing treatment as well,' replied Ethan. 'Sometimes, after she puts me down, I can see my mum is still bobbing as she creeps away from the cot, I often wonder how long she does it for. Look at those two, nattering away nineteen to the dozen. Do you think they know what we're saying?'

'No,' replied Oliver, 'They don't understand *"Glug"*, a language you must forget as you start talking, I suppose.

Speaking about talking, what sort of words does your mum use when she talks to you.'

'Oh, mum mainly talks to me as though I'm one of them, you know, things like *"Right, Kid, time for a run around the park."* It's granny who comes out with the amusing words, *"Oooos my booofy, booofy boy den?"* or *"Oooo wanna come to is Gwanma den?"* The one I like best is, *"Ickle, ickle on is tum-tum."* That one always makes me laugh, till I'm sick.'

'My mum's the same,' said Oliver. 'When she's changing my nappy she always says, *"Who's got a smelly welly bum-bum then?'* It's so embarrassing, and the worst bit is after she's cleaned me up and sprinkled the powder, she likes to kiss both of my bum cheeks. What's that all about? Imagine if I was sixteen and she did that in front of my mates.'

'My mum likes blowing raspberries on my tummy,' said Ethan. 'She lays me down on my back and goes, *"Brbrbrbrbrbrbrbrbrbrbrb,"* onto my tummy, till I laugh.'

'Ho, ho, look who's coming,' said Oliver. 'It's Alice. She's a stunner, she can rock my pram any day. Her mum's not so bad looking either.' A young lady was approaching with a pushchair which, for the moment, hid the baby within.

'Good morning Oliver,' called the new arrival from within the pushchair. 'I spotted you earlier when that smart pram of yours came into the park. We were over the other side of the lake.'

'Good morning Alice, you're looking pretty in that outfit,' returned Oliver as Alice came properly into view.

'Do you like it? My granny knitted it for me, first time on today.'

'It's rather ... pink? replied Oliver with a grin. (or was it wind?) 'Have you met my friend, Ethan?'

'My, he's a bonny boy,' replied Alice.

At this moment, the three young mothers were sitting together deciding who has the worst nights. Ethen, somewhat in awe of Alice, felt that he should try to impress her, so he started blowing bubbles and kicking his legs as far as his covers would allow. Clearly impressed by this behaviour, Alice did the same, that is, until her attractive mum stooped over her to wipe her face with a napkin. To cover her embarrassment, Alice said, 'We went to the weighing clinic yesterday, I'm ten, three now, whatever that means. They all seemed pleased. On Sunday we went to church and I was Christened. *"Alice Charlotte Goodman,"* I'm a Christian now. I don't know what it means, but I enjoyed the service. Lots of friends . . . . . . Oops, sorry, that was a number two, I needed that. Where was I? Oh yes, lots of friends and relatives there, most of them were on their mobiles all the way through the service. They looked up and laughed though, when I pulled the vicar's glasses off and dropped them in the water. Have either of you two been done yet?'

'No, not me,' replied Ethan. 'My mum likes to do her own thing. She likes to be different. My dad's a test tube. She says I'm the only man she wants in her life, doesn't bother about relatives.'

'My dad can be a pain,' chipped in Oliver. 'He likes rubbing my hands over his chin and saying *"Whiskers-*

whiskers-whiskers." I can't see the point. Then he holds me up in the air and zooms me around the room and up to the ceiling. I was sick all over his head last time he did it. I enjoyed that.'

'What's that your holding, Oliver?' enquired Alice.

'It's a teething ring. I can bite on it when I feel a pain in my gums.'

'My mum just gives me a spoon to suck,' said Ethan. 'She put something from a jar on it this morning so I spat it out all down my chin, just so she knows that breast is best.'

'I got hold of my mum's mobile phone yesterday,' said Alice. 'Much better than all those coloured toys she puts around me on the blanket. I was having a good old suck when a man's voice came out of it. He was saying, *"Hello? Hello? This is Warm Heart Dating. Can I help you?"* Can you believe it? At my age? They can't wait for us to grow up, can they?'

'Well I don't know about you two, but talking about sucking, I'm feeling a bit peckish,' said Ethan.

'And me,' replied Oliver.

'Come to think of it,' said Alice.

'Right then,' said Oliver. 'After three .... one, two, three,'

'Waa, waa, waa, waa.'

'Waa-waa-hic-waa-waa.'

'Waa, waa, hic-hic, waa, hic, waa.'

Out came two bottles and one breast as the dappled sunlight continued flickering through the tree above the six of them What a life!

The End

A SPECIAL DAY

This was going to be a special day. A day like no other. A day one can only dream about, knowing that the dream will inevitably pop. Just like that, … Pop! … Gone. To be replaced by reality. The reality of knowing that the crutches will be leaning against the bedpost, just like every other morning. The knowledge that the twenty-minute walk to school along the dusty track will take closer to fifty minutes. The humiliating taunts of cruel children who have never bothered to get to know the quiet, gentle girl who can never play their games because of her useless crooked foot. Reality was the slow process of washing and dressing, of descending the bare wooden stairs on her bottom. Reality didn't allow her to help her mother with the numerous chores which were the lot of a poor farmer's wife. Collecting the eggs was as much as she could manage between a breakfast of fried bread with dripping and setting out for school. Reality was the crushing fact that she was not able to attend the end-of-school-year dance that evening.

Beth never complained, seldom cried, and always had a smile in her eyes. Those eyes could, at times, be as deep as the ocean for any who took the trouble to look into them. They concealed a depth of wisdom and compassion that was far beyond the age and experience of the twelve-year-old girl. Having said that, there was nothing in her experience that would have suggested that on this day, the day of the dance, reality was to be turned on its head. This was indeed, to be a special day.

Beth loved her hard-working parents. She understood why they seldom had time to sit with her. Life on the leased farm was hard. From dawn to dusk, year's beginning to year's end, their work never stopped. Had they been fortunate enough to have had a healthy son, life may have been easier for them. That was not to be, however. In the hard winter of the year 1862, on that small farm, twelve new-born lambs survived, four died, and one baby girl came into the world. Ten tiny fingers, ten tiny toes, but five of those toes were attached to a foot that was so deformed it was only the toes that suggested it was a foot at all. It was due to her parents being so busy that, from an early age, the child was left for long hours with her maternal grandfather who was no longer fit enough to work the farm.

The old man was a great lover of books. Naturally, Beth acquired the same love of reading, although, to be truthful, there were never enough books for the two of them to devour. When not immersed in a book, grandfather and granddaughter loved nothing better than to sit together discussing, in great depth, what they had been reading. If there was one thing, they enjoyed even more than discussing, it was arguing over their separate understanding of the topics in hand. Grandfather would sit in his rocking-chair in front of the fireplace, contentedly puffing on his smelly pipe, while Beth sat at the table alongside. This is what Beth was anticipating at the end of this, the last school day before the summer break. Not, for her, the excitement of the music, and dancing through the evening along with the other children. Not possible! ……. Not possible?...... Didn't we hear that this was to be a special day?

Carefully, the man stepped onto a stump at the foot of the aged oak tree. With his other leg, he reached a low branch, before hauling himself further up. A second branch, a little higher, offered him another opportunity to rise further from the ground. He paused. His breath came in short gasps. He looked down. He felt giddy when he realised how high he was above the moss-covered ground. At least seven foot! But when you are only four foot-ten tall, seven foot is high, isn't it? The bee's nest was still some ten foot above him. He thought of the wax he needed, and gathered his determination to reach it. He would fall rather than give up. And he did. Fall that is, not give up. A fall of seven foot can be less than a pleasant experience. The little man's breath left his body as gravity completed its task of ensuring that the man would make hard contact with the ground. 'Ouch'. It hurt. Having regained his breath, the man tried moving his limbs. *Left arm? Okay; Right arm? Okay; Left leg? Okay; Right leg? …… Right leg? …… Not okay. Oh dear, it hurts. Now what?* Gingerly, the little man, with difficulty, sat up. *So far, so good. Now if I can get the good leg to bend, I might be able to stand up on that one before trying the bad one.* It worked, he was on his feet, or on one foot with the right one still in the air six inches above the ground. With his left hand resting on the ribbed surface of the oak tree, he slowly lowered the leg. Hurt became all-consuming agony. *Fluggaty floop!!! That's not good. How am I to get home now? Can't stay in these woods all night. Why didn't I bring Tapper? He would have sorted this ankle out in no time. Shame those kids passed through fifteen minutes ago, they might have helped. I suppose they are in school by now. Crawl. No choice, crawl or hop.* Just then, as that unpleasant thought passed through his mind, a blackbird, with a flutter of wings, settled on the low branch of the oak tree. For a moment, with its bright yellow eyes, it watched the struggle of the man who had, for so long, been scattering bread crumbs in his yard for his winged friends. As quickly as it had arrived the bird flew off with a throaty call.

On this special day, Beth was delighted when she found fifteen eggs hidden amongst the straw, three more than usual. Her mother, in a rare moment of relaxation from other chores, cooked omelettes for the old man and the young girl, to celebrate, before setting out to milk Buttercup, their one and only cow.

Grandfather leaned heavily on his crooked stick at the front door, shaking his head, as he sadly watched his beloved Beth slowly hobble down the lane to the school on the other side of the woods. As difficult as the walk was for the girl, she always enjoyed that time alone. She loved those enchanting woods with so many exciting things to gaze at with each passing season. The new buds of spring along with the carpet of bluebells and the yellows of early primroses, the opening of fresh green leaves. Summer had arrived. Insects busily going about their business with hums, clicks and buzzes. Squirrels scampering along the ground and up into the green canopy above, or simply sitting on their haunches nibbling on nuts held between their little paws. Grass-snakes slithering from shade to shade. Varieties of birds whistling their respective calls. Never a moment when there was nothing to take her attention. Half way through the woods however, a blackbird demanded Beth's attention in a most insistent way. It landed on her head.

The girl froze. She hadn't seen it coming. She had no idea what was on her head, but correctly guessed it was a bird. What else could it be? Slowly letting go of one of her crutches she raised her hand to her head until it came into contact with the soft feathers. Before she had time to move her hand away the bird had hopped onto her outstretched fingers. Moving it as slowly as she could, Beth lowered her hand to eye level. The bird sat there looking into her eyes. 'Hello little friend,' she said quietly. 'What are you doing here?' The blackbird sang its beautiful song for a moment, then with a sudden beat of its wings it flew along the track a few yards before landing on the ground. Once again it sang its song. Beth returned the crutch to its position under her armpit and hobbled forward. The bird remained where it had settled until Beth was nearly on top of it. With a trill of alarm, it flew further on and remained on the ground until Beth had reached it for a second time. This time, rather than fluttering further along the track, it flew up in front of Beth then turned and landed again, on her head. Before the girl had time to react, it took off and flew across nearby bushed to disappear from view.

That was strange, Beth thought. *I have never heard of that happening before. What was it doing? It was almost as though he was trying to tell me something. Well, it's gone now.* Suddenly, the sound of the blackbird singing amongst the bushes crowded Beth's mind. She remained fixed to the spot. She then noticed that all the other bird calls had ceased. Even the leaves in the canopy seemed to have stopped rustling. The hidden bird continued singing.

The little man was nearing exhaustion. His knees were bruised and sore. His ankle throbbed with pain. *Must be near the track now,* he thought, with hope, more than certainty. Everything looked so different at this level. Suddenly a blackbird settled on the branch of a bush alongside him and started his song. He looked up and smiled. Blackbirds had always been his favourite. One of them was frequently perched on his fence watching out for the bread crumbs. The bird continued its song in the silence of the woods, for all the other birds had ceased their songs. The man rested his head on his hands and listened. A rustling sound in the bushes distracted him. It was slowly coming closer. He was startled when suddenly, in front of his face, a thick stick descended onto the ground, then a foot, followed by another thick stick. The bird ceased its song as a sweet voice said, 'Oh my.'

'Good morning young lady. I would stand and bow if I could, but as you see, I'm a little discommoded. Tell me, why are you wandering alone in these woods, and off the track, such as it is.'

'I'm always the last to come along here to school. The others don't want anything to do with me, and they won't wait for me. I didn't mean to leave the track, but I was following a blackbird who seemed to want me to find you. Oh, you're hurt, how can I help?'

'Well now, that is indeed an interesting question. Do you perchance happen to have a cart? .... or a horse? ..... a donkey perhaps? .... No, I imagine you haven't, what a pity.'

'Sir, I see that you have hurt your leg. We need to get you home. Where would that be?'

'Near the school, sweet girl. Possibly the place you were heading for. I own the little shop opposite.'

'The cobblers! You're the cobbler?'

'Yes, why does that surprise you?'

'But, you're so ......'

'Small, you were about to say?'

'Oh no! ... Well, yes, I suppose I was. I'm sorry, I didn't mean to offend you Mr Cobbler. How did you hurt yourself?'

'I fell out of a tree, a big oak tree.'

'But what were you doing up an oak tree?'

'You are an inquisitive girl, aren't you? If you must know, I was after wax from the bees. Wax is good for my shoes.' Beth frowned and inspected the man's shoes. 'No, not these shoes, I mean the ones that I make. Now that I'm a little rested, I think I must crawl on. Can you help me up, please?'

'Oh, you don't have to crawl, Mr Cobbler. You can use one of my crutches. We can cobble ... I mean *hobble* .... along together.'

'What is your name, my dear?'

'Elizabeth, but my family call me Beth.'

Well then, Beth. Let's see how we get on with one crutch apiece, shall we?'

As they stood together, each holding a crutch, the blackbird sang a beautiful song for a moment before taking to the wing and disappearing amongst the trees. What a sight the two of them made when they arrived in the square. Each with one foot held in the air as they swung along together, chatting nineteen to the dozen. Beth followed the little cobbler into his shop in order to recover her crutch before entering the school, just as morning playtime started. All the children were excitedly talking about the forthcoming dance and what they would be wearing, and with whom they would have the first dance. They were not so engrossed however, that they forgot to jeer at the cripple who had come to school later than ever that morning.

The moment the door had closed behind his new friend, the cobbler found Tapper under some leather offcuts on the workbench. With the words, 'Hibberdy-jiggerdy, rumperty-foo, fix this ankle just like new.' he touched the ankle with Tapper, who was in fact, a little hammer made with the wood of a Snonker tree, which can only be found in Cobballand. The ankle was instantly snonked to perfection.

'Now, let's see what we can find in the loft for my friend,' said Mr Cobbler to Tapper. For the remainder of the day, the little shop opposite the school resounded to the sound of tap-tap, tap-tap, tap-tap, tap-tap. Beth, the last child to emerge through the school gate during the afternoon, stopped for a moment to listen to the rhythmic sound. Later, after finishing her tea of potato soup with chunky bread, Beth sat with her grandfather by the fireplace to tell him about the encounter with the blackbird and the cobbler.

'The cobbler, you say? Now there's a strange fellow if ever I saw one,' mused the old man. 'He seems to have been the same age for as long as I have known him.'

At that moment, there came a knock on the door. They both listened as Beth's father answered the door. Following a brief muffled conversation, the living room door was opened by Beth's father who said, 'A visitor for you, Beth.' It was the cobbler who stepped around her father with a smile on his face and a brown paper-wrapped parcel under his arm.

Beth rose to her feet, holding onto the table. 'Mr Cobbler! What a lovely surprise!'

'Hello Princess,' said the cobbler. 'I have something for you.' He held out the parcel.

'For me? But it isn't my birthday. I won't be thirteen till October,' replied the puzzled girl.

'Not your birthday perhaps, but for you, this day is even more special. Here, take it.' Beth looked first at the parcel, then at her grandfather who was sitting nodding, his pipe bobbing up and down. Then she looked at her parents, both of whom were standing in the doorway, smiling.

With trembling fingers, she took the parcel and carefully unwrapped it. 'Shoes!' In her hands were a pair of the most beautiful shoes she had ever seen. They were so delicate, they glistened in the light coming from the window. Each had a bow of velvet which contrasted perfectly with the deep red leather. A pair of shoes, indeed fit for a princess. A tear ran down the girl's cheek. The shoes were a wonderful gift that she could never accept. She had never, ever, worn a pair. She barely had a left foot upon which to fit a shoe. *So kind, but how could he ever have thought I can wear them? And even if I could, where would I wear such beautiful shoes?*

'Beth, would you do me the honour of trying on my humble gift?'

'But I can't, you see ...'

'Please? Try them on. It will be fine. You'll see.'

Beth glanced up at her mother. She was wringing her pinafore in her clenched fists and her face was crumpled in pain. Her father just stood in the doorway giving no clue to his feelings. She turned around and looked at her grandfather who simply said, 'Go ahead lass.'

The troubled girl sat down on the upright chair, rested her crutches on the corner of the table and slipped her right foot into the shoe. To her amazement, it fitted perfectly. She hesitated and looked up at her Mr Cobbler who, with a slight smile, nodded toward the left shoe which was sitting on the table where Beth had placed it. Slowly she removed the thick sock that covered her withered foot. With a sense of humiliation, having exposed the foot to a comparative stranger, and knowing that this was all a waste of time, she lifted the shoe and bent forward to fit it over the stub at the end of her leg. No one moved, or spoke, allowing the song of a blackbird in the garden to infiltrate into the silence.

'It fits,' breathed Beth. No one spoke. 'Grandpa! It fits! I can feel my toes wiggling inside, just like the other one.'

'Could you ever doubt that shoes that I have made, with the help of Tapper, wouldn't fit?' said the cobbler with raised eyebrows. Now, Princess, stand up and try them.'

Reaching for her crutches, Beth made to rise from the chair.

'No, sweet child,' said her new friend. 'Without the crutches. You no longer need them.'

'But ...'

'But me no Buts. Just stand and walk.' As he was saying this, the cobbler stooped down, looked into the bewildered girl's eyes with an encouraging smile and nodded. As Beth raised herself from the chair, her mother stepped forward ... to help? ... To stop her? But she was held back by her husband. Beth was on her feet ... both feet. She gingerly eased her weight onto the left foot before stepping forward with the right one. She then swung her weight onto the right foot and stepped forward again. She was walking. She was walking! She walked into the outstretched arms of her sobbing mother. The singing of the blackbird in the garden was drowned out as father, mother, grandfather and daughter all spoke at the same time. All were talking gleefully, all, that is, except the cobbler who stood there smiling while gently massaging the handle of his little hammer which nestled deep in his pocket. As the excited chattering ceased, he said, 'Beth, your foot is now sound and healthy, and will remain so. Now, if you would care to change into your best dress, with your parent's permission, I would like to take you to the school dance in a cart I have borrowed for the purpose. I will leave you there until it's time to bring you home. My dear girl, you are beautiful within your very being, and now you are equally beautiful on the outside. I imagine you will have no problem finding many partners for the dance this evening. I know you will forgive them for their fear of something they couldn't understand.'

'Thank you, Mr Cobbler, from the bottom of my heart,' replied Beth. 'And please thank Tapper for me, whoever he is.'

A blackbird was clearly heard by all, as the room fell silent on that special day.

The End

THE SPITFIRE

Dressed in an old beige gabardine mac, black wellington boots and a red woollen hat, rather like a tea-cosy, Mrs Coleman bent down to pick up her shears. Then, remembering her knitted mittens, she returned the shears to the ground and dug the green woollen mittens from her pocket and slipped them on. Satisfied, she again bent to retrieve the shears from the ground. All of this had taken a full two minutes. She stood for a moment and glanced at the length of hedging she had clipped in the last three hours. With a sigh, she turned and looked along the length of ragged hedging still to be trimmed. It was twice as much more than the section she had already done. Feeling somewhat daunted, she forced herself to recommence the mindless task she had set herself.

'You should have set a line across, Mrs.'

'What? Who's there?'

'You're not doing it straight. It's going all up and down like a roller-coaster. I could do it better, even without a string to guide me.' The old lady looked up to see a boy peering over the hedge. *Cheeky beggar.*

'Go on, be off with you. Less of your lip and get back to wherever it is you came from,' she shouted.

'Just suggestin' that's all. Your business if you wants a raggedy hedge.'

In exasperation, Mrs Coleman replied, 'There is nothing wrong with my hedge,' realising as she did so, that her hard work was resulting in a hedge which did indeed resemble a roller-coaster. 'Who are you?' she asked crossly. 'I'll come and tell your mother how rude you are. What is your name?'

'Ain't got a mum. Not no more. The bombs got her. Took the wardens and the brigade ages to dig us out. I 'ardly 'ad a scratch, but she was dead by the time they got to 'er. Me name's Norman.'

'Well, if you don't go away and leave me alone, I'll tell you father.'

'You'll 'ave to wait fer a bit. 'E's at sea in a frigate. Been gone since the funeral, ages ago. Me Aunt looked after me for a bit, then they stuck a label on me and put me on a train with lots of other kids, and 'ere I am, in the country, on a pongy farm.'

'Well, I'm sorry about your mother. However, I'm sure someone is wondering where you've got to, so run along and leave me to my work.'

'Okay Mrs, I get the message. You're not very friendly, are you?'

'Friendly? What use have I with friends? They just let you down when you need them most. Now, go away and annoy someone else.' With there being no reply, Mrs Coleman continued her clip-clip-clipping for a minute or two before curiosity got the better of her. She placed the shears on the ground and limped over to the solid gate, which she always kept closed. Quietly sliding the bolt, she lifted the latch and pulled the gate open. Standing in the middle of the lane, with hands in his pockets, was the grinning boy. He was wearing a grubby grey shirt, short trousers of an indiscriminate colour, and grey socks hanging half way down his thin lower legs which disappeared into his sandals. His brown hair looked as though it had not seen brush or comb for weeks.

'Hello Mrs. Thought you might come out fer a look.'

'The impertinence!' exclaimed the old lady. 'Why would I want to look at a scruffy urchin like you? As it happens, I just wanted to check the hedge from outside. Aren't you needed at the farm? I imagine it would be Coopers Farm to which you refer?'

'Yea, that's the one. Done all me chores fer the day. They won't want me back till tea-time.' At that moment the quietness of the morning was disturbed by an approaching aircraft. It was low and quite possibly heading for the nearby RAF airfield. Norman forgot the old lady in his excitement as he shielded his eyes to watch the aircraft pass close overhead. 'Cor! A spitfire. 'Spect he's been out shooting down jerry bombers. I'm gonna fly one of them when I'm older.'

'You're *going* to fly one of *those*,' corrected the lady.

'Yea, that's what I said din' I?'

'So, you like aeroplanes then?'

'Not 'alf. Spits are the best, but Hurricanes are okay too.'

Mrs Coleman looked at the boy for a moment, trying to come to a decision. He was scruffy and dirty, his vocabulary suggested that he was from a poor family, possibly from London, which was suffering so badly at the moment. He said that his mother was killed and his father is away. Poor lad, what harm can it do? 'Would you like a glass of lemonade, Norman you said your name is, didn't you?'

'Sright, and yes please, I 'ave got a bit of a thirst on. Shall I wait here, Mrs?'

'Mrs Coleman. My name is Brenda Coleman. You may call me Mrs Coleman. You can come up to the house, I have something you might like to see.' Brenda noticed the boy's hesitation and said, 'It's perfectly safe. You see, I used to be the well-respected village school teacher. That is, until …. Oh, never mind that. If you prefer, I'll bring your lemonade out here.'

'Naa, that's okay. I'll come to the 'ouse,' replied the boy, having made up his mind that, should it be necessary, he could easily outrun the old lady, especially if she expected him to do sums, or something rotten like that.

'Then follow me, young man.'

Having stepped through the gate, the boy gazed at the large three-storied house before him. It was surrounded by long grass which might have been well manicured lawns at some time in the past. There were a number of overgrown flower beds alongside the cracked drive which led to the ivy-covered house. The open front door was beneath a porch which was guarded by two lichen-covered stone lions. The old lady led the speechless boy through the front door into a large hall which contained a tiled fireplace, several closed doors and a winding staircase. The walls were hung with various paintings of severe looking people. 'This way, said Brenda. The kitchen is through here.' Norman followed her through one of the doors into a room with a large oak table in the centre. 'There's a sink over there,' Brenda said while pointing to a butler sink. 'You'll find a tablet of Pears soap. I suggest you might like to wash your hands before sitting here at the table. I'll pour us both some lemonade. Would you like a piece of jam sponge to go with it?'

'Yes please, Mrs Coleman,' replied the boy while turning on the tap.

A few minutes later, Norman was sitting alone at the table with a glass of non-fizzy lemonade. Also, with a china plate set before him, upon which sat a very large portion of jam sponge. His stomach rumbled as he waited for the old lady to return to the kitchen, having told him that she wouldn't be a moment. He wasn't sure if he could start without her, but decided he would play it safe. As he sat there gazing at the sponge, the sound of another spitfire passing overhead momentarily distracted him, wishing he could see it. With the aircraft engine noise diminishing into the distance, Brenda returned to the kitchen, holding something behind her back with both hands. 'Why, you haven't eaten you sponge, don't you like it?'

'I wasn't sure if I should wait. Can I start now?'

'Of course. Go ahead, do you want a fork?'

'Naa, you're all right, what ya got behind yer back?'

'Here.' Held in Brenda's hands was a perfectly carved model of a spitfire. She carefully placed it on the table near the boy's plate. The sponge was forgotten as Norman looked at the model in awe. *Undercarriage, prop, canopy, even a pilot under the Perspex. Painted with the right colours.*

'Wow! It's brilliant, just like a real one.' Norman leaned forward to take a closer look. 'It's even got tiny swastikas under the canopy to show how many enemy planes it's shot down. Where's it come from?'

'I can see that you're impressed. My late husband made it in his spare time. Like you, he loved anything to do with aeroplanes. He was a clever man.'

'Was he a pilot? Did he get shot down?' enquired the boy as he continued to stare at the model.

'No,' replied Brenda, 'He was the local doctor until …' She hesitated and picked up the model. 'He finished this model the day before the accident. He was well respected around these parts, even well loved, I would say. The village folk have never got over it. Some have never forgiven me. You see? I killed him.'

'Did you mean to?' asked the startled boy.

'He used to have to start the car with a handle. *"Winding up the springs",* he would say. It was being stubborn that morning. Although I can't drive, Clive asked me to sit in the driver's seat and press the pedals as he turned the handle. I don't know exactly what happened. All I remember was the engine starting and the car shooting forward. It's all a blank now. He died three days later in hospital. Pneumonia. It all happened over two years ago. That model has become very special to me. I keep it in the lounge.'

'Thanks for showing it to me, can I hold it?'

'Yes, Norman, I know you will be careful with it.' Jam sponge forgotten; the boy carefully lifted the model from the table, to examine the detail. 'You are the only other person to have seen it. In fact, you are the only person I have had a conversation with for over a year. Sad, don't you think? Now, eat your sponge, Norman. Then I should go out and tackle that roller-coaster hedge, and you must have better things to do than listen to a poor old lady sharing her woes.'

'Can I come again? Praps tomorrow? To look at the spitfire, I mean.'

'You would be most welcome, but promise me, you will ask Mr Cooper if that will be all right. Promise?'

'Oh, I'm sure he won't mind,' replied Norman as he reluctantly returned the spitfire to the table.

'Promise me!'

'Okay, Mrs Coleman, I promise.'

***

It was late into the evening, after the blackout curtains had been drawn, that Norman had the opportunity to talk to his hosts, Mr and Mrs Cooper. The day's work was done, although it was never finished on this hard-working farm.

Norman had been made welcome when he had arrived and been allocated to them. They encouraged the boy to undertake simple tasks around the farm, when not at the village school, tasks such as mucking out, sweeping the yard, or collecting eggs, but they were careful not to treat him as free labour, believing the boy should have some freedom to be able to recover from his loss. They had become fond of the lad and knew they would miss him when he eventually returned home to his father in London. Their own son, Robert, had been killed during the Battle of Britain while defending his airfield as a gunner. At this moment Norman was sitting at the kitchen table with the Coopers, enjoying a meal of stew made from leftovers.

'What have you been up to today, Lad?' enquired Mr Cooper while peering at Norman over the top of his spectacles.

'I walked over to the airfield this mornin' to watch the planes goin' in and out. Then, on me way back, I met a new friend, an old lady who said she used to be the village teacher, and her husband was the doctor.'

'That would be Mrs Coleman,' said Mrs Cooper. 'She's a bit of a recluse since the doctor died, blames herself for his death. Last time I saw her was in the village shop months ago, she didn't want to talk to anyone, she just took her change and left without a word. I remember that some of the folk around here were unkind to her because her husband was so popular.'

'That's right,' said Mr Cooper. Although the coroner's verdict was accidental death, some of them thought she should be done for manslaughter, as if she hadn't suffered enough. How did you get to meet her, Lad?'

'She was cuttin' 'er 'edge, but not gettin' it straight, so I told 'er 'ow to do it better.'

'That must have impressed her,' said Mr Cooper with a chuckle. Did she give you an ear full?'

'She invited me in to 'ave some lemonade and cake, and then she showed me a model spitfire that 'er 'usband made before the accident. It's brilliant.'

'She invited you in?' responded Mrs Cooper in amazement.

'Yea, she said I can come again, but only if you say it's alright.'

Both adults were lost in their own thoughts for a moment or two. 'Tell you what,' said Mr Cooper eventually. 'Tomorrow, you and I can take a drive over there in the old Austin. You can introduce us and I can have a bit of a chat with her.'

'That's a good idea, John. You could invite her back for tea,' said Mrs Cooper. 'The poor soul must be so lonely; it would be good to let her know that she's as much a part of our community as those who like to make trouble for folk'.

'What say you, Norman, is that a good idea, do you think?' asked Mr Cooper.

'Yea, that'll be great. Just one thing though. Can we take some shears with us, and a scythe, oh, and a ball of string? I might stay there for the day.'

***

The following morning, small fluffy clouds drifting across a blue sky, sparrows chattering in the hedgerow, an old Austin motor car chugged up the lane. The old lady paused from her clipping as a familiar scruffy figure alighted from the passenger side of the vehicle, which had come to a standstill by her gate. 'Good mornin' Mrs Coleman. This is Farmer Cooper come to 'ave a word. I've brought some sheers so I can 'elp ya. Then I'm gonna 'ave a go at ya lawn.'

'Bless my Soul,' muttered the bemused lady. *I imagine he has come to tell me not to encourage the boy. But then, why the extra shears, and, is that a scythe he's unloading?*

'Mrs Coleman,' said Mr Cooper while lifting his cap. 'Thought I would pop over and introduce myself, although we met when our Bob attended your school years ago. He thought you were the best teacher he ever had.'

'Yes, I remember Robert Cooper,' the old lady said with a smile. 'A nice lad and a pleasure to teach, although his spelling never improved, try as I might. I remember most of my pupils, you know.'

'Seems a long time ago now, a different world. Anyhow, young Norman here, has taken to you and has referred to you as his new friend. Well, any friend of his is a friend of me and the wife, Diane. We were wondering if you would like to join us for a meal this evening. If you would do us the honour, I'll come round at six-o-clock to pick you up. Meanwhile, the boy has said he wants to stay here for the day to help you. Does any of that suit you?'

With a tear threatening to spill from her eye, Brenda grinned and replied, 'It suits me very well indeed, Mr Cooper. It just happens that my late husband kept some very fine wine in his cellar. I have never touched it, so this may be a good time to take the dust off of one or two, which I shall bring with me. Does that suit you, Mr Cooper?'

'That will suit me very well indeed, Mrs Coleman,' replied a grinning farmer who hadn't tasted wine since before the war. 'The name is John by the way.'

The evening meal went well and lasting friendships were started. Later that night, after retiring to bed, Diane commented, 'Funny how it takes a child a moment to make a friend while us adults can take years. How do they do it, I wonder?'

The End

GOLD FEVER

The distant figure that Brett had first noticed over an hour ago hadn't seemed to come any closer. Even allowing for the heat haze, which distorted the image of anything over a quarter of a mile away, he thought the figure would have been more distinct by this time. Holding his hand up to shield his eyes, Brett peered intensely into the distance. The far-off mountains danced in the haze. A lake appeared in the desert-like prairie, a lake which wasn't there. Returning his gaze to the figure, he noticed, for the first time, the vultures circling in the air, four, no, more than four, closer to seven. Difficult to tell from this distance. Sitting in the shade of the wooden stoop, booted feet resting on the back of his slumbering dog, Brett continued studying the vague blob which should not be there. Nothing had changed, or perhaps it had. The vultures, they were circling lower. *Darn! Guess I'll have to go take a look. Something's not right out there.* Reluctantly, getting to his feet, the rancher nudged the panting dog and moaned, 'Come on Pip, time to move out of here.'

For his sins, Brett had been unanimously elected to be the Sheriff of the small single-street town of Two Rivers. He owned a small holding on the edge of the town, in which he bred horses, which were always in demand in that area of The West. He kept himself pretty much to himself, apart from two reliable and honest hands he had taken on in the earlier days of his business. He was also known to visit Morag, the Irish school teacher, on rare occasions. Not much was known about her. She had rolled into town some six or seven months after the previous teacher had died, and had been welcomed with open arms. She turned out to be a bit of a red-headed fire-brand who was not afraid to speak her mind, particularly in respect of the lack of a school building. She strongly objected to having to use one of the saloons, as there was not even a church in the town, which could have been used for the purpose.

As Sheriff, Brett had an office equipped with a single cell, a few doors down from the saloon. This was usually locked as Two Rivers was in the main, a law-abiding town. As it happened, this very day, he was looking forward to a meal at Morag's place. Brett regarded her amazing apple pies as compensation for the ear-chewing he would, no doubt, have to endure about the lack of civilised facilities in the town. In honour of the occasion he had had a shave that morning, the first for over two weeks. The last thing he wanted right now was to have to ride out, investigating something that could possibly ruin his plans for the evening.

Stepping off the stoop, Brett called out to the young man he had previously been watching. He was hammering nails into one of the corral fences which needed fixing. 'Slim, stop that for now, and saddle up. You and me have some riding to do.'

'Sure, boss. Where we going?'

'Don't rightly no yet, son. Best fill a couple of water pouches.'

Ten minutes later, the two riders set out from the ranch, heading for the place where Brett estimated he had last seen the unusual object through the heat haze. At that moment, it was no longer visible, although the hated vultures were still evident as they continued circling in the same area of sky. *Someone, or something's in trouble out there,* Brett was thinking. With a flick of the reins and applied pressure on his horse's flank, he eased it into a canter, closely followed by Slim who was wondering why they were out in the heat of the near-desert. He didn't have too long to wait for an answer however, for soon they were approaching their objective. Brett was the first to realise that it was a mule that had attracted the birds. The animal was clearly beyond help, as the vultures continued their quarrelsome feast. As he took in the gruesome scene, Brett was instantly alerted to the fact that the mule was harnessed and loaded with full saddle bags. Outraged, Slim sprang from his saddle and ran amongst the ugly winged creatures, kicking out and swinging his arms while shouting his hatred. Most of the birds took to the air, although they clearly had no intention of going too far away from their meal. One or two however, were too fully gorged to be able to leave the ground. These creatures had to hop as best they could in order to avoid being kicked by the young man. Satisfied, Slim returned, to see Brett standing in his stirrups peering around. It didn't take him long to see more vultures soaring a little higher, off to the right. That, and the dragging marks in the sandy soil, was all the evidence they needed to know where they would find the mule's owner.

He was an old man, a leathery face with peeling skin above a sun-bleached ragged beard. His head was bare, thin wisps of hair failing to protect it from the burning sun. His clothes were torn and filthy. He was slumped in an upright position, his back resting against a boulder. His eyes were closed, cracked lips slightly open. Brett dismounted and walked over to the still figure. A brief inspection told him that the man was still alive, although seemingly unconscious. Bending over to listen for any sign of breathing, he was startled when a weak voice whispered, 'Shoot me.'

'Slim! Pass me the water, quickly!'

With one arm around the man's shoulders, Brett poured a small drop of water onto his necktie and held it to the cracked lips. After a brief moment, the man's tongue appeared. It slowly licked the moistened lips. Brett poured more water onto the damp material and held it on the lips. Clearly with difficulty, the eyes slowly opened, although didn't focus on Brett's face. Taking the water pouch from Slim's outreached hand, Brett held the top to the moistened lips, allowing a trickle to pass into the open mouth. The man gave a weak cough, then sipped a little from the pouch. Brett was careful not to pour too much too soon. The man moved his face away from the pouch and whispered, 'Don't drag this out, stranger. Shoot me.'

'No one is shooting anyone, mister. You're alive and we aim to keep you that way. Can't say the same for your mule however. Sorry about that.' Turning to the lad, Brett said, 'Slim, ride back to the ranch and fetch the buckboard. Tell Jed to ride into town and find the doc to warn him were bringing this hombre in.'

As Slim rode away, Brett became concerned, as the old man appeared to become agitated and was clearly trying to say something. Leaning forward, Brett thought he detected the word, *"Mule"*.

'Don't you worry about that, friend, just concentrate on getting your strength up. Here, take another sip of water.' The man slowly slumped against Brett and it was clear that he had become unconscious again. It took nearly an hour for Slim to return with the buckboard. Between them, they lifted the unconscious man onto the blanket covered floor. Turning the team, Brett steered the buckboard in the direction of the dead mule, with Slim now riding Brett's mount. As they approached, the vultures were again ripping the innards out of the carcass. Slim once again expressed his revulsion as he swept into the feathery fray. Brett pulled up the buckboard and activated the brake handle with his foot before jumping down. 'Don't fret so much, Slim,' shouted Brett. 'They're doing what's natural, and keeping the prairie healthy at the same time. Leave 'em be. Now let's get that harness and saddlebags off.'

The old man remained unconscious throughout the journey over a bumpy track. Riding into town, Brett noticed the curious looks their passage was receiving from folk on the boardwalks as they passed along the dusty road between the wooden buildings. Pulling up at the doctor's house, Brett was relieved to see his old friend waiting expectantly in the open doorway. With the help of two passing cow-hands, they lifted the old man from the bed of the buckboard into the doctor's surgery. 'Okay, Doc, I'll leave him with you fer a bit. If you need me, send Rose over to my office. I'll take his saddlebags into safe-keeping and write up my report. See if you can git his name and how he came to be out there in that state.'

An hour or so later, Brett knocked on the doctor's door, to be let in by his housekeeper. 'How is he, Rose?' he enquired of the rotund lady whose gleaming teeth and whites of the eyes stood out on her smiley black face.

'Yo best be askin' the doctor, sheriff. His patient is in bed in de back room. Last I sees of him he wus alive and tryin' to say somethin', but he ain't got no voice back yet. No siree.'

'Thanks Rose. How's your Sam?'

'Oh, he be doin' alright. Enjoys his job in dat saloon, though he never touches none ob dat whiskey. Otherwise he don't get to share my bed fer a week.'

'Give him my regards,' said Brett with a chuckle. 'And tell him he's always welcome to visit the ranch, and you, of course.'

'I'll surely be tellin' him dat. Thank ye kindly sheriff.'

As the conversation came to an end, the surgery door opened to reveal the doctor in his usual waistcoat and leather neck-tie. 'Hi Brett. Reckon you found him just in time. Touch and go, though no obvious injuries as far as I can tell. We'll have to wait it out. He did try telling me his name though. Something like Teddy, I think. The other name sounds like Boyle, but I could be wrong.'

Later, with the sun touching the distant mountains, filling the sky with colours of gold, orange and finally, deep purple, Brett knocked on Morag's door and used his hat to brush away the dust from his jacket and pants, as he waited to be let in. He grinned at the handsome red-head as the door swung open. 'Howdy Ma'am, I hope you are still expecting me?'

'Good evening Brett, of course I am. Dinner's nearly done. Come on in and help yourself to a whiskey, you know where it is.' Morag quickly turned and left her guest to make himself at home as she rushed into the kitchen to save the gravy. Brett followed her in, and made for the sideboard where he poured himself a drop of the amber liquid before easing himself into an easy-chair. As he sat there enjoying his whiskey and listening to the busy clash of various pots and pans coming from the kitchen, his mind returned to the old man. *What happened? How did he come to be in that state? What was in the saddlebags, causing them to be so heavy?* Brett had resisted the temptation to open the worn leather bags before locking them into his safe. *Just hope the old man pulls through, that's all,* he mused as he emptied the glass.

'Anything I can do?' he called through the open door while appreciating the mouth-watering aroma filling the air.

'All in hand,' came the reply, a moment before a loud crash made Brett leap from the chair.

'It's okay,' called Morag. 'Dish was a bit hotter than I expected. No harm done. Just finishing, you can come and take a seat now.'

Brett needed no second invitation to come into the kitchen where he seated himself before a piled plate of steak with roast potatoes and various vegetables, all covered in a rich gravy. He was in his elements as he picked up his cutlery to tuck in.

'Haven't you forgotten something, Brett?' asked Morag, who had taken the seat opposite and was staring at her guest with raise eyebrows.

'Oh yea, the salt and pepper,' he replied with a grin.

'You know full well what I'm talking about Mr Yates.'

'Well, I did wipe my feet when I came in, can't think what ……'

'Brett Yates!' scolded Morag while folding her arms. 'If you continue to act like a heathen, that's how you will be treated, I'll put your dinner outside for you to scoff. Now, the grace, if you please.'

'Shucks ma'am, why didn't you say, if that's what you wanted?' replied Brett with a broader grin. Shutting his eyes, he said, 'For this here steak, and for the apple pie I know is coming, oh and for the cooking skill of this fine woman, Lord I give mighty thanks. Now, can we get started?'

The meal was every bit as good as Brett had anticipated. *Attractive, sassy, bright, and a good cook to boot, yes this was the night to reel her in and propose.* Cutting into the steak, Brett asked, 'What sort of day have you had?'

'Morag frowned as she replied, 'We're doing the best we can, but without a school building, or proper equipment, it's a constant struggle. I love the children, but, as things are, not the job. Sorry, I know you've heard all of this before, but you did ask. How's your day been?' she asked with a grin. 'Rounded up any rustlers? Or caught a gang of bank robbers? Or clapped some drunks in your jail? Or has it been exciting?'

'Well as a matter of fact, it's been kind of interesting. Brought an old timer in from the prairie, just short of the ranch. His mule had died and he was in a bad way, more dead than alive. He must have come from a fair distance to be in the state he was in. Doc's got him at his place, but it's a bit touch and go.'

'Poor man,' said Morag. 'So, you have no idea who he might be?'

'Well, apparently he had nothing in his clothing to give a clue, although he had some saddlebags, which are in my safe. If he doesn't come round, we'll have to see what's in them. That may give us a clue. In a moment of near consciousness, he apparently told Doc his name is something like Teddy Boyle, but he wasn't all that clear, so the Doc is unsure.'

'Oh my god!' gasped Morag. It couldn't be, could it? Brett, I have to see him!'

'What?'

'Now! Come on. We have to go now!'

'But we haven't finished dinner, and I've got something to ask …'

'Now!'

Darn it all, what's got into the woman? Haven't even got to the apple pie yet.

'Are you coming?' shouted Morag. 'Or are you going to let me walk down the dark street on my own?' She was already at the door, shrugging into her overcoat.

In less than ten minutes, Morag was banging on the doctor's door, with Brett standing behind her. He was still confused and a little concerned regarding the woman's behaviour. *Why would she want to visit a sick old man at this time of night?* he asked himself.

'Brett? Morag? What's happened? A shooting, or something? I'll get my bag.' The doctor had opened the door in his dressing gown and was peering out at the couple who had disturbed his end of day glass of Brandy.

Morag unceremoniously barged passed the startled doctor and turned to demand, 'Where is he?'

'Dear lady, would you kindly tell me who you are looking for,' said the doctor. 'I can assure you that no one has come into my house this evening.' Turning his eyes to Brett, he said, 'Perhaps you could explain this intrusion, sheriff?'

'Wish I could, Doc, I'm as much in the dark as you are, although I've a feeling it's got something to do with the old timer I brought in earlier.'

'That's right, Doc, said Morag. 'Sorry, that was rude of me. Can I see him?'

'You need not concern yourself, Morag,' replied the doctor. 'Mrs Jacklin has agreed to do any nursing that's required. Anyhow, he's asleep right now.'

'I understand, doctor, but please let me see him. I promise not to disturb him.'

'Well, if you insist,' replied the doctor, thoughtfully. 'I don't doubt you have your reasons, though I don't for the life of me …'

'Please! Take me to him. Please?'

'Very well, follow me,' sighed the exasperated doctor. 'You too Brett. Let's make a party of it.'

The doctor led the way to the room in which he kept his sick patients. The door had been left open to enable him to keep the old man under observation without disturbing him. He stepped aside to allow Morag to enter the room, and watched as the teacher stepped over to the bed where the unconscious man was laid under a blanket.

Looking down at the prone figure, Morag said quietly, 'His name isn't Boyle, it's Doyle, Paddy Doyle.'

'How could you possibly know …'

'He's my grandfather. I had given up hope.' Brett was fortunately close enough to catch her as Morag sank toward the floor.

***

'I don't understand any of this, Morag. How come your grandfather suddenly appears out of the blue, just like that? Why didn't you ever tell me you have a grandfather? For that matter, how come you arrived in Two Rivers alone? Have you got any other family tucked away somewhere?' The two of them were back in Morag's kitchen eating cold apple pie, having stayed with the old man for several hours in the hope he might wake up. It was only at the insistence, and reassurance of the doctor, that Brett could encourage her to leave her grandfather for the night, but with a warning from her, that she would be back very early in the morning.

Morag sat looking thoughtfully at Brett for a moment before saying, 'As you have no doubt realised, I'm Irish. Until the great potato famine back in 1850 I was teaching in our local village school and living with my parents and grandfather. We were in a rented cottage in the beautiful hills overlooking Donegal Bay on the west coast. We managed for a while, eating turnips and carrots, but as the crops diminished, and the second potato harvest failed, we starved along with thousands of others. My mother was the first to die. My father died shortly after. He just gave up the will to continue the struggle. We were not receiving any help from the British government. There seemed to be no end to the struggle. Then grandfather Paddy heard about the California gold rush. He was convinced that if we could only get across the ocean it could be our salvation. He had enough money saved to buy two one-way tickets on a sailing ship, in steerage. The voyage was a living hell, and food was almost non-existent. But we made it. Many didn't.' Morag stopped talking to wipe away tears that were spilling down her cheeks. Brett left his chair and moved round the table to put his arm around her.

'You don't need to go on, sweetheart. You're done in, you should get some rest.'

Morag rested her head on Brett's shoulder for a moment before blowing her nose into her handkerchief. 'It's okay,' she said. 'After we landed, Grandfather spent more money than it was worth buying prospecting equipment, before arranging for us to join a wagon train heading west. If I thought the ocean crossing was hell, this was something else entirely. Progress was slow, food, what there was of it, was poor, water was mostly green.

Grandfather was becoming concerned for my health, although he was determined to see the journey out. It all came to a head when two of the single young men began pestering me. At the first opportunity, he put me on a stage coach which, among other places, was bound for Two Rivers. He thought, correctly as it happens, that I would take care of myself here, and promised he would come here, once he had made his fortune. That was over seven years ago. I assumed he was long dead.'

Brett continued holding Morag as silence descended. Both were deep in their own thoughts. 'Thanks for telling me that,' said Brett softly. 'I can see that life's been hard for you, and it's sure made you a tough filly.'

'The answer's yes.'

'The answer to what?'

'You said earlier that you wanted to ask me something, well the answer is "Yes"

'But you don't know what I was going to ask?'

'Just make sure you let me choose the ring. I can read you like a book, you big lug. And why do you think I've been feeding you apple pie all this time? Now, if you don't mind, I'm off to my bed, and you'd best get home before they send out a posse looking for you.'

***

Early the following morning, Brett knocked on Morag's door. She answered it immediately and was already dressed to go out. Looking up at him, she said, 'You can kiss me if you like, since we're now engaged.' This was an invitation not to be turned down, as Brett had never before bucked up the courage to let Morag know how he felt about her, at least, he didn't think he had. He gently took the red-headed fire-brand into his arms and bent down to brush her lips with his own before pulling back.

'Was that it?' she demanded. 'You mean to tell me I've waited all this time for that?' Suddenly her hand was behind Brett's head and pulling it down till her lips crushed against his. Without conscious thought, he put his arms around her and responded with a more passionate kiss, savouring the taste and feel of her partly open lips against his.

'That's better, practice will improve. Let's go.'

The main street was yet to awaken as the couple stepped arm in arm along the boardwalk. In another hour the street would be bustling with horse-drawn wagons whose owners will have driven in to barter and buy provisions, cowboys in from the scattered ranches aiming to indulge in a fried breakfast they would prefer to the oats served up in their respective crew lodgings. Saloons would be swept. The barber's shop windows cleaned and the tooth-puller would be downing his first whiskey as he walked toward his dreaded Torture Chamber. A normal morning, apart that is, the sheriff seemed to be holding the arm of the school teacher as they headed along the street. A lady, out sweeping her steps, tutted as she thought to herself, *knew there was something dodgy about her, arriving in town from nowhere, just like that. Wonder why the sheriff's taking her in?*

'Mornin' Doc,' said Brett the moment his door swung open. 'How is he?'

'Morning Brett, Morag. Still not with us, but breathing seems easier. Not a stir during the night. Come in, come in. Morag, how old would you say your grandpa is?'

'I was thinking about that last night in bed,' she replied. 'He must be in his mid-seventies, I imagine.'

'That's what I assumed. His body, at that age, could just shut down after his ordeal, but that old timer looks like a tough character to me. I'm sure he'll come round, in the next day, in the next hour, who knows?' He's in the hands of the Almighty, so he couldn't be in a better place. That's an idea, I might preach a sermon on that, come Sunday. It would be a good thing if we could afford a preacher for this town, instead of me being expected to do it. Coffee?'

Two hours later, Morag was sitting alongside the bed, holding her grandfather's calloused hand. Brett had sat with her for a while, before excusing himself so that he could call into the sheriff's office to clear up any paperwork, mostly reports and posters. He had first gone along to the saloon to tell the assembled kids that there would be no schooling that day. He also took the opportunity to walk the street and alleys. Although he owned his own horse breeding ranch just on the edge of town, it was good for the folk to see the sheriff's star on the street from time to time. It made them feel safer in this uncertain land.

Meanwhile Morag's thoughts wandered to her home country, the small cottage, overlooking the Bay, the two mounds of earth, the last she had seen of her parents. She smiled to herself as her mind turned to Brett. *It sure took him long enough.* She was determined to be a good wife for that big gentle man. *Five children, I'll give him, or seven. Yes, seven's a good number, four boys and three girls, or four girls and three boys? A real family.* How she had missed being family. Quietly, Morag started singing one of the songs her mother used to sing to her at times when she needed comforting.

'Morag? Is that you?'

Startled, Morag snapped out of her dreams and looked away from the window, into the open eyes of her grandfather. 'Is that you, my dear?' The familiar voice, very weak, but the voice she remembered and loved.

'Yes, Grampa, it's me,' she whispered. She could not have stopped her tears from spilling over, even if she'd tried. 'Oh Grampa, you're awake. Morag leaned forward and took the old man in her arms. 'You're safe now,'

'It really is my Morag. Thank you, blessed Lord.'

'I like to feel I had something to do with it,' said the smiling doctor who was leaning on the door post with folded arms. 'So, our patient has decided to join us then, would you like to put him down, Morag, so that I can feel his pulse.'

'Who's there?' asked the feeble man.

'It's the doctor, Grampa. He's been looking after you. Grampa, can you see me?' asked the girl while releasing her hold and sitting back in her chair. The old man squinted in the direction of his granddaughter's voice.

'Morag, you mustn't tire him,' cautioned the doctor. 'Why don't you go out and get some fresh air for a bit, while I examine your grandfather? Perhaps you can find Brett and bring him back with you. He'll need to hear anything the old man has to say.' Reluctantly, Morag squeezed her grandfather's hand and said, 'I'll be back in a few minutes Grampa. The doctor is a good man, and a friend, he'll take care of you.'

Half an hour later, Morag returned with Brett. Her emotions were spinning. She was engaged to this man she had loved for a while back, although she had not told him. Her grandfather had returned from the dead, he was weak and possibly blind. How could she look after him and hold down her job, her only source of income?

'Ah, there you are,' said the doctor as Rose led them into the surgery.

'What's happened?' asked Morag, in alarm. 'Why are we in here? I want to see my grandfather.'

'Hush, woman. He's okay and he's sleeping,' replied the doctor as he took her hand and led her to a chair. 'I'm pleased to say, he'll live. He's weak, but will recover with more rest and some feeding up. Rose will take care of that. Unfortunately, I have to tell you that he is almost blind. He can only see moving shadows, changes in light, that sort of thing. He has cataracts in both eyes, must have been coming on for some considerable time. Operations are quite successful these days, I understand, but beyond my ability I'm afraid. He would have to go to the city for that, if he could afford it.'

'I reckon that could account for his condition when I found him,' reasoned Brett. 'He must have had a hard time finding his way here, from wherever it is he came. Doc, when is the circuit preacher due to come here?'

'A week on Sunday, Brett,' replied the doctor, confused by this turn in the conversation.

'Why, have you suddenly found religion?'

'Not yet Doc, but I recon it's just a matter of time before my wife sees to that,' Brett replied with a grin.

'Your wife? Since when have you had a wife, and why didn't I know about it?'

'You're the first to know, Doc. Me and this her gal are gonna be married on Sunday week.'

'You are?'

'We are???'

'Yep. Waited long enough, I reckon.' Brett took Morag's hand and asked, 'What do you think Honey? It was always gonna happen sooner or later. If we do it now, you and your Grandpa can move into the ranch. We can take care of him there. Might even find space for your schoolin' in one of the barns.'

'You take a long time to make your move, cowboy, but when you do it, you do it big time,' replied the grinning girl.

'That's on account of training horses. When you need to bring 'em down you have to rope 'em and throw 'em before they can scoot.'

'Are you comparing me with a horse, Sheriff Yates?' demanded Morag, hands on hips and foot stamping on the floor.

'No ma'am, horses are much better tempered … Ouch! That hurt!'

'Now then, you two,' said the doctor. 'I have things to do, even if you don't, so if you don't mind?'

***

'Well, what do you think? We'll be in my room, your grandpa in here. If he needs us, we'll be just along the hall.' The newly engaged couple were at the ranch where Brett, with Pip following behind, had shown Morag the spare bedroom. 'It solves a whole lot of problems, don't you think?'

'It's all a bit sudden, but it sounds wonderful to me. I love it here, have done since you first brought me over,' replied Morag. 'Are you sure you're happy to have my grandfather living with us?'

'Absolutely certain. After all, he'll be my grandfather-in-law, won't he? Although a bath wouldn't do him any harm.'

'You're a brute, Mr Yates, and I don't know why I'm even talking to you, let alone marrying you.'

'Cos you can't resist me, now give me a kiss, then I'll conjure up some lunch.'

A short time later, the two of them returned to the doctor's house where the door was opened by Rose. 'Good afternoon Sheriff, Ma'am,' greeted the smiling housekeeper. Doctor's with your grandpa, go on through.' As they entered the house, they could hear the old man's voice, stronger now, coming from the bedroom.

'Ah, here they are,' said the doctor. 'Brett, Mr Doyle is concerned about his saddlebags. I've told him that you have them safely locked away, but he wants to see them.'

'Sure, no problem. Be back in five minutes,' replied Brett, who was keen to know what the bags contained, although he was fairly certain that he knew the answer to that one. Morag went immediately to her grandfather's side and took his hands in her own.

'I'm so pleased to see you looking better, grandpa.' She said. 'You mustn't worry about anything, just concentrate on getting stronger.'

The old man squeezed his granddaughter's hands then reached up to gently touch her face before saying, with a rasping voice, 'You're a good lass to be sure. Can you ever forgive me for leaving you so long?'

'Nothing to forgive, grandpa. You did what you did, for the both of us, and for the best. I love you dearly and I'm never going to be parted from you again. Brett and I are to be married in a few days and you will have a home with us, you'll like it on his ranch.'

'I'm very pleased for you my dear, I look forward to getting to know this man of yours.' The old man was suddenly overcome by a coughing fit for a moment, then, with an apologetic smile, said, 'There's something in my saddlebags that's all for you, my wedding present to you both.' It was at that moment that Brett walked in with the bags, which he carefully laid on the bed in front of the old man.

'Open them, Morag, carefully. It's all yours.' Slowly, Morag reached her hand into the first bag and withdrew a pouch, tied with a draw-string. With trembling fingers, she untied the string.

'Careful, lass. Mind you don't spill it,' cautioned her grandfather. 'That pouch alone, is worth a small fortune. There are twelve in each bag. You are a very wealthy couple, and I thank the good Lord that he blessed my prospecting over all those years, and brought me safely back to you.'

Morag was speechless for a moment, as she continued peering into the pouch. Then, looking up at Brett, she asked in a subdued voice, 'Is this gold?'

'Don't you worry your pretty head about that, my dear,' said the old man with a rasping chuckle which brought on another coughing fit. 'It's all been checked, weighed and certified as pure.'

***

It was eight months later, that Morag and her husband walked into the city hospital to collect Grandfather Paddy, following his successful eye operation. The bandages had been taken off two days previously and it had brought joy to Morag to observe her grandfather's amazement to be seeing clearly again. For the duration of his confinement in hospital, the happy couple had been staying in a grand hotel not too far away. It was to that hotel that they were heading, on foot, as Paddy wanted to take in the sights of the city through his temporary smoked spectacles. Holding onto Morag's arm, he asked, 'Tell me again, what's the name of the young man we are to be seeing at the hotel.'

'The reverend gentleman's name is John Banks. He is newly trained and ours will be his first church. He comes highly commended.'

'I'm looking forward to being able to see how the church building is coming along,' said Paddy. 'I understand the tower is to be started next week, and the bell installed.'

'It's looking grand,' replied Morag. 'The organ is on order and should be installed by Christmas. Won't it be grand to be singing carols in our own church? The town folk are so looking forward to it. Also, the children are looking forward to your visit to the school, they have been very busy painting pictures for you to see.'

'It's been a busy time, Paddy,' said Brett. I can hardly believe how quickly the work has been done. It's all down to you, and the town is grateful. You and Morag have lived through real tough times, you've come through it and you've made good. I'm proud of you both, and I've never been so happy as I am now, and I can't wait to be back home to one of your granddaughter's apple pies.'

'He's thinking about his stomach again,' said Morag. 'Come on, Grandpa, let's go and try on your new suit, you'll be needing to look smart when they make you the first Two Rivers Mayor next month.'

The End

IMAGINATION

The nine-year-old boy, named Colin, reluctantly allowed his dream to fade away. He had been flying on the back of a huge golden eagle, its wings slowly beating as it searched the sky for a good thermal upon which to soar. Together, he and the bird had visited mountains which were high enough to enable their snowy peaks to point through the fluffy clouds. They had also zoomed into deep valleys, across thick forests, and over high waterfalls. Colin had not been afraid, for this was the same eagle that appeared in so many of his dreams. It was his friend. His dreams didn't always involve flying on his eagle. Sometimes he was a sailor who's ship had five tall masts. The sea was always blue and friendly, often with dolphins smiling up at him as he held the large spoked wheel. He was not able to remember if there were any other crew members on the ship, for he always seemed to be alone. One of his favourite dreams was the one where he was a train driver, steaming at over one-hundred miles per hour through the towns and countryside. The last time he was in that dream the steam engine became a bicycle at some point, but he couldn't remember when that had happened.

Colin had reached the point between sleep and being awake. He knew that he could stay on the eagle's back a little longer, or he could open his eyes and see his familiar bedroom. Only it would not be the whole of his bedroom he would see. He decided to stay asleep, that was better than looking at the place where the rest of his bedroom should be. It had been a while since his bedroom had been complete. He had almost forgotten what it looked like. He could remember a dressing table with a mirror, a wardrobe with a half open door, but little else. Trying to remember woke him up, the eagle had gone. He was no longer soaring amongst the clouds, just as well really, for without his feathered friend he was bound to fall down, down, down. But that would be okay, because he would fall into his soft comfortable bed.

The wide-awake boy was lying on his back looking up at the blue sky, but it wasn't, the sky had become a white ceiling. Not a whole ceiling unfortunately. A quarter of a ceiling. Colin would have loved to get up and go downstairs for his breakfast, but he couldn't. For that matter, he would have liked to go to the bathroom for a wee. But he couldn't. He was unable to do these things because the stairs, kitchen and bathroom were in the part of his cottage that wasn't there. Just as well that he didn't need to wee, or eat, or wash, or dress. He would not need to do any of these things until his bit was once again fitted into place like all the others. Then he would be free to be a forever nine-year-old boy again, free to eat, free to go out and explore, free to pee.

Colin hoped, each time he had a sleep, that this would happen soon. You see, he had good reason to hope. Was it only before this last sleep, or perhaps the one before, or the one before that, when he felt unusual movement, like things being shaken up? Also, a bit of a rattling noise. His bedroom was still the same, as he looked around, at least that is, the bit that was still there. One of the things he looked forward to the most, was the darkness outside the window changing into light. For how long had Colin been living in this way, you might ask? Well, apart from sleeps, time didn't exist. Yesterday could have been a minute ago, last week could be yesterday, last month could be last year. Do you get the point? You might be wondering if he was frightened, or lonely. No, he was neither of these things. He was safe, and secure in the knowledge that there would be a moment when things would all come back together, when he would be reunited with his parents and younger sister, when he could go out to play in the fields, or on the river again. As time didn't exist in his fragmented world, all of this could be before his next sleep, or after many more sleeps, it didn't matter, because it would just happen, like it did before, and would do again.

Dreams of the eagles, ships and trains awaited, but right at that moment, the shaking had started again. Could this be the moment when the light would return, as it had on previous occasions? Colin glanced at the bedroom window, well actually, only one half of it, as the other half was not there. More shaking and rattling. A loud rip followed by ...... light! Rattle, shake, rattle, more shaking, more light. Colin sat up in his bed to look at the light coming from the half window. His room had suddenly changed. Shadows disappeared. Grey changed to colour. Warmth spread through the quarter room. It was all happening again. A nine-year-old boy, who would never be older, beamed with pleasure and anticipation. Maybe on this occasion between sleeps he would be able to leave his quarter room. Or it might take a while longer, it didn't matter, the light was back.

***

'Wow, a jigsaw puzzle!' exclaimed the birthday boy who had just turned nine. It's a picture of a little house by a river, and look, there's cows and horses, and ducks on a pond. Can I do it now?'

'I'm sorry it's not a new puzzle,' said the boy's mother apologetically. 'The man in the charity shop said that all the pieces are there. I'm glad you like it.'

'I love it, mum. Thank you. I like all my presents, and you mustn't worry that they're not all new. I know you've had to work harder to sell your stories since dad died.'

'You're a good boy, Ron,' said his mother, planting a kiss on his forehead. 'One day, things will get better when an agent takes me on, then I can buy you lots of new things that no one has owned before.'

'I don't care about new things,' replied Ron wistfully. 'What I really want is a special friend. I don't seem to be very popular in my new school. Can I start my jigsaw puzzle now?'

'Yes, I know, my darling. It may be because they don't understand the way you can imagine things. You see things that they don't, because it's all in your mind. You have the mind of a writer, and I think you will create some brilliant stories when you are older, if that's what you want to do. I love the story about Pixies you wrote for my birthday. I've lost count of the number of times I've read it.' Placing her arm around her child's shoulder, she said reassuringly, 'You will find your special friend one day, Ron, you'll see. Come on, help me clear away this wrapping paper, then you can start your puzzle on the dining table while I make you a nice birthday cake for tea.'

***

Living in a small part of a two-hundred-piece jigsaw puzzle may seem odd, even weird. Words such as boring, restricting, confining, lonely, endless, meaningless, and such-like easily come to mind. The thing to remember is that, in the confined world of a fragmented part of a jigsaw, time is non-existent. Therefore, there can be no sense of the passing of time. We all live in a jigsaw world, a world with many more pieces than Ron's two-hundred. The difference is that our jigsaw world is indeed subject to time. We can seriously be affected by confinement of any sort. Our world is made up of pieces, just like the world in which Colin lives. The man who is the boss in a busy office, making important decisions, meeting familiar people, is living, at that moment, in a world far different to the same man who is wading in a shallow river casting his line, while enjoying the surrounding peaceful scenery. The severe glaring judge, who has the power to send a person to prison for twenty years, could be the same man who is sitting in his armchair, slippers on his feet, and with his toddling granddaughter happily bouncing on his knee while playing gee-gees, as he calls it. The strict highly respected math teacher, never to be crossed, might be the grown-up daughter who lives under her mother's thumb in the small cottage they share together. The country in which we live, for some of us, is our entire world, whereas, in fact, it is a relatively small piece of a much bigger world. Do you get the picture? No pun intended. We are all a small part of a whole, and our own individual small piece is also made up of separate parts. The essential difference is that time rules our non-jigsaw-puzzle-world. Not so for Colin. Now that things are being shaken up, he has no perception of waiting. He knows that soon his small bit of bedroom will, once again, become a whole room. He will be able to look out of a whole window and see a familiar view coming back together. The river, the pond, the cows, horses, ducks, clouds, trees, fields, flowers. He knows the house in which he lives will have all the rooms back, the toilet, the stairs, his sister's bedroom, the kitchen, his mum, dad, sister, puppy and budgie in its cage. All together, as though never parted.

***

Ron loved doing jigsaws. This one had two hundred pieces, the largest he had ever tried to do. He looked at the picture on the box. A thatched cottage in a pretty garden surrounded by brightly coloured flowers. Green fields with cows and horses. A river, a pond at the bottom of the garden with swimming ducks. What was that in one of the upstairs windows? A girl, or maybe a boy, looking out between the open curtains. Ron carefully removed the Sellotape and lifted the lid. He allowed his hand to sift through the shiny pieces. So many colours, mostly greens, blues and yellows. Knobbly pieces and pieces with straight edges. He liked those best because they were easier to fit together, except they were usually mainly sky and tree tops. Where should he start? Yes, the edge bits.

Methodically, Ron started sorting the pieces into knobbly ones and straight-edged ones, these he laid out on the table, while the others went into the box lid. Ron's world, at that moment, was confined to his careful sifting and the ten minutes it was taking. Whereas Colin's world was being shaking about, although he, of course, had no sense of the time it was all taking. The first connection was made, then the next and the next. All at the bottom of the picture. A part of the pond with the ducks. The boy could imagine the funny quacking and the splashing as his favourite birds swam amongst the swaying reeds. The two bottom corner pieces were in, so that he could build the sides of the picture. A bit of a wall, a river and something red on one side, and something that could be a part of a haystack on the other side. He was absorbed. Time seemed to stand still, but of course, it didn't. It took twenty minutes to complete the sky which, fortunately, had some white fluffy clouds in it to make the task easier.

Now the knobbly pieces. Ron started laying the pieces out, face up, on the table. He decided to start with the cottage. Lots of white bits, a brown door with red roses around it. Windows and a thatched roof. Slowly, the cottage came together. Ron could see that there were four windows, two up, two down. Now he could tell that it was a boy looking out of the window, a boy at around his own age, he imagined. That window with the boy in it was the final piece to complete the cottage. At that moment, his mother came into the room with a glass of lemonade and a biscuit for him.

'My word, you are getting on,' she said encouragingly. 'What a pretty cottage.'

'Yes, mum, can you see the boy in the upstairs window?'

Mother peered again at the cottage. Shaking her head, she said, 'No, I can't see anyone in any of the windows.'

***

Suddenly, there was a loud click behind Colin. He turned from the window to see that his room was again complete. A whole room. With a loud 'Whoop' he shot through the door, which wasn't there before, and ran down the stairs two at a time. At the kitchen table sat his mum and dad, with Bess, all eating a late breakfast.

'Good morning, Colin. Come and sit down while I dish up your bacon and egg. Do you want toast or fried bread?'

'Fried bread please, mum,' Colin replied as he took his place at the table.

'What do you want to do after breakfast, son?' asked his father. 'It looks like a nice sunny day, but then it always is isn't it?'

'I would like to play down by the river, if that's okay.'

'The river isn't there yet, nor the garden.' said mother who was peering out of the kitchen window.

***

Ron placed his half empty glass of lemonade down and peered at the bedroom window. 'That's funny, there was a boy looking out, I'm sure,' he said while perhaps feeling not quite so sure any more.

'You must be getting confused with the lady looking out of one of the downstairs windows,' laughed Ron's mother.

'Don't be silly, mum,' exclaimed the boy. 'There isn't anyone else looking out of windows, I checked.' Saying that, Ron looked again at the four windows, one, two, three, four. All clear of boys and ladies. 'There was a boy, mum, honest,' said Ron, looking up at his mother.

'You, and your imagination,' she replied while gently rubbing her son's head. 'Must go, I need to keep an eye on the oven. Let's see how much more you can do before I come back.' With the cottage complete, Ron started picking out the pieces which looked as though they could be a river, or possible a pond. He could see more ducks on some of the pieces. He realised after five minutes had passed that he was making both a pond and a river.

***

Having finished their breakfasts, Colin and Bess got down from the table and went to the front door which the boy opened wide enough for both to peer at the river. Colin longed to be able to go down there, but was unable to, as they were still separated by a gap 'Come on!' said the boy rather loudly, in frustration. 'We want the garden and the path, so we can get to the river.' To his satisfaction, bits of garden, with the path and gate, started to appear, making it possible to do what Colin most wanted, the rowing boat was what he had in mind.

***

The river was nearly finished. As Ron took another sip of lemonade and a nibble on his biscuit, a voice in his imagination said, *'Come on, we want the garden, and the path, so we can get to the river.'* The voice was so clear.

With renewed determination, Ron concentrated on the garden pieces. He was so focused, he failed to notice that the front door to the cottage was open and a boy with a small girl alongside him were standing on the step looking into the garden. At last, the garden was complete, including a path and gate. Ron was able to connect it to the river, including another piece of river he hadn't noticed before, perhaps because it was mainly a red piece. To his amazement he realised it was a rowing boat. Ron liked the rowing boat. In his imagination he could picture himself with two friends rowing on that river. One of his new friends would be a boy of about his own age, and the other would perhaps be the boy's young sister, yes, that would be nice. Ron was now totally absorbed in the picture. The pond was complete. He could see the two friends, now in the red boat, laughing as they splashed each other with their hands over the side, trailing in the water. More pieces were fitted into the picture. It was becoming easier as there were less pieces left on the table. The horses and cows were now in the field. *'Come on,'* said the boy in his imagination, *'let's go and feed the horses with grass.'* The rowing boat was, once again, tied to the river bank and three children, with long grass held in their hands, were walking up to the two shire horses who trotted over to meet them. With the horses fed and patted, the three children played hide and seek amongst the bushes as the blue sky filled the space above them. When they tired of that game, they found some good climbing trees, both boys helping the little girl to reach the second branch from the ground. There was much laughter as the children turned their attention to the haystack. The three of them delighted in each other's company and became firm friends.

'Here you are, Ron. Nine candles,' said his mother, walking into the dining room with the cake, 'See if you can blow them all out in one go and make a wish.' Ron took his eyes away from the puzzle and looked into the glowing flames. He took a deep breath and blew hard. The flames flickered before going out, leaving a small trail of smoke rising from each candle. 'Did you make a wish?' enquired mother.

'Yes, mum. I wished that this jigsaw puzzle could be framed and hung on my bedroom wall forever.'

'Well that might be possible. Let's wait until my next cheque. Meanwhile, we can leave it there with the table cloth covering it. I see that you've finished it. Well done. You've been sitting there for hours doing that puzzle, I looked in at you once or twice and saw you just staring at it. You seemed to be miles away, in another world. Let me have a look now that it's finished.' Ron's mother stooped over his shoulder for a closer look at the completed picture. 'That's strange,' she muttered. 'I didn't notice those three children playing in that field before. Let me see the box.' Mother picked up the box lid and gazed at it before turning her eyes back to the completed picture. 'I thought not, they aren't there on the box picture.'

***

Our new friend, Ron, often came to play with us. He particularly liked rowing along the river in our boat. And he always made a point of bringing apples to feed to the horses who would always trot over when they spotted him. He seemed to be getting older, then he stopped coming. We never saw him again. It's strange that our cottage never came apart after Ron's first visit. Sometimes I feel that he's still with us somehow.

***

My seventh novel is complete. My agent has been putting on the pressure a bit more than I would like, but my books are popular and selling well. Mum is retired now, and living with us. The children love her, it's always her that they choose to tell them stories when they go to bed. She often peers at the mounted jigsaw puzzle on my wall when she has brought me my morning coffee. She shakes her head as she heads for the door, saying, 'I'm sure there used to be three children in that field.'

The End

THE BENCHES

At this time of the afternoon, on a warm July Sunday, it is not at all unusual to see many people in this park. An elderly gentleman limps along, Golden Spaniel trotting at heel beside him. He is smartly dressed. Tweed jacket and tie, regardless of the warmth of the day. A trilby hat which he lifts politely as he passes the young lady who is seated on one of a pair of park benches situated on a low hill overlooking the bandstand. Taken by surprise by the unexpected gesture, she smiles at the gentleman's retreating back. He has paused to allow his dog to sniff a post which holds a rubbish basket.

The young lady checks her wrist-watch. *Twenty-five minutes. Time for a read.* She lifts her bag and takes out her paper-back novel, she opens it at the place where she had previously inserted a used bus ticket to mark her page. She is immediately transported to a Scottish glen where the main character has just agreed to marry her childhood sweetheart.

If the young lady was not so immersed in her romantic tale, she would notice, and be aware of the various uniformed brass-band members who are drifting toward the bandstand, some alone, others in groups, each carrying their particular instrument. She would also notice that folk are beginning to seat themselves on the collapsible wooden chairs which are strategically placed around the bandstand below her.

A little girl, who is holding an ice-cream cornet, oblivious of the creamy mess on her hand, chin and dress, skips over to the unoccupied bench next to hers and attempts to climb onto the seat. 'Not there, darling,' calls the mother. 'Come here, sweetheart, let's go down to the seats so that we can be closer to the band.'

Having reached the end of her chapter, the young lady closes the book with a sigh. She and her boyfriend, have been together for over three years. She is so much in love with him. One day perhaps. Thinking of Eric, she again checks her wrist-watch. *Four-thirty, he said. Still twenty minutes to go.* Her wistful thoughts are interrupted by the arrival of a man who is wearing a dog-collar. He steps passed her and seats himself on the other bench alongside her own. Smiling across to her, he comments, 'Lovely spot, isn't it?'

'Yes, it is,' she responds. Feeling that she ought to make further polite conversation with the clerical gentleman, she says, 'My boyfriend and I often sit here when the weather allows. He's meeting me here soon.'

'How nice,' replies the vicar. 'I don't often find the time to relax in the park. This is a treat for me. I was asked by one of my parishioners, after the service this morning, if we could have a chat. I invited him to come to the vestry but he suggested we meet here, as it's such a splendid day.' I'm so glad he did, much better than a dusty old vestry. I see that we are about to be entertained,' nodding toward the bandstand.

'Yes, they do it most Sunday afternoons during the summer months. There are three different bands that take it in turns. I like this one the best. They call themselves *The Toy Soldiers.*'

'I look forward to hearing them, in that case. How long have you and your young man been together, if that's not too intrusive a question?'

'Since my twenty-first, over three years ago,' replies the young lady. 'We met at my party, a friend of a friend.'

'Is it serious?'

'Well, I think so. He's very special, different from all the other boys I have been with. Impulsive, unpredictable, interesting, funny, gentle, sweet.'

'Bless my soul,' says the vicar with a smile. 'You need to marry that paragon, before he gets snapped up.'

'That's my intention, but I'm not sure if he knows that yet.'

At that moment, a middle-aged couple are approaching the benches. It becomes clear that they are intending to occupy a space, so the vicar gets to his feet and says to them, 'Have this bench, more room for you, I'm sure my friend here, won't mind me sharing the other one with her, since we already know each other.'

The couple gratefully settle on the, now vacant bench, while expressing thanks to the vicar. The young lady slides along to make more room for the clerical gentleman, hoping that Eric will come soon. The four of them sit there in an awkward silence. The young lady glances down at her closed book. *Would it be rude of me to continue reading?* she ponders. The clerical gentleman, having sat closer to the young lady at his own suggestion, asks himself, *Have I crossed a line here? Claiming to be her friend, asking questions, moving closer. She's looking a bit uncomfortable.* The middle-aged couple sit quietly without speaking. The wife is wondering about the other two. They are both looking as though they want to move on. She glances across her husband to the neighbouring bench and speculates. *Is the vicar bothering the girl? He claimed to be friends. She seems to want to keep her distance. Are they together? Have they had a falling-out? Does he know he has ice-cream on his bottom?* Meanwhile, her husband simply sits there, watching one of the band members setting up his drums. He is oblivious of the tension. His wife nudges him and nods toward the other bench. He looks round. She hisses, 'Don't look!' He looks back at her, thinking, *why don't I understand my wife after all these years?*

She can stand the silent tension no longer. Leaning across her husband again, she says to the clerical gentleman, 'I hope you won't mind me mentioning it, but it appears you have sat on some ice-cream.' She suddenly realises that she is seated on the spot where the vicar was previously sitting. She leaps to her feet, the vicar does the same, the young lady is reaching in her handbag for a packet of Wet-Wipes, the husband continues to concentrate his attention on the drummer who's clearly looking for something in his bag.

'It was a little girl, allow me …'

'Oh my, how embarr …'

'It's all over my nice …'

'I think he's lost his sticks.'

A moment later, a young probationary policeman approaches. He stops his much-practiced important walk, hands behind his back, chin pushed forward, as he spots a young lady who is wiping a vicars backside at one bench, a middle-aged lady who is bending over in front of a middle-aged man, at another bench, demanding that he forget the bl..bl..blessed drumsticks and look at her bottom. The policeman stands there for a moment, mouth open, eyes wide. Then, hoping not to be noticed, he quietly turns and walks back in the opposite direction, perhaps a little faster than his earlier approach.

'It was a little girl,' says the young lady. 'I should have warned you, I'm sorry.'

'Don't reproach yourself, my dear,' says the vicar. 'No harm done.' Turning to the couple, 'Are you okay madam? I hope …'

'Oh, no. It's fine, my husband assures me there is nothing on my dress, although it does feel a little sticky. It wouldn't do to meet our son with ice-cream all over us.'

'No, I suppose it wouldn't. Are you to meet him here?'

'That's what he said, didn't he Stephen? A pair of benches, on a slope, overlooking the bandstand. All a bit mysterious. We don't see him much; we've travelled down from Hull for the week. We've only been here for an hour. He's paid for us to stay in The Grand. We're having dinner together this evening. He says he has something to celebrate, most likely to do with his job. He's doing so well, you know.'

'Well, I hope you have a good time,' says the vicar. 'Funny enough, I also am to be dined this evening, one of my younger church members is feeding me. He says he has something to discuss, perhaps it's about the church music. He may have thought, meeting here and listening to the band might awaken my interest. In my opinion, you can't beat a lusty organ and the old hymns.'

'He's definitely lost his sticks. How's he going to play without them? That's what I want to know.'

Addressing the young lady, the middle-aged lady says, with a smile, 'That's two people being met here. What a coincidence. It would be funny if you were here to meet someone as well, wouldn't it, Stephen?'

'What's that, Mabel?'

'I said, "It would be funny if this young lady …. Oh, never mind.'

'Perhaps he's left them in his car.'

'What has who left in his car, dear?'

'His sticks. He's looking in his trouser pockets. He won't find them in there. Too long, you see.'

'As a matter of fact, I'm meeting my boyfriend here, any time now,' says the young lady.

Before Mabel has time to respond to this astonishing revelation, a smartly suited gentleman approaches the two benches and asks the group of seated people. 'I'm to meet a lady named Diane, here. Would that be one of you two ladies by any chance.'

'I'm Diane,' exclaims the young lady. 'But you're not my boyfriend!'

'Afraid not,' replied the newcomer. May I ask your surname?'

'*Don't tell him!*' warns Mabel. *He could be a stalker ... or something.*'

'I can assure you, madam, I'm nothing of the sort,' says the indignant gentleman. 'Now, Diane, would you kindly reveal your surname. If you are the person I am to meet, I have something I must give you.'

'It's Gibson … Diane Gibson,' says the young lady suddenly.

'Ah. Then my mission is accomplished. Miss Gibson, this is for you, and I hope you will be very happy. Good day to you.'

'But what? …Who? … I don't understand.' The man has gone, already fifty yards along the path.

'Open it, luv. What is it?' Mabel is unable to hide her curiosity, although she doesn't really try. The vicar frowns and says, 'Bless my soul' as he watches Diane shaking the envelope.

'They'll have to make do without them I suppose. Careless to lose your sticks, if you ask me.'

'It's a key,' exclaims the mystified young lady. 'It looks like a front door key. What on earth …?'

'Bless my soul,' says the vicar'

'Perhaps it's a prize from a game-show,' says Mabel. 'Here, they haven't brought back that Candid Camera programme, have they?' She's looking into the nearby bushes for a possible hidden camera.

As it turns out, there is someone in the bushes, someone with a huge grin on his face as he steps out into the sunlight. 'Hello Mum, Dad. Glad you made it okay. It's good to see you both.'

'Eric? It's Eric!' exclaims Mabel as she rushes over to hug her son.

'Eric? It's my Eric,' says Diane in amazement.

'Eric? It's the church member I've come to meet,' says an amused clerical gentleman. 'Bless my soul.'

'Having extricated himself from his mother's hug, and his father's vigorous hand-shake, Eric says, with a smile, 'I see you're all getting to know each other, that's good.'

'Eric, do you mind telling me what's going on,' says the vicar. 'I have to admit, I'm utterly confused. I gather these are your parents, but who is this young lady? And why am I here?'

'All in good time, Vicar,' replies Eric. 'I have something very important to do first.' Turning to Diane, who hasn't moved, or spoken since he joined them at the benches, Eric lowers himself to one knee, in front of her, and asks, 'Diane, will you marry me?'

'Oh, Eric, my darling, yes, a thousand times, yes.'

'You will? I love you, Diane. Wow, you want to be my wife. I'm so happy. I haven't got a ring as I thought you might like to choose it, but I do have a surprise for you, my love.'

'Would it be something to do with a front door key, by any chance?' says Diane with a glint in her eye.

'It's the key to the house you loved so much when we went for that country walk last month, the one with the "For Sale" sign in the front garden. Well, it's ours now, that chap was the estate agent. We can move in as soon as we are married.'

'Bless my soul,' says the vicar.

The couple rise to their feet and fall into each other's arms in a drawn-out kiss while their bemused audience look on. Eventually, after breaking apart, Eric turns to his parents and says, in a posh voice, Mother, Father, I would like to introduce you to my fiancé, Diane. Diane, my parents, Mabel and Stephen, who you will be addressing as *Mum and Dad,* as soon as my vicar here can give us the earliest date possible for our wedding.' Addressing himself to the clerical gentleman, he asks, 'I assume you have your diary with you, Vicar?'

Amidst the following laughter, back-slapping, hugs, and kisses, Stephen is the first to notice that the brass band has finished their tuning up. *Won't be much good without the drums* he thinks to himself. It's as that thought passes through Stephen's mind, that Eric waves down to the band leader who nods before turning to his players with both arms raised. As his arms drop for the third time, the band breaks into the song *'Congratulations".* The audience are quickly on their feet, including a little girl with ice-cream stains down her front, singing and clapping along with the music. Taking his fiancé by the hand, Eric leads the group down the slope to join the crowd in front of the bandstand.

As the song finishes, in a loud voice, Stephen calls to the drummer, 'You found your sticks then?'

'Never lost them, mate, why do you ask?'

'I saw you searching for them this passed twenty minutes.'

'Naa, it was my chewing-gum I was looking for. Can't beat the skins without chewing the gum, just wouldn't sound the same.'

Having thanked the band leader, and waved his thanks to the audience, Eric says to the small group, 'Well, folks, I think it's time we made for The Grand. You'll have plenty of time to get to know each other better over a few drinks before our meal. I have a table booked for the five of us, at six-thirty. I hope that's alright with you all.'

Why did I think it was his sticks he was looking for? Could have been.

The End

DEEP WATERS

A sequel to 'The Captain'

Captain Samuel Styles emerged from the shipping office bearing a huge grin on his weather-beaten face. He had just secured a cargo which was destined for Cadiz, in Spain, one of his favourite ports. His owners would be pleased with the speed in which he had secured his manifest, and the likely profit he would bring to the company in due course. In the few weeks in which his ship *Nimble Lady* had been tied to the jetty he had overseen the discharge of its cargo, the renewing of much of the running and standing rigging, and the repainting of the hull. Most of the credit for this work belonged to his first mate, Seth Jones, a valued friend and ship's officer.

Yes, Samuel had much to lift his spirits on this fine afternoon which was showing the first hint of spring, not that he, or his crew of twenty-five would see much of the English spring this year. For he estimated that, all being well, he would be sailing on the tide before the week was out. Dressed in his smart blue jacket with gold rings on the sleeves, and gleaming brass buttons down the front, he was aware that he must cut a fine figure amongst the stevedores, longshoremen, labourers and stall holders as he strode along the jetty. Now in his fortieth year, Samuel's one regret was that he had no family. Both of his parents were long in the grave, his father having fallen from a ship's mast, and his mother dying of a broken heart, shortly after. He had been on the other side of the world at the time, serving as a bosun on board a fast clipper, homeward bound in the Pacific Ocean. Life as a deep-water sailor offered little chance of meeting members of the opposite sex, apart from those he preferred not to be associated with. No, for him, a bachelor's life would be his lot, perhaps a good thing, as he was often away at sea for a year or more, depending upon the weather and the dictates of the owners.

If this voyage did well, it would take him a step closer to being able to afford to buy *Nimble Lady,* from the owners, a dream he had nursed for many years, and one that was coming ever closer. With luck, there would be a quick turn-around in Cadiz, which might well take his ship anywhere in the world. This was his life and within it, he was well content. Still smiling at the world in general, Samuel continued his walk back to the ship, unconsciously avoiding the many hazards to be expected on a busy jetty. It was as he drew closer to *Nimble Lady* that he noticed the lady standing alongside her. She was first peering down onto the deck and then up into the rigging. This curiosity would not be unusual for a man or a boy, but for a lady, possibly in her middle years, to show such interest, was indeed unusual. His own curiosity aroused; Samuel approached the lady, lifted his cap and said, 'Good afternoon, madam,' and at the same moment, recognised who she was. 'Why if it's not the lady of the basket, I trust you are feeling warmer now?'

The startled lady swung round to see the familiar figure standing before her with his cap raised respectfully. The grinning captain said, 'You seem to be interested in my little ship. Would you like to come on board and look around by any chance?'

Was it only last week when this same lady, while carrying her precious basket of eggs for trading, had accidently stepped on his foot as he had emerged from the tavern? She had clearly been very cold at the time, for snow was in the air, and he had impetuously offered to treat her to some hot food and drink at the nearby corn exchange. He had not been surprised when she refused his offer, claiming to be in a hurry to return to her sick mother. And now it seemed, he was about to be refused a second time.

'Oh, no, I couldn't.' she replied.

'Don't tell me, I know, you have to get back to your sick mother. I understand. Another time maybe. I have a cargo and we will be sailing to Spain once it's loaded, so best make it soon if you change your mind.'

Taking her eyes from his, and looking down, she replied, 'I have just buried my mother and …'

Before she had time to finish her sentence, Samuel broke in, 'Oh, my dear, I'm so sorry, I had no idea.'

Looking back up into his eyes, the lady replied, 'And why would you? Tell me, Captain …?'

Realising that she was asking for his name, he responded, 'Captain Styles, but Samuel to you and my friends.'

'Well then, Cap … Samuel,' she replied with a smile, the first he had seen on her attractive face. 'Tell me, do you take passengers on your ship?'

Taken by surprise by the question, he replied, 'Yes, we have a small cabin for that, and we provide victuals. Why do you ask?'

'Spain, you say?'

'That's right, Spain.'

The lady paused for a moment, looking back at the ship. Then, with a grin, she looked back into his eyes and said, 'I think, Samuel, that I would like to come on board and look around after all.' It was at that moment that Samuel noticed Seth looking up at him with an enquiring look on his face.

'Ah, Seth, this is ... I'm sorry, madam, I still don't know your name?'

'Nancy.'

'This is Nancy. She's coming on board to look around. You will be pleased to know we have a cargo. We'll start loading in the morning.'

'Okay, skipper,' replied the grinning first mate. 'I'll detail the crew.' Turning his attention to the attractive lady, Seth said, 'You are welcome on board, Nancy. Known the skipper long?'

'Oh yes, at least five minutes,' she responded with a grin.

Having negotiated the narrow gangway and stepped down onto the deck, Nancy was impressed by the confusing array of ropes above her head, and the ordered neatness of the way many of them were fastened along the deck. Several crew-members were busy with various tasks, both above and below, those who noticed her arrival, respectfully tugging their forelocks as she passed.

'This way, Nancy,' said Samuel who was pointing to a covered companionway which led to the deck below. 'I think it wise for you to go first, for the sake of decency. It's quite steep, so mind how you go. I'll be right behind you.'

So it was, that Nancy, having seen the clean and tidy passenger accommodation, made her life-changing decision. 'You mean to say you want to sail with us?' asked the astonished captain.

'Yes, Spain sounds wonderful. Can I move in straight away?'

'I hate to have to ask you, my dear,' said Samuel with some embarrassment. 'Have you the means of paying for your passage?'

'I'm afraid I have very little money in my purse, perhaps sufficient to purchase a few simple luxuries that a lady may require, but I do have this.' Thus saying, Nancy removed a leather pouch from her bag and held it out for the captain's inspection. 'You should open it over the table in case you spill any of them,' she cautioned.

'Diamonds, by god, do you realise this is a fortune? Where have they come from? Are they yours?' Samuel was clearly stunned as he continued peering into the bag and moving the stones with his forefinger.

'Yes, you can be assured that they belong to me. They were left to me by my late father, although I knew nothing about them until … well, recently. As to the value, that is still to be assessed, but I imagine it will be adequate to enable me to start a new life, perhaps in Spain, we will have to see. Do you happen to know where I could sell some of them? At least enough to pay for my cabin and food for the duration.'

'Well, I'm not in the habit of selling diamonds,' responded Samuel, while thrusting the closed pouch back into Nancy's hand. 'Perhaps the company's agent can help. He is a friend and an honest man. I'll take you to see him. Do me a favour Nancy. Tell nobody aboard this ship about these diamonds. If you feel you can trust me, I think it would be wise to place them in my safe until you leave us.'

***

On the following Friday, at mid-day, *Nimble Lady* eased away from the jetty. The top-sails on all three masts were released from their spars and already catching the light breeze. Nancy was standing on the aft deck, leaning on the rail as the gap grew wider between the ship and the jetty. She was fascinated by the activity aloft, and on deck, as more sails appeared against the clear blue sky. With admiration, she watched the captain as he handled the ship, shouting orders through a megaphone. Nancy had spent the last four days on the ship as it was being loaded and, during that time, had got to know most of the hands by name. They seemed pleased to have her on board and during their off-watch times vied with each other for her attention. The company agent had been most helpful in arranging the sale of a small number of her diamonds. She had been amazed at how much money she had received for so few of the smallest stones. She realised for the first time; just how wealthy she had become.

With all sails now fully set and catching the wind, which was stronger now they were away from the shore, *Nimble Lady* began to live up to her name. Soon the channel was behind them and the sea was beckoning them forward into the sweeping waves. With exhilaration, Nancy removed her head scarf and allowed her copper coloured hair to stream behind her as she looked up into the billowing sails. 'Enjoying it?'

She had not heard the approach of the Captain, due to the moaning of the wind in the rigging. 'It's wonderful, I love it,' she responded. 'I can see why you have spent your life at sea. I never realised how free you feel away from the clutter of the land.'

'Yes, it's a good life, mainly. I won't try to kid you that it's always like this. There are times when you would pay a king's ransom never to see the sea again, what with storms when it's constantly wet and cold on top of the danger of floundering, then the doldrums when you fry in the heat while praying for a breath of wind to get you moving again. But I wouldn't change it for the world. Nancy, I wonder if you would join myself and Seth for dinner in my cabin this evening? Nothing grand, but we can enjoy the vegetables while they are still fresh.'

'Why, that sounds lovely. How can a lady resist? I would love to join you both, thank you. But who will be in charge up here, with you two below?'

'It'll be the second mate's watch for a while, before Seth has to take over for the first watch at eight-o-clock, so no problem,' replied Samuel.

Later, after an exhilarating few hours standing on deck watching the land slowly slip beneath the distant horizon, and feeling the ship coming alive as it elbowed its way through successive waves, causing spray to fly over the bows, Nancy couldn't remember ever feeling happier, or more alive. All too quickly it seemed, it was time to go below to change for dinner. As it happened, there was little choice in the matter of what she would wear for the occasion, for she had had little time to shop for additional clothing. A quick inspection in the small mirror provided, revealed the tangled mess the wind had made of her hair. She burst out laughing when she remembered the looks, she had received from grinning crew members, including

Samuel, as her hair had been the last thing on her mind during that wild and wonderful time on deck. Her amusement was interrupted by a knock on the cabin door. Nancy was delighted when, upon opening the door, a boy was revealed holding a jug of warm water and fresh towels. 'For you miss,' he said. 'Captain told me to let you know dinner will be ready in his cabin in half an hour.'

'Thank you, Tommy. I remember you joining the ship, along with your chest, yesterday. Is this your first time at sea?'

'Yes, miss.' The boy replied stiffly. 'I'm an apprentice. My father is one of the company directors. I'm to learn the business from keel to boardroom, he says.'

'Oh, and how do you feel about that?'

'Not sure about the boardroom bit, but I love being here, at sea. I think I would rather be a captain, like Captain Styles. He says he'll give me all the help I need as long as I work hard. If I end up like him, that's what I want.' Nancy took the jug and towels from the boy, noticing how the stiffness had left him as he talked about Samuel. 'Thank you, Tommy, I think you and I will be friends as we learn together, don't you?'

'Yes miss, and thank you,' he replied with a smile that lit up his young face.

The meal turned out to be a most enjoyable evening. The food was plain, although not a problem for Nancy as she was well used to that. However, the company proved to be both stimulating and interesting. Samuel and Seth were clearly close friends of long standing, with the formality of rank having been left on deck. Nancy was well entertained by their stories of adventures in foreign ports around the world, of people they had met, and of places they had explored. She had been thrilled, rather than scared, as they relayed accounts of storms they had fought together, when the ship had been tossed around like a cork in a mill-race. All too soon, it was time for Seth to relieve the watch, leaving her and Samuel alone to enjoy a glass or two of Port with a rather fine cheese.

'Well, I can see you have enjoyed your first day at sea, my dear,' said Samuel. 'It has been ideal conditions for passing through the Channel, but I must warn you, that once we reach the Bay of Biscay, things can be very different. I've told young Tommy to put some wet-weather gear in your cabin this evening. You may be needing it.'

'Thank you, he was telling me earlier that he would like to grow up to be a captain. Is that possible?'

'He has much to learn, seamanship, navigation, trading. He can do it, if he sets his mind to it, and as long as his father allows him the freedom to remain at sea. He's a bright kid.'

'Would you be happy to teach me some of those things whenever you have time?'

'Bless you, Nancy, of course. I would be delighted. If you're serious, you can join us at two bells during the forenoon watch, that's nine-o-clock to you. I'm intending to go through the rudiments of navigation with the young fellow. You may want to shoot the sun with us at mid-day if we can see it.'

'Shoot the sun? That sounds interesting. I assume you don't mean literally?'

'You'll see, it's all about finding where we are.'

'Don't you know?' replied Nancy in mock alarm.

'Yes, by dead reckoning, but shooting the sun gives us confirmation, along with the chronometer of course.'

'I see I have much to learn if I intend a life at sea.'

Samuel thought for a moment, before asking, 'Nancy, have you any idea what you intend to do when we get to Cadiz?' I mean do you know anybody in Spain? Family, friends perhaps?'

'No Samuel, I don't know anyone and I have no idea what I'll be doing. I joined you on impulse. I just needed to get away. Going to sea sounded exciting, still does. Does that sound foolish and pathetic?'

'Frankly, yes. Do you really think I will be comfortable with the thought of leaving you alone in a strange country with no one to meet you, and a fortune in your bag? Do you even speak Spanish?'

'No, I don't, and it's kind of you to be concerned, thank you.' Nancy sipped from her glass, allowing the warming liquid to slip down, as she considered what Samuel had said. If she were being honest with herself, those thoughts had been niggling at the back of her mind since that heady moment when they had set sail.

Several days of fine weather followed. An easterly wind had kept the temperature down, sufficient enough to require warm clothing while on deck. On the plus side, the wind enabled *Nimble Lady* to carry mountains of white sails on each of her three masts and from her bowsprit. Nancy enjoyed the lessons she shared with Tommy. Sometimes taught by Samuel but often by John, the bosun. She took pride in the fact that she had mastered both the bowline and clove hitch and was looking forward to having a go at the sheet bend. The worry of what was to happen in Spain was shelved as each day brought fresh experiences. She was falling in love with this life of freedom and beauty. However, invariably things can change quite rapidly at sea, and this was something Nancy was to discover on the fourth day out. The easterly wind had dropped during the night, to be replaced by a strengthening south-westerly. Having finished a light breakfast of bread spread with plum jam, Nancy emerged from the companionway to see that the sails had been trimmed and swung round to catch the wind from a different direction. She also became aware that the bows were dipping and lifting with each passing wave, and that the ship was heeling over in a way she had not seen before.

'Morning Nancy.' It was Seth who was holding the forenoon watch. 'Feels like we're in for a bit of a blow. You may want to ensure that you are holding on to something solid if you remain on deck. Should it become livelier, you'll be better off below. Nancy found that the situation, far from causing anxiety, was in fact, quite stimulating. However, an hour later, it became clear that the situation was becoming more alarming. There were now two men manning the wheel. In spite of a further reefing of the sails, the ship was leaning far enough over to allow the sea to flow over the leeward decking and out through the scuppers. Samuel had come up from below, although Seth was more than capable of handling the ship in those conditions.

Climbing the deck to where Nancy was firmly holding on to the rail on the windward side, Samuel shouted above the shrieking wind, 'Time for you to go below, Nancy. You should have been told to go earlier. Hold on to me, I'll see you safely to the companionway.' It was immediately clear to Nancy that the captain would brook no argument, so reluctantly she did as she was told. It was to be a long day for Nancy, being confined to her cabin, not being able to see what was happening. At some point, Tommy knocked on the door to offer her some bread with a knob of cheese.

'Thank you, Tommy,' she said, glad of a moment's distraction. 'How are you coping, up there?'

'The skipper said I must be quick, as he needs all hands on deck to reduce the sails again. The wind is stronger now, and the waves are huge. I'm okay though, just glad that I don't have to go aloft yet.'

'Well, you take care, we don't want any accidents, do we?'

'I'll be okay. I'll let the skipper know you're all right. He asked me to check.' Apart from the lively movement of the ship, the thing that surprised Nancy most in her forced confinement was the noise. Above the shrieking of the gale in the rigging and the crashing of the sea on the hull next to her ear as she laid on the bunk, there was the overriding noise of the ships creaking timbers which seemed, to her inexperienced ears, to be coming apart. It was while Nancy was endeavouring to eat her bread and cheese, that she became aware of loud shouting coming from beyond her closed cabin door, followed by a scuffling noise amidst a chorus of grunts. Quickly, Nancy was on her feet and clinging onto her bunk as she made for the door. She was alarmed by the scene in front of her as the door fell open. Two deckhands were struggling with the prone figure of Tommy, with Samuel following.

'In here,' she said. 'Bring him into my cabin, quickly! On the bunk.'

'I think he may be dead,' said Samuel as the still figure was laid on the bunk. 'He went over the side when he got his leg caught in a severed rope. He was dragged below the surface for a while before we managed to haul him out. He doesn't seem to be breathing.'

'Stand out of the way, all of you! Let me see! It took Nancy just a few seconds to see that the boy was indeed not breathing. Without hesitation, she looked up at Samuel and said, 'I saw old Mrs Harris do this to a child who was dragged from a flooded river, it worked.' Holding the boy's head back, and pinching his nose, she took a deep breath before breathing into the boy's mouth. She was not aware of the gasp that came from one of the men as she repeated the process, then again, and again.

'Nancy, are you sure this ...' Samuel hesitated, mesmerised and shocked by what he was witnessing as Nancy thumped Tommy's chest very hard several times before continuing with the breathing. He was about to pull Nancy to her feet, when suddenly Tommy gave a loud cough, as sea water spurted from his open mouth.

'Turn him onto his front,' commanded Nancy to no one in particular. The two men did as she had said, then watched as Nancy thumped the boy between his shoulder blades several times. The boy entered a spasm of coughing as more water soaked the mattress.

'Well, knock me down with a feather,' said Samuel in disbelief. 'He's alive! You've done it!' You actually breathed life into him. It's a miracle!'

'I want dry towels, a night shirt and a mattress quickly!' said Nancy. 'And a tot of brandy if you have any on board.'

'Okay,' responded Samuel. Addressing the men, he said, 'I'll get the brandy, you two find the rest.' Two minutes later, Samuel was back with the brandy and two glasses. 'Thought you might like a tot, as well as the boy. You've earned it. Thank you, I'm in your debt.'

As suddenly as the wind had come up, so it eased throughout the remainder of the day. The last of the sun managed to break through the cloud as it surrendered itself to the horizon. Although the sea was still restless,

Nancy left the sleeping boy in her cabin and made her way to the aft deck where she found Samuel gazing at the crimson sky. They were alone, apart from the helmsman and the second officer further forward. 'How is the boy?' enquired Samuel.

'He's sleeping. He'll be fine. The young have a remarkable ability to recover.'

'Well, I imagine you won't want him moved, so you can sleep in my cabin tonight. I'm on watch after midnight, then I can bunk down in my chart room for the remainder of the night. I think the weather should hold now until we turn the corner off the coast of Portugal.'

'How long have we got till we reach Cadiz?' enquired Nancy quietly.

'You can never be entirely sure at sea, my dear, but I think we should manage to land in two to three days, all being well. Have you had any further thoughts about what you will do?'

'No, I'm afraid not. Do you know for how long you will be in Cadiz?'

'I'm hoping to be able to purchase barrels of wine which should raise a good price in New York. It's all down to how well the negotiations go with the Spanish suppliers.'

'That sounds interesting. I like to do a bit of bargaining. That's how I spent much of my time when looking after my mother, and running the homestead.'

'Would you like to accompany me to the meetings, Nancy? You would be most welcome. In fact, you might even be a positive influence.'

'Yes, I would, Samuel. And if my presence would help, although I can't imagine how, that's all to the better.'

The sun was well down, and Nancy gave a brief shiver as what little warmth there had been, dissolved. 'Here, let me put my jacket around you,' said Samuel with concern. Thus saying, he quickly shrugged out of the jacket and placed it around Nancy's shoulders. As he did so, he allowed his arm to linger on her shoulder for a moment. It was at that point that a larger wave passed beneath the ship, causing Nancy to lose her balance and stumble against Samuel. Suddenly, she was in his arms, looking up into his eyes, which she could see in the glow of the aft lantern. She made no effort to pull away, he continued to hold her. Both were frozen in the moment. He leaned down ... hesitated ... his lips close to hers ... then started to pull back. Without conscious thought, Nancy quickly stretched her head up and kissed his lips. His arms tightened around her as he returned the kiss. She had never been kissed by a man before. His lips tasted of salt. She placed her arms around him and allowed her body to relax against him. She was lost. The ship continued its movement, rising and falling, the breeze whipped her hair, a loose rope slatted against the mizzen mast, the timbers creaked, the ships bell rang the half hour.

It was fully dark when Samuel escorted Nancy to his cabin, opened the door for her, stepped back to allow her into the lantern-lit space, and returned up the companionway to the stern rail where he stood gazing at the rising silvery moon.

Cadiz harbour, with its towering fortified walls, glittered in the morning sunlight as the ship, bearing British colours, sailed sedately through the entrance.

Many eyes watched with interest as the gleaming sails were efficiently furled as *Nimble Lady* swung round and dropped her anchor with a splash as her forward momentum ceased. Soon the harbour master's boat was seen to be rowing out to the vessel, followed, at a respectful distance, by hopeful traders in their smaller rowing boats. On the aft deck, her captain was to be seen, pointing out various buildings to a lady who was standing closely alongside him. Shortly after, the vessel was towed to a quay where she was secured by a number of thick cables.

The captain, with megaphone in hand, having satisfied himself that his ship was secure, started issuing orders to his crew to ensure that all was ship-shape and tidy before the off-watch crew members could go ashore to the delights of Cadiz.

***

'You were amazing, my dear,' said Samuel in admiration two days later. 'You had him eating out of your hands. How you managed to talk him into reducing the prise by a further eight percent I will never know. I was just about to accept his terms when you interrupted me. You're an amazing woman, do you know that?'

'I won't take the credit entirely,' replied Nancy with a grin. 'He was a walkover. Couldn't resist a sweet smile. Simple really. It's how I always used to get a good deal with my eggs.'

'Walking together, arm in arm, along the quay, Samuel said, 'Unloading will be finished by the end of the day tomorrow. The wine consignment won't be here for at least three days. So, we have some time to spare. Would you like to accompany me for a stroll around the city tomorrow? Lots of narrow streets, shops, waterfront bars and taverns, street entertainment. Plenty to see. It may help you to decide what you intend to do now you are here.'

'Yes, I would love to accompany you. Thank you so much for asking. As it happens, I have already decided what I want to do. I'm sailing with you, if that's okay. I still have sufficient cash to pay for the cabin. I assume it isn't booked?'

'You are? Well, knock me down …'

'Yes, with a feather, I know,' said Nancy with a smile.

***

The following day was enjoyed by both of them. Nancy loved the shops, combined with the fact that she now had funds to make the odd purchase or two, mainly in clothing shops. Samuel, on the other hand, resisted the temptation to purchase any of the items he spotted and clearly admired. The afternoon merged into evening. Samuel was pleased to be able to recommend a tavern he had used on previous occasions. Selections having been made from the menu, Samuel filled both glasses and asked Nancy how much she had enjoyed her day.

'It was wonderful,' she replied. 'Thank you for the invitation. It's a grand old city, and such interesting history. As you saw, I have enjoyed topping up my previously meagre wardrobe. I couldn't help noticing that you didn't buy anything, Samuel. Were you not tempted?'

'No, not really. You see, I've been banking my money with the intention of, one day, being able to afford to buy *Nimble Lady*. It's taking a long time, I'm half way there now. A few more years should do it.'

'Sounds interesting. You think she will be a good investment?'

'She'll be a good start to building my own shipping company. I will be making profits for myself, instead of owners. Steam will be the future in shipping. I hope to invest in a steam driven ship one day, but that's well into the future.'

***

Cadiz was now three days behind them. To Samuel's amazement, Nancy was already competent with the handling of his sextant during the noon sightings. She was also coming to terms with the complexity of plotting the ship's position on the chart. Meanwhile, young Tommy was gaining in confidence working aloft with the topmen.

He had the makings of a good seaman and Samuel hoped he would be allowed a life at sea, by his father, if that turned out to be the boy's choice.

He and Nancy had now developed the habit of meeting at the stern rail each evening, to watch the sunset together, each willing the other to take the lead in a repeat of the outward voyage. However, there was something unspoken between the two of them. Having faced the possibility of finding herself alone in a strange country, regardless of her wealth, Nancy's heart had warmed to this kind and gentle man and his ship. As she peered out to the beautiful changing colours of the horizon at this moment, and listened to the rush of the sea below her feet, she could think of no other place she would prefer to be.

Samuel's thoughts, however, were in turmoil. He was in love. Nancy had come into his life the moment she had accidently stepped on his foot outside a tavern weeks ago. She had remained in his mind from that moment. Chance had brought her on to his ship. If it had not been for those diamonds, he might have allowed himself to show Nancy how much she had begun to mean to him. As things were, she would inevitably think that it was her fortune that was attracting him if he allowed his feelings to become clear.

'Samuel.' Nancy hesitated for a brief moment. 'I have something I want to ask you.' She turned to face him so that her silhouette was framed by the yellow, orange and purple horizon. He was mesmerized. Unable to speak. 'Samuel,' she reached forward and took his calloused hand into her own. 'How would you feel if I were to suggest a partnership? If I were to contribute to the purchase of *Nimble Lady?* Joint owners?'

'But, why would you do that?' asked the perplexed captain. 'You sailed with us to Spain on an impulse, not really knowing why. Now you are suggesting part ownership of a ship, without knowing why. No, Nancy. I won't even consider it.'

'You say I don't know why. Well, for your information, I do. I have fallen in love with the sea, with *Nimble Lady,* with this life, and …. with you. Samuel, I love you, can't you see that? I also think you are in love with me, but you're afraid to say it, because of what I may think. I know I have been fickle, but in this, I'm sure. I want to remain on this ship, to build a company with you, to be your wife. Samuel ... Will you please propose to me before I push you over this rail!'

The tension was broken as they both burst into laughter. 'You are an amazing lady, Nancy, did you know that? First you bring a boy back to life, then you breathe new life into my dreams. What can I say? You walked into my life on that freezing cold day, had you agreed to accompany me to the corn exchange for that hot potato, as I suggested, I would likely have proposed to the poor egg lady then and there. Why would I not propose to the same lady now? I do love you, as indeed do most of the men on this ship, I suspect. I can't imagine life, or *Nimble Lady*, without you. Nancy, will you do me the honour of becoming my wife, and my partner?'

'Yes, Samuel, I will. New York sounds like a good place to have a honeymoon, don't you think?'

The End

I hope you have enjoyed reading my short stories, all of which have emerged from my imagination.

We all have an imagination which stays within us throughout our lives. Our minds are the source of our creativity in whatever form it takes. Our minds are constantly active, even in sleep. Imagination is the recreational side of our thinking. It is the channel of escapism. It is the playtime of the mind.

Watch a child at play for a while. Imagination is at the forefront of all they are doing. This was a time in our lives when our own imagination was most active. However, it doesn't need to be confined to those informative years. Our ability to reason, to think, to calculate, to remember, all need to be exercised, and it's the same with our imagination. What better way is there other than to record the best aspects of our imagination? With surprisingly little effort we can all create a story either as a picture or in the written word. It doesn't have to be a highly acclaimed product admired by others. The important thing is to enable and encourage the imagination to arise from the ashes.

All fiction, be it in a book, a play, a film, or a bed-time story, is born in the imagination. We can all do it. Why not give it a try? The next time you have a little time on your hands, pick up a pencil, a paint-brush, a pen, a sheet of paper. Or sit down at the keyboard. Let your mind drift off to another place, a different time, or try allowing yourself to become a different age, a different gender, a different person, even an animal. Who knows? Perhaps you will discover that book we are all said to have within us.

Enjoy your imagination and allow the child within to come back into the game of life.

Paul Ludford

Paul.ludford45@gmail.com